Praise for Anita Kelly

Something Wild & Wonderful

"A gorgeous, curative read about the new identities people create by giving themselves permission to heal from the pain of the past and what can be discovered as they immerse themselves in the vast, untamed, wonderful wilderness. A deeply satisfying, romantic story worth getting lost in." —*Kirkus*, starred review

"*Something Wild & Wonderful* is so sweet and satisfying that you'll want to read it again and again." —*BookPage*, starred review

"This steamy, opposites-attract m/m romance is impossible to put down. Highly recommended." —*Library Journal*, starred review

"Brimming with tenderness, hope, humor, and healing, this romance is truly something wild and wonderful. A must-read for those looking for stories with a big heart."
—Ashley Herring Blake, author of *Astrid Parker Doesn't Fail*

"*Something Wild & Wonderful* is my favorite kind of romance, a tender, achingly beautiful journey of love and healing—harrowing passages through grief, thrilling ascents of growth, that glorious vista of recognition that these two people are exactly where they're supposed to be, exactly as they are, learning to love themselves, to love another, to let themselves be loved, too."
—Chloe Liese, author of *Two Wrongs Make a Right*

"I can't get enough of Anita Kelly's writing. As I followed Ben and Alexei on their journey, I was enthralled by the palpable care and tenderness that went into both the tiniest details and the most sweeping emotions, creating a stunning romance that feels epic and intimate all at once. *Something Wild & Wonderful* made my heart ache in the best way possible."

—Ava Wilder, author of *How to Fake It in Hollywood*

"A heart-tugging triumph! Every step Ben and Alexei take on the Pacific Crest Trail reverberates with vulnerability, adventure, and sweaty, crackling tension. *Something Wild & Wonderful* is the rare romance where the characters feel like new friends and also kindred souls you've known your whole life. Kelly never fails to bring the perfect combination of humor, swoons, and grounded emotion."

—Timothy Janovsky, author of *Never Been Kissed*

"Filled with unforgettable and shimmering moments of hope, bravery, and the reminder to live life as authentically as possible, Anita Kelly's *Something Wild & Wonderful* overflows with a soft but undeniably sexy tenderness—one that shines with the magic of falling in love on your own terms."

—Chip Pons, author of *You & I, Rewritten*

Love & Other Disasters

"An essential read."   *—USA Today*

"This chef's-kiss debut . . . brilliantly explores the idea of being true to yourself with insight and compassion. In between all the deliciously snarky wit, simmering sexual chemistry, romantic yearning, and quippy banter, Kelly also delivers some moments of romantic hope and happiness that will long resonate with readers."

—*Booklist*, starred review

"A delicious confection of a story: savory, succulent, and also a bit salty in spots… The only bad thing about this book is that even after you've gorged on the whole thing, it'll leave you wanting more."

—*BookPage*, starred review

"Kelly will whet your appetite from the first page, capping off the wonderful feast with the absolute sweetest of happy-ever-afters."

—*Kirkus*, starred review

"A stunning debut."   —*Library Journal*, starred review

"This debut is delicious in every way."   —BuzzFeed Books

"*Love & Other Disasters* is by turns funny, sweet, and hot, but Anita Kelly's emotional river runs deep—this romance will stay with readers long after they've turned the last page. A deeply emotional yet buoyant romantic comedy about finding love and self."

—Shelf Awareness

"A sweet debut… a nonbinary protagonist in a mainstream romance is cause for excitement and the characters spark with chemistry."

—*Publishers Weekly*

"Sweet and sexy and wholly delicious. I'm head over heels for these two delightful disasters… Anita Kelly writes with tremendous warmth and care, and these pages shine with joy."

—Rachel Lynn Solomon, author of *The Ex Talk*

"With only one book, Anita Kelly has landed among my all-time favorite authors."

—Meryl Wilsner, author of *Something to Talk About*

"Kelly writes wildly charming, exquisitely vibrant, and achingly tender prose and has a unique gift for making readers feel safe, loved, and understood within their pages. This story is both fantastically fun and crack your heart wide open vulnerable."

—Rosie Danan, author of *The Roommate*

"This book is sweet, steamy, and absolutely delectable! With relatable main characters, vivid (and delicious) descriptions, and beautiful queer representation, this is a book you both want to savor and consume in a single bite."

—Alison Cochrun, author of *The Charm Offensive*

How You Get the Girl

How You Get the Girl

ANITA KELLY

FOREVER
NEW YORK BOSTON

Forever
Hachette Book Group
1290 Avenue of the Americas, New York, NY 10104
read-forever.com
@readforeverpub

First Edition: February 2024

Forever is an imprint of Grand Central Publishing. The Forever name and logo are trademarks of Hachette Book Group, Inc.

The publisher is not responsible for websites (or their content) that are not owned by the publisher.

Forever books may be purchased in bulk for business, educational, or promotional use. For information, please contact your local bookseller or the Hachette Book Group Special Markets Department at special.markets@hbgusa.com.

Library of Congress Cataloging-in-Publication Data

Names: Kelly, Anita (Romance author), author.
Title: How you get the girl / Anita Kelly.
Description: First edition. | New York : Forever, 2024.
Identifiers: LCCN 2023032051 | ISBN 9781538754917 (trade paperback) | ISBN 9781538754924 (ebook)
Subjects: LCGFT: Romance fiction. | Lesbian fiction. | Sports fiction. | Novels.
Classification: LCC PS3611.E4457 H69 2024 | DDC 813/.6—dc23/eng/20221013
LC record available at https://lccn.loc.gov/2023032051

ISBNs: 9781538754917 (trade paperback), 9781538754924 (ebook)

Printed in the United States of America

LSC-C

Printing 1, 2023

For Mom
a natural at all of it

and for every queer and trans person in Tennessee
your joy will outlive the cruelty of your government

CHAPTER ONE

T he angry girls always made her smile.

There were other truths Julie Parker had learned during her first season as head coach of the East Nashville High girls' basketball team. That she was officially too old to understand what teenagers were ever doing on social media. That the smell of a high school basketball court—stale sweat and floor wax—never, ever changed.

But more than anything, she'd discovered that the players who approached each team huddle with a scowl were the ones who lingered in her brain. Who most often made her burst into unexpected laughter.

It was the honesty, the openness in showing their annoyance and their fear.

And every afternoon, from mid-October through February—March, if you were lucky—Julie got to toss a basketball around with them for a while. Spend a couple hours a day being a bit more honest.

So even though Julie knew she should have been irked by the front office throwing a new player onto her team today, a full two weeks into practices, she struggled to keep her face stern as Vanessa Lerner stomped across the court toward her, BTS T-shirt damp with sweat.

"Sorry, Miss Parker," Vanessa huffed. "But I'm not doing this shit."

The tips of Vanessa's dark blond hair were dyed lavender: pretty pastel pops inside her messy bun that seemed incongruous with the stomps and grunts she had filled Julie's gym with for the last two hours.

Julie bit the inside of her cheek to keep from grinning.

"As I've told you three times today, Lerner, call me Coach. And sorry to say, this is how we end every practice. If you want to be part of the team, you have to be *part of the team*."

Julie opened her palm toward the endline, where the rest of her players were shaking out arms, stretching hamstrings before the ritual end-of-practice sprint. Throwing looks at where Julie and Vanessa stood outside of Julie's minuscule office.

The questions on their faces were warranted, and Julie didn't have answers. Yet.

Because Julie wasn't sure Vanessa *did* want to be part of the team. All Chloe from the front office had said was "Trust me, you gotta take her," before scuttling away at the beginning of practice.

But almost despite herself, Vanessa had put in the work today. She wouldn't be as sweaty and disgruntled in front of Julie right now if she hadn't.

Which was why, no matter the reason for her appearance, Julie knew she had to get Vanessa to stay. Because if she stayed, Julie could show her how a perfectly executed pass, a shot that *swooshed* just right, could take all that anger and make her feel like a badass instead.

If only Jacks were here.

Julie had led these initial weeks of practice pretty well by herself. At least, she liked to think so. But she couldn't deny that she missed her assistant coach. That there were moments, like now, where she longed for the extra hands and comfort of Jacks's steady, no-bullshit presence. Jacks could've led the sprint while Julie had a heart-to-heart with Vanessa, helped figure out her deal. And then, after they'd all run off to the locker room, Jacks would turn to Julie to say, in her signature rocks-in-her-throat rumble, "Well, that was a hell of a thing, huh?"

But Jacks wasn't here. And they hadn't been able to fill her position in the entire month it had been posted on the district website. Julie was on her own.

"Yeah, sorry," Vanessa said again, scratching her elbow and sounding not very sorry at all. "But I think I'm done."

Julie glanced once more at her team. They'd gone along with Vanessa's presence today, most likely because Julie had pulled aside her co-captains, Ngozi and Sasha, and asked them to help keep the peace.

But the peace was getting restless.

"We all want to be done." Julie kept her voice low and calm. "But we're not. Not yet. This sprint is hard, but doing something hard when you're already beat is what makes a great basketball player."

Vanessa rolled her eyes.

"Whatever," she muttered, before shaking her head and adding, "No, you know what? That's nice and easy for you to say, *Miss Parker*, when you're just standing here on the sidelines. But we're the ones who actually have to *do* that hard shit. And sometimes, you're just beat."

With that, Vanessa returned to scowling into the distance.

Julie tilted her head. Considered her.

Don't smile, she commanded herself. *Do not.*

Because Vanessa Lerner, angry BTS fan, would likely read a smile as condescending. A challenge. And the Vanessas of the world didn't need challenges. They only needed to be listened to.

"All right," Julie said. "Fair point."

She joined her players on the line.

"Listen up, Bobcats." Julie nodded to her left, her right. "Let's see if any of you suckers can beat Coach."

She stretched out a knee. Made sure Vanessa had made her way to the line, too.

And then she blew her whistle.

And Julie Parker ran like hell.

To the foul line, and back. To the half-court line, and back. To the opposite endline, and all the way back. She repeated the routine again, sneakers squeaking against the court, the players around her huffing and puffing, the thud of her own heart pumping against her chest.

Laughter from the pure, painful joy of it bubbled up her throat.

Ngozi passed Julie at the timeline, a full court length ahead. She grinned and clapped her hands, braids slapping her back as she yelled across the gym: "Come on, Coach!"

Julie groaned as she pivoted for the final stretch.

This had been easier when she was sixteen.

She propelled herself toward the endline anyway, leaning her body to help spur on her feet. Her players pumped fists, hollering where they waited for her.

Maybe it was a small thing, coaching a high school basketball team.

Certainly smaller than the things Julie's closest loved ones had been doing these last few years—appearing on nationally televised cooking competitions, hiking the Pacific Crest Trail, starting dream careers—while Julie sat in the same cubicle at Vanderbilt University where she'd sat for years, completing the same tasks she'd never truly cared about.

But for a few months out of the year, Julie also helped a few teenagers get a bit better at this one thing. Watched them make friends. Taught them what it meant to be part of a team.

Maybe it was a small thing.

But it was important to *them*.

Julie glanced to her right in the final stretch, at the only player left sprinting across the court. Made sure Vanessa's sneaker toed over the line a split second before hers did.

And the Bobcats burst into applause.

Their laughter reverberated in Julie's chest, cementing her determination more than ever.

Her first season with the Bobcats had been okay, record-wise. They'd won more games than they'd lost, which Jacks had assured Julie was a more impressive showing than the previous few years.

But Julie wanted better than okay for Ngozi, for Sasha. For Katelyn, for Gray. And for Vanessa now, too.

She would get the East High Bobcats to district playoffs this year.

"Next time, Lerner." Julie breathed heavily, resting her palms on her knees. "I'll get you next time."

Vanessa rolled her eyes, walking off the sprint in a circle.

"You're corny, Miss Parker," she wheezed. "Shit," she added a second later, for good measure.

Julie straightened.

"All right, everyone, you're done for the day. Lerner, hang back a sec."

Vanessa trudged over, chin tilted toward the scoreboard on the wall.

"Look. I have a feeling you don't want to be here," Julie said as her own heart rate galloped back to normal. "But you had a good practice today."

Another eyeroll.

"Pretty sure I came dead-ass last just now."

Julie gave her a look. "Pretty sure that was me."

Vanessa threw the look right back, eyebrow raised. Like she knew Julie had made sure that was the case, and was here to call her on it.

Julie bit her cheek again.

"You'll keep improving. But, Vanessa, you have to curb the cussing. The team's been practicing together for two weeks; they're already confused about why you're here—"

"Join the party," Vanessa muttered.

"—and if you keep breaking my rules, the ones they've already learned, they're going to be even more annoyed. I fully understand you're going to *want* to cuss me out, possibly frequently, so I suggest coming up with some special words of your own to get your feelings out. That way, when you're pissed at me, you can just say something like... *snap crackle pop* instead."

Vanessa stared at her.

"Snap crackle *what*?"

Julie bit her lip, trying to think. "Maybe... balderdash?"

Vanessa backed away, shaking her head.

"Just think about it!" Julie shouted, pointing finger guns in encouragement.

"You're weird, Coach."

And with another headshake, Vanessa disappeared into the locker room.

Julie raised her fists in triumph.

Vanessa had called her *Coach*.

Vanessa was going to be just fine.

"Excuse me... Coach Parker?"

Julie twirled, dropping her hands.

And promptly swallowed her tongue.

"Holy *shit*," she breathed, breaking her own rule immediately.

But snap crackle fucking *shit*.

The face of the woman in front of her appeared older than the last time Julie had seen it on TV, although her body was the same. Tall, lean, fit as hell. Olive skin, with the lightest spattering of freckles underneath those electric-blue eyes. Sharp cheekbones, strong jaw.

The biggest difference was her hair. No longer swept up into a thick ponytail, it was cut neat and clean over her ears. On top, black tangles curled over her forehead. Julie couldn't stop staring at the surprising streaks of silver that popped now among those curls.

She wore slate-gray slacks, a white dress shirt opened at the collar.

In short: she was hotter than she had ever been.

The words tumbled out of Julie's mouth.

"You're Elle fucking Cochrane."

CHAPTER TWO

Later, Elle would wish many things had been different that day she met Julie Parker.

Mostly, that she hadn't been distracted by the familiar beginnings of a migraine.

That it had been even just a few more days since Vanessa had come into Elle's care. That she would have been less overwhelmed, more in control.

And last, that Julie would not have recognized her so instantly. That she would not have called her *Elle fucking Cochrane.*

This one was the most complicated. Because that *Elle fucking Cochrane* had also made a frisson of flattery zip up Elle's spine.

She was recognized less and less these days, a fact Elle normally welcomed. But she was also human. A very gay human, to be exact. And, well. What queer woman wouldn't feel a bit of a thrill, being greeted with an emphatic *fuck* by a pretty girl?

Because Elle wasn't confident about many things that day. But she had known, the second she'd walked into the East High gym, that Coach Parker was pretty, in a way that was specific to Elle. In a way Elle hadn't let herself observe in a long time.

She held herself with the poise of every baller Elle had ever known, spine straight under her well-worn T-shirt, those loose, men's style basketball shorts that signaled Coach Parker was either nostalgic for the game of the nineties—and who wasn't—or also extremely gay.

In the case of women Elle had most frequently been attracted to in the course of her life, both things tended to be true.

And when Coach Parker talked to her team, her confidence was underscored by humor, a kind, charismatic enthusiasm. Traits Elle increasingly found captivating on a basketball court as she got older, the years perhaps making her soft. Her former ruthless competitiveness stripped away by time.

Not that Elle had spent much time herself on basketball courts, these last eight years.

To be more precise, she had spent...none.

Which was maybe one reason why, when Coach Parker stared at Elle with her jaw dropped, her eyes so wide, so clearly stunned, that it should have made Elle want to laugh—

Elle could only stare back.

Those wide eyes were the most arresting shade of hazel, peppered with flashes of gold, complementing a face full of freckles that Elle, helplessly, could only classify as *adorable*.

Then there was the hair. Sunset-colored, thrown into a ponytail, glowing in the fluorescent lights.

It was close to physically impossible to look good under the lights of a high school gymnasium. But somehow, Coach Parker was pulling it off.

And the longer Elle took her in, the more she realized there was something vaguely familiar about those freckles and that hair. A ghost of a memory flitted through Elle's brain, even though Elle was fairly certain she'd never seen her before. This woman with huge, New Year's Eve confetti eyes. Elle would have remembered.

"That's me," Elle eventually replied, once her senses returned to her. She tried to ignore the impending migraine's pull behind her eyes, the reality of standing on a basketball court again, as Vanessa's coach continued to gape.

Elle opened her mouth to explain about Vanessa, and—

"Oh my god. You used to be my *idol*."

Elle blinked.

She should have been ready for it. The *used to*.

Coach Parker *used to* think Elle Cochrane was special.

Along with the rest of Tennessee.

"Yes, well—"

"I had posters of you on my wall. Next to my posters of Pat Summitt. It was like, Pat, Pat, Elle, Pat, Elle."

Elle rubbed a hand over her forehead.

"Elle Cochrane," Coach Parker went on. "Elle Cochrane is *in my gym*." She broke eye contact to touch her own forehead. "Elle Cochrane is in my gym, and I'm wearing my boob-stain shirt."

Elle's mouth opened before she could stop herself. "Your—"

And then good sense kicked in once more. Elle glanced at Coach Parker's faded Kacey Musgraves T-shirt for exactly one second before snapping her mouth shut.

"My boob-stain shirt," Coach Parker repeated, gesturing at herself, her own mouth apparently heeding no such command. "Dropped some pulled pork right on my left nipple two years ago. Knew it was hopeless as soon as it happened. But it's such a good shirt, I could never let it go. Always just hope the general public is too distracted by Kacey to notice it."

Coach Parker stared past Elle, scratching her head, eyes gone hazy.

For a second, Elle was so fully focused on not looking at Coach Parker's left nipple, she was almost able to forget her migraine, or the court around them—or anything, really—entirely.

"Anyway," Coach Parker said, still staring at something beyond Elle's vision, "remember when you took that last-second shot against Notre Dame in the Elite Eight?" An unnatural laugh escaped her lips. "I almost passed out. God, you were—"

Elle closed her eyes.

She did not, in fact, remember taking that last-second shot against Notre Dame. She remembered the aftermath, the feeling in her ribs when Mara had collided into her side. The din of the locker room, after. The flash of cameras.

But like the majority of her most noteworthy moments on the court, it always felt to Elle, even back then, like she had simply blacked out. That she ran so fully on gut instinct in those moments that the memories weren't so much tangible, but rather like the impressions of a phantom limb.

Mostly, she tried to not remember them at all.

When Elle opened her eyes, the gym had gone suddenly blurry, the lighting piercing into her skull.

She'd hesitated, fifteen minutes ago, when she'd texted Rose that they might need a ride, but now she was glad. It would only be minutes before the migraine collapsed everything good. And while Elle hated asking her mother for help, especially last minute, when she didn't know what Rose's pain levels had been like that day, she'd promised she'd keep Vanessa safe. And driving home with a migraine wouldn't keep anyone safe.

Even after a lifetime of living through them, every migraine was frustrating, somehow felt like a failure. Like her body had once again overpowered her current medication, which was supposed to reduce their frequency.

And lord help her, if Elle had to switch up her medication again, she might lose her mind.

Distantly, she realized Coach Parker was still saying something. About UConn, and the Vols, and—and Elle could no longer make out the gold in her eyes.

Just like that, the low-level panic that had ruled her system for the last week took charge once more.

And only once it returned did she realize. That these last ten disconcerting minutes standing in front of Coach Parker—her eyes and her freckles and her nervous, charming energy—were the first time that low-level panic had receded at all, in the five days since she had received the call from the Department of Children's Services.

But that call, she'd do well to remember, was why she was here.

"I'm here about Vanessa," Elle made herself interrupt. And, okay. If she had to analyze the tone of her voice there, perhaps the sentence had been more of a bark. An air-stealing, unintentional reprimand.

"Right." Coach Parker's voice immediately sounded so much smaller. "Of course."

Dammit.

Elle wanted to explain. About her head, her desire to not relive her past. But there wasn't time. She knew getting Vanessa onto the team late was inappropriate, and she needed to at least provide Coach Parker with the basics before Vanessa came out of the locker room.

"I wanted to apologize," Elle went on in a more Reasonable Human Being tone of voice, "for putting her into your program two weeks late. Vanessa was only put into my care recently, and I needed somewhere for her to go after school, and..."

And the truth was that Elle had realized picking Vanessa up from school directly conflicted with her daily three o'clock work meeting. And while she knew Vanessa could take the bus and take care of herself until Elle was done with work, the social worker had explained that Vanessa should be watched as closely as possible, since this was her first time in the system and her flight risk was uncertain.

And so, even now... Elle's only solution had been basketball.

"I thought it might be good for her," she finished. "I appreciate your accommodation."

Coach Parker nodded, bringing her hands to her hips.

"So you're her... foster parent, then?"

"Yes. I think. I mean, yes."

Double dammit. Elle hated tripping over her words. It simply still felt so strange, hearing the word *parent* applied to her. Hearing the word *foster* in relation to Vanessa.

"Sorry. I'm technically her foster parent at the moment, yes. But Vanessa's mom, Karly, is my cousin. I'm only helping Karly out for a while, while she takes care of some things."

And Elle needed to shut her mouth now. For heaven's sake. One of the first things Elle had learned from the gentle CPS woman on the phone—whose name she still couldn't remember, because her brain had only been half-functioning, as it apparently still was now—was that she shouldn't overshare Vanessa or Karly's business, to protect their privacy and the process. But Elle hadn't yet found a neat, tidy way to explain the situation.

And it felt less awful, less awkward, when Elle explained they were related. Like this was some voluntary arrangement she'd made with her cousin, to be helpful while Karly moved houses or started a new job. Like there were no state agencies involved. No addictions, no shady ex-boyfriends. Like it hadn't totally upheaved Elle's—and Vanessa's—and Karly's—world.

"Got it. And you're Elle Cochrane, the best basketball player this state's ever seen, so that's why the office was so desperate for me to take her on."

Elle at least had the self-awareness to blush. At least she thought she was blushing. Mostly, she was trying to not pass out underneath these excruciating lights.

"I'm sorry; I wouldn't normally... This isn't—"

"No, no." Coach Parker waved a hand. "It's totally fine. I'm just processing all of this out loud. I'm happy to have Vanessa join the team."

"Really?" A lightbulb of hope flickered on, dimly, in Elle's brain. "So she did okay?"

"Oh, well, she freaking hated it. Has she ever played basketball before?"

Elle blushed a bit more, opening her mouth to respond, hoping something would appear in her mind to say in the next 0.2 seconds that wasn't *I dunno*. Since, upon trying to ask Vanessa that same question yesterday, the only response she'd received was *whatever*. A word Elle was becoming intimately familiar with.

But before she could come up with something that sounded like she sincerely knew the child under her care, Elle was saved by the bell. Or rather, the distant clanging of ancient lockers slamming shut, the rumble of teenagers pouring back onto a basketball court.

"She'll be fine," Coach Parker said quickly, tone closer to what Elle had heard when she'd first slipped into the gym at the end of practice. Both authoritative and reassuring. "If we're both patient with her. All right?"

"Thank you—I'm sorry, I didn't catch your first name." The office had only told Elle to go see *Coach Parker*. And she hadn't thought to ask. She was going to kick this migraine in the shins.

"Julie."

"Julie. Thank you again."

And for a small, yearning, irrational moment, Elle wished she could listen to Julie talk, about Kacey Musgraves or basketball or anything at all that wasn't related to Elle's current life, for just a bit longer.

Because those ten minutes without panic... they had been nice.

"Um. Are you... okay?"

No, Elle wanted to say. *Not even a little.*

"Um," Julie said, again, when Elle didn't respond. "Vanessa just walked out of the gym. In case... you wanted to know."

Shit.

Elle turned, pain racking her head, a roil of nausea hitting her stomach.

It was only when she'd caught up to Vanessa, almost to the parking lot, that she realized she hadn't even said goodbye.

CHAPTER THREE

Julie pulled out her phone and dialed London's number halfway up the stairwell, a sudden thought entering her mind.

"Listen, you guys aren't, like, doing it right now, are you? Because I'll be at your door in two seconds, just FYI, so get ahold of yourselves if so."

London's sigh rattled in Julie's ear.

"We are fully clothed. Well, mostly. Thanks for the head's-up, though; truly, you know I just love spontaneous, unannounced—"

"Visits from your twin sister?" Julie finished, stepping through the door as London opened it. "I know. But I had an emergency. And what are you talking about?" She shoved her phone back in her bag. "You're totally fully clothed."

London scratched at the back of their head, nodding toward the couch. Where their girlfriend, Dahlia, was sprawled, drooling onto a pillow. One of London's T-shirts covered her torso, but her bare legs stretched across the gray cushions.

"Please." Julie waved a dismissive hand. "I've seen Dahlia in her underwear before. I know how she feels about pants."

"Pants bad," Dahlia mumbled.

A thud sounded from the bedroom, followed by the scuffle of paws making their slow way across the hardwood floor.

Julie sighed in relief as she scooped up the ugly, one-eyed dog, shoving her face into his wiry fur. She had been in desperate need of a Schnitzel hug.

"What's the emergency then?" London perched on the piano bench in the middle of the room, which accompanied the baby grand hardly anyone ever played. But London still owned it, because they were London, and they were the worst, and Julie loved them terribly.

"So."

Julie dropped her messenger bag and began to pace the length of London's annoyingly hip apartment, Schnitzel stuffed under an arm. The personality she'd been able to craft, somehow, in the East High gym these past couple of years, the one she put on for the team, where she was a competent, mature adult worthy of respect, had disappeared the moment she'd walked through London and Dahlia's door. Now, she could simply be herself. Which was...the opposite of all those things.

"So Elle Cochrane showed up at my practice tonight, and I think I possibly talked to her about my nipples."

London stilled.

"You—" Their face went blank. Before their lips contorted in the way Julie knew meant they were trying not to laugh. "Julie. I'm going to need you to go back and start that story over."

Julie groaned before letting Schnitzel go and flopping onto a love seat, covering her face with her hands.

Dahlia rose to a sitting position with a yawn. "What's going on?"

"What's going on"—and now London was not even trying to keep the laughter out of their voice—"is that Julie's teenage idol supposedly showed up at her basketball practice tonight. And apparently Julie said something about her breasts, but I'm ignoring that little factoid for now."

"The teenage idol's breasts or Julie's breasts?" Dahlia asked, suddenly alert.

"Mine."

Julie dropped her hands from her face to gesture to Kacey Musgraves.

"My idol appeared in front of me, and I realized I was wearing my boob-stain shirt. Which I think I might have pointed out. Out loud. I don't know. I sort of blacked out."

Dahlia leaned forward, squinting.

"Oh yeah. I see it now."

"You can't unsee it once you do. Which means I can never wear this shirt in front of Elle Cochrane again. Which is a sentence I never thought I'd say. Are we by chance living in an alternate dimension right now? Would there be signs?"

"I don't know, but I, for one, would like to stop talking about your boobs," London said.

"Oh, shut it. Having a boob-stain shirt is a universal experience." Julie scowled, hugging a throw pillow to her stomach.

"Okay." Dahlia held up a hand. "Let's go back and have someone explain to me who Elle Cochrane is."

"It is extremely offensive to me that you've lived here for over a year and don't know who Elle Cochrane is," Julie grumbled, her annoyance at herself and how she'd reacted back in the gym spilling over to anyone in her general vicinity. "That's like saying you don't know who Pat Summitt is."

A silence filled the apartment.

Julie turned her head slowly.

"I'm concerned that you're not saying anything," Julie said.

"Um." Dahlia blinked.

"Oh my *god*." Julie threw her head back against the love seat. "I do not have the capacity to process this right now. London, how the *hell* did you let Dahlia move here without telling her...anything."

London held up their hands.

"I don't know how I'm a part of this."

Julie glared. "You are my *twin*. Bonded by blood. You should know that falling in love with someone requires you to give them at least a bare minimum history of the Tennessee Volunteers before you introduce them to me."

"Obviously." London rolled their eyes. "What was I thinking."

"*Guys.* Jesus. I'll google Pat. Someone tell me who Elle Cochrane is."

Julie gave London one last look. "Obama gave her the Presidential Medal of Freedom, you know."

"Elle Cochrane," London said on a weary sigh, moving from the piano bench to the couch to drape an arm around Dahlia's shoulder, "was the star point guard of the Tennessee Vols when we were teenagers, leading them to two Final Fours and one national championship. The Tennessee Vols, made legendary by Pat Summitt, who never coached a losing season. Who coached an Olympic team to a gold medal. And who was apparently also given the Presidential Medal of Freedom."

"Thank you," Julie muttered.

Dahlia turned to London, a curious look on her face.

"I didn't know you knew sports."

London shrugged, face smug. "I know some stuff."

"Hot," Dahlia assessed with an approving tilt of her chin.

Now Julie rolled her eyes. London only knew whatever stuff they'd learned from Julie.

"Can we please get back to me completely humiliating myself in front of the hottest person in the world?"

"We've been *trying* to," London said, at the same moment Dahlia abruptly turned on the couch and said, "She's hot?"

"Well." Julie sank further into the cushions. "Yes. Obviously. Like, that is another fact. About her."

London raised a brow.

Julie picked up Schnitzel, who had retreated to the corner of the love seat, and placed him back in her lap. That sentence about

Elle's hotness had just sort of...plopped out of her mouth, and its existence left Julie...disconcerted. Julie wasn't typically a person who examined people's hotness out loud.

Mercifully, London cleared their throat.

"Did you know she was coming to the practice? Is she doing outreach to local high schools or something? I haven't heard anything about her for a while."

"No, that was the shocking thing. I had absolutely no idea. I just turned around and she was there." Julie ran her fingers through Schnitzel's fur. "She's a foster parent of this girl who was just added to the team."

"Oh," London said. "Huh."

"Yeah."

Julie bit her lip, feeling squirmy inside, like maybe she shouldn't have shared this. Squirmier than she had already been feeling. A different variety of squirm.

"So what was she like?"

"I..." Julie's fingers paused behind Schnitzel's ears. "I don't know."

London removed their arm from Dahlia's shoulder, eyes sharpening. "What do you mean?"

"Well. So, I saw her. And kind of lost my shit."

Dahlia nodded. "Referenced your boob stain."

"Yeah. And then, like, rambled about how amazing she is, I think. Again, it's all kind of a blur."

London frowned. "Did she not react well?"

"The thing is, she didn't really react at all? She just sort of stared at me while I blathered on, before she cut me off and was like, 'I'm here to talk about Vanessa.' So we talked about Vanessa for a couple of minutes, and then she stared at me with that weird look on her face again, and then...she was gone."

"Huh," London said. "I'm so sorry, Julie."

"No, no, it's okay," Julie said quickly. Maybe she'd explained it wrong. "She wasn't, like, *mean*. It just..."

"Wasn't how you expected meeting Elle Cochrane to go," London supplied.

"Yeah," Julie agreed.

"To be fair," Dahlia said, tucking her legs underneath herself, "no offense, London, but you don't always react perfectly when people approach us, either."

London and Dahlia had met on the cooking show *Chef's Special*. Nashville was a town that took food—and fame—seriously, and accordingly, they had achieved instant local celebrity status. And while Dahlia normally handled it well, everyone knew it wasn't London's favorite thing.

"I know, but...I don't know, this feels different. Most of the people who talk to us just want selfies, and they'll probably forget us in a few years. Elle Cochrane really meant something to Julie."

London looked at her, sympathy in their eyes.

"And Elle hasn't been a public figure in a while, so I'd think she could handle a fan being excited to see her every now and then."

"It's okay," Julie said again. "It was weird. I guess that's why I came here, to process it. But..." Julie rested her head on the back of the love seat again, staring at London's high ceiling. "It was embarrassing. And she's going to keep picking up Vanessa from practice, which means I'm going to keep seeing her, and—" A frustrated sound escaped her throat. "I don't know how to act around her! And oh god, if my players see me being all flustered and weird around her, they are going to give me shit about it *forever*."

Julie was starting to flounder now.

Even if it wasn't who she truly was, Julie *liked* being Coach Parker. Liked feeling competent on a basketball court. Being worthy of her players' respect. She didn't want to be disconcerted.

Dahlia sat up.

"So you fangirled in front of your teen idol and she was weird about it. It happens."

Julie huffed out a half laugh. She didn't actually think such a thing happened all that often, but sure.

"What you do," Dahlia continued, invested now, "is you take the weekend to process that you're going to be seeing her now. You remember that you are a grown-ass adult and a great basketball coach. And then you go in there on Monday and act like today never happened, like the boss you are."

Julie kept staring at the ceiling. It made her happy, sure, but she didn't think being a high school basketball coach qualified as being a *boss*. She had never even contemplated being a coach at all until Iris Caravalho, her best friend Ben's mother who used to run the East High front office, had talked her into it last year.

But damn, Dahlia was a great cheerleader.

And in that moment, Julie missed her, in the same confusing way she often, these days, missed London, missed Ben, even when they were right in front of her.

Dahlia had worked with Julie, briefly, when Dahlia first moved to town. Julie always knew she'd never last, that someone like Dahlia was above the administrative tasks that consumed Julie's days. It only took a few months for Dahlia to finally accept that her increasing income from her YouTube cooking channel and food writing gigs, along with London's regular income as a sound engineer, was enough to live comfortably, and she'd left Vanderbilt behind.

Julie was happy for her. As she was happy for London, working in a music studio like they'd always dreamed of, and Ben, who was in his hard-earned first year of residency as a geriatrics nurse. Julie was happy, truly, that her friends were living their dreams.

It had simply been nicer than she'd even realized, those few months when Dahlia had been at Vandy. Having someone to laugh with in the break room, to vent about passive-aggressive emails with during post-work drinks, to share memes with in very professional private messages throughout the day.

For a time, even though Dahlia had been stationed two floors away, Julie's cubicle had felt a bit less lonely.

"Okay," Julie said eventually. "Thanks."

"You're welcome," Dahlia said. And then, a moment later, eyes alight: "Wait. You still need an assistant coach, right?"

Julie eyed her warily.

"Yeah..."

"Okay, so, make sure she's not actually a jerk first, but if she's not...why don't you ask Elle?"

Julie snorted.

"Right. Ask one of the best players Tennessee has ever seen to assist *me*. At East High."

"Yes." Dahlia practically bounced on the couch in excitement. "You know you need an assistant, Julie, and clearly she knows the game. And she already has a connection to the team!"

Julie looked to London for assistance.

They merely shrugged.

"It's not the worst idea I've ever heard. It's not often you get the chance to work with your heroes. I would emphasize making sure she's not a jerk first, though."

Julie stared at them both, incredulous.

"She would *laugh* at me."

Being laughed at by Elle Cochrane would be even worse than... whatever had happened today.

"If she does," Dahlia said, eyes serious again, "then I will turn completely to London's side in hating her. But I've seen firsthand how you refuse to ask for help—"

Julie made a sound of grumbly protest. Maybe she shouldn't have vented about Vandy stuff to Dahlia all those months ago after all.

"*So,*" Dahlia continued pointedly, "at least think about it. Okay?"

There was no way Julie would think about it.

"Okay," she said.

After a prolonged moment, Dahlia burst out, "Okay, but you have to try these canelés London made last night. They are for sure the prettiest things I've ever seen, and I'm still kind of mad about it."

As they indulged in caramelized French pastry and rum-soaked custard, Julie told herself that Dahlia was at least right in her first piece of advice.

Julie could get over this, the reality of Elle Cochrane in her life.

Elle was simply another parent, and Julie would treat her as such. She would be cool and collected. She'd allow herself to freak out, when she needed to, in the privacy of her apartment and the comfort of her cat, Snoozles.

Julie would put today behind her. Focus on getting to districts. Playing good, fair, beautiful basketball.

And maybe, if she was lucky, getting Vanessa Lerner to laugh along the way.

CHAPTER FOUR

Elle was not being a creep.

At least, she was actively trying to convince herself she wasn't being a creep.

She knew this habit she'd developed of running out of the house as soon as her last meeting ended to sneak into the East High gym and watch the end of practice each day was a bit odd. Most parents and guardians who picked up their kids simply waited in their cars. She knew Vanessa might view it as obsessively hovering.

Being that Vanessa had said, at one point over the last week, "I know those people probably told you to watch me like a hawk, but seriously, if you don't leave me alone soon, I'm going to freak the fuck out."

Still, Elle couldn't stop herself from being interested in how Vanessa was doing, making sure she wasn't completely miserable on the team. Which, as far as Elle could assess, she…well, she didn't appear any more miserable than she appeared elsewhere, which Elle tried to take as a win. She was slower on the court than the other players, but she had, Elle thought, impressively good ball handling skills.

And maybe, beyond Vanessa's well-being, in the secret pockets of herself…Elle knew the other reason she rushed here each day.

Coach Parker blew her whistle to end the scrimmage.

Her hair bounced in its ponytail, that particular hue Elle found herself occasionally daydreaming about: not quite red, not quite blond.

But even more than her hair, or those firecracker eyes, what continued to catch Elle's attention about Julie Parker was...everything.

The way her lips were almost perpetually curved in a smile. Until they weren't, when the smile fell and Julie's brow creased in focus as she watched a drill play out. Elle could practically feel the wheels turning inside her head. How seriously she took the game and her players, while still maintaining a warmth in her communication with them that made something in Elle's chest ache.

It was an ache Elle didn't want to examine too closely, for a variety of reasons. But one she found herself leaning toward anyway, in the hectic confusion of her current life, like a spring daffodil inching toward the sun. An ache that made Elle somehow okay with sitting here, observing, listening, after eight years of avoiding basketball courts.

"All right, Bobcats! One more sprint, and another practice down. We're gettin' there."

The team lined up under the far post, Julie alongside them. She said something to the player next to her, the one with rambunctious dark curls Elle was pretty sure she'd heard Julie call Moskowitz. Moskowitz laughed. Julie grinned, extended an arm over her chest to stretch her shoulder.

And Elle, as with every time she'd watched Julie make a player laugh, felt her own mouth curve.

This wasn't the gym of Coach Snyder or Coach Davis, who had influenced so much of Elle's young basketball career: serious men who had taught Elle the skills she needed. How to block and rebound, how to dribble effortlessly with both hands. The art of the fake pass and the pick-and-roll. To carry yourself on and off the court, through the wins and the losses and the bad calls and the pure luck, with dignity.

To never let them see you cry.

Coach Parker's gym, in contrast…

Coach Parker was somehow, simultaneously, deadly serious and goofy as hell.

And against Elle's better judgment, she couldn't get enough of it.

Surely, it was okay to soak in a few minutes of that joyful dichotomy each day. And along with it, perhaps enjoy Julie Parker's calves. The occasional thrilling sight of quads peeking out from underneath those long basketball shorts. The length of her neck, exposed by the ponytail that bright hair was always captured in. Her freckled forearms and round cheeks, usually pink with the efforts of coaching her players.

She leaned forward now, whistle approaching her equally pink lips. And even as she shot across the court, arms pumping, those lips curved into that smile.

Elle watched Julie run, Vanessa always a foot or two behind her, and flashes of the last two weeks played in her mind.

That first frenzied trip to Target after receiving the call from CPS, frantically grabbing anything she might need in order to convert her home office into a bedroom for a teenager.

The trip to the mall last Saturday for all the things Vanessa actually needed, that she hadn't packed in the two bags she'd shown up to Elle's house with: Vanessa's preferred brand of tampons; a new charger for her Chromebook; art supplies for a school project. Proper basketball shoes, even if Vanessa's eyes had bulged at the price. But footwear was important. Elle could barely think about the fact that Vanessa had raced around the court last week in *Vans.*

All of the phone calls and emails, reaching out to Vanessa's teachers and school counselor, making the doctors' appointments Vanessa apparently hadn't had in too long, contacting the CPS-mandated therapist.

And then, last night: the first scheduled phone call from Karly's rehab facility. The first time Vanessa had talked to her mom since arriving at Elle's. The call was meant to be supervised, but Elle had put in her earbuds, puttering around the kitchen, listening to a podcast she didn't comprehend a word of, allowing Vanessa privacy in the adjoining den.

While Elle hadn't been able to hear the words, she'd seen Vanessa's face afterward. The way she'd run the sleeve of her sweatshirt under her nose as she shouldered past Elle and barreled upstairs to her room.

The Bobcats' sprint neared its end, the gym thundering with the exhausted but exuberant yells of teenagers. Vanessa and Julie were still always the last to cross the line, and watching them sprint down the court together tugged on that ache in Elle's chest each time. The weight on her shoulders lifting an inch, knowing someone else was pushing Vanessa, supporting her. That Vanessa wasn't alone out there.

Elle barely wanted to admit it to herself, but this new daily routine of watching Vanessa's practices was making it dangerously easy to remember the beauty of sports, whether you were on or off the court: a respite from the world. A few hours where all that mattered, all you had to think about, was the game.

"Goooo, Bobcats!"

The final huddle broke, and Julie's players headed toward the locker room, a few lingering to talk to Coach. Elle stood.

Each day, her need to actually talk to Julie again, to apologize for the way she'd handled their first interaction, intensified.

But Coach Parker had thus far avoided Elle's efforts.

On Monday, Julie's eyes had darted toward Elle countless times. But the moment Elle moved from the bleachers at the end of practice, Julie had disappeared into her office. Yesterday, another parent had dashed in at the last second, engaging Julie in a conversation that lasted until Vanessa emerged from the locker room, even as Elle hovered an obvious I-need-to-talk-to-her-too distance away.

It had been evident Julie and this parent knew each other; Julie's body language relaxed as they chatted. At one point, the other woman had rested a hand on Julie's arm, and Elle's chest had flared with jealousy.

Today, though, Elle was the only guardian in sight, ready to once more make her move, when Julie herself turned toward the bleachers. And after a moment's obvious hesitation, she crossed the court.

"Um." Julie paused a few feet away and waved. Like they were children, passing each other on the school bus. She seemed to regret the gesture immediately, face stricken as she shoved her hands in the pocket of the sweatshirt she always threw on after practice. "Hi."

And with the absence of migraines, with the court emptied of everyone but the two of them, the cuteness was almost too much to handle. Elle couldn't hold back her grin.

"Hi," she answered. And after a beat, "I hope it's okay I've been checking out the ends of your practices."

"Oh. Uh." Julie went to tuck her hair behind her ear, before seeming to remember it was already up. "Sure."

"I'm glad you came over," Elle continued, sticking her own hands in the pockets of her joggers. "I've been wanting to apologize about last week. I know I was short with you, when we first met, and—"

"It's okay," Julie interrupted. "I know I was being—"

"No, no, you were fine. I was just having an off day. I get migraines, and I can become kind of a monster when they hit. Which isn't an excuse. I'm sorry."

"It's okay."

"I also, generally"—Elle was careful to keep her voice gentle—"prefer to . . . keep my basketball past in the past, you know?"

Elle did want to apologize. She wanted to converse, carefree and casual, like that parent who had gotten to touch Julie's arm.

But she also needed to set boundaries for herself.

Julie shifted, staring at the floor. A frown ghosted over her features before it disappeared.

"Okay. Um. Understood."

"But thank you, again, for allowing Vanessa onto the team."

"Yeah, that's why I—" Julie gestured vaguely before clamping her hands over her elbows. She glanced, briefly, at Elle. "She's a hard worker. That's what I wanted to tell you."

A swell of pride crested in Elle's chest. She couldn't wait to repeat the compliment to Karly. Whenever she actually got to talk to Karly.

"She also...seems a little terrified of shooting the ball?" Julie ventured, and Elle laughed.

The sound seemed to ease the tension in Julie's shoulders. Her mouth even came close to its natural curve.

"I've noticed that, too," Elle admitted. "Even though she appears to have ball handling down."

"Oh, absolutely," Julie agreed, letting go of her elbows. "She has fantastic control. She just doesn't trust herself."

A moment of silence transpired, an awkward beat too long.

It was an astute observation. The observation of a good coach.

Just one Elle had no idea how to fix.

"Do you teach here, as well?" Elle asked at length, noting how Julie's sneakers were inching away, her mouth clearly opening to end the conversation.

But Elle wasn't quite ready for Julie to leave yet. For the real world outside of East High to return once more.

"Oh, no." Julie shook her head, staring at the empty court. "Just coach. My day job is at Vandy."

"Huh." Elle smiled. "Me too."

Julie's head jerked. For the first time this week, those hazel eyes stared straight at Elle.

"What?"

Elle's grin crept a bit higher on her cheeks.

"I don't work for their athletic department, if that's what you're worried about. I'm not a traitor to the Vols. I actually work for the hospital, doing admin work. I'm in medical billing."

Julie's face had not changed.

"What?" she asked again.

Elle's grin gradually fell away. She had spent the past eight years avoiding exactly this—explaining her new life to old fans.

But, Elle reminded herself, Julie Parker wasn't only an old fan. She was Vanessa's coach. And like Vanessa's teachers, like Vanessa's caseworker Amber and Elle's foster certifier Camryn, like Vanessa's doctors, Julie was a part of their team now.

"I wanted a job where I could work from home," Elle forced herself to say, "after..."

And not even a full sentence in, she trailed off. But certainly, Julie already knew about Elle's departure from the WNBA. She pushed on.

"I wanted something simple, where I could be anonymous. I didn't necessarily plan on working for the hospital, but I enjoy it. I mean, medical billing is...well." Elle tried on a self-deprecating smile she hoped was charming. "It's depressing, and horrible, really. But when I can get past my specific job, it's been interesting, learning how the hospital works. And I've always liked working with numbers."

Julie only continued to stare. Elle cleared her throat.

"I do have to go in, sometimes, for trainings or meetings. I had actually just run here from the hospital last week, when we first met. Typically, I'm less frazzled. And"—Elle gestured to her sweats—"this is more my daily attire."

Even though Elle privately liked when she had to go in to the hospital, when she got to dress up a bit. Elle liked dressing up.

"Anyway," she continued when Julie clearly had nothing to say about medical billing. Which was fair. Elle knew her life was boring now. Boring was exactly what she had wanted. "You work at the university?"

"Um." Julie blinked, finally breaking her stare, looking once more toward the court. "Yeah. Alumni relations. Fundraising and stuff. It's boring as shit. I mean—fuck." Julie winced. "I'm not supposed to cuss on the court. It's just—" Julie scratched her head, looking anywhere but at Elle's face. "I'm just really fucking nervous around you."

And Elle did not want Julie to be nervous.

But this open honesty made something inside Elle melt like snow in the South.

She cleared her throat again, around a smile this time.

"You don't have to be nervous around me, Coach Parker. You're not nervous out there." Elle nodded her chin toward the court. "Don't think of me as Elle fucking Cochrane. She doesn't exist. I'm only Vanessa's aunt. In fact—" A thought occurred to her. "Can you make sure you refer to me that way, to the rest of the team? Vanessa's aunt? It's who I am, in the first place; the fostering situation is new for everyone, and I don't want Vanessa to feel...embarrassed, about anything."

Elle could barely get a word out of Vanessa, when it was just them, about how she was feeling about everything. She could only imagine how Vanessa would feel if her teammates, her classmates, started asking about her *foster parent*.

"Oh, of course." Julie looked almost at ease for the first time since walking over here. Like she was on the same page, at least when it came to discussing Vanessa. "Absolutely."

Beyond Julie's shoulder, Vanessa emerged from the locker room. A twinge of disappointment hit Elle's gut. Julie had just started to possibly relax around her.

And something in that flash of disappointment, that slightly panic-filled regret at having to return to the real world, made Elle reach out a hand and place it on Julie's arm.

Except while that other parent's gesture had seemed nonchalant, a tiny blip in the conversation, it turned out nothing felt casual about Elle's hand on Julie's bicep. Elle knew it, as soon as her hand reached toward Julie's sweatshirt. But her arm was already in motion, brain powerless to stop it.

"Thank you, again, for all you're doing for Vanessa."

And then, horrifically, Elle's thumb made a truly unnecessary journey, swiping up, down, up again against the soft fabric. Before finally, her fingertips dropped away, trailing down Julie's sleeve.

Julie stared, unblinking.

"You ready?" Vanessa asked, before glancing at Elle. And Julie. And back again.

"Of course."

Elle managed a last smile, heart thumping in her chest like an awkward teenager, before turning and walking with Vanessa out of the gym.

They made it to the parking lot before Vanessa said, "Elle, were you just putting the moves on Coach?"

And while Elle had been busy berating herself—apparently she could only act inappropriately cold or inappropriately warm toward Vanessa's coach—to her own surprise, a laugh escaped her throat.

"Do you think it worked?" she couldn't help but ask.

"Ew," Vanessa responded, chucking her bag in the back seat. "How am I supposed to know?"

Elle bit back a smile the entire ride home.

CHAPTER FIVE

J ulie walked into her apartment, scooped up Snoozles the cat, and
exhaled long and hard into her gray fur.

After a full minute of Snoozles breathing, Julie set her back onto
the couch. She walked to the kitchen, dug out a slightly freezer-
burned veggie burger, and tossed it in a pan.

And once her hands were still, once she had nothing to do but
watch the veggie burger cook, she reached for her phone and opened
her group chat with London and Dahlia.

Julie: HELLO. ALERT. MAYDAY.

Dahlia: omg what's happening

Julie: elle cochrane

Dahlia: ohhhh! was she a bitch again!! tell us everything!!

Julie: no

Julie: I tried to treat her like any other parent

Julie bit her lip. This felt like a bit of a fib. At least, she hoped she did not act like such a nervous fool around other parents. But she supposed it was an accurate statement. She had, indeed, tried.

Julie: and she was NICE TO ME THIS TIME

Julie: which was SO MUCH WORSE

Dahlia: . . . it was?? 👀

Julie: she TOUCHED MY ARM

London: oh my god

London: this is incredible

Dahlia: so did you ask her to be your assistant coach??

Julie typed what? no, wtf before deleting it.

Julie: i did not

Dahlia: omg DO IT

London: agreed, do it

London: this is the workplace romance i didn't know i needed

London: im crying

Dahlia: fact check for your feelings—they are not. They're smirking, a little

Dahlia: it's cute :)

Julie almost threw the phone across the room. "Dahlia!" she shouted at its screen instead. "Fucking focus!"

She took a breath before typing again.

> **Julie:** seriously though, I don't think I can treat her like a normal parent. I tried and I failed
>
> **Julie:** what do I do??
>
> **London:** find a tree
>
> **London:** sit in it
>
> **London:** I believe the next part is k-i-s-s-i-n-g
>
> **Julie:** London I swear to god

Julie could see Dahlia typing something else, but she tossed the phone on the kitchen counter, angrily grabbed a seltzer from the fridge, and wondered why she'd texted any of that in the first place.

London normally didn't give Julie a hard time about...about whatever. *Romance.* She assumed most people in her life thought she was ace. Charlotte, their mom, had stopped asking if Julie was seeing anyone years ago, although she still gave her *looks* sometimes whenever other relationships were brought up that made Julie's stomach sink.

And maybe Julie was ace. Who the fuck knew.

She was a big fan of masturbating—huge, really—so she knew she had a sex drive. She was attracted to people. Or, well, some people. Sometimes. She was attracted to Elle Cochrane, had been attracted to Elle Cochrane since she was fourteen, and also, Manny Jacinto. Julie knew she landed somewhere on the queer spectrum, a fact she'd always somehow inherently known. Possibly because most of her friends were queer, so it had always felt like an open option, a concept that made sense.

But she had yet to find an "Into Both Elle Cochrane and Manny Jacinto, Specifically" sexual identity category, so she'd never been able to land on a more precise label, something that truly seemed to fit *her* in the way she'd watched everyone else find their labels over the years.

Which she possibly obsessed about, sometimes.

Either way, label or no label, she had never been able to figure out the translation between possibly being attracted to certain people and...everything else.

And she'd never found anyone she was interested in *enough*, who was interested in her back, to fill that gap.

Her lack of experience always made her feel like a bit of a freak— an imposter for even wanting to claim a particular queer label in the first place—as she faded into the background each time a discussion veered into friends' sexual and romantic trials and tribulations. Julie loved giving advice, listening, ever the Supportive Friend.

But she always wondered if everyone else thought it was weird. That she was never an actual player in the conversation.

She *had* kissed someone, once. The kissing itself had been...you know. Fine. But everything that had happened afterward—the consequences of actually acting on an ill-advised attraction—had only been embarrassing. And frankly, it all just seemed like a lot of work, thinking about trying that again, a lot of work that made her itchy and sweaty if she thought about it all too hard, and Julie didn't like being itchy and sweaty.

She didn't like who she'd been around Elle Cochrane, this week and last. The itchiest and sweatiest.

Even though Julie had been pumping herself up about acting normal. And, okay, avoiding Elle. Who was apparently going to be one of the most supportive Bobcat parents ever, which was...good. It was good! That Elle was apparently going to be there, every practice! It was especially good for Vanessa, and Vanessa was what was important here.

But when Julie hadn't been avoiding Elle the last few days, she really had been preparing. Playing out hypothetical conversations in her head. Ready to channel Dahlia's advice and act like a professional-ass coach in front of Elle Cochrane.

The only problem—or, at least, one of the problems—was that Elle kept showing up to Julie's gym in...athleisure wear.

Loose gray joggers. Sweatshirts so smooth they looked fresh off the rack. Coral pink sneaks, which added a surprising touch of softness. And hotness.

Julie could accept, in an intellectual way, the Elle Cochrane she'd met last week, in slacks and a crisp button-up. The Elle who had always handled postgame interviews with a calm, whip-smart swagger. Who never lost her head, even in the midst of a celebration. A pillar of strength. A queen.

This casual, comfortable Elle Cochrane, made for binging Netflix and eating nachos with, made Julie crawl out of her skin.

And the anticipation of seeing her every day, the anxiety of not knowing if it would be today that they actually talked again, needled inside Julie's brain every night she fell asleep and each morning she woke up. She felt, sometimes, as obsessed with Elle Cochrane as she had been when she was fifteen.

Except it felt weirder and more creepy now.

She almost looked forward to going to work, so her brain could be filled with things that were not Elle Cochrane, or even Elle Cochrane–adjacent. But then she'd find herself staring blankly at her computer, remembering the way she'd been able to see the freckles that peeked from the open collar of Elle's button-up last week, that trailed up the side of Elle's neck from her collarbone, light enough that Julie didn't remember seeing them on her TV screen, but impossible to miss in person. The way she still seemed to hold herself with such poise, even in joggers, but just...in a *grown* way now. Not quite the same person Julie had watched as a teen at all. Like her face alone—those eyes, so piercingly blue Julie could barely look at them—could tell you stories. Stories Julie wanted to know. And, just—it was just—

Just a parent, Julie's ass.

She realized she had somehow consumed her entire veggie burger and didn't even remember eating it.

Her phone buzzed on the counter. She picked it up as she tossed her plate in the sink. She flopped onto the couch, disturbing Snoozles, whom she scooped up once more.

The new text was from London.

> Hey Jules, sorry if I was being an asshat just now. You having a crush—on your crush—just really tickles me, but I'll shut my mouth if that's what you want. For the record, I'm sure you're acting totally fine around her, and I do still agree with Dahlia that you should ask her about coaching. It could be cool, and you need (and deserve) some help. Okay, love you, tell me you're not mad at me or I won't let you hug Schnitzel for two weeks

Two weeks!

The gall.

I'm not mad at you, she typed. She was close to adding, *and I don't have a crush*, but god, she did, didn't she? That was what this was.

Not that this crush actually meant anything, because Elle was Elle Cochrane, and Julie was just Julie, so she *really* wasn't going to get anything out of it, but still.

And the assistant coach thing…man, if they *did* exist in a parallel universe where Julie felt totally normal around Elle, she had to admit it would be nice. She was still managing the team okay, but as their first game against Hillcrest approached next week, she was also starting to low-level panic. Practices went by so fast, and she simply didn't have the ability to give the attention to every player like she knew she should, like she wanted to, like she had been able to last year with Jacks.

She'd been leaving East High later and later each night, addressing parent concerns, answering emails from East's athletic director, making sure everything about the season's schedule and transportation was squared away.

There was so much else she wanted to do—ways to truly build a unified basketball program at East, across gender lines—if she only had time.

But maybe they'd have better luck finding a new assistant next year. She could focus more on some of those goals then.

Love you too, Julie eventually typed to London, before once more throwing her phone to the side.

Okay.

She could do this.

Maybe she just had to level up her practice.

"Snoozles." She stood, situating Snoozles on the windowsill, and grabbed a bag of cat treats. "You're gonna help me out here. Pretend you're Elle Cochrane, all right? And I'm going to talk to you. I'm going to be so totally, completely, awesomely normal."

Snoozles swiped at the bag of treats.

Julie stuffed them under an arm as she walked to the opposite side of the living room. She closed her eyes, taking a deep, Zen-filled breath, before she twirled on her heel and approached Snoozles with a confident smile.

"Hey, Elle," she said. "I know I've acted super embarrassing each time we've talked before, but those days are behind us. We're cool now. And—" She put a hand to her heart, accidentally dropping the treats in the process. Snoozles meowed in outrage. "I promise to never bring up your legendary basketball career again. Including but not limited to the time you led the Vols to victory over UConn in the national championship, the single best thing that has ever happened to me, personally."

Julie still couldn't understand this, *at all*. But she would respect it. And try to forget the way she had felt scolded when Elle had talked about it today. Even though Elle had said it nice. But scolded Julie had still felt, an extremely squirmy sensation she cared to not visit again.

"I will also," Julie went on, "come to terms with the fact that you *also* work at Vandy? And that"—she waved a hand around, a movement Snoozles tracked avidly, until she got distracted by a dust mote drifting through the air—"our lives have apparently followed a weirdly similar trajectory? Which makes me feel...I don't know, a certain kind of way."

Julie had started working at Vandy six years ago now, when she'd moved back home after graduating from the University of Tennessee. After she'd admitted to herself she had no idea what to do with her bachelor's in psychology. Or at least, after she'd admitted that all of the job options available to a newly graduated person with a psych degree in the American mental healthcare system were too intimidating and sad. And securing an office job felt like the thing you were supposed to do, after earning a bachelor's you didn't know how to use.

She'd moved into this apartment with Snoozles as soon as she'd secured the Vandy position. It was close to her office on campus, and living across the river in Hillsboro felt like enough of a difference from where she'd grown up in East Nashville to signify that she was still moving forward, finding her own way, even if she was back home. It was a simple apartment in a large complex of simple apartments: nondescript, perfectly livable.

Julie had known it didn't quite fit her the moment she'd moved in. But she could afford the rent on her newbie admin salary, and it was close to Kroger and the Pancake Pantry, so it had seemed ideal.

"Well," Julie continued, finally rewarding Snoozles with a treat, "I suppose our lives have followed a weirdly similar trajectory except for, you know, the part where you went to the WNBA while I rode the bench at Thompson-Boling, but I can't talk to you about that either, even though you have to know I am *dying* to know why you left! You could have come back easily from that injury!"

Julie stopped herself. Planted her hands on her hips and took another Zen breath.

Truly, the fact that Elle Cochrane was not buying mansions and selling shoes like Lebron but instead working in *medical billing* made Julie want to actually strangle something.

"But again"—Julie returned an apologetic hand to her chest— "I respect it. So." Snoozles jumped off the windowsill and started meowing at Julie's shins. "I will ignore my undying admiration of you, and simply treat you as Vanessa's aunt. And foster parent. Even though I have a ton of questions about that too, questions I know aren't any of my business, but like—is everything okay? Are you okay? Do you need support?"

Julie plopped herself on the floor.

"Anyway. Vanessa really is great, so maybe if I can focus on that, talking to you will be easy. Did I tell you she's started using *fork* any time she wants to curse at me? Which"—Julie smiled and gave Snoozles another treat—"I found lacking in creativity at first. Although when I made a *Good Place* reference she only gave me a blank stare, so maybe it is a little creative. Either way, I have to admit, any time she looks at me all exasperated and says, 'What the *fork*, Coach,' it makes me laugh so hard."

Julie already had an idea for the end-of-season banquet. She'd visit Goodwill, buy a bunch of mismatched forks, wrap them with a bow like a bouquet, and present them to Vanessa in front of the team.

Because there was nothing that glued a team together like inside jokes.

"Ooh, maybe I can start a rewatch of *The Good Place* tonight instead of thinking weird, useless things about Elle Cochrane. Now, there's a good idea. See?" Julie nuzzled her knuckles between Snoozles's velvety ears. "You're always so helpful, Snoozles. Which I know is because you love me deeply and sincerely. Not just because of this Friskies Beachside Crunch Party Mix."

Snoozles made a low growling noise when it became clear Julie wasn't going to reopen the bag. She moved away to lick her butthole.

Julie sprawled on the couch and clicked on the TV, scrolling until she found Eleanor Shellstrop. After a few minutes, she picked up her phone.

Julie: how exactly is manny jacinto so hot

Julie: also I miss you

Ben texted back immediately.

Ben: JULIE I MISS YOU SO DUCKING MUCH

Ben: work has been…intense

Ben: can we plan a bad movie & buffalo wild wings date soon, PLEASE

Julie laughed out loud.

Ben and Julie's first Bad Movie & BW3s Day had been years ago, during a particularly rough period at work. Julie had been working on a big event where it felt like every single thing was going wrong: a typo on the invites, a scheduling snafu with the venue, nagging emails from her nemesis Lorraine at all hours of the day. Ben had demanded Julie take a mental health day. And they both agreed there was nothing better about being a grown-up than being able to go to the movies in the middle of the day on a weekday.

Adding on Buffalo Wild Wings had been Julie's idea; she and her dad used to go there sometimes to watch games. And there was something about heading out to the suburbs—they always went to the movie theater and the BW3s down by Franklin—that was an inexplicably good time. Ben always lifted both fists in the air and yelled "Sports!" as they walked through the parking lot to the restaurant. And again when they sat at their favorite booth.

The idea of a Bad Movie & BW3s Day made something settle so firmly and happily into Julie's chest that she could almost forget Ben was leaving. Moving to Portland, Oregon, to live with the love of his life, whom he'd met while hiking the PCT.

Just after New Year's, two short months from now, her best friend would be a cool 2,348 miles away.

Did they have Buffalo Wild Wings in Oregon?

Probably.

Maybe Ben would drag Alexei to one, one day. Alexei, a quiet man who preferred the company of birds to humans, would hate it. But maybe he'd go anyway, for Ben. And Julie liked to think it would make Ben happy, being reminded of her.

Ben: also, it's obviously the cheekbones

Ben: although I have more thoughts

Ben: including questions about you texting me this important query at all

Julie rolled onto her side.

If there was anyone she could talk to about her confusion about herself—a confusion she was normally pretty good at shoving to the back of her mind, until this old-new crush on Elle Cochrane pushed it all to the surface—it would be Ben Caravalho, whose main traits were being incredibly kind and incredibly gay.

But she and Ben had been friends since second grade. She'd never talked to him about having a crush before. She was still, if she was honest, slightly confused about what having a crush on Elle Cochrane now—a few shades different from daydreaming about a poster on her teenaged wall—even meant. And there was something so epically embarrassing about discussing a crush for the first time when she was almost thirty years old, when Ben had had approximately two hundred relationships since the second grade, that her cheeks flamed even thinking about typing the words.

She brought up her work calendar instead.

> **Julie:** what days are you off next week? i could probably play hooky on thursday

> **Julie:** we'd have to hit the first possible show, so i could get back in time for practice

Snoozles strolled up, headbutting her on the chin.

Things were back on track, she assured herself. She'd only talk to Elle Cochrane about Vanessa. About the team. About the things that actually mattered. She was pretty sure she could do that.

And she had a date with her best friend.

She curled her arm around Snoozles and hit rewind to catch what she'd missed.

CHAPTER SIX

Coach Parker jogged over to Elle the next day before the Bobcats' practice was even over, a smile on her face. Easy and wide and natural, as if the scene had been plucked straight from Elle's dreams. As if the nervous woman from only the day before had disappeared. It lit up her face like a sunrise.

She slowed to walk the final few steps, hands on her hips, those baggy shorts swaying over her thighs. Her old Vols T-shirt was pulled forward just enough for Elle to catch a glimpse of collarbone.

Something stirred low in Elle's belly. A sensation beyond casual admiration that she hadn't truly felt in . . . god, years. A desire to grab Julie Parker by the hips, so strong her fingers tingled.

"Great news." The smile didn't drop from Julie's face. "I think Vanessa's making friends."

Elle finally stood from the bleachers, tearing her attention away from Julie's collar to glance at the court. "Yeah?"

"Yeah." Julie turned to stand at Elle's side, so they could watch the scrimmage together, shoulder to shoulder. "I caught her *laughing* with Evans earlier. Katelyn," she supplied.

Elle turned her head.

"Laughing?"

Julie raised a hand, three fingers up. "Scout's honor."

Elle returned her gaze to the court. Vanessa sat on the sidelines, looking perfectly disinterested. Elle wouldn't dare bring up this supposed instance of laughter later. But she let this small win settle in her chest.

"So we've now got"—Julie opened her palm, counted off on her fingers—"ball handling skills. Excellent attendance. Inside jokes."

Elle's head snapped toward Julie again. Julie had inside jokes? With Vanessa?

"And"—Julie's eyes sparkled—"friendship. Lerner's journey to becoming a Bobcat is firing on all cylinders."

Elle looked once more at Vanessa. Who was picking at her fingernails, not even watching the game.

But Julie was still smiling at her like a proud mom.

Elle almost huffed a laugh, the warmth in her belly kindling further, spreading in different directions.

"The rest of the team, on the other hand…" The smile on Julie's face faltered. Elle could feel its disappearance, somehow, even before she looked over to confirm, like the lights had dimmed.

"They seem pretty solid," Elle said.

"Yeah, they're great. It's just—" Julie moved her hands back to her hips with a sigh. "I don't know. I don't have a handle on how we're going to gel this year. We have our first game next week, and I still don't have my starting lineup finalized." A small shake of her head. "I had an assistant last year, Jacks. She wasn't here when I was a player, but—"

"You played here?" Elle interrupted.

"Yeah." A different kind of smile. Smaller, wistful. "I guess she started shortly after I graduated. She had become the backbone of the program. One of those quiet coaches, no-nonsense, but she *saw* everything, you know? Like she could sit back and watch a practice and know exactly what we needed to do for game day."

Elle nodded. She did know.

"I can run drills, joke around with them, but I feel like…I just don't have *time* to sit back and analyze and figure it all out. I don't know." Julie sighed again. "Jacks really should have been head coach. I didn't know what the hell I was doing when I signed up for this last year. I told her that, over and over, but she'd just say—" Julie's voice turned to gravel, low and rough and, Elle assumed, exaggerated. But then again, having known her fair share of women's basketball coaches, maybe not. " 'And deal with the parents and the paperwork? No thanks, Chicken.' "

"She called you Chicken?"

"Yeah. 'Cause I was a spring chicken." A whisper of the smile returned.

"Did Jacks resign?" Elle asked after a minute, watching the scrimmage, mind ticking.

Julie shook her head.

"Got ovarian cancer. Moved up to Lexington to be closer to her daughter for treatment."

Elle sucked in a breath through her teeth.

"And they didn't get you a replacement?"

"No. It'll be okay. I'm just getting in my head."

Elle frowned. She'd actually wondered about Julie's lack of assistants. In any level, whether it was professional or biddy basketball, you needed more than one person. At least, if you truly cared about shaping your players. One person couldn't do it all.

"Well," Elle said after another moment of silence between them, of sneakers squeaking across the gym. "You've got Ngozi at point."

"Right. And Mosk on center. Moskowitz," Julie added. And a second later, in case Elle might need further explanation: "Sasha."

Elle smiled at the obligatory sports hierarchy. Nickname, last name, first name. "Right."

"They're both solid on those positions from last year," Julie continued. "But—"

Abruptly, Julie blew her whistle. Elle nearly jumped.

"Good setup, but you can't move like that once you're planted!" Julie yelled. Elle thought *illegal screen* to herself, helpless to not think it, as Julie continued to shout. "You know this! Chin gets two shots."

Mosk groaned but didn't object.

"Now, Chin—Gray—has the potential to be the three," Julie said to Elle, voice back at a reasonable level, like their conversation had never been interrupted. She rubbed a hand along her jaw.

"I can see that." Elle watched Gray take the free throws, trying not to think about Julie's jaw. Or her hands.

It only surprised Elle a little, how much she realized she already knew about the team from her practice observations. And she remembered what Vanessa had said last week, after that first practice, when Elle had asked if she'd met anyone cool: *I didn't meet anyone cool, Elle, because I already fucking know all of those girls. Except Gray isn't a girl, but—I already go here, remember? God.*

"But I need them and Mosk to work better together, and I don't know if they're there yet."

"You can get them there," Elle said, voice confident. Julie shot her a little grin.

"That's nice of you to say."

Elle lifted her shoulders. "You can."

And maybe because Elle could sense that their time here was probably up, that Julie would leave to start the final sprint soon, and Elle didn't want her to—she opened her mouth and said, "You know, before last week, it had been a long time since I'd set foot on a basketball court."

Julie went still.

"Yeah?" she eventually asked, voice cautious. Elle smiled at the restraint, the respect in that caution.

"Yeah."

Julie didn't need to know exactly how long. That it had been, in fact, as long as the last time she'd left the Milwaukee Shipwrecks Arena. But maybe Julie already knew it.

Elle shrugged.

"Maybe it's the fact that it's a high school court that's made it feel…okay. But every time I walk in here…" Elle's smile curved further. "It's the smell."

"Oh my god." Julie dropped her arms and turned toward her. "Right?"

And even though Elle was aware she was being ridiculous, that *right?* made the tingle reappear in her fingertips.

Right? said in that way felt like it was only made for…people on your level. People you wanted to curl up on a couch with, bitching about people you both knew.

Elle returned her eyes to the court, uncertain about whether she had been looking at Julie's face for too long. Unsettled that she was uncertain, that she was perhaps losing track of herself. She should have let Coach Parker return to her team.

"It's exactly the same," she finished.

"*Exactly* the same." And Elle couldn't help but glance back, again, at Julie. Her eyes were full golden sparklers in twilight.

Maybe Elle should start waiting in the parking lot, after all.

Another honk of Julie's whistle helped break the spell.

"Good job, Bobcats! Go ahead and line up!"

Vanessa stood, casting Julie a questioning look as she walked toward the endline.

"I'm sitting this one out," Julie called. "You got this, Lerner."

Vanessa only scowled.

Elle thought she heard Julie suppress a laugh.

Another blow of the whistle. Julie and Elle settled back into silence as they watched the Bobcats fly across the floor.

And with each second that passed, as they stood there side by side, Elle could feel the space between Julie's shoulder and her own—mere inches—like a caress.

She was about to tear herself away, to make an excuse about something she left in the car, when Julie said, eyes still on the court, "If you ever need any help with Vanessa, you can ask me. Even if it doesn't have anything to do with basketball. I don't know anything about the situation, and I'm not asking to know. But I imagine inheriting a teenager, even if it's temporary, is a lot. So if the two of you ever need anything, I'm here."

Elle stared at her. Julie had to feel her staring, but she only tracked her players' progress on the court, hands on her hips again.

For a moment, Elle was speechless.

And then she heard herself say, "Are you free tomorrow night?"

Julie turned to her then.

Heat crawled up the back of Elle's neck. "I have to go to a class, for foster parents. I was going to ask my mom, but my mom is…" The heat on her neck intensified, crawled around to her ears. It truly *had* been too long since Elle had interacted with a pretty girl. Said pretty girl threw her one line of kindness, and Elle had hooked it around her wrist, tugging and spilling unasked-for information about her family history without thought, like a wide-eyed baby queer. "My mom has some health issues and already does more than she should. And I know Vanessa's old enough to not need a babysitter, but I've been advised to not leave her alone, and…" Elle shook her head. "But it's super last minute, and probably more than you—"

"Sure," Julie interrupted. And when Elle was able to properly focus on Julie's face again—things had gone kind of hazy, as she'd been rambling—she saw a small, reassuring smile there. "I'd love to hang with Vanessa for a few hours."

"Yeah?" Elle asked, a small battle playing out in her chest between embarrassment that she'd asked at all and relief that Julie could do it. "It wouldn't be getting in the way of your Friday night plans or anything?"

Julie's smile grew at that, her eyes drifting back to the court as the shouts coming from the endline increased in volume. Julie stepped away to join in, leaning forward and clapping her hands as Vanessa sprinted the final stretch.

"That's right!" Coach Parker yelled, as Vanessa dropped her head back and groaned. Julie ran to the endline for a quick huddle before the team scattered into the locker room.

Julie jogged back to Elle.

"My only Friday-night plans were continuing my rewatch of *The Good Place* with my cat," she said. "So no, hanging with Vanessa won't be getting in the way. Just tell me where and when."

Elle almost asked if she was sure one more time. But instead, she mentally shook herself, remembered she was Elle Cochrane, who made decisions and stuck by them, who had the ability to accept kindness when it was offered, and she said, "*The Good Place* is an excellent show. Is five thirty too early for you? I know it's right after practice, but I have to drive to—"

"Nope, that works."

And then they were exchanging numbers, and Elle was texting Julie her address and hoping Vanessa wouldn't hate her for this. Elle promised she'd leave money so they could get pizza, which for some reason made Julie laugh, and a second later, Elle laughed a little herself, realizing that, for the first time in her life, she felt like a mom from a nineties sitcom.

"It'll be fun," Julie said.

Elle, in fact, wasn't entirely sure if *fun* was the accurate word for this at all; she was more concerned it was a massive overstepping of boundaries.

But then Vanessa emerged from the locker room, and Elle

remembered the whole reason Julie had started a conversation with Elle today in the first place was because she'd seen Vanessa laugh. And while she still scowled at her phone as she walked toward them, Elle thought Vanessa's shoulders did, perhaps, seem a little less bunched. Elle remembered that her most important job right now was helping the stress on those shoulders ease as much as she could.

And maybe *fun* was exactly what Vanessa and Elle needed.

CHAPTER SEVEN

J ulie stared at the steel-blue door.

It had a pretty square window, a curving dark bronze handle. There was a wreath of twisted twigs and fall leaves on a hook, a pumpkin on the stoop.

Elle Cochrane's house sat at the end of a dead-end street in a cozy East Nashville neighborhood. It had a red maple in the front yard, a perfectly landscaped mix of shrubs. While there were neighboring houses on either side of the property, the land behind the house dipped over a hill, a copse of trees visible beyond the backyard. The almost-winter sun was already low in the sky, glowing orange in the distance.

It was, clearly, much more a *home* than Julie's IKEA-clad, white-walled apartment. It was nice, like HGTV-shows-made-for-moderately-incomed-people nice. *Lovely*, really. Julie couldn't believe she was standing in front of it.

And still, the fact that Elle Cochrane did not own a house filled with sports cars and cascading waterfall features and whatever the hell else Elle Cochrane might have wanted, as other world-class athletes did, once again made Julie want to scream.

But she was not going to scream. Or pass out. Or do anything weird. She was going to channel the Coach Parker of yesterday, who had somehow manifested her own plan, and focus on only talking to Elle about Bobcat basketball–related things.

Standing on Elle's front stoop as just Julie, though, felt approximately one hundred light-years away from standing in the East High gym as Coach Parker.

Julie took a deep breath. Elle had a Ring doorbell; Julie hoped she hadn't been looking at her camera for the last five minutes, watching Julie excessively exhale and talk to herself.

She was here for Vanessa. Her interactions with Elle would probably only last ten minutes, tops, as Elle left and then came back home. Julie could handle this.

She rang the doorbell.

Her breath caught when Elle opened the door, back in her sharp business attire: crisp slacks and a button-up, but a gayer button-up this time, patterned with tiny elephants and buttoned all the way up. It was topped off by a coal-gray blazer, those shot-with-silver curls Julie was still getting used to appearing freshly gelled.

Had she said she was going to a *class*? Because by all accounts, it appeared to Julie like Elle was going on an extremely hot queer date where everyone else in the room would be jealous and overheated.

"Hey." Elle attempted a smile, but her face looked tight. Like she was possibly regretting inviting Julie to her home. "Come on in."

Julie stepped into the small foyer and slipped off her sneakers, but Elle was on the move before Julie could even get it together enough to return her greeting. Julie hustled after her, through one of those perfectly arranged rooms that lacked a TV or any sign that human beings actually spent time there. Even though the couch and chairs within it looked quite sittable, soft blankets neatly folded over their backs, an artfully faded rug running along the hardwood floor. Dark blue bookshelves lined one wall, but before Julie could even peep at what books they held, Elle was already through the next open doorway into the kitchen. Where Vanessa sat on a stool at the large island, shoulders slumped over a laptop.

"Hey, Coach," she drawled without looking up. "Ready to babysit me?"

When Julie glanced at Elle, the pinched look on her face twitched even tighter.

Yeah, maybe whatever was going on with Elle's face actually had nothing to do with Julie at all.

"The pizza's already been ordered," Elle said, voice strained as she picked at the inside of her bag. "It should be here within a half hour. There's—"

"Where'd you order from?" Julie asked.

"Five Points."

"*Sweet.*" While Elle's head was still stuck over her bag, Julie thought her lips twerked, more naturally this time. "Did you get garlic knots?"

"Duh," Vanessa said, voice just as deadpan, but perhaps slightly less angry.

"Man. I haven't had Five Points in forever."

Elle hefted her bag over her shoulder. "I hope you enjoy it. Feel free to watch whatever you want." She gestured behind Vanessa, where the space opened up to a den, a step down from the kitchen. Julie peered around Vanessa's head to see the leather couch and huge TV, a coffee table scattered with signs of life. "I shouldn't be gone more than three hours."

Julie nodded. "We'll be good."

Elle hesitated in the doorway, glancing once more at Vanessa, even more quickly at Julie.

"Call or text if you need anything."

"Will do."

And with another not-really-a-smile-at-all, she was gone.

Julie waited until she heard the front door click to take a good look around the kitchen, whistling low.

"Dude," she said. "I can't believe I am in Elle Cochrane's *house*."

Vanessa released a small huff, still hunched over her computer. "Yeah," she said. "Me too."

Julie paused before she walked around the island, plopping herself at a stool.

"You know your aunt is like, a legend, right?" she asked, picking up the textbook lying next to the computer.

Vanessa was silent for a beat before answering, voice completely neutral, "Sure."

All right, then, apparently Julie wasn't going to be able to gossip about Elle's storied basketball career with Elle *or* Vanessa. Which, considering there were clearly some complicated family dynamics going on here, was fair, and Julie should keep her mouth shut.

Except then Vanessa said, "And even if I didn't know, she has that huge box of trophies in the closet."

Julie's hand froze on the textbook. "What?"

"The closet across from the bathroom." Vanessa motioned with her head toward the den behind her. "Huge box. Full of dusty trophies."

Julie frowned.

She didn't like the sound of that.

But instead of leaping off the stool to go inspect said box of trophies immediately, Julie resumed paging through the textbook, attempting to play it cool.

"Who've you got for history this year?"

"Delgado," Vanessa answered with an eyeroll. Julie laughed.

"Oh my *god*, Ms. Delgado is still there? How old is she now?"

"Like, twenty years past ancient. She can't hear shit. I mean... stuff."

Julie pressed her lips together to hide her grin at Vanessa watching her language, even here, off the court.

"We're supposed to just use the online textbook," Vanessa said, scratching at her scalp underneath her loose bun. Like Julie, she was still in her clothes from practice. "But I don't know, I can't concentrate on the screen for that long, and I'm like, ten assignments behind, so I got that copy from the library for the weekend."

"Makes sense." Julie flipped through a few more pages. "I couldn't do textbooks online, either."

"I'm not, like, a bad student or anything," Vanessa went on, an unnecessary defensiveness creeping into her voice. "It's just that everyone in that class are assholes—I mean, jerks—since Delgado's so old and oblivious, so I normally just watch YouTube so I don't have to deal with them." Her leg bounced on the foot of the stool, her words coming quicker. It dawned on Julie, then. That for whatever reason, Vanessa was nervous. "But I feel like I have to catch up now. To show..."

Julie paused her perusal of the textbook, turning her head toward Vanessa.

"What do you have to show, Vanessa?"

Vanessa swallowed, still staring at the computer.

"To show that I'm being good. Maybe if I get caught up in everything, and show Amber I'm doing okay, maybe they'll let me go back."

Julie's heart sank into her stomach.

"Vanessa," she said carefully, "I don't know anything about what's going on with you. But...I don't think that's how this works."

Vanessa's eyes shot toward her.

"You don't? Know anything that's going on, I mean? Elle hasn't told you anything?"

Julie held her eyes as she shook her head. "No, Vanessa. You can tell me anything you want, but Elle hasn't told me anything. I'm just here to hang out."

Vanessa stared at her another second, eyes big and vulnerable, the mask she wore every day on the court simply gone. Until finally, she sighed as she looked away.

"Okay," she said, half-heartedly clicking on the mousepad again. And then, casting Julie a much more Vanessa-like look of skepticism, she added, "You're totally babysitting, though. Which is weird."

Julie laughed, looking around the kitchen again, at the window above the sink that looked onto a patch of winterberries. The light wood of the butcher block island. The white tile of the backsplash along the counters, offsetting the darkness of the steel-blue cabinets. The cabinets matched the front door, Julie realized, while also complementing the blues visible in the sitting room. The kitchen, aside from the sweaty T-shirts Julie and Vanessa were wearing inside of it, appeared almost appallingly clean.

She hadn't known what to expect as she'd driven here from East High, her body a bundle of nerves. But she was not at all surprised that Elle Cochrane lived in a perfectly coordinated HGTV house. And now that she was here, inside of its clean-but-warm ambience, she felt, all at once, that she never wanted to leave.

"I'm not babysitting you," Julie countered. "I'm just hanging out and eating free Five Points."

Vanessa snorted. "Sure. You going to go eat pizza at Ngozi's next?"

Julie grinned. "If she asks me to."

She was about to respond to Vanessa's eyeroll when the doorbell rang. Julie threw her hands in the air with a whoop and leapt off the stool. A minute later, she ushered the food into the kitchen with a little dance, humming a little made-up song.

"Just..." Vanessa hugged her forehead with her palms. "So corny."

Julie dropped the goods onto the island, immediately reaching in to pull out a garlic knot.

"Fu—*fork*, that is hot." Julie fanned her mouth with a hand. "And *delicious.*"

She rinsed her greasy hand in the sink before opening a cabinet. "Maybe plates would be good?" Julie assumed Elle did not run an eat-your-pizza-over-the-open-box kind of household. If Julie got a grease stain on anything in this place, she would never forgive herself.

She meant to continue looking for plates, but she was stopped short by the cabinet in front of her: the most meticulously organized cabinet she had ever seen. Most of the...food? Julie thought it was probably food—was in clear containers, oats and flakes and grains in an almost confusingly pleasing variety of beige.

She pulled out a labeled bag.

"What the hell is bulgur? I mean," she amended hastily, "what the *heck* is bulgur. Is what I mean. Obviously."

Vanessa snorted.

"I don't know. I don't know what half that stuff is."

"Huh."

Helpless to stop her curiosity, Julie opened the rest of the cabinets, until finally, she found Oreos and bags of chips in garish colors.

"Oh, thank god," she breathed. "She is human."

"Nah." Vanessa stood. "That's my cabinet. Or—"

She froze. Only for a second, but a long enough second that Julie was able to glance over and see the look on her face. The slight panic, and confusion, at saying *my*.

"You know," she said, turning to open the cabinet next to the fridge. "The cabinet where she's letting me store stuff that doesn't taste like hay."

Julie watched Vanessa get down two plates and serve herself a slice of cheese. Slowly, Julie closed Vanessa's snack cabinet, and did the same.

After grabbing a seltzer from the fridge—Elle seemed to have a preference for Polar over LaCroix, and her favorite flavor appeared to be pomegranate, not that Julie was taking notes or anything—she resumed her seat at the island next to Vanessa.

"Wait," Vanessa said after a second, a delayed lightbulb going off. "You went to East, too?"

"Yup. Bobcats forever, Vanessa. Bobcats forever. Had Delgado my senior year."

"Damn. She really is ancient."

Julie laughed. "I'm not *that* old, Lerner."

"Did you play on the team when you were a student?"

"Yeah." Julie grinned. "I was good."

Another small snort. "At least you're humble."

Julie took a bite of carbohydrates and cheese.

"You shouldn't always be, Lerner, when you're good at something. I mean..." She took another bite, swallowed. "You don't have to be a jerk about it. But it's important to know your worth. To know what you're good at, and be proud of it."

Vanessa picked at her crust.

"I don't really know what I'm good at." And then, "It ain't basketball."

Julie knocked her shoulder against Vanessa's. "You're getting there, though, Lerner. For real. And it's okay to not know your thing yet. You'll figure it out."

A second after she said it, Julie wondered if she was full of shit.

It had felt genuine, coming out of her mouth.

But Julie wasn't a high school basketball star anymore.

And years later, she hadn't figured out what her thing was at all.

"Do you think... I'll get any playing time at our first home game next week?"

Julie looked at Vanessa, surprised. "I mean, yeah. I try to make sure everyone gets some. Do you *want* playing time?"

"No." And then Vanessa laughed a little, and Julie laughed with her. "It's just... my mom will be there. We worked it out that she can come to my games. And I guess I don't want her to be completely bored, ya know."

Ah.

Suddenly, Vanessa's disgruntled efforts at practices—her almost surprising commitment to not completely hate basketball—made a lot more sense.

"Cool." Julie took another bite of pizza, keeping her voice casual. "I'm looking forward to meeting her."

Vanessa glanced at her, quick and away. "She's not a bad person," she said, so quiet Julie almost didn't hear it. "I know...she was gone too long this time. But she's going to fix it."

Julie bit her lip. Struggled to not reach over, grab Vanessa's hand, and squeeze tight.

She was gone too long this time.

After a moment, Julie settled for an equally quiet "I believe you."

They finished their pizza in silence. Julie grabbed another garlic knot before she spoke again.

"You know Elle doesn't actually think you need a babysitter, right? I think she's just trying to do the right thing. Follow what she was told."

Another huff of breath. A shake of Vanessa's head.

"I know she is, Coach," she said, frustration clear in her voice. She turned to look at Julie. "And do you know how fucking weird that feels?"

Julie didn't reprimand her for the curse. They weren't on the court anymore, anyway.

"No," she answered, voice soft. "I don't. But I hear you." It must have been hard, to feel like you were a problem a team of strangers was trying to solve. "I get it."

Julie was surprised, but grateful, at how much Vanessa was sharing. How fully her guard was down, slumped on the stool next to her. Because while most of Julie's nerves on the way here had been over seeing Elle Cochrane outside of a basketball court for the first time, she'd been anxious about hanging out with Vanessa, too.

Julie might have respected the angry girls, but she also wasn't made of steel. If Vanessa had only spent the night staring daggers at her across the room…well, it wouldn't have felt great.

But instead, Vanessa seemed almost eager to say things. It made sense, when Julie thought about it. Vanessa was separated from her mom; she was angry at Elle by default. Julie was a neutral adult in Vanessa's life. Someone safe to confide in.

Julie was glad she'd agreed to come to Elle's house tonight.

Not even a second after Julie thought this, Vanessa slammed her laptop closed and stacked her textbook on top of it.

"I'm going to work on homework in my room," she said as she dumped her plate in the sink.

And before Julie could protest, Vanessa was racing up the stairs off the kitchen.

Julie sat a moment, garlic knot paused halfway to her mouth. She laughed to herself before rinsing her hands in the sink again.

Nothing left to do but creepily explore the home of her idol, she supposed.

After sticking the leftovers in the fridge, Julie wandered through the first floor, lingering longer now in the sitting room. The books, she discovered, were a bit disappointing, albeit unsurprising. She'd hoped for some saucy romances or cozy mysteries, a genre Julie had only recently discovered and couldn't get enough of. Alas, there was no *Sconed to Death* or *Thread on Arrival* here, only a lot of nonfiction: history, sports memoirs. Cookbooks. Queer shit. An intriguing number of medical tomes.

And then there were the elephants.

Figurines of the stately animals were everywhere, on almost every shelf, crafted of wood and plastic, stone and glass. Julie picked up one made of smooth marble, rubbing a thumb over its side, thinking of the elephants on Elle's shirt tonight. A smile lifted her mouth before she returned it to the shelf.

A bay window jutted out to meet a hydrangea on the side of the house. Julie could picture reading here on lazy Sunday afternoons, cocooned by sunshine and tiny elephants and high-quality furniture.

She was about to wander into the hall when a framed photograph on a side table caught her eye.

It showed Elle and her mother—or at least Julie assumed it was her mother. The older woman was wearing a green dress and delicate gold jewelry. Julie remembered Elle saying her mom had health issues, but the woman here looked free from pain. She was short, with trim gray curls and a kind, open face.

Elle wore a fancy dress, too, although hers was purple. They stood on grass littered with flower petals, white chairs in the background. Elle looked hot, of course, in the purple dress. Although the longer Julie stared at the photograph, the more she studied Elle's muscular shoulders, she found she most wanted to see Elle—if she had options, if she could choose—in an expensive suit. Elle Cochrane fit best in sharp lines and authority.

What was most striking about the photograph, though, wasn't the dress, or Elle's impressive biceps. It was her face, turned toward her mom, tilted downward in a laugh.

She still had long hair, swept into an updo, no traces of gray, so this must have been several years ago. But what felt most familiar about Elle in this photo was the easy look on her face, the happiness in the curve of her lips. This Elle was the same one Julie had watched, countless times, with a basketball in her hand, dribbling slowly, naturally, on her way down the court. One arm outstretched as she called out to her teammates, setting up a screen.

Elle Cochrane on the court had been cool as a cucumber. And when she won, when she walked off the court at Thompson-Boling Arena, it wasn't arrogance that radiated from her like waves. It was joy.

Julie had only been able to catch a glimpse of that Elle this past week, in the small smiles she'd thrown Julie's way yesterday. But even those glimpses hadn't been like this. And the rest of the time...

Elle, now, mostly seemed to be composed of a clenched jawline and tight shoulders, stress lines etched in her forehead.

Julie returned the photo to the table, a slick of guilt sliding down her back. Like she'd seen something she shouldn't have.

A feeling that only intensified as she stepped into the hall and paused outside the closet opposite the half bath.

She continued to the den.

It was by far the most lived-in room on the first floor. Julie tried out the leather couch, groaned out loud at its perfection. Studied the art on the walls, a mixture of artsy photographs and framed vintage postcards. And then, above the light switch at the edge of the room, a rustic wooden frame different from the rest.

It surrounded a yellowed square of fabric. *Elle Loves Elephants* was cross-stitched down its center in slightly uneven lettering, accompanied on both sides by a rendering of the animal in gray cotton floss.

Something hot kindled behind Julie's ribs.

She stared at the cross-stitch for likely too long. Memorized the imperfections that only made it more charming. This obvious token of Elle's childhood. This piece of Elle Cochrane—not just a basketball player, but a person, someone who used cookbooks and loved her mom and had an apparent penchant for large mammals—that somehow, even though Julie knew she'd be entering her home tonight, Julie had never expected to see.

She turned away. Stepped through a door in the corner, next to the TV, that opened to a deck. Julie took a deep breath as she looked over the extensive backyard, the rolling green hill that led to the trees. Waiting for the scenery to calm her heart. Before eventually, shivering in the slight chill, head still in tangles, she headed back inside. She poked her head into the laundry room that rounded out the first floor.

And found herself, again, in front of the hallway closet.

Maybe this wasn't the closet Vanessa had referenced at all; maybe it was simply a door leading to a basement, and—

There it was.

Before she could stop herself—even though she knew she was already too mixed up about this whole night—Julie was on her knees, dragging the box closer to the light.

She didn't touch a thing. But she recognized all of it.

MVP awards. Championship trophies. Some high school ones, but also a decent number of golden plaques emblazoned with the NCAA logo. More NCAA plaques than Julie had ever received, that was for sure. With a gasp, Julie realized that the crystal globe sticking out of one corner was an ESPY. Best Female College Basketball Player, as voted on by both fans and sports journalism experts. In Elle's junior year at Tennessee, she had been deemed the best female player in the country.

And now the evidence of it was sitting in a cardboard box, hiding in a closet. Inside a house that would only ever be one-tenth the size of Lebron's.

Quickly, Julie pushed it back into its corner.

She hurried back to the den. Clicked on the TV. Flipped through channels until she found a football game. She didn't care about the game in the least, but the sound of the announcers' voices was familiar and soothing.

She'd made a mistake. Elle had explicitly explained her boundaries. She didn't want to talk about the past.

But Julie knew she'd never be able to forget that box.

She didn't understand a single thing about that box.

But suddenly, Elle didn't seem larger than life anymore.

Like with Vanessa, all Julie wanted to do was reach out her arms and give Elle Cochrane a hug.

A soft bang in the kitchen startled Julie awake. She blinked, not remembering falling asleep. She shouldn't have been surprised; she was exhausted constantly during basketball season. Vandy allowed her to adjust her hours so that she could haul it to East High in time for practice each afternoon, which she was grateful for, but it also meant starting her work days at the ass crack of dawn. If given the opportunity, she'd sleep on this couch for twelve hours straight.

She stretched her toes, mind calm and quiet from the nap, ready to bug Vanessa again—maybe there were some video games in this place they could play—before she stood and realized the noises in the kitchen had come from Elle.

Who had cracked open a pomegranate Polar and was leaning against the fridge, smiling at her.

Oh god. Did Julie have drool on her face? She pawed at her cheek just in case.

Okay. Maybe Elle was still a little bit larger than life.

"Hey," Elle said. "Everything go okay?"

"Yeah." At least, Julie assumed everything was still okay, that Vanessa hadn't run away while Julie had passed out to Al Michaels. She stepped up into the kitchen, out of the darkness of the den. "How was the class?"

Elle took another sip of seltzer.

"It was good. Depressing. Interesting."

She'd taken off her blazer, revealing that her button-up was short-sleeved. There was a tattoo on her right arm. A rose, high on her forearm. The thorns wrapped around her elbow, disappearing up her sleeve.

Julie must have been staring at it, and Elle must have noticed, because she said, "It's for my mom. Her name is Rose." A small smile. "Not very original, I know. My goal is a sleeve." She looked down at her arm. "But I'm not sure what I want next."

Julie swallowed, thinking about the picture of who she was pretty sure was Rose in Elle's sitting room. Imagining Rose cross-stitching *Elle Loves Elephants*. And as she looked at Elle, standing in her kitchen, with her new hair, and her new tattoo, Julie suddenly felt...she didn't know what she felt. She wished, in that moment, that she had never watched Elle Cochrane on TV. That Julie was a different, braver person, someone who knew herself better, someone Elle hadn't met in a high school gym. That Elle hadn't had to go to a foster care class tonight. That she had gone to a bar instead, and Julie could have been there, to see her walk in. And Julie would have said...something, something that would have made Elle laugh, like she was laughing in that photograph, and maybe it would have meant something. Maybe it would have helped Julie understand what she wanted.

"Thanks again for coming over," Elle said, and Julie finally looked away, moving to pick up her bag.

"Of course," she said. "It was nice."

Even though Julie wasn't sure, at that moment, if that was necessarily what it had been.

"You don't have to run off," Elle said, pushing away from the fridge as Julie walked toward the doorway. She gestured toward the TV. "If you want to finish the game or anything."

"No." Julie scratched at her neck. She couldn't even remember who was playing. "That's okay." Snoozles was probably wondering where she was.

She paused in the doorway, looking into the sitting room, the dark bay window in the corner, before she turned.

She didn't know why she said it. Why it came out of her mouth now, when she had really never been planning to ask at all.

"I know this is probably a long shot, but...would you have any interest in helping coach the team? Fill Jacks's position, at least for the season? I feel weird asking you to be an assistant, when you're... But it wouldn't have to be like that. We could be co-coaches. It would just be good, I think, having some help."

And when Julie finally took a breath and let herself look at Elle, she saw it. What she should have looked and seen from the second she started talking. Elle's face, scrunched in uncomfortable pity, her fingers messing with the tab of her seltzer.

"I'm sorry, Julie," she said, voice gentle, "but I have work meetings around the time practices start, and I—"

"No, no." Julie was already backing away. "I get it. No worries. Forget I asked." By the time she said "I'll see you next week," she was already in the sitting room, halfway to the door, talking to empty space, away from Elle's clear secondhand embarrassment.

She turned as soon as she reached the foyer, slamming her feet into her shoes and escaping to the dark, jumping into her car and backing out as fast as she could, back to her boring apartment across the river, away from Elle Cochrane's cozy den and her bright, clean kitchen.

CHAPTER EIGHT

Elle sat in her car in the East High parking lot on Monday afternoon, drumming her fingers on the steering wheel.

She was twenty minutes early, as always. Wanting to go inside and watch Julie Parker run up and down the court, as always. Maybe catch Vanessa in a smile.

It had been a decent weekend: a quiet Saturday, as Vanessa holed up in her room with homework and Elle aggressively cleaned, her favorite stress-relieving activity. Yesterday, she'd dragged Vanessa along to yoga with her and Rose, a practice Elle pushed Rose to do as often as possible, as it helped her fibromyalgia pain. Vanessa had rolled her eyes as they left the house, but when they got back in the car afterward, Vanessa had said—so quietly Elle almost didn't hear it—"Thanks."

Yet, all weekend, even in the middle of savasana, Elle hadn't been able to shake the vision of Julie standing in the doorway of her kitchen. Shrinking into herself as she asked Elle a favor Elle couldn't say yes to. Disappearing immediately afterward, even though Elle hadn't wanted her to.

Elle had probably liked it a little too much, coming home to Julie Parker asleep on her couch.

An image that danced in her brain still, as she watched dusk settle over the parking lot.

Maybe she should start putting some distance between herself and Coach.

Another minute passed. Elle fiddled with the radio.

And then she turned off the car and crossed the lot.

If she didn't go in, she reasoned, her absence might make Julie even more embarrassed about asking her about coaching, and Elle didn't want Julie to be embarrassed. It had been a fine question. A logical one Elle had likely brought on herself. Christ, she was the one who kept showing up to practices. Julie needed help, and there Elle was, lurking on the bleachers.

If only Elle wasn't Elle. If only she had more time in her life. If only she hadn't sworn off basketball. If only she was 20 percent less attracted to Julie.

It was the basketball thing that made it an automatic no, of course, but the attraction would've made it a bad idea regardless. Elle needed to focus on Vanessa right now. On her family. Not on... everything she wanted to do to Coach Parker.

Elle settled into her regular spot in the bleachers as the team scrimmaged. They were looking good, she thought. Still needed some help in transition, but what team didn't?

Maybe she'd ask Julie, after the final sprint, how the starting lineup was looking. How she was feeling about their first game on Wednesday. Make sure Julie knew, no matter how the night had ended on Friday, that they were still...

What were they, exactly?

Elle was contemplating the answer—was there a level between *acquaintance* and *friend*?—when there was a sudden cry, followed by a blow of Julie's whistle.

Elle looked up to see blood on the court. And without further thought, her feet were moving.

Julie was running toward the endline, where Gray was bent over, holding their nose.

"I'm so sorry, Gray!" Katelyn's voice was high-pitched, eyes frantic. "I didn't think I—"

"Not your fault," Gray said, voice muffled through their hand. Blood trickled down their wrist, dripping onto the floor. "You barely got me. I just get nosebleeds sometimes."

Elle breathed out, pausing a few feet away. She'd seen her fair share of what a good elbow could do on a basketball court, incidental or otherwise. For Katelyn's sake, she was glad it was only a nosebleed. Even if . . . wow. It was—

"*Fork.*" Elle looked over to find Vanessa at her side, an impressed look on her face. "That's a lot of forking blood."

"Oh my god." Another player whose name Elle forgot put a hand to her chest, face draining of color. "I can't . . ." She shook her head, whispering, "Blood."

"Okay, everyone, give some space," Julie called, hand on Gray's shoulder, voice strong and assured. "Mosk, get Bianchi to the bleachers before she passes out. Williams, go get some paper towels from the locker room. Everyone else just take a break, all right?"

Julie's eyes snapped onto Elle's. Something flashed there, a glint of gold. Something like relief.

"Elle. Can you keep an eye on the team while I go with Gray to see if the health room's open?"

Elle nodded. "Of course."

As soon as Ngozi handed Gray a wad of paper towels, which they promptly stuffed under their nose, Julie led them Elle's way, a steadying hand on their back.

"Just make sure everyone stays away from the blood on the floor, all right? I'll get in deep shorts if they don't."

Elle nodded again. Without another glance Elle's way, Julie and Gray were gone.

And Elle was left alone with a restless basketball team.

They broke into small groups, some joining Sasha in comforting

Bianchi, some stretching quads and chatting. Vanessa drifted over to Katelyn; they stubbed the toes of their sneakers against the court. Elle's chest lifted when Katelyn laughed at something Vanessa said. She glanced away, determined to give Vanessa space.

And looked right into the eyes of Ngozi, who was staring at her. Quickly, Ngozi turned away, whispering with the girls next to her. But every few seconds, her gaze darted back to Elle.

Elle had to admit she had wondered, over the past week of sitting in this gym, if any of the teens recognized her. If maybe they had older siblings, aunts or uncles who had watched Elle play. It was the same feeling she had whenever she caught someone staring at her a beat too long at the grocery store, at the park, when she walked through the hospital. A prickling at the back of her neck, followed by a self-conscious worry that she was overinflating her own importance.

The first few years after returning home to Nashville from Milwaukee, the neck prickle had been tinged by shame. A certainty that whatever stares she received were stares of pity. It was partly why she rarely left her house those first few years: a new, quiet life, one she could build from the ground up.

Basketball had made all of Elle's decisions for her for so long. It had taken those first few years to even feel like she knew who she was without it. But slowly, she'd found her footing, crafted a life defined not by shooting percentages but by each square inch of her house that she remodeled, that she made her own. By her competence at her job. Taking her pills and talking to Mara. Through yoga and exercise that didn't tax her joints. Cooking the foods she discovered she liked to eat, not because of any trainer or dietitian's plan, but because it made her happy.

The attention, too, had gotten easier as time went on, even if she still struggled sometimes. Most of the people who recognized her now, like Julie, simply wanted to wax nostalgic about UT. And Elle, more than anyone, understood that impulse.

She had simply found that, like any good heartache, sometimes a clean break was the healthiest way forward.

When Ngozi broke away from her circle, though, dribbling a ball toward her, Elle knew.

She knew even more when Ngozi stopped a yard away, holding the ball on her hip, and looked Elle in the eye.

Chin raised. Eyes fierce, jaw set.

It wasn't defiance, at least not exactly.

It was *I see you.*

It was *This is my court.*

It was *What you got?*

It was a look Elle had seen countless times in her past life, from any opponent who gave a damn. Ngozi knew who Elle was, had probably, like Julie, been overly aware of Elle sitting in the corner. And suddenly, a new flash of shame slashed through Elle's gut. She hadn't meant to be a distraction. From day one, she should've stayed in her car.

But she was here now. And Ngozi, in her teenaged bluster, wasn't intimidated.

She was only here to play.

And that look in her eyes made a small compartment in Elle's heart open wide, swift and surprising on a rusted hinge, revealing something soft and tender.

Without a word, Ngozi passed the ball. No easy bounce pass, but hard and fast, direct to Elle's hands. It made Elle's fingertips sting.

She contemplated the ball, the familiar texture on the pads of her fingers. Danced it back and forth between her hands like she'd never left. Like it wasn't the first time in eight years she'd held one.

And then she squinted at the court, the clusters of girls watching her. Thought about how Julie had left with Gray. Calm and decisive, indisputably in control.

But she was only one person. Only able to be in one place at a time.

Elle glanced at the clock. Fifteen minutes left of practice.

They couldn't keep scrimmaging, at least not full court, since the endline with the drops of blood was out of play. Elle looked toward the opposite basket. Paused the bouncing of the ball between her fingers. Holding it still.

She looked at Ngozi and felt her lips tilt into a grin.

"Layups?"

By the time Julie returned with a somewhat-cleaned-up Gray, the team was in the locker room, and Elle was standing at center court, staring at the scoreboard.

"Hey." Julie jogged over, blowing a stray hair out of her face. "Thanks. You were a lifesaver. Now I just have to fill out an incident report and clean that up and we can all move on with our day. Gray was more embarrassed than anything. Was the rest of the team all right?"

Elle stared at her. At the whistle hanging over her chest. The wisps of strawberry hair haloing around her cheeks. Her easy smile, one that began to fade the longer Elle stared at her without speaking.

"Did..." Julie twisted her bottom lip between her teeth, a move Elle silently tracked, cataloging it somewhere in the back of her mind, to be reexamined later. A crease of worry appeared on Julie's forehead. "Did something happen with the rest of the team? Were they weird to you? Or, fork, did Anushna bring up that thing about the yearbook again with Bia—"

"I'll do it," Elle interrupted.

Julie blinked.

"You'll do it?"

Elle nodded. The words had left her mouth before they'd fully formed in her brain. But she knew, even with all the promises to herself she was breaking, that they were the right words. That they'd been forming since Ngozi threw her that ball. Maybe before then.

"I'll be your assistant coach."

Julie's jaw dropped. She snapped it shut a second later, bringing a hand to rest on her hip before dropping that, too.

"You'll—" She frowned. Elle should not have liked watching flustered Coach Parker as much as she did. But by now, Julie's fidgeting was close to feeling familiar, like a scene from a favorite movie, one that always made you laugh. "Really?"

"Yeah." Elle nodded. "Really."

Julie made eye contact then, as if searching Elle's face for something. After a moment, she nodded back, her movements stilling.

"Okay," she said, her coach voice creeping back in. Elle tried to hold back her smile. "You'll want to contact the office first thing tomorrow so you can fill out the paperwork. I think they'll need a background check."

"I can do that."

"I thought you had a work conflict?"

"I can work it out."

And the moment she said it, Elle knew she could. Her work week had felt near impossible to manage since Vanessa's arrival. There were so many things Elle had to do—like visiting juvenile court next week, a place she never thought she'd have to go, to update a judge on Vanessa's well-being—and every new appointment, each new thing, seemed to fall during business hours. Elle wasn't sure how other working foster parents managed it. How any parent managed anything, really. How society even functioned.

But the idea had been floating there, in the back of her mind, ever since Vanessa had shown up at her doorstep.

Elle would take a leave of absence.

She knew her benefits. Knew she'd been a diligent employee for a long time. Had hardly missed a day.

She had savings now, enough to cover the mortgage for at least a few months.

Vanessa was in her care because Elle's family had gone too many years not looking out for her. Not being there for Karly. Too distracted by their own lives to investigate further when Karly and Vanessa missed another holiday, another party.

Elle wasn't going to be distracted anymore.

And if Vandy didn't like it, Elle could always take her diligence elsewhere. She'd actually been itching for a while to make a move anyway, learn something new in the medical world beyond deductibles and payment plans. Learning all the ins and outs of the hospital these last eight years had made her curious. If there were other ways she could help people.

In addition to everything else—this might be the break Elle hadn't let herself believe she needed.

"Okay." Julie looked at her for another long moment. Elle looked back, heat licking up the back of her neck as the moment stretched.

She liked when Julie looked at her straight on, when her gaze didn't flitter away. Elle had never loved the attention of strangers, even when she'd been a star. But Elle wanted Coach Parker to look at her.

"First game's on Wednesday," Julie said eventually. "Bus leaves at two fifteen."

Lord. Elle couldn't believe she was going to be stepping onto a school bus again.

Elle couldn't quite believe any of this.

But a steady hum of adrenaline ran underneath her skin anyway.

She held Julie's gaze.

"I'll be there."

CHAPTER NINE

By the time Vanessa tromped up to bed later that night, the adrenaline inside Elle's veins had faded.

She sat at her kitchen island, laptop open, blue light glasses perched on her nose.

She'd already sent an email to her boss and a leave of absence request to HR, all typed in haste after dinner, before she lost her nerve. It would take a few days, she knew, at the least, to get the request approved, to wrap things up. But she went ahead and requested enough PTO for this week to get the paperwork for East High done, to make it to the Bobcat practices and games.

She'd dropped the news to Vanessa, worried she would think it was yet another way Elle was intruding in her life.

Instead, Vanessa had only said, "I mean, you could just ask Coach if she wants to make out. But sure."

Elle hadn't replied to that. Mostly, she just felt thrilled the response hadn't been *whatever*.

But now, staring at her reflection in the dark window above her sink, Elle's earlier nerve was nowhere to be seen.

She barely knew how to talk with Vanessa. Did she really think she could coach a whole team of teenagers? And sure, holding that basketball today had felt more natural, less traumatic than she had anticipated. An old memory come to life, as surprisingly vibrant as if she'd never left it.

But she'd held that ball for ten minutes. Had barely even dribbled it, as she'd watched the team make baskets and run their final sprint.

Had she truly believed those ten minutes somehow signaled she was ready to immerse herself in the game again? All this time, all this discipline, shaping a life for herself outside of basketball. Toppled by a competitive teenager, ten minutes, and a charming coach with pretty eyes.

Elle closed the laptop and picked up her phone, scrolling to Mara's number.

Mara Daniels had been Elle's teammate, roommate, and best friend at Tennessee. And even though every player she'd played with at UT would always be family—distant family, now, but still family; Elle had never gone back on that—Mara was the only one who remained present. She'd been there, with champagne, when Elle signed with the Shipwrecks. Mara flew to Milwaukee to be at the hospital when Elle tore her ACL. It was Mara Elle first confided in, even before the ACL, that she was pretty sure the Wreckers were going to drop her. That if they did, she didn't think she'd object. That for the first time in her life, Elle Cochrane wanted a break from basketball.

Elle still considered Mara her best friend, even if the last few years had stretched the distance between them. Mara still lived in Knoxville, but it wasn't so much a physical distance; Elle could probably make the three-hour drive between Nashville and Knoxville in her sleep. But Mara and Dikembe had gotten married three years ago, and after having Quisha a little under a year ago, Mara had less time to catch up over the phone, to make the trek herself for a weekend of dancing or TV-binging.

God, Elle couldn't remember the last time she'd been dancing. She hated navigating around the endless gaggles of bachelorette parties that descended upon Nashville every weekend, but dancing with Mara had been one of the only things, after giving up basketball, that still made her feel truly free.

Point was, Mara was busy. And explaining everything about Elle's current life, even to Mara, felt like...too much. Even if Elle knew it shouldn't feel that way, that she shouldn't be ashamed or embarrassed or...whatever it was she was feeling about Vanessa and Karly. People unexpectedly helped out other people in their lives all the time. Addiction ran in so many families. Sometimes life was messy.

Still. It was difficult, sorting through the strings of how her life had changed over the last few weeks, figuring out where to start.

Elle stretched out her back. Listened to the muffled K-pop blaring above her. And longed, fiercely, for Mara's room-filling laughter.

Maybe she should simply start the conversation. The words would come to her.

Elle: hi

Mara responded immediately. Hey! What's up??

The time stared at Elle from the digital clock on the stove.

The words did not come to her.

sooo, a hi with no punctuation followed by a weird silence, Mara filled in. is this one of those you-want-me-to-ask-you-something-but-don't-know-how-to-ask situations

Desperately, Elle responded. Yes.

Mara: All right, let's go through it. Everything okay with Rose? Tricia and the kids?

Yes, Elle answered. They're all fine.

Mara: You seeing anyone new?

And Elle hesitated before she typed, no.

Mara: Work? The house?

Elle: Also fine.

As soon as she typed that last fine, the question jumped into her brain, unbidden and unsettling.

How much of Elle's life was *just fine*?

It was what she'd wanted. A normal life, where she was in control. Better for her brain chemistry, too. But something about it felt off just then, a slightly sour taste in her mouth.

Mara: Okay I'm out. Tell me what's up, Cochrane

Elle took a breath. Maybe I should just call? If you're able to talk?

Mara: Already dialing

A second later, Mara's voice was in Elle's ear, and Elle's body finally relaxed.

Keeping her voice low so Vanessa wouldn't hear, even though the music from the floor above continued, Elle filled Mara in on becoming a foster parent.

"Makes sense they called you," Mara murmured. "Probably wasn't enough room at Tricia's. And Rose would've said yes, but shouldn't."

"Exactly." Elle's family tree was small and largely lopsided toward the branch her older sister Tricia had grown with her husband, Akhil. While their four children were delightful, Elle couldn't imagine Vanessa would've felt exactly comfortable inside their happy family unit. And Rose needed to focus on her own pain management, not on taking care of a teen.

"Do you need me to come down there?" Mara asked after a minute. "Give you a break? Maybe I could take Vanessa to get a manicure or something."

"First of all, no. Please, you have Quisha to take care of—"

"Whom *I* could use a break from, just sayin'."

"—and secondly, Vanessa is not the sort of teen who would enjoy a manicure." But here, Elle paused. "Or maybe…she would? She likes jewelry. Fuck, Mara." Elle rested her forehead in her palm. "I've known her since she was a baby. She's lived with me for over two weeks. How can it be that sometimes I feel like I don't know her at all?"

"Elle," Mara said softly. "I think even regular parents could say the same things about their teenagers."

And Elle knew that was true. But still, it didn't feel right. That Vanessa—and Karly—could feel like such strangers now.

Karly had gotten pregnant when she and Elle were barely adults themselves. When Elle had been consumed with dreams of getting to the University of Tennessee, of cutting down the net at the Final Four. It had been bewildering to hold a tiny, sleeping Vanessa in her arms when Elle and Rose had visited the hospital, knowing Karly's world would now be consumed with diapers and daycare instead.

But before then, before life stretched them further and further apart, she and Karly had been close. Karly was her only cousin, only a year older than Elle; she and Elle and Tricia had spent every holiday together as kids, countless summer sleepovers. Movie nights, swimming together at Percy Priest Lake.

And even when their roads had taken Karly to parenthood and Elle to UT, Elle had still witnessed Vanessa growing up. At those same holidays, at Tricia's wedding, at family get-togethers. Had seen her, in those once-or-twice-a-year gatherings, grow from that pudgy red-faced baby to the tall, lanky young woman with cautious eyes, clothes a size too big, a purple dye job fading from the tips of her hair.

"It just feels like...we all let her and Karly slip through our fingers or something. Makes me feel like shit."

"You didn't know. I know you, Elle. You would've fixed it, if you knew, if you could, but some things aren't easily fixable. You have to just keep doing what you're doing. Which is enough, by the way. More than enough."

"I miss you," Elle blurted.

"*Elle.* I miss you, too. Shit. Can we go dancing sometime? Have Rose or Tricia keep Vanessa company for a night? This mama needs to go *out.*"

Elle laughed, tired but happy as the weight of the day hit her, as she remembered what it felt like to be on the same page with someone you loved.

"Yes. I don't know when, or how, but yes."

"I'll look at my calendar as soon as I hang up. We're making it happen, Cochrane."

"Good." Elle took another deep breath. "Okay, and there's something else."

Trying to revive that former nerve back to life, Elle made herself talk about the Bobcats. How she'd agreed to be Julie's assistant coach.

This time, Mara only answered with silence.

And then: "Hold up, girl. I'm going to get some wine. Quisha can drink formula tomorrow. Kembe!"

Elle waited, heart thumping as she listened to Mara mumble in the background to Dikembe, a brief cry from Quisha, a dim clatter as Mara got herself a glass of wine.

"Okay, my love," Mara finally said once she'd returned. "I'm going to say a few things that might seem contradictory, but stay with me here."

"Always," Elle said.

"First: fucking finally. I could not have predicted your way back to basketball would be through a public high school team, but honestly, maybe that's exactly what you need. Just the game without any of the bullshit."

"I mean, I wouldn't call it my *way back to basketball*. It's not like I'm playing or anything. Julie mostly needs someone to help supervise, to analyze and strategize for games."

"Mm-hmm. Which is more than you've done in...?"

"Eight years," Elle muttered.

"It's been *eight years* since—" Mara's voice rose, sounding alarmed. "Shit, that can't be right. How did we get so old?"

Elle only smiled, standing and moving to the stove, putting on the kettle to make herself tea.

Sometimes, for her, those eight years felt even longer. Sometimes, Elle thought she had felt old for a very long time.

"Anyway," Mara continued, taking an audible slurp from her wine. "I'm excited, Elle. For you and for me. I understood your need to go cold turkey, after Milwaukee and the ACL and Sophie and everything; truly, your commitment all these years has been very Elle, but shit, girl. Do you know how hard it's been to not talk about basketball at *all* with you?" Her voice went soft. "It was our *life*, Elle."

Elle swallowed, fingers faltering in their search through her box of tea.

She had always known, when she left basketball behind, that she wasn't the only person it affected. She had been overly aware, in fact, that she wasn't the only one who had lost something.

She knew Rose mourned, even if she tried, poorly, to hide it. Supporting Elle's career had been, for all intents and purposes, a full-time job for Rose for more than a decade of her life. Even while Elle had always felt guilty that doing so kept Rose from pursuing an actual career for herself, only ever able to pick up part-time work here and there from employers who would accommodate Rose's commitment to Elle's basketball schedule. Even while Elle worried, now, that they should have been paying more attention to Rose's health than to Elle's basketball life... she knew Rose loved the game as much as Elle had. The rush, the constant adrenaline of a basketball game. The culture, loud and alive; the community connection. That she missed it.

And then there was Mara. Their friendship had been solidified outside the court, but it had been born on it. There had never been anyone Elle loved playing with more, no one she had ever been so in sync with. Even though their relationship had always been platonic, Elle was pretty certain she had never been as deeply in love with anyone as she had been with Mara Daniels.

And while Mara didn't pursue the WNBA after graduation, even if Elle was certain she could have, the game had still been a beating heart between them. They'd walk to the park whenever Elle was able to get back and visit Knoxville, throw around a ball one-on-one, backing their hips into each other, laughing even as they were serious about it. They'd still spent most of their conversations back then reminiscing about UT, talking about where the rest of the team was now, gossiping about the fates of their old fiercest rivals—some of whom were then kicking Elle's ass back in Milwaukee. Being with Mara in those fraught post-signing days was the only way Elle had still been able to grasp some joy from the game, from the life that used to be theirs. Until that summer eight years ago.

When Elle had taken that beating heart away from both of them and locked it neatly away.

Elle wouldn't have been surprised if their friendship had faded after that, but Mara's life had been evolving too: she met Dikembe, moved up in the marketing firm where she worked. Bought her own house in Knoxville a year after Elle had moved home and started renovating hers in Nashville, and suddenly, they'd had plenty to talk about again. Learning how to set tile together, cursing and laughing over FaceTime with grout stuck under their fingernails. Complaining about the cost of everything, about the trials of finding contractors, plumbers, electricians; commiserating about the abject terror of crawl spaces.

"Oh my god, Cochrane," Mara burst out now, excitement vibrating in every syllable. "Does this mean we can watch March Madness together again? Have you been following this Shanice Jones at LSU? Because *phew*, she—"

"Maybe," Elle interrupted, "we take it one step at a time?" But another smile made its way to her face. She poured water into her favorite mug.

Mara exhaled.

"Yeah, shit, sorry. That was actually going to be the other part of my speech; I just got excited."

"I get it."

"So, as much as I welcome this surprising development in your life... it is still your life, Elle. And if it starts to not feel right? If never stepping onto a basketball court again *was* the right choice for you? You can step back off it, okay?"

Elle dipped the tea bag in and out of the water.

"Yeah," she whispered, before clearing her throat. "I know. But thanks for saying it."

"Tell me more about this team. They any good?"

"Honestly? Who knows. The coach knows what she's doing, and they seem to have a couple ringers, but they haven't played any games yet. And it's been a long time since I've been on a high school court, so I have no idea what the landscape's like. Julie's going to have to fill me in on the competition."

A small giggle escaped from Mara. Elle set her mug on the counter.

"Did you just *giggle* at me, Daniels?"

A louder laugh filled Elle's ear drum. "I'm just picturing it. You're going to scout out all the other sixteen-year-olds in the league, aren't you? You'll have one of those little coach's notebooks and be making diagrams and charts within a week. I know your study habits, Cochrane."

Elle took a slow sip of tea.

"Well," she said, "if you want to get a job done, you have to do it right."

She could somehow hear Mara's smile across the line.

"There she is."

The music in Vanessa's room fell silent. The house felt suddenly hushed, still.

"So"—another slurp of wine on Mara's end—"tell me about the coach."

Elle took a long sip of tea and glanced toward the ceiling.

"Her name is Julie Parker," she said, slow and careful. "She used to have pictures of me on her bedroom walls."

A snort from Mara so loud Elle had to momentarily lift the phone from her ear.

"So you're saying she has sense. That's a good start."

"Maybe." Elle swirled her tea. She could say nothing, because her attraction to Julie meant nothing. Or rather, nothing actionable, anyway. Nothing Elle had time or space for. She was doing this because Julie clearly needed help, and Julie had been kind to them. She was doing this because she needed to focus on Vanessa, and this could be a good way to get closer to her, to make sure she was doing okay.

Mara didn't need to know about Julie's freckles, or her eyes, or how when she flapped her hands around when she was nervous, Elle wanted to grab them and lightly bite down on her fingers.

Elle sighed.

"Mara, I think I'm in trouble."

Elle was so busy the next day, sending emails and filling out paper-work for both East High and Vanderbilt Hospital, that she had little time to continue second-guessing her choices.

And when she reached the East High gym that afternoon, a few minutes late, the music was so loud there was little room left in her brain for pretty much anything.

"Hey," Julie called over the blaring playlist, mouth curved in an easy smile. Elle's stomach relaxed at that smile, as Coach Parker watched the team warm up. She appeared unbothered at Elle's late-ness, even though Elle had been sweating for the last ten minutes as she'd raced over here. "You're getting to start on a Mosk day. I rotate through letting each of them choose the warm-up music. Moskow-itz always chooses the good shit. Or—" Julie grimaced. "Sorry. The good shorts? Man, I'm still getting used to that one."

Elle glanced around the gym, taking in the warm-ups. The music was heavy on the bass, fast on the lyrics, the kind of rap that had defined much of her own basketball practices in her former life. She typically listened to folksier stuff on her own time, but something about knowing Julie Parker considered this *the good shit*—a bit of a surprise, after seeing her Kacey Musgraves shirt, but somehow also not a surprise at all—made Elle smile.

"Has Vanessa gotten to choose yet?"

"Oh yeah." Julie grinned. "Last week." She glanced at Elle. "It was this super pop-y stuff? She loved it. Was *smiling* the whole warm-up."

Elle laughed.

"Amazing."

"Yeah." Julie turned back to the court. "It was."

"So." Elle stood a little straighter. "What would you like me to do here?"

"I was thinking we could strategize tomorrow on the way to Hill-crest about how exactly we want this to work," Julie said without hesitation, voice all Coach Parker. "What you're comfortable with. Today, I'd love if you could just observe, see what we're missing, what's not working, what's working well. I'm gonna go right into scrimmaging here in about..." She glanced at the clock. "Five minutes. And then I'll break early to give a big pre-first-game motivational thing. I'll take any feedback you have on that, too."

"I'm sure you've got it handled."

Julie opened her mouth, skin crinkling around her eyes, as if she were about to make a joke at her own expense. Elle was glad when the door to the gym opened, distracting Julie from her train of thought.

"Ah," Julie said instead. "And you get to meet Blake."

A cheery white girl bounced into the gym—literally bounced, sneakers jumping off the floor with each skip—over to where Elle and Julie stood.

"Hi!" she shouted over the music.

"Hey, Blake." Julie smiled. "This is Coach Cochrane."

"Oh," Elle said, surprised, even though she shouldn't have been. "You can just call me Elle."

"Okay!" Blake chirped. "Hi, Elle!" She gave a little wave with the hand that wasn't clutching a sticker-adorned notebook to her chest. Elle waved back.

"The scorebook's in my office," Julie said, "if you want to get started. There's a printout of the team roster somewhere in there, too."

"Awesome! Thanks, Coach! Good to see you!"

Julie smiled as Blake disappeared into the office.

"Team manager," she supplied to Elle. "And possibly nicest person to ever exist."

"And as team manager," Elle asked, in case anything had changed since she was in high school, "her duties are..."

"Filling out that scorebook at every game." Julie nodded toward Blake as she bounced back out of the office and plopped her backpack at the foot of the bleachers before settling in with a thin forest-green notebook on her knees. She removed several packs of pens from the backpack, placing them neatly beside her.

"Wow." Elle blinked in hazy recognition at the old-school scorebook. "They still use those?"

"Yep." Julie grinned. "Blake definitely knows the game, but mostly, she is just really into stationery supplies. The Bobcats have the prettiest scorebook in the league, for sure. Possibly in the history of high school basketball."

As Julie spoke, Elle watched Blake lean her face close to the book and carefully apply a sticker. Elle's mouth twitched into a smile.

"And I think"—Julie moved an inch closer, shifted her voice an inch lower—"there's something going on between her and Gray?"

Elle's eyes searched the court until she found Gray, who was currently staring openly at Blake, while a bounce pass sailed straight past their hip. They blinked, running to catch it while Ngozi cursed them out. Elle's smile threatened to spill over into a laugh.

"I try to stay out of their personal lives," Julie said with a shake of her head. "But sometimes they just..." She shivered. "Tell me things."

"They trust you," Elle said. She thought back to her own high school days and couldn't quite imagine telling any of her coaches about crushes she might have been suffering through. They were too focused on getting Elle to the McDonald's All-American, preparing her for recruiting. It was a different world.

Julie lifted a shoulder. "Or they're just into oversharing. Who's to say. All right, time to get this started." She moved from Elle's side, blowing her whistle, and Elle wondered if Julie was always this adept at sidestepping compliments, or only when they came from Elle.

Julie organized the team into opposing sides, tossing out colored pinnies, while Elle wandered past Blake to hover on the sidelines near center court. From the pocket of her sweatshirt, she removed the small notebook she'd started making notes in last night, compiling some thoughts she'd had about the brief moments of play she'd seen so far.

"Okay, Bobcats." Julie bounced the game ball once on the timeline. "We're playing like this is the real deal, like we're stepping out onto Hillcrest's court. All in. And for the love of god, let's try to rebound, okay?"

Elle looked down at her notebook, where first on her list, she'd written: *Rebounding.*

She shook her head and stuffed the notebook back in her pocket.

Forty minutes later, the Bobcats sat in a haphazard circle on the floor, stretching limbs, while Julie wheeled a whiteboard out of the office.

"All right, friends." Julie sat on a chair Blake pulled out for her. "Time for my first-game pep talk." A scattering of lighthearted groans. Elle stood behind the circle of players, opposite Julie, eyes trained on the whiteboard. Julie pointed to her first rule.

"*Every minute counts.* I know everyone talks about last-minute shots, but listen, it's not actually buzzer beaters that win games. It's every minute *prior* to that buzzer beater that brought the game to that point in the first place. If you half-ass it in the first half, you don't deserve a win, and probably won't get close to one anyway. Every. Minute. Counts."

Vanessa's hand shot into the air.

"Ass," she said simply. Julie sighed.

"You find me a better phrase for telling y'all not to half-ass it, Lerner, and I'll use it. Number two. *Ref etiquette.* There are going to be calls you disagree with, calls that are flat-out wrong. You can voice your frustration, once, if you need to, but then let it go. Sports are good preparation for life not being fair. The ref's call is the ref's call. Their job is hard; Bobcats are kind to people whose job is hard. Which reminds me, make sure you thank our bus drivers on away games, always."

Julie ran through the rest of her rules. *Play together, not against each other. Remember, it's just a game: make sure you have a little fun.*

A reminder Elle couldn't quite remember hearing from her own coaches. At least not for a very long time.

And finally, again: *For the love of Pete, rebound.*

Elle smiled as players asked questions, mostly logistical things about the game tomorrow—*Can't we leave during fifth period instead? Mr. Hall's class is the worst*—and Julie answered each one with good humor.

Last night, as Elle had fallen asleep after talking to Mara; today, as she had rushed around town…Elle had started to feel, almost, maybe, like she did have something to contribute to this team. Beyond being the right thing to do in helping Julie, beyond being a way to help support Vanessa. Maybe this actually could be a way to return to basketball.

But Julie, as Elle had known from the first time she'd walked into this gym, had it well in hand.

Elle was just along for the ride.

But maybe that was okay, too.

Elle hadn't been on a ride in a long time.

"Oh yeah," Julie said as she stood. "I forgot to mention. We have another coach to help us out now. Everyone, say hi to Elle."

As one, the team turned to look at her. Elle wanted to search out Vanessa's eyes, but also didn't want to make Vanessa feel weird, so mostly, she just looked back at Julie.

But somehow, she could feel Ngozi, staring her down.

"Anything to add, Elle?" Julie asked.

"Nah." Elle attempted to throw the teens a smile. "I'm good. It's nice to meet you all." And then, because she felt she should add something else: "Let's go, Bobcats."

And when Julie smiled back at her, that golden twinkle in her eye visible even from here, it was possible Elle's stomach flipped, the tiniest bit.

"Let's go, Bobcats," she agreed.

CHAPTER TEN

T his smells the same, too."

Elle's voice was far too close to Julie's ear, her breath a whisper on Julie's neck. Julie glanced over her shoulder to see Elle smiling, looking out over the school bus.

"Sure does," Julie managed, moving into her seat, giving space for Elle to take the one across the aisle.

The rest of the team settled behind them: earbuds in, knees propped on seats, eyes on their phones. Julie had decided early on last year to stay quiet on the bus, after a few failed attempts at screaming motivational words down the aisle while Jacks snorted at her. Let the travel time belong to the players. She'd say everything she needed to on the court.

She usually spent bus rides now checking her Vandy email or attempting to read. She'd prefer sticking her own earbuds in like everyone else, but she had to keep her ears open, in case any nonsense broke out she had to mediate. She preferred to keep Bobcat bus rides as peaceful as possible for the drivers.

Today, Julie simply prepared to stare out the window for the next twenty-five minutes. She didn't want to think about Vandy, and she knew she wouldn't be able to concentrate on *Board to Death*.

She'd been a little proud of how well her focus-on-the-Bobcats plan was continuing to work while existing around Elle. It was almost weird, actually, how easy it increasingly became to pull off. But apparently sitting on a bus with Elle Cochrane stretched Julie's boundaries, just as the visit to Elle's house had, and Julie was immediately squirmy again.

Which she could've attributed, she supposed, to nerves about the Bobcats' first game, but that would've been at least a half untruth. It was more likely because she'd learned, when Elle had just hovered behind her, that Elle Cochrane smelled really good. Like some gender-neutral cologne full of pine cones and fancy shit that did weird things to Julie's stomach.

"Hey."

Julie almost jumped as the fancy pine cones hit her full force. Elle was picking up Julie's bag, moving it to the seat across the aisle.

"Okay if I sit here? I figured we could go over how you want this all to work, like you said."

Had Julie said that? Was it okay if Elle sat here? No. Julie felt quite confident, suddenly, that no one had ever sat so close to her in her life.

"Of course," Julie said.

"So." Elle was wearing slacks again, a button-up covered with an expensive-looking sweater. Like she had dressed up for game day. Julie was wearing what she always did: shorts and a hoodie. Looking at Elle made her want to explode. "How can I best support you?"

"Uh." Julie scratched her arm. "I have to be honest; I'm still struggling with the whole *you* supporting *me* thing. Are you on board with calling ourselves co-coaches?"

Elle tilted her head and gave Julie a look, one that seemed almost full of...affection? But that didn't make sense. Elle still hardly knew her.

Julie looked away.

"We can call ourselves whatever you want, Coach Parker. But it's still your team."

"Okay." Julie blew out a breath. "So ideally, as *co*-coaches, you'll help me analyze during games. And during practices, maybe we can do more targeted skill work if we're both there to work with small groups."

Elle nodded. "I'm here for whatever. I actually had some ideas about lineup..." Elle reached over to her bag, pulling out a mini whiteboard, marked with the outline of a basketball court. Just like the ones Julie had in her own bag. For the first time since sitting down, a smile tugged at Julie's lips.

Until Elle settled back in again, leaning toward Julie as she explained her thoughts. Her knee bumped against Julie's as she did, her arm brushing Julie's each time she gestured.

Julie's smile dropped away. Due to the fact that she was having a weirdly difficult time breathing, and her mouth suddenly didn't know what to do with itself. Was this a heart attack? She'd read symptoms could be confusing.

Thankfully, as Elle went on about Bianchi being a good backup to Chin at small forward, or something or other, Julie's body grew more accustomed to fancy pine cones and the surprising softness of Elle Cochrane's forearm—67 percent more, as a guesstimate— so that she was pretty sure she wasn't experiencing cardiac arrest. Accustomed enough that she thought she made conversationally appropriate *uh-huh*s and *yeah, I hear that*s and *cool*s. Possibly too many *cool*s, but whatever, pobody's nerfect.

Ten minutes post Elle sitting beside her, though, Julie's blood still felt too warm underneath her skin, like a charger left too long in a MacBook. She hoped that by the time they reached Hillcrest, she'd be able to pop that sucker out of the port, her battery reloaded and ready to cool the hell off.

"I know you're running the show," Elle said after a stretch of silence. "And I don't know a single thing about this league yet, but." She tapped her long, graceful fingers on the whiteboard and gave Julie a sheepish look. "I feel a little nervous."

This startled Julie enough to finally return to herself.

She contemplated how to respond. Her initial reaction was to make a joke, as the idea of Elle Cochrane, ESPY winner, being at all nervous about an East-Hillcrest game seemed ludicrous.

Except then Julie remembered that box of trophies in Elle's closet. The comments she'd made about how long it had been since she'd been on a basketball court. And Julie realized that Elle Cochrane might, in fact, be nervous.

For a beat, Julie was again overwhelmed with that irrational desire to comfort her.

But if Elle was nervous, it meant she cared. That she wasn't simply here out of pity.

An idea that made that overheated feeling ramp up, concentrated somewhere near Julie's chest.

Because the Bobcats deserved someone who cared.

"Yeah," Julie eventually said. "That never goes away either."

The Bobcats left the Hillcrest gym with a W, but barely.

Which was exactly how Julie liked it. You didn't want a confidence-crushing loss to kick off the season, but you didn't want an ego-inflating blowout, either. This matchup had been spot-on, not boring for a second. Luck went their way, built-up anticipation exploding at that last buzzer, relief and pride radiating off every Bobcat's face.

Even Vanessa. Even if her version of radiating appeared via a few limp claps and a smirk, Julie saw it for what it was.

"Take it it was a good night, Coach?" Howard, their bus driver, asked as Julie and Elle lumbered on after the players.

"It was indeed, How." Julie clapped him on the shoulder. Howard was one of her favorites. "Thanks for hanging around."

"My pleasure, boss."

The volume level of the bus was distinctly louder than it had been before, as the Bobcats sang at the top of their lungs to whatever song Mosk was playing from her phone. Julie took her seat and smiled out the window. She propped her knees up, letting out a long, satisfied breath. As long as it didn't get too out of control for Howard, this time was for them.

Five seconds later, Elle dropped into the seat next to her.

"Hey," she said with a grin. "You were right."

Julie tried to be less startled this time, to cool her temperature and her heartbeat, but it was difficult, being as Elle settled in even closer than before. She mirrored Julie's position, slumping down and resting her knees alongside Julie's. Shoulder to shoulder, hip to hip.

Jacks had always sat on the opposite side of the aisle, snoring the whole way to and from the opponent's gym.

"Fork," Elle said, still grinning. "This position is going to be horrible for my back now, isn't it?"

"What?" Julie said, with eloquence.

"Slouching down like this. I know it's how we always used to do it, but I'm going to have to navigate myself out of here carefully."

"No," Julie said, "what was I right about?"

"Oh." Elle smiled bigger, staring past Howard's head. "That basketball can be fun."

And Julie's heart almost broke. Of course basketball could be fun. How could Elle of all people even—

She shook her head, tearing her eyes away from Elle's profile. *Not your place, Parker.*

"Well," she said instead, "it was fun because it was a good game and we lucked out with Hillcrest missing that last shot. It'll be markedly less fun next time we're on this bus and aren't leaving with a win."

"Yeah." Elle nodded, her smile dimming but still there, a

nostalgic-looking curve of lips. An ease in those blue eyes Julie couldn't quite remember seeing in person yet. "Yeah, I remember that, too."

A beat went by before Elle turned, the movement pressing her bicep against Julie's.

"Okay, but the turnovers, though."

And somehow, a laugh fell out of Julie's mouth.

"Yeah. I know."

"Were they always that bad, when we were in high school?"

Julie smiled and shrugged. Except doing so rubbed her arm against Elle's, and even if their skin was separated by layers of clothing, it felt illicit anyway. Her smile disappeared, replaced by a furious blush Julie prayed the dark of the bus would hide.

"Will they get better?" Elle asked.

Julie didn't dare move this time, even if her true answer, once again, was a shrug. "Hopefully," she managed to say. "If we do our jobs."

Elle faced forward again. Tapped a finger against her knee.

"I was thinking," she said. "Would you mind if I worked one-on-one with Ngozi sometimes? If Ngozi was cool with it?"

"Oh my god." Ngozi had the potential to be something special, and even more importantly, the fire to make it happen. Julie had never, even last year, had the time or skill to truly give her what she deserved. "Absolutely. Please do."

Elle lapsed into silence. Julie resumed looking out the window at the blur of lights whisking by in the darkness, trying to not focus on all the places she could feel her heart beating where she'd never felt it before, like her elbow, and the outside of her thigh, and pretty much anywhere that currently touched Elle.

And suddenly, the exhaustion of the day swept over her, as it often did at the end of the day during basketball season. The early mornings, the long days of being on both at work and with the team, the adrenaline of the game. And gradually, hazily, the lights outside, the landmarks she'd been driving by her whole life grew blurrier still, and Julie wondered what Snoozles was doing, and felt a random pang of missing Ben even though he wasn't gone yet, and realized she was quite hungry but needed to go grocery shopping, and remembered a joke from her *Good Place* rewatch that had made her laugh, and thought, for just a moment, about the rose inked on Elle's skin, before the lights dimmed completely.

A nudge woke Julie as they were pulling into the East parking lot.

A nudge from Elle's knee, knocking against her own.

"Hey." Elle's voice was soft, and entirely too close, and—

Fork.

Julie bolted upright, mouth dropping open and snapping shut again.

"We're here," Elle said, unnecessarily, and it was too dark and Julie was still too half-asleep to make out Elle's face, but it sounded like she was smiling.

Julie blinked out the window until the familiar approaching building was no longer blurry. Until the whoops and hollers from the team, renewed by arriving home, filtered through her brain enough to wake her up.

She had fallen asleep *on Elle Cochrane's shoulder.*

Howard brought the bus to a stop with a groan of the brakes.

Julie didn't have time to process this right now.

"Okay, Bobcats!" She took care to keep her body away from Elle's as she stood. "Great job tonight. Go get her."

One by one, the Bobcats trooped off the bus, running up the sidewalk to smack the head of the bronze bobcat that stood sentry outside East High's main doors, its head shiny from the hands of every student who paid her a celebratory visit after every Bobcat win, at the last curtain call of every school play.

Julie slung her bag over her shoulder and stuck her hands in her pockets, chilled by the night as soon as she exited the bus.

She couldn't meet Elle's eyes as she called out a goodbye and headed toward her car. But she had seen, from the way Elle had welcomed Vanessa into her home, from the fact that Elle was part of this team at all now, that Elle contained kindness and grace. And she hoped Elle would employ some of it for Julie now, and never mention the events of this bus ride again.

CHAPTER ELEVEN

An hour later, Julie could still feel the ghost of Elle's arm against hers.

"I know." She scowled at Snoozles, who was sitting on the windowsill and swishing her tail. "Stop looking at me like that. God, you can be such a bitch sometimes."

She crumpled up the silver wrapper of the Pop-Tarts she'd eaten cold for dinner and threw it, half-heartedly, Snoozles's way.

Snoozles was unmoved.

Julie sighed and collapsed back on the couch.

And remembered falling asleep on Elle's couch, last week.

Falling asleep on Elle's couch. Falling asleep on her shoulder. Shit, Julie was turning into Ben, who had this weird habit of falling into a dead sleep whenever he was stressed. Julie had spent half of high school shaking him out of unconsciousness. But like anything Ben Caravalho did, it had been somehow charming.

Julie wasn't sure if she had ever felt charming. She certainly didn't now.

She was past ready for bed, even if it was still technically early. But instead of making any move to brush her teeth or wash her face or any other number of things she should be doing, she stared at the ceiling, TV off, apartment quiet.

Her body still hummed with awareness, a low-grade fever born of Elle's nearness, the press of her against Julie's side.

It was a fever Julie didn't quite know what to do with.

She thought again of that moment last week in Elle's house, when she'd seen Elle leaning against the fridge in her short sleeves, and she'd felt the possibility of...something, something that didn't normally make it through to Julie's brain. The moments in the East High gym that seemed to stretch between them, the air too thick, Julie's lungs too tight.

Elle had talked about liking numbers; Julie liked numbers, too. She wished there was some kind of computer where she could input how it felt to have Elle's thigh pressed against hers, or that nanosecond when she realized her cheek was smooshed onto Elle's shoulder, the feeling of Elle's breath hovering above her cheek.

And after a few minutes, said magical computer would spit out a clear, understandable analysis: 15 percent general queer, 10 percent lesbian stereotype, 20 percent ace, 55 percent dumbass.

If she had stayed at Elle's house that night, when Elle had invited her to...would they have sat on opposite ends of the couch and finished the football game?

Or would Elle have sat as close to her as she had on the bus?

Would Julie have wanted her to?

Julie's phone rang, interrupting her thoughts. She leaned over to grab it from the coffee table.

London.

Panic bubbled in Julie's chest, wiping all other frivolous concerns away. Like her, London never called when the option of texting existed.

"What's wrong?"

"Hey, Jules. I'm fine. No one died."

"For fork's sake." She leaned back against the throw pillows, clutching her chest. "If you were here, I'd hit you over the head with my teakettle."

"Sorry, sorry. I just…" A sigh. "Are you busy?"

"Nope. Just got home from a game." *Actually, I got home forty-five minutes ago, and have been lying on the couch ever since, eating Pop-Tarts and feeling confused about pine cones.* But that was more than London needed to know. "What's up?"

"Would you maybe want to come down to the studio?" This request was followed immediately by "I know it's late. You don't have to."

Julie frowned. She'd been to the studio where London worked a few times before; one of the best perks of living in Hillsboro was that it was close to Music Row. And even though she knew a matter of geography probably didn't hold true meaning, it had made her feel closer to London since they'd gotten the job there. But she'd never stopped by the studio at—she leaned up to check the clock—nine forty-five p.m.

"Yeah, I can do that." Exhaustion, and everything else, could wait if London needed her. "You sure nothing's wrong?"

"Yes." Another *huge* sigh. Julie rolled her eyes now. The *drama* of London sometimes. "This band has been on break forever, and I'm all hopped up on caffeine alone in the booth, and I've been thinking about this thing, and I just…wanted to talk to you."

Like that, Julie didn't care about magical identity computers or falling asleep in inappropriate places. She was already slipping on her shoes.

"Be there in fifteen."

"Jules."

London jumped from their chair as soon as Julie walked through the door. They wrapped her in a hug, arms squeezed tightly around her shoulders.

Any other day, Julie likely would have laughed about the overly enthusiastic greeting—clearly London was in a mood—but tonight, she merely hugged them back a bit tighter. Let her eyes drift closed, breathing in the comfort of her person.

She tried not to dwell on it, but a bittersweet ache often settled in her bones these days, a subtle but ever-present awareness that she was no longer as needed by the people she loved most. That London had Dahlia now, as Ben had Alexei.

She wasn't sure if it was jealousy, exactly, as much as a quiet acceptance. That Dahlia was who London ran to first, with their problems or their triumphs. Alexei, whom Ben first sought comfort from, who first heard about his day.

Julie was no longer the recipient of the first tellings of stories.

But London had called her tonight.

And though she still didn't know why, what mattered was that they had called her.

"Hey," she finally replied, blinking away whatever this long, strange day was doing to her eyes before throwing herself onto the worn couch along the wall. "Who've you got booked tonight?"

"These Little Things. You'd like them. Some First Aid Kit vibes for sure, but they mix it up sometimes." London swiveled back and forth in their chair, laughing a little. "It's probably partly their music that's got me all..." They flicked their wrist. "Weird."

"Hit me with the weird, then."

London stared through the glass that looked into the studio, the temporarily silent guitars and mics, a drum set and keyboards.

"I want to ask Dahlia to marry me."

Julie shot off the couch.

"*London!* Of course you do! God, *finally*."

Julie almost laughed in relief. This was not what she had been expecting. London had been trying to schedule top surgery for months, but kept running into insurance hassles and scheduling setbacks and the Tennessee legislature's attempts to invalidate their existence. She had been worried this late-night phone call had something to do with that, and she was already fed up enough with everything on their behalf that she wanted to break things.

London wanting to marry Dahlia? That was easy.

"But." London covered their face with their hands. "But she's divorced, Jules. She got divorced because she didn't want kids and all the trappings of marriage. What if I'm just being a complete idiot? Playing into the patriarchal bullshit she hates?"

"Yeah, Dahlia's divorced." Julie sank back on the couch, crossing a foot over her knee. "But she got divorced because she married the wrong person. You know what you have is different from what she had with Whatever That Dude's Name Was."

London dropped their hands and leaned forward.

"But if that's true, if we're so solid, why do we need to get married anyway? What if I ask her and she thinks...that I *am* like David? That I need some external validation of our relationship or something."

"Well." Julie tilted her head. "How would you answer her? *Do* you need external validation? Or something else? You know I would be thrilled if you and Dahlia got married; that would be a fucking fun wedding. But it also shouldn't matter what anyone else thinks. Why do *you* want to marry Dahlia?"

London sighed, shoulders drooping as they looked at their hands.

"I don't know," they said quietly. "I just...can't stop thinking about it. I've been thinking about it for months and months. I wish I had better words to describe it, but I feel like it would just be... nice. You know?" They glanced at Julie, bouncing their knee. "To get dressed up and stand in a forest with her somewhere and promise we'll always be each other's person. And I know we don't need legal paperwork to do that, but..."

"London." Julie put her hand on London's knee. "It's okay to want cheesy stuff. Okay? Who cares if the institution of marriage started as patriarchal bullshit. Who cares if people on the internet would judge you for wanting to get married. I was just asking those questions to help you out, in case Dahlia asks. But if you want this, you can let yourself want it, okay?"

They breathed out.

"Yeah. Okay. Thanks."

"And it's not like if Dahlia says no, you'll leave her, right?"

London shook their head. "Come on."

"Exactly. Look, I think you're getting yourself all worked up over this, when all you have to do is *talk to her.*" Julie cocked her head again. "It's like I've had this conversation with you before."

But Julie smiled as she said it. Julie loved giving London a hard time. Loved being the person people turned to for advice. She felt more at home in her body, more fully herself here in this recording studio past her bedtime than she had in weeks.

London laughed, wiping a hand over their eyes.

"I know. But apparently...even if you love someone, and are around them all the freaking time, it's still...hard to make yourself talk to them about things? I don't know. Brains are weird."

"Yeah," Julie agreed. "But you gotta do it anyway. Don't do the whole...get down on one knee proposal thing. You're right; Dahlia probably doesn't need that again. Just tell her how you're feeling. Talk it out."

"Yeah." London bit their lip. "You're right. I know you're right."

"Obviously I'm right." Julie huffed out a breath, affronted. "I'm always right."

"I was thinking maybe I could offer," London moved on, ignoring her offense, as they had so expertly, annoyingly done for the last three decades, "if she does say yes...the idea of having a really small ceremony? Like, just us. So she knows it's only about her and me."

Julie stretched an arm across the back of the couch.

"Okay. But is that what you want? Or would you want a bigger thing? You should be honest about what you want, if you're going to do this."

"Yeah. I don't know." London fiddled with some knobs on the equipment in front of them. "Fuck, I'm messing up the levels." They clasped their hands back in their lap. "I . . . keep researching stuff? Like, venues and cakes and—" They covered their face again.

"You've been researching *cakes*?" Julie squealed, leaning forward again. "Oh my *god*, London. You are in *deep*."

"It's awful. I'm constantly worried she's going to find out. Like she's going to open up the laptop to edit her latest video and a page full of engagement rings will pop up. I have to keep clearing my browser history."

Oh, this was gold. Julie could make fun of London about this *forever*.

"It's especially dumb," London went on, laughing now, "because the whole thing is just . . . gender torture. Bride and groom this, bride and groom that. Even the gay marriage industry is all tied up in the binary. Like, yes, I *am* excited you can now buy a wedding cake, even in Tennessee, with two ladies on top, but that's still not really helping me here."

"Oh." Julie's smile faded. "That must be super annoying, London."

"It's fine." London waved a hand. "We can figure out our own thing. I'm used to it. But . . . I don't know. I would like our friends and family there, probably. But if Dahlia wanted it to just be us, I would be okay with that. Although . . ." They grinned. "Dahlia does like a party."

"Oh my god." Julie's eyes widened. "London. Dahlia knows, like . . . everyone in Nashville now. London, if she *does* want a real wedding, you are going to have to invite . . ." Julie trailed off, trying to calculate it. "A hundred million people."

"I know." London laughed.

"London. That would be your *nightmare*."

"I *know*." London laughed harder. "Dahlia is the worst." They hung their head in their hands. "I love her so much."

Julie sobered, staring at her twin sibling's hair, the same shade as hers but styled in such a hipper way.

Suddenly, the room felt too small.

Julie looked away, staring through the glass.

An hour ago, Julie had been having an identity crisis over... what? Sitting too close to someone?

Meanwhile, her twin sibling was preparing to *marry* someone.

Julie hated how bitter it felt in her stomach just then, the fact of how drastically her and London's roads had diverged, somewhere along the way. She'd always felt a few steps behind them, never quite measuring up to their accomplishments. God, they were discussing London's possible marriage while sitting in a *Music Row studio*, where London was living their absolute dream career.

But this felt... different.

Julie was used to feeling behind in this, to somehow never Getting It, through middle school and high school and college, when everyone around her coupled up while she only ever wanted to listen to music and play hoops. It was a reality that didn't bother her, most of the time, because listening to music and playing hoops was awesome.

But there were times—like right now, like her twin getting married while she was melting down over brushing elbows; like when she'd contemplated telling Ben about her crush while he was preparing to move across the country for love—when the embarrassment was almost overwhelming.

"Anyway," London said. "You're right. I'll figure out a time to talk to her. Thanks for coming here and talking to me about it. Sometimes I just... need to talk to you, you know?"

"Yeah," Julie managed to say, even though her throat felt thick and strange. "I know."

"And I feel like you disappear sometimes during basketball season." London nudged her foot with their own. "How are you? How's coaching with Elle Cochrane going?"

"Oh. Uh." Julie blinked, thrown further off-kilter by the mention of Elle's name. London and Dahlia, to their credit, had been relatively chill when she'd texted them earlier in the week about their plan of asking Elle to coach actually paying off. But it felt like such a ridiculous change of topic. There were fucking Grammys in glass cases in this room. London was going to get married. There was no way they actually wanted to know about a high school basketball team. "Fine."

London raised a brow.

"Julie—"

A loud knock sounded on the door.

"Hey, London," Robin, one of the managers of the studio, poked her head in to say. "We're on again in ten."

London nodded, straightening. "Got it."

"Hey, Jules," Robin said with a smile. Julie waved before Robin retreated.

"I should get going anyway." Julie stood, gathering her bag.

"You can stay, if you want." London nodded their head over their shoulder, toward the glass. "I'd love to have you hang and listen for a while."

"Nah, I'm beat. Thanks, though." She hesitated before heading toward the door. "And thanks, London. For calling me."

"Thank you for coming. Seriously." London pulled her into another hug. Marriage talk had *definitely* gotten into their brain.

"Yeah." Julie forced a small smile.

London ruffled her hair as they pulled away. Julie groaned.

"Why do you always have to mess up my ponytail? God."

"Because you always make that face. Hard to resist, really."

"I hate you."

"I love you, too. Listen, it's late, and sometimes drunk tourists wander over here from Broadway...Text me when you get home?"

"I will."

"And Julie?"

Julie paused, already halfway through the door. "Yeah?"

"You know you can talk to me about anything anytime too, right?"

"Yeah, London." Julie swallowed. "I know."

She stepped into the hallway without looking back, closing the door with a soft *snick*.

CHAPTER TWELVE

Y ou okay?"

Julie's eyes remained on the Bobcats, practicing layups while the McDougall Raccoons did the same under the opposite basket.

But clearly, Julie had noticed Elle—and Vanessa—glancing toward the doors of the gym approximately every thirty seconds.

Elle sighed.

"Her mom's coming today. Karly."

Julie nodded. "I know."

Elle hadn't been entirely certain Karly would be released from rehab in time for this first home game, a fact that had been keeping Elle awake the last several nights, running through worst-case scenarios about how much her absence might affect Vanessa.

But late last night, she'd received an email from Amber: Karly will be at the game with her sponsor, José. Reminder that all contact between Karly and Vanessa currently needs to be supervised, and limited to the game. I won't be able to be there; please let me know how it goes.

"Rose is coming too," Elle added, her nerves propelling more words than were probably necessary out of her mouth. "Which should be interesting, considering she's been...well...she has a lot of thoughts about the situation."

Julie's mouth curved in sympathy. "Moms do tend to have a lot of thoughts."

Elle sighed again. "Yeah."

Rose was glad Vanessa was safe and believed in Elle's ability to take care of her. But she possessed an anger about the situation—an anger toward Karly—that Elle herself didn't want to fully feel. Elle only had the capacity to focus on what was happening now. How she could help.

But Rose, above all else, identified as a mom, a single mom who had dedicated her life to Elle and Tricia, for better or worse. The joyful grandparent, now, for Tricia and Akhil's kids: Sanjana, Sid, Luna, and Jeremiah. Always available to babysit, even when she was in pain, to lavish gifts she couldn't necessarily afford.

Rose could not understand leaving your child at home, pulled by the lure of addiction or a toxic boyfriend or both—Elle herself was still learning the details, had been counseled by Amber to accept that she might not ever have all the details—and not returning for weeks.

Until a neighbor made a call to CPS because they were worried the teenager next door was living alone. That she might be running out of food.

"If you need to," Julie said, "you can sit with them. I can make it through this one without you, if that works best for y'all."

"No, no," Elle said. "It's fine. It'll be fine."

Julie was silent a minute, before she blew her whistle.

"Williams! Lead dribble passes!"

Ngozi looked over her shoulder and nodded, switching the drill.

"If it helps," Julie added, finally glancing at Elle, "everyone is nervous today. Some of our parents travel for away games, but for most of the team, this is the first time this season that their parents, their friends, their classmates might be watching them play. And McDougall…" She blew out a breath. "Shorts. They're looking good."

Elle grimaced. "Yeah."

Julie had warned Elle yesterday that the Raccoons were consistently one of the best teams in the league. Even though Elle had already learned, in her current-state-of-Nashville-high-school-basketball research, all about the McDougall program. While both teams had only engaged in warm-ups so far, as the scoreboard counted down to game time, Elle could already tell how much tighter their passing was. Their shots smarter and smoother.

Their coaches, too, looked more severe, an older man and woman standing in matching Raccoons warm-up gear, serious looks on their faces.

The familiarity of those looks—of the expectations that probably hung heavy on the Raccoons' shoulders—sent a shiver up Elle's spine.

"Think we could get matching Bobcats tracksuits?" she joked, in an effort to distract herself from the tension creeping dangerously up her neck. Elle did not want to get a migraine tonight.

Julie smiled.

"Yeah, not sure the Doc would approve that budget request." Elle had met Dr. Jones, the principal of East High, when she'd filled out the paperwork for the position. The Doc had a strong handshake and eyes that brooked no argument. Elle, naturally, had been attracted to her energy immediately. Although she was positive that for a student, she was probably terrifying. Elle hoped Vanessa never got sent to her office.

"I'm going to go make sure Blake's all set." Julie motioned to where Blake sat at the scorer's table. "If Karly shows, Vanessa should know she's free to go say hi too if she wants."

Elle took a deep breath. "Thanks."

A batch of cheerleaders walked through the door, shuffling red and silver pom-poms, setting up at the edge of the bleachers.

And then they all walked in together—Karly and a large man Elle presumed was José, followed by Rose, leaning on a cane.

Elle cursed under her breath. She should've brought her walker; her walker had a padded seat that folded down. These bleachers were horrible for Rose's joints.

Elle closed her eyes before she walked over. Took just a tiny moment to let herself sink into the memory, as she had any time she'd needed a breather over the last forty-eight hours, of the warmth of Julie's temple resting against her shoulder. The softness of Julie's hair against Elle's jaw.

Julie falling asleep there had been an accident. Even if Elle had doubted it, the way Julie had run off afterward, without a single second of eye contact, had confirmed it. Elle knew she should keep her distance, next away game. Not sit so close.

But she couldn't help remembering how those fifteen minutes had felt anyway.

"Hey, Mom," she said, meeting them at the bleachers. "Good to see you, Karly."

And it was. Even if it was hard.

Elle had prepared herself for Karly possibly looking rough, but the reality still felt like skipping a step, a small jolt of panic. She looked so much skinnier than Elle remembered, smaller, somehow, in general, like life had shrunk her. She wore skinny jeans and a purple sweater, dark hair pulled back in a tight bun. She tilted her chin in the air, jaw set, eyes guarded. It was so similar to how Vanessa had held herself when she'd first arrived at Elle's house that it almost made Elle crack.

"Good to see you too, Elle."

Elle heard the waver in Karly's voice, saw her eyes widen a second before Vanessa crashed past Elle, slamming into her mother in a hug.

Elle stepped back, trying not to stare at the way Karly's eyes squeezed shut, at the way she tilted her head over her daughter's shoulder and breathed her in.

Elle hadn't been sure, exactly, how Vanessa would react to seeing her mother again. She avoided all touch, all signs of affection so diligently that it had simply been hard to imagine her...like this. In the middle of a hug.

But of course. Of course this was what Vanessa needed.

Elle looked away. Introduced herself to José. Wished they could be having this meeting someplace quiet, not in the middle of a loud high school gym whose bleachers were rapidly filling with strangers.

But when Karly patted her eyes and said, "All right, Ness, get on back out there now," when she took a deep breath, her shoulders relaxing after Vanessa listened, Elle realized that maybe it was okay. To have that hug here, in a place full of activity. Where Karly could sit and blend into the crowd, find a little breathing room.

She turned to Elle, damp eyes still on guard, but the tiniest bit more open.

"She doing okay?"

"Yeah." Elle nodded. "She is."

Karly nodded back. Her voice was quiet when she said, "Good."

And even though Elle knew she herself wasn't nearly the most important part of the equation here, she had privately been so worried, all this time, that Karly was angry with her. For going along with CPS's orders. For stealing her kid.

Truthfully, she still couldn't quite tell. Maybe Karly was only being polite right now because she knew she had to be, because José was here, because she had to go along with CPS's orders now, too. But Elle allowed a bit of relief to enter her system anyway that Karly at least didn't appear to want to punch her. That Karly had shown up. A bit of hope, that they could find their way forward from here.

"I can't believe I'm here again!" Rose said, bright and loud, followed by her signature crackly cackle. As if nothing was out of the ordinary. "More basketball to watch with these old bones. Who knew?"

Elle knew the words weren't directed toward her, weren't meant to inflict guilt. Were said only with excitement and not *you took this away from me*. But she held in a wince anyway.

Rose leaned forward, narrowing her eyes.

"I hear McDougall's top of the league. What do you think our chances are?"

And at that, Elle was finally able to take a full breath, huffing it out as she said, "Mom, how do you even know that?" Elle had gone to a private high school on a basketball scholarship at the opposite end of town. Rose shouldn't know a thing about the current standings of Nashville public high schools, but of course she did.

"Oh, please, child," Rose scoffed. "You know I have my sources."

Elle could only smile, unable to deny it made her heart warm, Rose asking about *our chances*. Automatically adopting East High as her own, even if she'd never stepped inside this gym before today.

"I honestly don't know," she answered, glancing at the court. "We won our first game, but the season's just started. Mom," she couldn't help but say as she turned back just in time to see Rose grimacing as she finally sat down. "You should've brought the—"

"Oh, you hush right now, Elle Belle." Rose waved her off. "Bleachers haven't killed me yet." She turned to Karly, motioning at her to sit. "Always nagging me, this one," she said, leaning toward Karly, who managed a small smile.

The horn sounded, signaling the game was set to begin.

"I have to get back. It was really nice to meet you, José."

"It's special for me to be able to meet you, Elle," José said, voice earnest, dark eyes kind. Elle's throat, for just a moment, threatened to close with an emotion she couldn't name.

"I'm glad you're here," she said again to Karly.

She should have expected the retort from Rose, audible as she turned away: "What am I, chopped liver?"

The game was a slow-moving train wreck.

Occasionally, a fast-moving one.

The Raccoons didn't only outshoot and outscore the Bobcats, but they were stronger on defense, and they were fast. Julie had to use three of her time-outs in the first half alone, just so everyone could take a breather and cool the fork off.

When Julie put in Vanessa in the second quarter, Vanessa's face was white with terror. She'd played a few minutes against Hillcrest just fine, but Elle knew the stakes here. She wanted to reach for Vanessa's hand so badly—to reassure her there would be other games Karly got to see her play, that Karly wouldn't care whether they lost every single one—that she had to turn away while Vanessa waited to be called in at the scorer's table.

At halftime, Julie did her best to rally the troops in the locker room. Elle even jumped in, for the first time, with some areas where she'd seen opportunities for the Bobcats to strengthen their defense. Elle knew, like everyone in the locker room knew, that they were going to lose, but it could still be a good lesson in defense. The players nodded as she talked, seemed to understand her points. And when Julie looked over at her, eyes bright with gratitude, Elle, once again, had to turn away.

Ngozi and Sasha kept up a good fight; Gray subbed in for most of the second half and became a beast at perimeter guarding.

But for the most part, the third and fourth quarters were that most painful of pursuits: continuing to have to put in the work, up and down the court, even when you knew it was a losing battle. It was especially hard, Elle knew, as a young player, to be able to fight off the embarrassment, the anger and disappointment, enough to still make your legs move, make your arms try.

Elle tried to limit her glances at the bleachers. Each time she gave in, she watched Rose talking animatedly at Karly, while Karly sat very still with her hands clasped between her knees. Her face never lost that tightness, but every now and then, Elle saw her smile at whatever the heck Rose was saying.

In the end, the Bobcats only lost by eighteen points. Which, considering, Elle thought was a pretty impressive showing. As did Julie, even if the team didn't seem to quite believe them, eyes downcast in the locker room.

Vanessa sat apart from everyone, back to Elle, staring at her locker.

Karly, Rose, and José were waiting when they reemerged onto the court, Rose leaning on her cane.

"Hey, kid." She slung an arm around Vanessa's shoulders. "Y'all put up a good fight out there."

Vanessa shrugged, head drooped, eyes glancing to Karly.

"Although I do have a few choice words about those McDougall coaches." Rose turned her keen eyes toward Elle, pointing a finger toward the empty court. "And the refs—"

"All right, Mom." Elle couldn't help her smile, even in the heaviness of the moment. It made her chest tight, but she knew how happy Rose was, loss or not, to be back in her element. "Let's save those thoughts for later, shall we?"

"Ah, fine." Rose waved a hand. "You know what I'm thinking? I'm thinking we all deserve some ice cream."

Karly tensed. Even more than she already was.

"Mom." Elle glanced at Karly and then back at Rose. There were clear rules in place here. Karly was allowed to come to games. Any other time Karly and Vanessa spent together had to be planned, reported. "I'm not sure—"

"Oh, fiddlesticks." Rose waved her off again. "It'll be fine."

Elle took a deep breath. She should have expected this. It wasn't that Elle didn't want to get ice cream with Karly, but if Karly somehow got reprimanded for it . . . Amber had made it clear, how the best thing for Karly right now was following the rules.

José held up his hands when Elle glanced at him. "I don't work for nobody," he said. "I'm just here for y'all."

"I knew you were a good man," Rose said. "We're family," she added, to Elle, voice softer. "Family can get ice cream together."

Elle forced her temper away. She looked at Karly, and then Vanessa. "What do you guys think? It's up to you. We can always plan an ice cream outing for another time, too, if right now doesn't seem right."

Karly cleared her throat. "Your call, Ness."

Vanessa bit her lip, raising her head to glance at everyone in their small circle before her eyes landed on her mom. A tiny smile lifted her cheek before she said, "I could eat some ice cream."

And when an equally tiny smile flitted across Karly's face, Elle knew she couldn't say no.

"Then it's settled!" Rose clapped her hands. "Let's get outta here."

Before they could, Julie appeared at Elle's side, messenger bag slung across her chest. "Hey there, folks. Just wanted to say hi, since I didn't get to before the game. Karly, right? And Rose?" She leaned forward and shook each of their hands in turn before introducing herself to José. Rose absolutely preened at Julie already knowing her name, and for some reason, Elle felt herself blush.

"It was a tough one out there today, Coach," Rose said, approval in her voice, like she wanted Julie to know she'd done her best. "But you'll get 'em next time."

"That's right," Julie agreed with a smile.

"We're getting ice cream," Vanessa blurted, and Julie only smiled bigger.

"Now, that is exactly the kind of thing you should do after a game like this. What's your favorite flavor, Lerner?"

"Mint chocolate chip."

"Excellent. Get an extra scoop of mint chocolate chip for me, okay?" Something behind Rose caught Julie's attention. "I have to head out, but it was really nice meeting y'all. I'm so glad to have Vanessa on the team. We'll see you Tuesday?"

"You'll see us," Rose responded with enthusiasm, at the same time Karly said, quietly, "Thank you, Coach."

Elle watched Julie walk toward a pair of men waiting at center court, throat tight again at how easily Julie had just pulled another fact from Vanessa that Elle hadn't known. Throat tight at how kind and casual she had been to her family, even after such a crushing defeat. Throat tight at how good she looked, walking away with her hands in the pockets of her basketball shorts.

The first man drew Julie into a hug, the second bumping her knuckles and doing some elaborate handshake, followed by a solid thump on each other's shoulders, like they were ballers who'd been playing together for years. The men looked like they might be brothers, a familiar look in their faces. The first man's hair was much longer, held in a sloppy bun, while the fist-bumping one's was buzzed short. Something about this second man seemed particularly familiar, but Elle couldn't place him. Perhaps because her jealousy and her nerves about ice cream were making her mind hazy.

"Hey, Coach Cochrane!" Elle jerked at her mom's words. When she looked back, Rose was smirking, and Karly and Vanessa were almost to the door. They walked side by side, talking quietly while José followed a step behind. "Stop slacking over there!"

Elle huffed out a half laugh and walked over to loop Rose's waiting arm through hers.

Three hours later, Elle once again sat alone at her kitchen island, staring out the dark window and tapping her fingers against the counter.

Ice cream had been fine. Good, even. Rose had filled the space for them, peppering Vanessa with questions about school and the team, which Vanessa answered in uncharacteristically rambly terms. Elle could feel the nerves rolling off her in waves. Or maybe Elle had been projecting. Either way, it allowed Karly to sit mostly in silence, smiling at Vanessa's answers, eyes hardly leaving Vanessa's face. And the sweetness of the ice cream had melted away, a little bit, the loss of the game, the complicated realities of the night.

Elle still wasn't sure if going to ice cream had been the *right* thing to do. But she couldn't deny Rose's assertion that it had been a good thing to do.

Yet Elle's anxiety had only intensified since leaving the ice cream parlor. Vanessa had been silent the whole way home, which Elle had expected. Hadn't said a word before she ran up the stairs to her room. Hadn't made a sound since. No blasting music, no rush of the shower.

Elle couldn't stop thinking about how Vanessa had hugged Karly before the game, the look on Karly's face at the moment of contact. How out of place Elle had felt all night. How helpless.

She had felt, every now and then over the last couple weeks, that she and Vanessa were settling into a routine. A rhythm that felt okay. The leave of absence from work had helped Elle immensely. It was already almost difficult, remembering what her house had been like without Vanessa there.

But seeing Karly tonight reminded her—had likely reminded Vanessa, too—how in flux everything was. How maybe finding a rhythm in this situation wasn't even possible.

Elle picked up her phone. They hadn't had a real dinner, just the ice cream, which now sat in the pit of her stomach, empty and overly sugared. She contemplated ordering something, but couldn't decide on what. She scrolled to Mara's number, but her thumb hesitated over their last messages, not knowing what she even wanted to say. Not knowing how to describe what she was feeling. What she wanted to hear.

A text appeared on her screen before she could figure it out.

how was ice cream?

Elle blinked.
Julie.

Elle watched as typing bubbles appeared underneath. They paused and started again about five times until finally: sorry if that's invasive to ask. you just looked like you were uncertain about it all.

Elle released a breath, amused despite herself. Coaches. Always observing.

Not invasive, she typed back.

But even if Elle truly didn't find it invasive, responding to Julie's question felt . . . different.

Other than their first real conversation, when they'd discussed both working at Vandy, Elle and Julie had stuck, mostly, to talking about basketball. About Vanessa and the team. Sticking to the team felt safe.

It was okay, she typed. Even if it felt inadequate, like she was brushing off the question. It was simply the most accurate answer.

Where'd you go? Julie asked.

Mike's, Elle answered. I prefer Jeni's, but it's Rose's favorite.

Julie: Oh man, can't remember the last time I had Mike's. What'd you get?

Elle: A scoop of honey pistachio and a scoop of banana pudding :)

Elle didn't know why she'd included a happy face. She felt ridiculous as soon as she sent it.

Julie: FOOORRRRRK THAT SOUNDS GOOD dang I want ice cream now

Elle smiled. Thank you for saying hi to Karly and my mom

Julie: Of course. How's Vanessa doing?

Elle took a deep breath. Okay, I think. Could've gone a lot worse. And then, before she could second-guess herself, she found herself typing, I wish she could talk to me.

Julie took a second to reply.

I know, she said. But you're doing your best, Elle

> **Julie:** And that's all you can do right now

> **Julie:** She's safe with you. That means so much

> **Julie:** Even if she's angry, even if she can't say it

Elle had to put the phone down. She blinked a few times, staring blurrily at her fridge, before she was able to respond.

> **Elle:** Thank you, Coach.

Julie responded with a :). Elle stared at it for a long minute, warmth stirring in her chest, spreading dangerously down her shoulders.

It was a good place to end the conversation. A nice note to finally fall asleep to.

But there was something else Elle needed to ask.

Speaking of invasive questions, she typed slowly. Can I ask who those guys were that you were talking to, when we left?

> **Julie:** Oh, that was my best friend, Ben, and his brother, Tiago

Elle closed her eyes and cursed under her breath.

She had placed his face, finally, halfway through ice cream, and it had made a shard of panic jolt up her spine. But she'd forced it back down, forced herself to focus on her family, until right now, when she remembered.

Elle: Tiago Caravalho, right?

Tiago Caravalho was indisputably Nashville's finest sports writer. He had only been writing a few years, hadn't covered her when she was a player. But as opposed to what Mara thought, Elle did still follow sports, in her own way. Tiago covered all kinds of things, but she could tell, in the passion that came through, that basketball was his favorite. Reading his work was one small piece of that world she still privately allowed herself, even if it sometimes felt like grinding a small, masochistic screwdriver into her heart.

Yeah, Julie replied. That Tiago Caravalho

Elle almost wanted to laugh at the fact that Julie was apparently friends with him. Because of course. And she wanted to trust Julie, 85 percent of her *did* trust Julie, which was why she'd shoved it away at ice cream, but she probably should have talked about the media with Julie in the first place, when she said yes to this, should have—

Julie: I told him not to talk about you

Julie: I hope that's okay? I meant to check in with you tomorrow about it all

Julie: I mean, he doesn't cover much high school stuff these days anyway

Julie: But he asked if you'd be interested in doing an interview and I said absolutely not but as I am typing this I'm realizing it's probably a bit weird that I just spoke for you like that so

Julie: If you ever want to do an interview, I know a guy

Elle's heart thumped in her ears.

Not weird, she typed. Perfect. And then, thank you.

The warmth was spreading from Elle's shoulders to her finger-tips. Warm enough to turn off the light and go upstairs. To say good night.

How was your evening? she typed instead.

> **Julie:** Well, Snoozles is pretty pissed about those Raccoons

Julie sent a picture of a fluffy gray cat sitting on a windowsill and looking unimpressed.

> **Julie:** So we've just been licking our wounds together. You know, same old, same old

Elle smiled. Tell Snoozles I commiserate

> **Julie:** She says brrrrrrgggghhhhrrrr which means 'go bob-cats, you got this,' approximately

And because Elle was a fool, she typed, Where are you and Snoozles in your Good Place rewatch?

And somehow, the night disappeared from there.

CHAPTER THIRTEEN

I can't go in there." Ben bent over his knees. "I can't let the baristas see me like this."

"Ben." Julie wiped an arm across her forehead. "These baristas see sweaty people all the time."

"And they are privately grossed out each time. I know these people; I have an image to maintain. *Fuck.* I'm on my feet every day. How did I get so out of shape?"

Ben sagged further toward the ground. Until his knees hit the sidewalk, and with a twist, he was splayed on his back outside of All People Coffee.

"That's it. Just leave me here."

Julie rolled her eyes. Her post-run adrenaline was the only thing giving her the courage to possibly talk to Ben about this, and she needed him to get into the coffeeshop before it disappeared.

"We need to do this more before I leave for Oregon. Lex got to know me when we were hiking twenty miles a day. I was *lithe*, Julie."

"Alexei does not care about your litheness, Ben. How's he doing, by the way?"

"Oh, you know." Ben waved a hand and gave a dreamy sigh. "Perfect."

This was how Ben always answered this question. Julie would've rolled her eyes again, except for the fact that it actually made her deeply happy each time he said it. Ben deserved perfect.

But he still needed to get his ass up.

"Ben. I need caffeine."

"Give me a minute."

"People are going to think you're seriously injured, and I'm just standing here like an asshole."

"It's cool, I can give people a jaunty little wave for reassurance." He demonstrated to the woman currently walking behind Julie, who gave a confused smile before stepping into the shop. "See?"

Julie crossed her arms over her chest. She squinted into the November sunshine.

"Say you've been texting with this person a lot," she said after a minute. "And it doesn't even matter, really, because they are the most unattainable person in the world, but...you think it's making you feel something."

Ben's arms fell to his sides. A beat passed.

"Julie Parker," Ben said. "I'll be damned." And then, "We need caffeine."

"Yeah," Julie said as Ben shoved himself off the sidewalk. "Figured that would work."

By the time they got in line, Ben's eyes had grown entirely too bright for Julie's liking.

"What?"

"I am...so excited."

Julie sighed. "Once we get our drinks, I'm going to talk to you about this for ten minutes, max, and then I'm done. Just as a warning."

"Got it."

When they settled themselves at an outdoor table with their iced coffees, Ben didn't waste a single second.

"Okay. So how, exactly, is this person unattainable."

Julie groaned. "They just...are."

"Are they already in a monogamous relationship or otherwise unavailable?"

"No, I mean—" Oh god. Julie had no idea. It was entirely possible Elle had a partner. How would Julie know? "I don't think so. They're just, you know. Super hot and impressive and amazing."

Ben squinted at her, tapping a finger to his lips.

"And you don't think you deserve super hot and impressive and amazing."

"Just...next question, please."

"Okay. You said the texting has made you feel something. How exactly has it made you feel?"

"Weird. And happy. And..." Julie searched her brain for better words. "Good. And freaked out." So that was a negative on better words then.

"And how did this texting start?"

"I sent her a message because I could tell she had been...stressed. About this thing. So I just wanted to make sure she was okay."

Julie had thought, then, that their texts had perhaps just been a late-Friday-night aberration.

But yesterday, they had just...kept happening. All day.

"Hm." Ben settled back in his chair, folding his hands over his stomach.

"*What?* I can tell you're dying to say something."

"Oh, I'm just wondering how in love with you this person already is."

Now Julie did roll her eyes again. "Please. She is not."

"And how do you know?"

"Because she's not."

Ben steepled his fingers, bringing them to his lips before he spoke again.

"Julie. You do know that you are a very lovable person?"

Julie took a sip of her coffee and stared over Ben's shoulder. He was wasting time. Trying to talk about this out loud was exactly as awkward as she had expected it to be.

"Like..." Ben went on, "you know Tiago used to have the biggest crush on you, right?"

Julie almost spit out her coffee. "Fuck off."

"I'm serious."

"All I've ever done with Tiago is fuck around and shoot hoops."

"Yeah," Ben said pointedly. "And your adeptness at fucking around and shooting hoops is, to Tiago and likely lots of other people, extremely hot."

Julie's mouth hung open for a fraction of a second before she snapped it shut.

"Oh my god. It is not. You're making fun of me."

"I'm *not*. Julie. You were a star basketball player, you're gorgeous, you're extremely kind and funny. I bet you a million dollars if you texted Tiago right now and said, *hey, wanna have sex?*, he'd be here in five minutes."

"Oh my god." Julie wrinkled her nose. "Don't be gross."

"I think the question here, Julie, is if this person who's making you feel weird and happy texted *you* asking if you wanted to fuck, what you would do."

A blush swept over Julie's face so swiftly—so fiercely that it even surprised herself—that she knew it answered Ben's question for her.

She cleared her throat, staring once more at the street.

"Well." Her knee bounced under the table. "I don't predict that ever happening, but... say, in this hypothetical dreamland, this person is into me. But what if—" Julie took a deep breath. Forced herself to think, *It's just Ben.* "What if they tried to... ask me out, or... touch me, or something, and I had to be like, oh, by the way, I have no idea what I'm doing or if any of this will even work for me, because I've never done this before." She covered her face with her hands. "Ben. It's mortifying."

"Julie. Listen to me."

Ben leaned over the table and clasped her wrists, dragging her hands away.

"Julie. I should say, first off, that wanting to be asked out and wanting to be touched are two different things. And maybe you want both. Maybe you want one and not the other. Any answer is okay. But I'll also say…Lex had never been in a relationship before, either, and that didn't affect how much I wanted him for a single second. Just like he didn't care that I'm—how did you phrase it to him?—kind of a slut."

"I apologized for that."

"And you didn't need to, because it's true. If you like someone, it doesn't matter what did or didn't happen in their past. Unless, you know, said previous sluttiness resulted in some slight emotional trauma"—Ben waved his fingers in jazz hands, singsonging the word *trauma*—"that you get to watch your partner go to therapy for."

Julie knew Ben was trying to get her to laugh, but she looked down at her lap, fidgeting with her shorts.

"The thing is, Ben, even that makes me feel kind of dumb. I mean, I'm not glad you have emotional trauma, obviously; I hated watching you date all those awful guys, but…" She shook her head, not sure how to put it into words. "At least you knew yourself enough, or were brave enough, or something, to make those bad decisions. You've been out there doing shit while I've been…" Julie shrugged. "Watching TV with Snoozles."

"No." Ben shook his head. "I mean, I understand what you're saying, but the comparison is not valid, Julie, at least in terms of one being better than the other. Because the time you and Lex spent trying to figure out your shit while I just followed my dick—" Ben scratched at his hair. "It's all valid, Julie, is what I'm saying."

"But I *haven't* figured out my shit," Julie cried, embarrassment hitting her cheeks at the unplanned rise in the volume of her voice. She took a quick sip of her coffee to recover. "I don't even know if I'm...bi, or a big lesbo, and maybe a bit ace or—whatever. And you and all the other queers we know have had it figured out for ages! You know what? I think I'm done talking about this now."

"Okay, okay, that's fair, but let me float one more possibility."

Julie took another sip of coffee.

"Maybe you are a little or a lot ace. And maybe these tingly excited feelings you're having any time your phone lights up with a new text are tingly excited Important New Friendship feelings. Because that is absolutely a thing, too. Honestly, sometimes shit is even *deeper*, more fraught, you know? When they're friendship feelings. Or maybe they *are* romantic feelings, and when you get there, the sex stuff doesn't really work for you."

Jesus, Julie almost interrupted Ben to say. Like, she got it. There were a million options and every option was great. Queerness and sexuality were all rainbows and endless freaking options.

Sometimes, that felt like the whole problem.

"But I don't think you would be talking to me about all this, for the first time since we've known each other, if you didn't want to at least find out. So maybe you should try. To actually find out. Because any relationship that's worthwhile, whether it's friendship or romantic or sexual, only really works when you try. Even if truly trying can be..."

"Humiliating?"

"I was going to say really hard, sometimes, but yeah, that, too."

Julie took another deep breath. She swirled the melting ice in her cup and was as awkward as possible when she said, "Um. Okay. Thank you."

"Thank *you*."

"I'm ready to talk about anything else now." She stood, chair scraping against the patio.

"Sure, but." Ben stuck his straw in his mouth, jogging to catch up. "You gonna tell me who she is?"

"Not yet."

Ben gasped, holding a hand to his chest. "Oh, that's better than I was expecting. Can I guess?"

"*No.*"

"There it is."

"Literally anything else, Ben."

"Okay. Um...how about them Titans?"

"I'm going to make you run back to the car."

"You wouldn't. Except you would. God, I love you so much it hurts."

For the first time all morning, Julie grinned down at the sidewalk. "Yeah. You too."

Julie: How was court?

Julie placed her phone back on her desk.

She knew Elle wouldn't be out of court for a while, but Julie had worked diligently for like, two hours now—a personal record for this week, thus far—so she deserved to send it anyway. Just in case.

Twenty minutes later, the screen lit up.

Elle: It was...okay. Karly was there.

Julie: How's she doing?

Elle: I wish I knew :(but she answered all the judge's questions well, I thought, even when it felt like the judge was being…judgy

Julie: ♥

Elle: I'm glad it's over. Now I at least know what to expect for next time

Julie: Definitely. You should do something nice for yourself now. Cook yourself some particularly tasty barley or something

Elle: Barley?

Julie: Look, I've seen your kitchen cabinets. I don't know all what's in there but it seemed barleyish

Elle: I'll have you know I can eat irresponsibly when I want to. I had ice cream just last week!

Julie: Elle. I have ice cream every night.

Elle: Wait. Really?

Julie: Life is short Elle

Elle: 😊

Elle: How's Vanderbilt Alumni Relations?

Julie cringed. She could not think of a question she wanted to answer less. How was Vandy Alumni Relations? Well, other than stewing at a new passive-aggressive email from Lorraine, Julie had spent most of this morning in a Teams "brainstorming" meeting for event ideas for next year, where she'd phoned it in so hard she'd started to wonder why the hell Raquel, her boss, hadn't fired her yet.

Julie looked around her cubicle, as if a more impressive answer could be found there.

Eventually, she texted Elle a picture of her stapler that was shaped like a dachshund.

> **Julie:** Looking at this is pretty much the highlight of all my days
>
> **Elle:** Of course it is. That is adorable.
>
> **Julie:** Office supplies truly are the best.
>
> **Julie:** The one thing You've Got Mail got right
>
> **Elle:** Firstly, they call them school supplies in You've Got Mail
>
> **Elle:** Secondly, you don't like You've Got Mail??
>
> **Julie:** He SHUT DOWN HER BELOVED SMALL BUSI-NESS, Elle
>
> **Julie:** Her life's work!!
>
> **Julie:** "I wanted it to be you"?? she should have PUNCHED HIM IN THE FACE
>
> **Elle:** 😄

Julie contemplated typing *What is your favorite rom-com?* or *You're hotter than Meg Ryan* or *Why didn't you sit next to me on the bus again?* but in the end, placed her phone back on the desk and took a deep breath.

Julie had been taking lots of deep breaths these days.

It probably didn't mean anything that Elle had stuck to her side of the aisle on the bus during their away game yesterday. She likely just didn't want to risk Julie drooling on her shoulder again. Which was reasonable. Totally fine. Julie hadn't missed the heat of her body at all.

She opened up a budget document to answer a question Raquel pinged her.

And then she picked up her phone again.

> **Julie:** I feel the need to clarify that I do not actually condone punching Tom Hanks in the face
>
> **Julie:** Like, ever
>
> **Elle:** Noted.
>
> **Elle:** I do think you need to rewatch the movie, though
>
> **Julie:** Maybe.

And Julie, like a professional-ass adult, kept working on the budget document for a solid half hour.

Until Elle texted, I got tacos for myself! Completely free of barley

> **Julie:** Okay but from where
>
> **Elle:** . . . the wild cow

Elle: But they are delicious okay!

Julie: I am positive your vegan tacos are delicious. Still dubious anything from there wouldn't contain barley though

Elle: They're sweet potato and black bean. With lime slaw and pumpkin seeds

Elle: They're really good :(

Julie: ♥

Julie stared at the screen. She was starting to text too many hearts. She knew this. And that frowny face had made her stomach feel squirmy again, in a *Was that a flirty frowny face?* kind of way. Even though, objectively, it was just a fucking frowny face. There was no reason for it to make her nauseous.

But maybe the truth was that Julie actually felt squirmy all the time, these days.

She shut the phone inside her drawer.

Many hours later, Julie opened her text chain with Elle once more.

Julie would wonder, later, why she hadn't texted London or Dahlia or Ben.

But no matter what the texting with Elle actually meant, it had somehow become second-nature this week. And even though it was late—Julie had gotten home from practice hours ago—and she knew Elle might already be asleep, she texted with her heart in her throat anyway.

I think something's wrong with Snoozles.

CHAPTER FOURTEEN

E lle sat up in bed.

Elle: What's happening?

Julie: She threw up when I got home, which isn't totally unusual, but she's barely moved since then

Julie: Which…also isn't that unusual, she's a lazy bitch, but she just doesn't seem like herself

Julie: I thought I was making it up but I just tried to give her a treat and she didn't even move to try to get it, just stared at me from the floor

Julie: Fuck I think I'm freaking out

Elle was already throwing on clothes.

Elle: Take a deep breath. We'll take her to the emergency vet. Just sit with her and I'll be there in a bit, okay?

Julie: Okay

Julie: Wait, no

Julie: What about Vanessa?

Elle paused, biting her lip. She thought it over for a second, and then—

Elle: I think…it'll actually be good to leave her by herself for once. Show her that I trust her, you know? Because I do

Julie: I know you do

Elle: I'll leave her with Rose and Tricia's numbers. I'll let them know what's going on too

Elle: Text me your address

Julie: I live all the way over in Hillsboro

Julie: It's too much

Elle: Hillsboro isn't far away, Julie

Elle: Text me your address

Elle: Okay, heading over now

Elle: It'll be okay, Julie

Elle knocked on Julie's door.

Julie opened it, took one look at her, and promptly burst into tears.

"Okay there, Coach." Elle rushed in, wrapping an arm around Julie's shoulder. "Hey. Shh. Everything's okay. There's an emergency vet not far away." Elle had asked Siri on her way over. "Have you called them?"

"Yeah." Julie sniffled, swiping at her face with a shaky hand, and Elle's heart broke into a thousand pieces. "They said to bring her in right away. That she might have ingested something."

"Then we'll leave right now. Is she ready to go?"

"Yeah." Julie hung her red, splotchy face in her hands, and Elle had to lean in to understand her. "She let me put her right in the carrier, like it was nothing. She barely meowed. And she *hates* the vet; they have to use these special cat gloves so she doesn't kill them, but she didn't even fight it when I—"

"Julie. Hey. Look at me." Elle shook Julie gently by the shoulders. "Can you breathe for me?"

Julie nodded.

"She'll be okay. But we need to get her to the hospital. I'll drive. Want me to carry her to the car?"

"No." Julie shook her head, backing out of Elle's grasp. She wiped once more at her eyes before standing straight, shaking out her shoulders. "I got it." She picked up a large cat carrier from the couch. "Let's go."

They were quiet on the elevator ride to the parking lot of Julie's building. Quiet as they clicked themselves into Elle's car and drove onto the street. Until Julie asked, voice small, "Do you have any Rihanna? Rihanna is Snoozles's favorite," and Elle directed her car's stereo to make it happen. Until Julie gasped and said, "Not the Wakanda one! It's too emotional!" And Elle frantically skipped to "Only Girl (In the World)" and Julie breathed out, leaning against the headrest. "She loves this one."

Elle was torn between laughing and reaching over to caress Julie's tear-streaked cheek.

Julie unzipped the top of the carrier, dipping in a hand to rub Snoozles's back.

"You're taking care of a full-blown human," she said after a few minutes, voice still too quiet. It felt strange that Elle had listened to her yell at top Coach Parker volume mere hours ago. "You must think I'm ridiculous."

Elle kept her eyes on the road, listening to Google Maps' directions.

"For the record," she said as they pulled into the emergency vet's parking lot. "I have never once thought you were ridiculous, Julie."

Julie stared out the window, making no move to unbuckle herself.

"Anesthesia is really dangerous," she said.

"Come on." Elle opened her door. "They'll take care of her. Promise."

And even if Elle knew it wasn't a promise she was completely qualified to make, she would revive Snoozles's heart herself if she had to, to make it true.

Julie got out of the car.

Inside, Julie talked to a receptionist while a vet tech took Snoozles to the back. Elle settled into a chair in the corner and attempted to cool her heart rate.

Julie slumped next to her a few minutes later.

"They said we could wait but it might take a while. That we could leave and they'd call us." Julie bounced her knee. "I said we'd wait. Is that okay?"

"Of course it's okay, Julie."

"They're going to give her some fluids and take X-rays."

"That sounds like a good start."

"I'm sorry," Julie said after a minute.

"Why are you sorry?"

"I don't know."

Finally, Elle reached over and grabbed Julie's hand.

"Julie." She intertwined their fingers. Julie let her. "It's going to be okay."

Julie's chin quivered, but she nodded. Elle didn't quite know how she was ever going to recover from seeing that chin quiver.

She sat back, gazing at a faded poster of a waterfall. She thought maybe the receptionist was staring at her, but she ignored it. She rubbed her thumb against Julie's forefinger, and she thought about how underrated holding hands was. How intimate it was. How lovely and important. Everyone was always hyping up sex, but Elle, at that moment, would take a hundred ballads about the feeling of Julie Parker's fingers inside hers.

Julie only let go when a doctor emerged, inviting them into an exam room.

And Elle remembered, quite suddenly and clearly, that she should be thinking more about Snoozles, less about Julie's knuckles.

Inside the room, Dr. Mendoza turned a computer screen their way, showing an X-ray of the beloved Snoozles, and the perfectly round ring in the middle of her abdomen.

"Is that—" Julie started.

"A hair tie, most likely," Dr. Mendoza confirmed.

"Whoa." Elle leaned forward to see the scan better. She'd always been fascinated by her own X-rays—and she'd examined plenty, over the course of her basketball career—but she'd never seen a cat's before. It was incredible; you could see every—

Elle looked back at Julie's face and quickly retracted whatever statement had been about to tumble out of her mouth.

"That's mine," Julie whispered, eyes wide and glassy. "I almost killed my cat."

Elle opened her mouth to disagree, reaching for her hand again, but Dr. Mendoza spoke first.

"You didn't. It's actually extremely common. Cats love playing with them, and occasionally, swallow them by accident. We've extracted countless hair ties here over the years, I promise. Sometimes foreign bodies will pass through an animal's system on their own, but with her current symptoms, and the way it's situated in the abdomen, we will have to put her under for extraction."

Julie's hand squeezed Elle's. Hard.

"Okay," she whispered.

"There are, of course, risks associated with the anesthesia and the procedure. But again, I promise it's one we've completed successfully many, many times. We'll keep you updated if there are any complications whatsoever."

"All right," Julie agreed, barely audible.

"All right." Dr. Mendoza smiled reassuringly. "Luckily, we have a surgery room available now, so we can get started right away. My assistant will be in momentarily; she'll take you through the consent forms we'll need you to sign." She twirled the computer screen back around, typing briefly on the keyboard. "We'll take good care of her."

With another smile, Dr. Mendoza exited the room, closing the door quietly behind her.

"I can't believe I almost killed Snoozles," Julie said.

"You didn't. Dr. Mendoza—"

"It's my fault! If I didn't have such dumb hair I never know what to do with—"

"Your hair," Elle cut in, thoroughly offended on its behalf, "is not dumb."

"What almost-thirty-year-old just wears their hair in a ponytail every day?" Julie's voice rose in despair.

"I think a lot of people, actually."

"I've never known what to do with my hair. Or my clothes. Or my face. I only learned how to use makeup because London was into it, and it always looks good on *them*, but—"

Elle wanted to interrupt and ask who this London was, because something about that name rang a bell, but Julie was talking too fast, and suddenly, her hand was reaching toward Elle's face, and Elle's brain plum ran out of thoughts.

"Or *this*," she said, fingers just barely grazing Elle's curls. "This is so fucking cool. How do I figure out how to do something like this?"

Elle swallowed.

"Um. You go to a gay stylist and ask for something gay."

Julie's eyes, if possible, turned even more miserable. She dropped her hand and flopped back in her chair. Her left hand still clasped Elle's right.

"I know," she said. "But that's even more—"

And then the door swung open again, and a cheery doctor's assistant walked in with forms and information Elle should have paid more attention to, but she couldn't stop wishing Julie had actually stuck her fingers in her hair. Couldn't stop wondering how Julie had been about to finish that sentence.

"We're all set," the assistant said, an untold number of minutes later. "We'll keep you updated."

Julie let go of Elle's hand as they walked back to the lobby, resuming their seats in the corner.

"They said it's a common surgery," Julie said, more talking to herself than to Elle. "They do this all the time."

Elle nodded, thoughts still in a haze. "All the time," she repeated.

Elle didn't reach for Julie's hand again, and Julie didn't reach for hers. Elle retrieved her phone from her bag, made sure she hadn't missed any texts from Vanessa. Tried to keep her thoughts to herself.

But eventually, she broke.

"Can I ask," she said slowly, "what you were going to say back in the room?"

"Huh?" Julie glanced her way.

"When we were talking about hair," Elle said. "And I said you could request a gay haircut, you started to say something."

"Oh." Julie stared forward again. Opened her mouth and closed it.

"You don't have to say anything you don't want to talk about," Elle said quickly. "Forget I said anything."

"No, it's okay," Julie said. "I mean, shorts, we have the time, right?" She sighed, leaning her head against the wall. "I don't honestly know what I was going to say back there. Probably because I don't know..." She waved a hand. "I just feel, to get a gay haircut, you have to really be confident in the kind of gay you are."

Elle nodded. Even though she had been partly joking when she'd talked about the gay haircut. Hair, objectively, couldn't be homosexual. She had changed hers after the WNBA because, like anyone going through a slight emotional crisis, it had felt like a good idea at the time. And then she had simply gotten used to it. She saved a ton of money on conditioner.

"And you...aren't? Confident?"

"Is anybody?" Julie said, exasperated, until she sighed again. "No, a lot of people are. That's the thing. Like you. You're a huge lesbian, right?"

A loud, completely unoffended laugh burst out of Elle's mouth.

"Yes, yes I am. But for what it's worth...I think being as sure as I am isn't necessarily common. Some of us are just born with extreme dyke genes. It doesn't make me...a better gay."

"Yeah," Julie said, like she didn't believe this at all.

Elle held her tongue, waiting to see if Julie would say anything else. There were so many things she *could* ask, that she *wanted* to ask. But she was still slightly confused about what Julie was even trying to say here. The ball was in her court.

And what Julie did say next wasn't what Elle had expected at all.

"This is why—" Julie took a shaky breath and covered her face with her hands again. "This is why Snoozles can't die. Because she's the only person who's ever loved me, and I was supposed to die first, so she could lovingly eat all my organs. Oh god." Julie lurched forward, hanging her head between her knees. "I'm going to die alone."

Elle blinked at the back of Julie's head.

She wasn't sure what to start with. The fact that Snoozles wasn't a person, or that, statistically, Julie dying first had never been very likely, or . . .

"Julie, I am positive Snoozles is not the only one who loves you."

Julie popped back up, face red.

"I know. Like. I know my siblings and my parents and Ben love me, but like . . ." She stared forward. Her shoulders deflated as she seemed to decide something. "I've never dated anyone. Or not-dated anyone. Hooked up or whatever. I kissed someone, once, but it ended up being embarrassing and made me feel miserable for like, months, so, yeah. Even if I did know what kind of gay I was, there's never been anyone to be kind of gay *with*, so. It is what it is. I'm just saying. Snoozles is it for me."

Elle's brain tried to process everything Julie had just said, but it kept getting stuck on wanting to find whoever had gotten to kiss Julie Parker and then made her miserable—for *months*—and have a serious conversation.

"Have you . . ." Elle cleared her throat. "Not wanted to be with anyone? Because that's okay."

Julie scratched the top of her head.

"I mean, a lot of the time, I don't even really think about it? So I think I might be kind of ace. But sometimes—" Her mouth opened and shut again, cheeks pinkening. "Maybe. Yeah."

Elle could not stop staring at her.

"I just don't really know how..." Julie messed with the hem of her sweatshirt. "To like, make that happen."

Elle knew she should say something. But there were so many things whirring inside her brain, inside her chest, that she didn't even know where to start. She had to pinch her thigh to keep herself from reaching over and touching her.

"Sometimes, I just feel like..." Julie bounced a knee, leaning onto the opposite arm of the chair and biting her thumb. And now Elle couldn't stop staring at that thumb. "Say, with sports, right? You have to try out before you make the team. You have to practice before you play the first game. And even before that, before you even know you want to try out, you do a trial run to get your feet wet and figure out if you like the sport at all." Julie shifted, gaining momentum. "You do biddy basketball, little league, rec league soccer. I just wish there was like...a little league of dating."

Elle bit her lip. Because Julie looked serious as sin. And if Elle laughed, and it made Julie stop talking, she would never forgive herself.

"Or a biddy maybe-I'm-bi," Julie continued. "Or..." She gazed into the distance, brow furrowing in thought. "A kind-of-ace rookie league. Or whatever. A chance where you can try it out, see if it works for you. I feel like...everyone I know has been able to just jump into the big game. And I..."

She trailed off, her hands turning to fists.

"You're not ready for the game," Elle supplied.

"Yeah. Maybe." Julie licked her lips, voice reedy. "Or maybe I am. But I know most people joined the game when they were like, twelve, so it feels like the more time goes on, the more impossible it'll be to even walk onto the court without everyone laughing at me."

"Julie."

"I just want some practice, you know?" Julie ignored Elle's stern look. A tinge of desperation entered her voice. "I just want to be able to try out, see what I like. And if it's not meant for me, that's fine, you know? I'm good at being a spectator! I love cheering people on about their shit!"

"I know you do, Julie."

"Or maybe…" Julie stilled. "I don't know. Maybe I'm just chickenshit."

Julie's voice warbled on *chickenshit*, like a lump in her throat had risen to greet her unexpectedly.

Elle's chest whirred so hard it hurt.

She wanted to say… that being uncertain about relationships was one thing.

But that when it came to identity, when it came to queerness, the whole point was that there *were* no tryouts. If you were even thinking about it, you were already on the team. That labels weren't meant to confine, only to bring comfort to those for whom they were useful. That Julie didn't need to ascribe to any of them if she didn't want to.

Elle wanted to say that, label or no label, hearing Julie just describe relationships and sexuality in sports metaphors was the gayest thing that had ever happened to her. And she had spent half her life dedicated to women's basketball.

But it was clear that everything Julie had just said was important to her. That it bothered her. Elle didn't want to meet that vulnerability with a lecture.

More than anything, at that moment, Elle wanted to make that lump in Julie's throat go away.

"You just want to be able to practice," Elle summarized.

"Yes."

"Well," Elle ventured, "what if you could?"

Julie turned. There was a sheen to her eyes that hadn't been there before, and it only made Elle more desperate to soothe her.

She shrugged, attempting to seem casual. "What if we practiced dating?"

It was, objectively, a ridiculous sentence. Elle should have felt ridiculous asking it.

Maybe it was only the adrenaline of the night that made Elle feel...not like that at all, actually.

Maybe a no-pressure kind of situation was what Julie needed.

And maybe a no-pressure kind of situation could allow Elle more time with Julie—which every honest bone in Elle's body wanted—without being distracted from Vanessa.

Maybe it could be safe for both of them.

Julie stared. "We. Like...you and me."

"If you wanted to."

Julie stared at her for another long beat.

And then she said, "You serious, Clark?"

Elle's mouth curved. "I am. Although I have to say, your pro–*National Lampoon* and anti–Tom Hanks inclinations are making me consider rescinding my offer."

"Oh my god. I never said I was *anti*..." Julie closed her eyes and took a deep breath. "What would practice dating even look like?"

Elle shrugged again, heart beating faster in her chest as the idea took shape.

"Whatever you want it to look like. Whatever you want to find the answers to, at least the parts that I could possibly help with. I mean." Elle cleared her throat, attempting to school her features as images of what she'd be willing to help Julie with flashed through her mind. "I can't help you find your right labels; that's a personal journey. But if you just want practice in *dating*, testing out engaging with a romantic relationship...we could start with the basics. Go on some practice dates. A judgment-free zone to practice whatever relationship things you want to test out."

"I don't..." Julie shook her head. "Honestly, I feel like I don't have a good handle on what *relationship things* even are. Other than what

I've seen in movies, and with people I know, but... I am never going to be good at like, calling someone sweetheart or whatever. Not that that's what encompasses a relationship, but—you know? I'm going to stop talking."

"Well." Elle attempted a charming grin. "That's where I'd come in. I could take you on a little tour of all my favorite ones. Minus cutesy nicknames; I'll mark that one right off the list. But I think we might already have a good start, really. Because one of my very top relationship things? Is this."

She reached for Julie's hand. And once again, Julie's fingers slid right on through, like they belonged there, intertwined with Elle's.

"Calling the other person when you need them," she said softly. "Holding their hand when they're scared."

Julie stared at their hands, Elle's thumb rubbing against her forefinger.

"Yeah," she finally said, voice hoarse.

And that was when the receptionist shuffled across the room.

Julie slipped her hand away, straightening. But Elle already knew, from the way the receptionist was fidgeting, the way Elle had felt her eyes darting toward her all night, that this wasn't an update about Snoozles.

"Hi," the receptionist said, squeezing a Sharpie in her hand. "I'm so sorry to bother you, but... you're Elle Cochrane, right?"

Elle finally tore her eyes away from Julie's profile, forcing a smile on her face.

"I am."

"I know this probably isn't a good time, but... well, my girlfriend loves you a lot, and her birthday is coming up, and I was wondering if you could sign..."

She held out a pad of paper.

"Sure." Elle took the proffered marker and paper. And stared at them.

She wanted to sign the damn thing and shove it back, return to this much more important conversation with Julie, but...

She simply never knew what to write. If she should write some inspirational quote. But it never made sense, since she wasn't an inspiration anymore.

"What's her name?" she asked.

"Ava."

Elle scribbled *Happy birthday, Ava*, signed her name, and handed it back.

"Thank you so much."

Elle pasted on another smile. The receptionist bit her lip on her own genuine grin before returning to the front desk.

A beat went by before Elle said, "That really doesn't happen much anymore."

Julie didn't say anything. And as the silence began to stretch, Elle worried that she had freaked Julie out. That she had crossed some invasive line, should take it all back, make a joke.

But then Julie turned, eyes soft as she asked, "Why?"

Elle met her gaze.

"Why would you do this for me?"

"Because. You've already done so much for us—"

Julie interrupted with a disbelieving snort.

"You came over to watch Vanessa when I needed it."

"I did that once, and it wasn't a big deal."

"Well, get ready." Elle smiled. "Because I have to attend another class soon, and I've just been waiting for a good time to ask you to do it again."

Julie rolled her eyes. "Again, not a big deal. Your house is awesome. Vanessa is awesome. I would hang out there all the time."

"You accepted Vanessa onto the team."

Julie smacked Elle on the arm. It surprised a half laugh out of Elle's mouth.

"You agreed to *coach*. You took a fucking leave of absence to help me. These things are not the same."

"The leave of absence was for me. And anyway. We're friends, and I want to."

And because, Elle didn't say, *ever since I met you, I have felt so much lighter.*

And I think I'd forgotten. What lightness can feel like.

When Julie didn't have a comeback, Elle said, instead: "So there." She settled back against the wall.

After a moment, Julie did the same.

Elle let a few minutes tick by before she said, "So, Saturday night? You pick the restaurant. I'll have Rose watch Vanessa. She knows I've been holding back from asking her for help, and she's starting to get crotchety about it."

Julie breathed out before she said, "It's a date."

After another few minutes, Elle said, "You should take the day off tomorrow. Stay home. Be with Snoozles. I can catch up on sleep during the day and cover practice."

Julie took another deep breath, her shoulder slumping ever so slightly against Elle's on the exhale.

"You sure?"

"Yeah." Elle snaked her hand over to Julie's, slid their fingers together once more. "I'll probably just make Ngozi lead everything anyway. It'll be fine."

She'd been working one-on-one with Ngozi this week, sometimes with Mosk, talking through different sets to try, with Julie's approval. Once they got each one down, Ngozi taught it to the rest of the team.

"You're already helping her be a better leader than I ever did," Julie said, voice suddenly sleepy. Elle glanced over to see her eyes fluttering closed.

"She's already a leader. I'm just giving her a nudge."

Elle could tell Julie was already half-unconscious when she mumbled, "I'm so glad I coerced you to be my assistant coach."

As Julie's breaths deepened, as her head slumped toward Elle's once again, Elle ran her thumb over Julie's, over and over, smiling to herself over the fact that, in her exhaustion, Julie had finally said *assistant*.

CHAPTER FIFTEEN

Julie blew a gust of air out of her cheeks. Checked her phone, again, for any updates from Dahlia, who was cat-sitting Snoozles to make sure she didn't rip out her sutures. The only thing Julie saw was the same picture Dahlia had sent ten minutes ago: Snoozles sitting in a corner and looking pissed. Maxin' and relaxin', Dahlia had texted.

Julie resumed dancing on the balls of her feet.

Elle was right. They were friends now, and this wasn't even a real date. Julie shouldn't be nervous.

But as she leaned against the red brick of Bella's Italian Eatery, her body couldn't quite be convinced of that.

Even if Elle *was* her friend now, she was still *Elle*. Someone strangers approached for autographs.

She was also older than Julie by four years, which wasn't a big deal, but suddenly Julie could only think about how it was four more years of Elle being more experienced than Julie in...everything. Elle had likely dated a ton of hot women, probably banged a ton of hot women, and—and she was walking down the street toward Julie right now, and Julie was going to die.

Because Elle looked like she was walking straight from a *Sports Illustrated* cover, one of the oddly sexy ones Julie never knew exactly how to feel about. Crisp linen pants and a silky, sleeveless cream-colored blouse. She held a blazer tucked under one arm, being that it was unseasonably warm today, which meant that all of those defined biceps—that tattoo—were on display, her skin tan and smooth.

Panicked, Julie looked down at herself. She was wearing a sweater—one of her nicest, although she was now sweating profusely inside of it, being that it was unseasonably warm—and jeans. Again, her nicest jeans, but oh god.

"Hi," Elle said, stopping in front of her.

"Hi," Julie said.

And then...they just stood there. Julie's brain scrambled for speech, but apparently she had lost the ability to produce sentences. All that came to her head were random words and phrases. Pigeon. Roller coaster. Donut. Ebenezer Scrooge. A-boom-chick-a-boom.

"Ready to go in?" Elle asked.

Hey, there was a sentence! Elle really was better at everything.

"Absofuckinglutely," Julie said.

Elle's mouth quirked.

And then they were inside, and being greeted by a hostess, whom Julie almost hugged for granting her a few seconds in which she didn't have to converse with Elle and Elle's shoulders, and then a waiter was filling glasses with water at their table, and they were looking at menus, and menus! What an amazing invention! You could simply stare at them and not have to look at the superstar supermodel in front of you even a little bit!

"You okay?" Elle asked, nudging Julie's foot with her own under the table.

"Yup," Julie answered, still staring at her menu.

"Julie," Elle said, voice soft, nudging her foot again, and Julie almost snapped at her to stop, because she was pretty sure most first dates didn't start with footsie, and this was probably her one chance to practice this. Elle had placed a once-in-a-lifetime opportunity in

Julie's lap, and while Julie had flip-flopped all day yesterday between calling the whole thing off and actually taking it seriously, she'd eventually committed to the latter.

Fortunately, the waiter returned, asking about drinks, and Elle dropped her foot back to the appropriate side of the table. And as Julie continued to study the menu, a burst of inspiration rushed into her brain.

"Should we order a bottle of wine or something?"

A bottle of wine was definitely date-ish, right? Plus, maybe if Julie got drunk, this whole night would go by way faster.

No, she shouldn't think like that. She was taking this seriously. She could do this.

Except. Elle's face looked pained as she replied, "I'm actually trying to not drink at the moment. But you can absolutely order something if you'd like."

Shit. Shit shit shit.

"No, no," Julie said quickly, horrified. "No worries at all. Forget I said anything. Just the water is fine."

She thrust the magical menu into the waiter's hand.

"Oh," he said, surprised. "Do you know what you'd like to eat?"

And, right. They hadn't actually ordered their food yet.

"Uh, the gnocchi, please," Julie managed, hoping they still had the gnocchi, as she hadn't actually comprehended anything on said menu.

"And for you?"

Elle ordered something with pesto without missing a beat, like Julie wasn't acting like a weirdo, and Julie both despaired and internally cried in relief that Elle was so goddamn smooth.

"I'm sorry, Julie," Elle said as soon as the waiter walked away. "I made a vow to myself when Vanessa came to live with me that I wouldn't consume any alcohol, or anything else, as long as she's with me, in case it triggers something for her. But I truly don't mind if you want to drink something."

"No," Julie said again. "It's fine, really." And it was. Of course that explanation made sense. It was thoughtful, and made Julie's heart squeeze a little.

"I know Vanessa's not here, so it might seem kind of silly, but... my brain"—Elle made a funny little circling gesture around her face—"tends to commit once it's made a decision."

"I get it," Julie said. "I'm glad you're doing that."

"Anyway," Elle said brightly, clearly trying to start over. "How was your day?"

"Fine," Julie said. Her nerve-addled brain almost blurted *I missed you*, but by the skin of her teeth, she kept her mouth shut. Because that would be a wild thing to say. Even though, over the last two days of doing nothing but sitting in her apartment staring at Snoozles, her text chain with Elle less active than it had been earlier in the week, Julie *had* missed her.

But that was a Julie problem, and not something Elle needed to know.

It took Julie longer than it should have—a horrible beat of menu-less silence—to think to ask in return, "How was yours?"

"It was okay," Elle said.

"That's good," Julie said.

Was it? Was an okay day good?!

Julie took a long sip of water and stared at the wall sconces beyond Elle's shoulder.

"So," Julie said casually as she placed her water back on the table. "I'm nervous as fuck."

Elle laughed, leaning back in her chair.

"You know," she said, "you should say the same thing on a real date, if it's true. It shows you're okay with being vulnerable. You're an honest person, Julie; it's one of the most delightful things about you. And if the other person is nervous, too, your honesty could help them relax. You'd already be killing it. Or..." Elle paused to take a sip of her own water. "If the person *is* put off by your honesty, then you'd know you're just not a good fit."

"Oh my god," Julie said. "I can be rejected before they've even brought out the garlic bread?"

"Oh yeah." Elle smiled. "Sometimes you know right away. But it's almost a relief, you know? For it to be clear. That's why my number one rule is to be picky about the restaurant, if you're meeting at a restaurant. Choose someplace you know you already love, or a place you've been wanting to check out. That way even if the date is rough, you at least get a good meal out of it."

Julie blinked at her a few times. And then she nodded.

"I do already love this place," she said, picking up her napkin to smooth it over her lap. "So. One point for me, I guess."

"Definitely. And if it helps, I'm a little nervous, too."

Julie looked up. "Really?"

Elle lifted a sheepish shoulder. "Yeah. It's your first practice date. I want to make sure it's good for you."

Julie glanced at Elle's silky blouse again and made a slight *harumph* of disbelief.

"Trust me," she said. "It's already good. You look—"

And then—thank heaven for 7-Eleven—the waiter reappeared with a basket full of garlic bread, the interruption alerting Julie's brain to shut the hell up. Her face bloomed with heat anyway.

"Thank you," she said to the waiter, who threw her a kind smile. Julie could have kissed him. If she knew more about kissing.

She shoved a slice of bread in her face before he'd even left the table.

"Anyway," she said, mouth still half-full, "what do people talk about on dates?"

Elle was tilting her head at her, a grin curving her mouth. After a moment, she grabbed a slice of her own.

"On a first date, normally the basics. Where you work, which we've already covered. I think for you and me"—Elle pointed between herself and Julie in a way that made Julie's stomach wobble nonsensically—"we should make a promise to not talk about the Bobcats. This is a date, not a planning session."

Julie blew out a breath. That sucked. She was good at talking about the Bobcats. "Got it."

"Hobbies," Elle continued. "Family. Maybe we could start there, with you telling me about yours? You've already met my mom, and Vanessa, and Karly, so you know more of my story than I do yours."

"Okay." Julie nodded, ready to get her head in the game. Family was easier than work anyway. "Um. I have a twin, who lives here in Nashville, too, and two older sisters who moved away years ago. They're cool, just a lot older than us so we were never super close. Uh. My parents do smart stuff with pharmaceuticals that I don't understand and have always just sort of hoped isn't too egregiously unethical. We have Sunday supper at their house every week, and my mom usually invites neighbors and friends and sometimes it feels like half of Nashville is there. Which is sometimes annoying and sometimes nice. All my grandparents are dead except for Grandma Nora, who's kind of mean and will probably live until she's a million years old. Um. I have cousins and aunts and uncles and stuff, although some of them live in Kentucky..."

Julie shut her mouth when she realized Elle was laughing. Or, no, not outright laughing. Holding it in, lips tight and eyes twinkling, which almost felt worse.

"Sorry." Julie leaned back. "I suppose you didn't need to know my entire family tree."

Elle shook her head, chin propped on her fist.

"Don't stop. I was enjoying it."

Julie rolled her eyes at herself.

"Right. I'm sure you want to hear more about Aunt Meredith and Uncle Charles in Bowling Green."

"I do!" Elle said, eyes bright. "I do."

"Well, Meredith is a first grade teacher, and Charles is super into rock climbing. They live in this adorable house and have three very small dogs." Julie took another sip of water. "Your turn."

Elle leaned back.

"Honestly, my family tree sounds much less exciting than yours. Never knew my dad, never cared to. My grandparents have also passed. Rose is estranged from Lulu, Karly's mom, so I barely remember her. The biggest branch in the whole tree is my older sister, Tricia, who's married to Akhil. They have four kids."

Elle grabbed another piece of bread, tearing it into pieces.

"Yeah?" Julie prompted. "That's a lot of kids."

"It is. One of the best parts of coming back to Nashville has been getting to watch them grow up. Sanjana was born when I was still in Knoxville, then Sid when I was in Milwaukee. I had to miss a lot of holidays, birthday parties... but Luna was born six years ago, and Jeremiah soon after that. I get to be there for everything, now, these past eight years." Elle smiled to herself, looking down at her bread plate. "It's been nice."

"I'm so glad." Julie's voice came out hoarse. Apparently her throat was affected by the vision of Elle playing with a bundle of nieces and nephews. She took another sip of water.

Elle propped her elbow on the table again, a look in her eye Julie couldn't read.

"This is probably more a second-or-third-date kind of thing, but sometimes, you also talk about relationship history."

That was when the food decided to arrive.

Seriously, this waiter deserved the world. It was like he knew Julie's pulse had just spiked and needed a moment. She hoped he had someone at home who loved him very much.

"Yeah, well." She picked up her fork once the waiter had walked away. "You know I don't have a relationship history, so."

"Right. But." Elle twirled linguine around her own fork before she glanced at Julie. "You mentioned, at the vet, that there had been a kiss."

Julie swallowed her first gnocchi before she'd finished chewing it.

"Did I? I should mention I was halfway out of my mind at the vet. I barely remember half the things I said."

"You definitely mentioned a kiss. And I just feel," Elle said, voice light—*too* light, "that to properly help guide you on your journey here, I need to know all the facts."

Julie narrowed her eyes before leaning back and crossing her arms over her chest.

"Okay, Cochrane. How about this. I tell you about my mortifying first kiss, and in return...you tell me why you left the WNBA."

It was a gamble, one Julie felt in Elle's immediate wince. But it was a gamble that felt worth it to make. Julie never talked about the kiss, hardly thought about it. She had never even mentioned it to London or Ben; it was too humiliating. If she was going to tell Elle Cochrane about it, of all people, she deserved something in return.

"Fine," Elle conceded. "But fair warning. It will take far less time to explain, and be far more disappointing, than you think."

"Fine," Julie agreed.

"All right." Elle picked up her fork again. "Tell me about this person who wronged you."

"She didn't *wrong* me; I was just..." Julie stabbed at her gnocchi. "Dumb. So, I was a freshman at UT."

"Oh." Elle's brows lifted in surprise. "You went to Tennessee, too?"

"Yeah." Now Julie winced, shifting in her seat. "I, um. Was on the team, too."

Elle put down her fork. "The basketball team?"

Julie laughed a little. "Yeah, the basketball team. I just missed you. I was a freshman the year after you graduated."

A crease appeared in Elle's forehead. "You did seem familiar to me, somehow, when we first met. Maybe that's why. I do still follow the team, always have; I just didn't—"

"No." Julie waved her off. "You wouldn't have known. I was a star when I was at East, but I was a benchwarmer at UT. All four years." She shrugged, averting her eyes so she didn't receive Elle's pity. "I knew that would probably be the case. It was my choice. I got scholarships to other schools, schools where I could've gotten a lot more playing time, but..." Another shrug. "I'd always dreamed of being a Vol. I don't regret it. It was special, just getting to be there, you know?"

She glanced at Elle. Wordlessly, Elle nodded.

"So..." Julie took a breath and continued. "I was a freshman. And even though Knoxville is only three hours away, and I'd been there plenty of times before, it was still strange, being away from my people. My twin had stayed in Nashville, went to Belmont, and Ben was still here, too, and I felt...unmoored, without them. Anyway." Julie pushed the sleeves of her sweater up her forearms. "That's neither here nor there. I'm feeling nervous again, sorry. This story is dumb."

"Freshman year is really hard," Elle said. "It's not dumb."

"Right, so, my roommate was always off somewhere getting high, and basketball stuff had barely started, so I hadn't had a lot of the college bonding experiences I'd hoped to have yet. But there was this girl who was down the hall from me. And *her* roommate was always crying on the phone with her hometown boyfriend, so she spent a lot of time in the common room on our floor, binge-watching *Real Housewives*. And I was lonely, and she...didn't seem to mind it when I joined her."

Julie poked around her plate with her fork.

"She was so...interesting. Her parents were diplomats? Or in the military or something? The details are fuzzy at this point. But she had been all over the world. And I had traveled a decent amount, too, but she could, like…speak three languages. And my world felt so small, right then, and she was…"

"Ah," Elle said softly. "The Very Interesting Girl. Been there before."

"Yeah." Julie's lips twisted. "And the fact that a Very Interesting Girl actually paid attention to *me*, when no one ever had before, made me feel…anyway."

She stuffed some gnocchi in her mouth.

"I feel quite positive," Elle said, just as soft, "that people must have paid attention to you before, Julie Parker."

Julie remembered what Ben had said about Tiago. She wasn't sure if it made it any better, that she might have simply been oblivious instead of ignored. Like there was still something broken inside her brain, when it came to understanding any of this. Her stomach squirmed again.

"Maybe. But not in a way that…I felt it, anyway. If that makes sense. Like…I had never felt…attended to? I guess? Or *wanted* to be attended to? Before that."

Elle nodded. "Okay."

"So anyway." Julie talked quickly. "We were both at a party once, and we made out. And I thought it meant something, but it turned out she was just drunk. She was still nice to me, afterward, but it took me a while to figure out that like…I don't know, we weren't in love. A week after the party, we were back in the common room and I was making all these plans about what we could do together on fall break, and she just looked at me like…like she felt sorry for me, and was all, 'Oh, Julie.' I've never felt so dumb in my whole life. So." Julie let out a small, embarrassed laugh before taking another sip of water. "I can't believe I told you that, honestly. Pretty boring story, but you asked."

"It wasn't boring," Elle said, voice quiet. "And you weren't dumb."

When Julie finally found the courage to look up, Elle was staring at her, face serious.

Julie looked back down, taking another bite of her food, desperately wanting to move on now. She knew it was, in fact, a boring story, one that probably happened to 87 percent of college freshmen. The only unique part about it was that Julie had never found another, better story to erase it with.

Finally, Elle fell back against her seat. Her eyes looked far away.

"But...you were on the *team*. I don't know how you got through four years as a Vol without half the team dying to make out with you."

At this, Julie burst out laughing. It felt good.

"Sure," she said, stuffing another forkful in her mouth. "Everyone had the hots for the awkward benchwarmer." She almost choked as a thought occurred to her. "Wait. Did *you* make out with half the team?"

"Oh yeah." Elle smiled as she brought her water glass to her lips. "We all did." Julie's mouth fell open. "I mean..." Elle laughed, placing the glass back on the table. "It was the best time of my life. But it was also..." More barely suppressed laughter. "*Extremely* messy."

"Okay." Julie put her fork down, raising both hands. "Hold up. I know we still have to get to the WNBA, but...I need to know. Who would I be most surprised by? That you made out with."

Elle's eyes twinkled again as she took another sip of water, and Julie knew, in a distant kind of way, that she'd feel depressed about this later, the fact that all of her suspicions about how much more experienced the world was than her—how far, exactly, Elle Cochrane was out of her league—were correct.

But right now, Elle was acknowledging her life at UT. And *smiling*. Julie never wanted the moment to end.

"Trinity Waters," Elle said eventually, and Julie almost flipped the table.

"Trinity *Waters*?" she screeched, leaning so far over the table she was probably getting tomato sauce on her nicest sweater. "But she played for *UConn*!"

Elle only grinned harder. "I know." She waved a hand. "The messiness wasn't contained to UT."

"But... *UConn*," Julie whispered.

"I know." Elle laughed. "It wasn't my finest moment."

"But—" Julie continued to sputter, memories rushing in. "But there was that game, in the Sweet Sixteen, when she *shoved* you, Elle. Like, egregiously shoved you."

"I know she did." Elle smiled over her glass. "Got ejected for it, too."

"Man." Julie's back hit her seat as she absorbed this. "Huh. Okay. So why did you leave the WNBA?"

"Oh." And there was still laughter in Elle's voice when she said, "I wasn't good enough."

"What?" Every bit of wonder left Julie's body in a flash. "No. No way."

Elle's laughter faded, the twinkle in her eye blinking out. She shook her head.

"I knew you would say that. But it's true."

"You were barely in there, barely had time to develop—"

"I had two years, Julie."

"But maybe the Wreckers just didn't know how to use you. I bet if you were able to get traded—"

"Julie." Elle leaned forward, eyes serious once more. "This is the way it happens. Some people burn brightest in college, and some people find their place in the league. Every now and then, someone can shine at both, but..." She shook her head. "Whatever I had at UT...I lost it."

"But..." Julie shook her head in return. She had to admit that she hadn't watched much, when Elle was in the W. She'd been busy getting her own bearings at Tennessee. And whenever she had tuned in, she got so angry about Elle normally being benched that she'd eventually turn it off in a rage.

"I know there were other things I could have done. I could have gone overseas, could have tried to get traded, could have even lived a quiet life in the D leagues. Anything you think of saying, it was said to me, by old coaches, trainers, friends. Rose. I said it to myself. But when I tore my ACL and was sitting in that hospital...I just felt done, Julie. My body knew it. My brain knew it. I struggled in Milwaukee, and not only on the court."

Elle balled her hands, resting on the table, into fists, and looked down at her food.

"I still feel bad that I never really gave the city a chance. I think there were a lot of things I would've liked about it if I had been in a better place. I liked walking by the lake. There was lots of good food. But...I've always struggled with depression. Sometimes I'm totally okay, sometimes I'm not. Mara helped me get on meds in Knoxville, which helped, but in Milwaukee, it was like nothing helped. I was never okay. I..." Elle bit her lip, as if contemplating what she wanted to say. "I was in a not entirely healthy relationship at the time. I missed home. It was so fucking cold."

She threw Julie a wry smile before looking back down.

"I had barely any money. My contract gave me enough for a down payment for my house, the one here in Nashville, which I'll always be grateful for, but then just enough to cover the mortgage and the tiny apartment I rented in Milwaukee. I still feel selfish that I bought my house first, even though..." She grimaced. "I know it's a cliché, but I'd always dreamed of buying Rose a house when I really made it big. She wouldn't have accepted it, but still."

She gave a sad little laugh.

"My game was off, and my game had become my life, so without it, I felt...empty. Sometimes I wonder, if I hadn't had Mara checking in on me the whole time I was there..."

Elle didn't finish her sentence. Julie's chest ached, as if a boulder had rolled over her torso. She could barely breathe.

"Mara Daniels?" she asked, voice hoarse again.

Elle glanced up, a small smile whisking some of the darkness away from her features.

"Yeah. She's still my best friend."

And somehow, this nudged the boulder off Julie's chest, just a bit.

Mara Daniels had been Elle Cochrane's number two. Elle on her own was a force, but Elle and Mara together on the court had been... magic.

It made Julie glad, that she and Elle were still close. That Elle hadn't said goodbye to every part of her former life. That she'd held on to the important things.

"How's she doing these days?"

"Great." Elle's smile grew, the shadows almost completely receded. "She's still in Knoxville. Has the cutest little girl, Quisha. Don't tell Tricia I said this, because all of her and Akhil's kids are cute, too, but... Quisha is *cute*." She emphasized it, an invisible capital letter, her eyes bright once more, and she was so pretty, her sharp face soft in the dim light of the restaurant, skin golden from the candle in the middle of the table, that Julie's boulder almost threatened to steal her breath again.

"Do you want kids of your own?" The question burst out of Julie without thought, and Elle's brows raised in surprise.

"Sorry," Julie said immediately. "That's probably a, like, twentieth-date question. You just... light up, when you talk about Quisha and your nieces and nephews."

"Oh." Elle blinked. "I... don't know. I honestly haven't thought about it much. I've been so focused on getting my own life in order, since leaving Milwaukee..."

She stared to the side before looking back at Julie.

"Being an aunt is different from being a mom. And I don't even know if I'm that good at being an aunt. I love watching my nieces and nephews and Quisha grow up, but I don't... play video games or do funny voices or know the right toys to buy. And then with

Vanessa…" Elle was quiet a moment before she repeated, "I don't know."

"That's fair," Julie said. And then, "Thanks. For telling me all that, about the Wreckers."

"You're welcome." Elle refolded the napkin on her lap. "I guess I just want you to know…I don't regret my decision. Things didn't work out how I'd dreamed them. But I got to take control of my own life. And I'm okay with that. That's why I like…living in the present. You know?"

Julie took a deep breath.

She didn't regret asking, even if it had clearly brought Elle pain to explain. She was glad to know. Because while part of her still wanted to protest—that Elle still could've come back from the injury, that she could've had it all, that she had been, still was, and always would be the greatest player Julie had ever seen—she accepted it.

Elle had let it go, eight years ago.

And now, Julie would, too.

Elle's box of trophies belonged to Elle. It was hers to do with as she wished.

"Yeah," Julie said. "Okay."

She held Elle's eyes. Hoped she could express how hard she had listened—how special she felt, knowing that Elle had trusted her enough to tell her any of it—when she said it again.

"Okay."

CHAPTER SIXTEEN

Elle's linguine had gotten cold.

She took another bite of it anyway.

She hadn't meant to say all that. She'd meant to say some of it, of course—Julie was her friend, and she was actually glad, at this point, to put the subject to bed for her—but not...all of that. And how had they gotten on the subject of having kids?

Time to steer this ship back on course.

"I think we should make a goal," she said.

When she glanced up, Julie was still staring at her, in that deeply kind way Julie's eyes conveyed, and Elle had to take another sip of water. She was wearing a soft orange sweater tonight, Julie, because what former Vol didn't own a strange number of orange garments? The color had never looked particularly flattering on Elle, but on Julie, it only made her hair even brighter, her eyes even warmer, like a sunset made human.

"A goal," Julie repeated.

Elle didn't know why it unsettled her so much, that Julie had played for the Vols. It wasn't that she didn't believe Julie had the talent—even benchwarmers had to be good to make it onto the team in Knoxville—it was more that Elle should have known, should have recognized her right away. And now that she knew...

Elle might have liked to keep the past in the past. But it made her feel even closer to Julie, knowing that she knew, too, what it was like. To be in that locker room, to walk through that tunnel. It felt almost impossible that she could share that with Julie, too.

"Yes." Elle cleared her throat, sitting straighter. "For you." She pushed away her plate, rested her forearms on the table. "Let's say we try out relationship things until the end of the season. And if relationship things aren't for you, then that's fine. But if you think they could be . . . you ask somebody out."

Julie's eyes flared in panic.

"I ask somebody out?"

"Sure." Elle shrugged. "I'm sure there's someone out there you could ask out. Or!" Elle smiled. "We'll sign you up for a dating app. Have you tried any of the apps?"

Julie made a funny expression, like she'd just eaten something upsetting.

"No."

"Perfect. I'm sorry to tell you that at least downloading an app is a necessary relationship thing in the modern age."

Julie's expression turned into an outright grimace.

"Barf."

And Elle laughed out loud—who actually said *barf*?—as the waiter returned to take their plates.

"Can I interest you in any dessert this evening?"

"I'll have the cannoli," Elle said, still holding in laughter.

"Me too," Julie said. Once the waiter left, she turned to Elle with a smirk. "Ice cream *and* cannoli, all in the same month. You're living on the edge, Elle."

"You know." Elle lifted her glass, feeling like she was walking a tightrope in a dangerous, deliriously fun game. "You say you're not good at relationship things, but you're already very good at that."

Julie's brow furrowed.

"At what?"

"Flirting."

Julie's mouth dropped open. "I—what?"

"The teasing. You only have to add a *little* more of a smile and a wink with it, and it's knockout level already. Well, winking is debatable. Has mixed results. Maybe hold off on the winking for now."

"But—" Julie sputtered. "You've seen your kitchen cabinets, Elle! They are infinitely teasable! You have something called *teff* in there, labeled in a little clear container."

"Oh, teff!" Elle grinned. "It's a tiny, nutty grain. Full of fiber and vitamin C."

"It sounds like a British cough."

Elle stuffed down a snort. They had perhaps gotten off course.

"Let's not focus on my teasability, specifically. I'm just saying, when you connect with someone on an app and go out on a real date, a lot of people find teasing flirtatious and charming, so you'll already be a pro."

Julie collapsed back in her seat, looking dazed. "Right."

"Or," Elle ventured, laughter dying away. "We can not do this at all? If you don't want to date, Julie, you don't have to date."

"No." Julie rubbed the back of her neck. "I might want to date, and I think this will be helpful." She gave Elle a weak smile. "Thanks. Again. For helping me."

"Is there anything specifically you want to get out of this? That I could make sure I help with?"

Julie bit her lip. "No. Like...figuring out literally anything will be good. I know this won't answer everything, but...like, even understanding that I like holding your hand feels like one less thing to worry about."

Elle stared at her lap as their cannoli arrived. Reminded herself that this was *practice*. For Julie. That Julie confirming, out loud, that she liked holding Elle's hand should not make Elle's chest fill with firelight.

They ate their cannoli quietly, until Julie started telling a story of when her family had visited Boston when she was in high school, and they'd waited in line for cannoli in the North End, and everyone was tired and grumpy and she and her twin had gotten into a huge fight about something neither of them could remember now, but whatever it was, it must have been good, because Julie started laughing so hard at the memory that she had to put down her nearly finished cannoli and cover her face. When she was finally able to get herself together and drop her hands, her cheeks were red, eyes wet with glee as she sucked down water to calm herself, and Elle felt herself floating away, untethered from the tightrope completely, to someplace full of glitter and helium and Julie Parker's unrestrained laughter.

"Here's the thing," Elle said once they reached the parking lot, after they'd settled the bill and left their cozy table. The night had cooled; Elle slipped on her blazer. "I keep thinking about your story."

Julie's eyes snapped up to hers; they had been traveling somewhere down the length of Elle's arm.

"The Boston one? Sorry I lost it back there; I know it wasn't even that funny. I just hadn't thought about it in a long time, and I kept picturing London's face—"

"No," Elle interrupted. "The story about the kiss."

"Oh." Julie's shoulders scrunched around her neck as she stuffed her hands into the pockets of her jeans, folding into herself as she had when she'd told the story in the restaurant. "That's...too bad."

Elle shook her head.

"The thing is," Elle said, "a drunk freshman kiss, from someone who did not deserve it, is not really a kiss at all. Trust me on this. So the question is...which roads do you want to go down here, Julie? If you want to just keep going on dates, we can do that. But if you want to test out what a real kiss is like..."

Julie froze, orange fuzzy sweater still at her ears.

"You're saying—" she started.

"I'm saying we could practice a real kiss." Elle shrugged, willing her blood to calm. "If you want to. No pressure, though, if you don't."

She really had only planned on taking Julie to dinner tonight. She'd hoped Julie would take the lead, give signs as this dating practice progressed, about any other things she was curious about. Things she might want, that Elle might be lucky enough to help with.

But it simply wasn't right that Julie had been treated so carelessly. Everything inside of Elle itched to show Julie, right fucking now, how not right it was.

Julie only hesitated a moment more before she nodded.

"Okay," she said.

"Yeah?" Elle asked, to confirm.

"Yeah." She said it with Coach Parker–level confidence, a confidence that made Elle believe her, that made Elle halfway want to take her right there, against a stranger's car.

But no. She was going to do this right, for Julie.

"Excellent." Elle glanced around them. "Would you like to practice inside-a-car kissing, or against-a-wall kissing? I have to say inside-a-car never feels as comfortable to me as the movies suggest, but it's your call."

"Um." Julie joined Elle in surveying their surroundings, hands finally falling out of her pockets. "Against a wall sounds good."

Before she'd even finished the sentence, Elle grabbed one of her hands, leading her behind a row of cars. They found a spot just inside the shadows, close enough to the floodlight of the parking lot that Elle could still make out the flicker in Julie's eyes, the softness of her lips, slightly parted, as she stared back at Elle.

Perfect.

Even as Elle knew, distantly, that this was all possibly a horrible idea, at the moment, it only felt perfect.

She advanced slowly, Julie shuffling backward, breath quickening, until she was right where Elle wanted her: shoulders against the brick, bracketed by Elle's hands.

"Still okay?" Elle asked.

Julie swallowed, tongue darting out to lick her lips, and it killed Elle that she probably didn't even know that was sexy.

"Still okay," Julie confirmed.

Elle traced her fingertips down Julie's freckled cheek. Pushed back an escaped lock of strawberry hair from her temple.

"You are very kissable, Julie Parker," she murmured.

Julie's lips parted further on an exhale. Stayed there, as if she needed to draw in the extra air. Elle ran her thumb across that open, plump bottom lip.

"But it's okay, too," Elle said, "if it turns out you just don't like it. Tell me if you want me to stop, okay?"

"Okay," Julie said, her voice a whisper now, and Elle loved it, the vulnerability in that barely there sound.

They had been standing a mere inch apart, but Elle leaned in now, pressing her thighs to Julie's, torso to torso. Ran one hand down Julie's shoulder, the fuzzy material of her sweater tickling Elle's palm, while reaching the other into Julie's hair, underneath her ponytail.

"I like to start slow," Elle said, voice soft. "Part your lips for me, Coach Parker."

Julie's lips *had* been in perfect position, but she had clenched them shut as Elle had gotten close, closer, closest. So Elle waited, nose brushing Julie's, nails continuing to scratch lightly at her scalp. Until, swallowing, Julie did as Elle asked.

"Perfect," Elle whispered, before dusting her lips over each part of Julie's, one at a time: the neat bow at the top. The luscious fullness of that bottom lip. A light touch to each side. And *oh*, Julie Parker's lips were soft. Elle knew, now that she had felt them—as she had known even before that—that she could do this all night.

She kissed down Julie's jaw, light and careful. Absorbed, with satisfaction, the quickness of Julie's breath, the warmth of her flushing cheeks.

"And then…" Elle's mouth returned to the prize, pressing against Julie's lips. "We do this—" She broke away and pushed in again. "Until you're ready for more."

The kisses were chaste, gentle. But when Julie pressed back, cautious but there, when she snuck her hands underneath Elle's blazer, fingers exploring the silk against Elle's side, Elle felt every movement, every slide, simmering under her skin. A glow, radiating through her rib cage, at the *trust* Julie was granting her in this moment.

And then, suddenly, the kisses weren't chaste anymore at all. Elle wasn't sure who had changed the dial, whether it had been her or Julie who'd snapped, sliding them firmly into *making out* territory, Elle's favorite stage. Mouths open wider, hotter, lips sliding against each other with force, tongues meeting in the middle. Julie's hands pressed harder, one against Elle's back, one sliding up her side, and Elle thought *yes, touch me, hold me closer*, and she knew, in the back of her mind, that she should stop, because the victorious feeling roiling through her veins was burning too hot, making her want to shove her thigh between Julie's legs, to grind her into the fucking wall, to make that hitch in Julie's breath go higher, higher, until Julie shattered beneath her, right here. She could picture it now, how beautiful Julie would look when she came, face flushed, skin tacky next to her strawberry hair, mouth open, and Elle wanted to see it while she wore this sweater, an actual firework, a flame against Elle's chest, burning underneath her tongue.

Elle's hand slipped underneath the hem of Julie's sweater, her thumb swiping over the soft skin above Julie's hip.

Julie moaned into Elle's mouth, shivering against Elle's fingertips, and god, if Julie reacted like that to the barest swipe of Elle's thumb along an innocent patch of skin, how would she react to other things? To Elle replacing her thumb with her mouth? To moving that thumb, down, down, to—

Julie released Elle's mouth with a gasp, shoving her gently but firmly away.

Fuck.

Elle took another step back.

They stared at each other for a long beat. Julie's face was so open, and Elle was so relieved to see that she didn't look upset, just... just...Elle was too turned on to interpret Julie's face as displaying anything other than *want*. But she had pushed Elle away, so Elle was probably projecting, or maybe she wasn't, but—space. They needed space.

"Okay," Julie said eventually, closing her eyes and wiping a hand over her face. "Um. That was...helpful."

A strange noise crawled out of Elle's throat that was maybe laughter, but ended up sounding half-strangled. She ran a hand through her hair. She had to—*had to*—get ahold of herself here.

"I'm glad," she managed, taking another step back. "Thanks for a great night, Julie."

She retreated one more step.

"I'll see you on Monday, Coach."

And then she turned and walked into the parking lot, away from the temptation of where Julie was still slumped against the wall, before Julie could read the want reflected on her own face, infused into every inch of Elle's body.

CHAPTER SEVENTEEN

Julie thought maybe all of her molecules had been rearranged.

It was the only explanation for how she was able to still exist in this world, side by side with Elle during the game against Rockland on Monday, without combusting.

Sure, she couldn't look at Elle without her face turning to fire, but at this point, that reality shouldn't have been surprising to either of them. The only thing that truly surprised Julie, after the kiss against the wall of Bella's Italian Eatery on Saturday night, was how okay she was.

She should have been freaking out, like she had freaked out so many times after interactions with Elle over the last month. But her overall thoughts about the kiss were that it had been...super awesome.

Like, dizzying, and overwhelming.

But awesome.

She had kept herself busy yesterday, so she wouldn't overthink it; started the day with a long run before inviting Ben over to watch trashy TV and help keep an eye on Snoozles's incision. She had wanted to tell Ben about the kiss, about all of it, but she'd ended up keeping it to herself. Because that was the thing of it, maybe the reason she'd been able to be so okay: while her heart had hammered from the moment Elle had suggested it in the middle of the parking lot, once Elle's hands landed on her, once she touched Julie with such care... Julie had only been overcome with a sense of *why the hell not?*

It was just between them.

It wasn't *real*. Sure, it had *felt* real, every electrifying second of it, but Julie had only been able to give in to that electricity because there was no pressure, no expectations. An opportunity to try.

She still wasn't quite sure *how* she had convinced Elle to be so kind to her. But god, if she couldn't grab hold of the pressure-free chance to kiss the literal woman of her dreams—well, maybe that would've answered some of her questions for her.

But she had wanted to. And she had. And maybe the euphoria of letting herself do so was simply overriding all of the other ways this was probably a bad idea.

But whenever her eyes snagged on Elle tonight, all she could think about was whether they'd be able to do it again.

Ben, to his credit, had only pushed once: *You still texting your girl?* And when Julie had answered, *Not my girl, but yeah*, and changed the subject, he'd let it go.

There had been moments, of course, over the last forty-eight hours, where overthinking had crept in. About the brush of Elle's mouth down her jaw, the press and weight of Elle's body against hers, the silk of Elle's shirt in Julie's hands. Remembering the touch of Elle's thumb along the tender, private skin of Julie's side.

The way Julie's body had reacted to all of it. Light-headed and hot and *wanting*.

These moments of remembering were tinged with an almost slight delirium. A *what the fuck* sensation where she thought, *I could have been a slut, too. This whole time.*

Except each time, she'd think about it a bit more, and she still wasn't sure. Maybe the kissing had only felt so awesome because it had been with Elle.

The buzzer rang, signaling the end of the third quarter. Julie clapped, motioning the Bobcats into another huddle. Her players were wheezing, but they were also smiling.

"You're looking good," Julie said, leaning in. "Really good. No matter what happens in this last quarter, I am *proud* of the fight you've shown today."

The game had felt good from the first buzzer, the pace fast but not sloppy, the score tight. The Bobcats were communicating so well, Ngozi and Sasha in perfect form. They'd stayed out of foul trouble. It hadn't been perfect; no game was, and Julie wasn't foolish enough to be certain they'd walk away with the W. But she could *feel* the confidence radiating from the team, the belief they had in themselves that their house was truly theirs today. The gym buzzed with energy; the crowd loud, the cheerleaders hardly taking a rest.

Elle jumped in with a few pointers, and then the refs were calling them back.

"Chin," Julie called, "take a rest. Lerner, you're back in."

"Yeah?" Vanessa glanced at the scoreboard before looking at the stands. "Score's pretty close."

Julie almost ribbed her about never questioning Coach, but instead only gave her a small pat on the shoulder as she walked toward the scorer's table. "Yeah. You've been clutch tonight, Vanessa. You got this."

And she had been. Vanessa Lerner was becoming a quiet star of defense. And while she was still afraid of shooting the ball, she was a special key on the offensive end, too, perhaps the best passer they had after Ngozi. She didn't want to take the shot, but she somehow knew how to get it to the player who did. You couldn't win without a player like that.

Maybe the Bobcats looked so alive because they were so close to Thanksgiving break. One more practice tomorrow, and then school was out until next week. Even the team had a few days' rest, until their next game on Saturday.

Whatever the reason for the mood, as Julie settled back on her haunches to watch the fourth quarter play out, she knew the real win today was Karly sitting in the bleachers again for this one. Vanessa getting to do her best for her this time.

Julie could tell within the first five minutes of the quarter that Rockland was getting frustrated. They were a good team. But the Bobcats had never let them get more than three points ahead, and they were currently down by five. The whistles started breaking up the flow of the game as Rockland's bumps and pushes got rougher.

Julie waited a few more minutes, monitoring the energy of her players as they absorbed the fouls, their confidence turning testy, Ngozi's eyes a little too full of fire, before she called for a time-out.

"Listen." She leaned into the huddle, voice at her most serious level of Coach. "I know they're getting rough out there. They're frustrated, because they know you've got them. But you can*not* let them get to you. If they want to dig themselves even further in the hole by giving us endless free throws, that's their call. Even if it doesn't feel right, don't react. Just keep your cool and keep playing Bobcat basketball. All right?"

The Bobcats nodded, resting their hands on their knees, breathing deep. Julie was about to motion them to put their hands in when Ngozi cleared her throat.

"I have an idea," she said.

Julie glanced up. Ngozi stood tall, hands on her hips. And Julie almost laughed at herself, that she had been worried Ngozi had been about to fly off the handle. Because now, her face was all smiles. And the only thing sparking in those brown eyes was mischief.

"I'm half-scared to ask," Julie said. "But go for it."

"Let's up the ante."

Julie raised an eyebrow, motioning for her to go on.

"We win this game," Ngozi said, "we get to take a break tomorrow. And watch you two"—she pointed at Elle and then Julie—"go one-on-one."

Julie didn't even get a split second to react. To gauge Elle's reaction. The roar that immediately went up from the entire Bobcats bench was too raucous to focus.

"And if we don't win?" Julie managed to ask through the hullabaloo.

Ngozi shrugged, easy, like she wasn't truly concerned. "Then we'll do extra sprints."

The yells turned into groans.

Julie cut her glance to Elle. Everything she knew now about Elle's history with the game churned in her brain. Elle handled the ball, demonstrated plays to Ngozi and the rest of the team during practices, but Julie wasn't sure if Elle would count any of that as actual playing. And there was nothing, really, more pure basketball than one-on-one. Even if it was only one-on-one in front of a bunch of teenagers, Julie knew it simply wouldn't be in her abilities to half-ass it, and she had a feeling that, even now, Elle would be the same.

Whatever I had . . . I lost it.

"Elle?"

Elle looked back. Julie gave a small nod, hoping it properly conveyed *your call*. It was hard to read Elle's face, her brow slightly furrowed, eyes serious. And for a second, Julie started to panic. If Elle said no, it would make Ngozi feel bad, and the team was so hype—

Elle's mouth curved into a smile.

"Sounds fair to me," she said.

The Bobcats cheered even louder. The ref said, "Coach, time to go," and Julie put her hand into the huddle.

"You got yourself a deal, Williams."

The Bobcats beat Rockland 57-50.

"My Julie." Charlotte Parker held Julie's face between her hands. "I'm so proud of what you're doing here."

Julie rolled her eyes before pulling away. "You just chose a good one to come to, Mom."

"I gotta run to the studio," London said, pulling on their coat. The rest of the East High gym streamed around them, parents hugging Julie's players as they came out of the locker room. "But that"— London threw an arm around Julie's neck—"was fucking awesome."

"Language," Charlotte *tsk*ed. After London kissed her cheek and took off, she leaned in toward Julie while glancing to the side. "She looks so different."

Julie tracked Charlotte's gaze to where Elle stood at the opposite end of the gym, deep in conversation with José.

"Uh," Julie said. "Yeah."

"I like it." Charlotte motioned to her own gray bob, looking back at Julie with a twinkle in her eye. "Do you think I could bring one of your old balls next time and have her sign it? I'm sure we still have some in the garage—"

"*Mom.* Please don't." Julie thought she'd already gone over the please-don't-freak-out-over-Elle-Cochrane rule at Sunday supper. In like, explicit detail.

Charlotte held up her hands in innocence. "Fine, fine. I'll be good." She rustled in her purse for her keys, mumbled something that sounded like "Although I can't make any promises for your father."

"What?"

"Oh, nothing. Truly, Jules, it's been fun getting to sit in this gym again." She procured her car keys and squeezed Julie's wrist with her free hand. "We'll see you around eleven on Thursday?"

This, of course, was a Southern mom's way of saying *Be there by eleven, or I'll publicly shame you.*

"Sounds good."

"Love you, honey."

Not a second after Charlotte walked away, a voice called out "Coach!"

Julie turned to see Rose Cochrane walking toward her, a wince on her face with each step.

Mothers everywhere, up in this gym.

"Sorry," Rose said with a wheeze. She leaned hard on her walker. "These old bones acting up again today. Just wanted to say good game."

"Thanks." Julie smiled. "It was."

"I've also been meaning to thank you," Rose continued, even though she was clearly in pain and should have been getting on home. Julie's smile faded in concern. "For what you're doing for Vanessa, and for my girl."

It took Julie a second to realize *my girl* meant Elle.

"Oh," she said, uncertain what to say. "I'm just so grateful Elle's been able to help out. She's been a real lifesaver for the team."

"Ach." Julie couldn't quite interpret the noise Rose made, or the look she threw Julie's way. "I'd say it's more likely the other way around, love. I know she wouldn't want me to say this." She scooched her walker closer. "But I was really starting to think she'd never look at someone else again the way she looks at you, after that whole mess with Sophie."

Rose smiled up at her, a hopefulness smoothing away, momentarily, the lines of pain. Julie could only gape at her, utterly unable to take that hope away from her, before Rose patted her arm and pushed away.

"You have a good holiday, Coach."

Julie stood another minute more, staring at nothing.

She had never heard Elle mention a Sophie before.

But Julie knew who Rose had been talking about.

More words from Saturday's dinner came back to her. When Elle had talked about being very much not okay in Milwaukee.

I was in a not entirely healthy relationship at the time.

And as Julie paused now, frozen in the aftermath of Rose's cryptic words, she wasn't so much concerned with what, exactly, Rose saw in Elle's face when Elle looked at her. She knew, with a twinge of guilt, that whatever hope Rose was feeling was misguided, whatever she thought she saw a trick of the eye.

What Julie suddenly needed to know, in a way that threatened to consume her, was what the hell Sophie Holiday had done to Elle Cochrane.

Elle stretched out a hamstring.

"Mosk, you're in charge of music," Julie called, stretching her own legs on the other side of the timeline.

"Please," Sasha said, scrolling on her phone. "Already on top of it."

"Can you make it Rihanna heavy?" Elle asked. "For Snoozles."

Julie threw her a quick smile before stretching down toward her toes.

Elle exhaled. Her nerves were pulled tight, a bowstring stretched from her stomach to her throat. She still couldn't quite parse, as she hadn't been able to all day, whether they were nerves of apprehension or excitement.

I have somehow agreed to a game of one-on-one, she'd texted Mara this morning. In front of an audience of teenagers. Against a woman I am extremely attracted to. On a scale of 1-10, how horrible of an idea is this?

Mara had texted back a GIF of Chris Evans scream-laughing and said, Cochrane, all I can say is I WISH I could be there

"Oh, come on." Julie threw her hands in the air as Evans and Bianchi came hollering through the door, each holding a piping-hot bag of popcorn. A second later, Mosk's playlist blared through the gym.

Julie pointed at her players, arranged in varying levels of teenage lounging on the sidelines, and shouted over the bass line. "If you smoosh popcorn on my court, I swear to god, I'll throw in an extra practice on Sunday."

"Sunday is the Lord's day, Coach," Katelyn shouted. Before throwing popcorn into her mouth.

"Says you," Sasha shot back.

"Why don't we keep all lords and saviors out of this," Julie said. "Just be careful with y'all's snacks."

"Hi, Coach and Elle!" Blake said with a wave as she walked by. "Good luck!" She sat next to Gray and promptly opened up a planner and five gel pens. Gray stared at her and blushed.

Ngozi strolled out of Julie's office with the game ball dancing atop her fingers, a whistle around her neck.

"I take it you'll be officiating," Elle said with a wry smile once Ngozi stood at center court between her and Julie, shoulders back, spine straight.

"Obviously." She blew her whistle and yelled at Bianchi and Mosk, who were dancing to the music under a basket. "Clear the court! And Mosk, turn it down a little. Jesus. I have to concentrate here."

Vanessa walked through the door, fifteen minutes late. Elle frowned.

"Hey," she said as Vanessa passed on her way to the sideline, backpack slung over her shoulder. Elle forced a smile into her voice. "Who you rooting for?"

"I'm just here for the popcorn," Vanessa said, voice dry.

Elle held in a sigh. Yesterday had been such a good day. But from the moment Vanessa came down to breakfast this morning, Elle knew something was up. It was her last day of school before Thanksgiving break; she should've been celebrating.

But Elle was pretty sure it was actually Thanksgiving break that was making Vanessa shut down.

"She okay?"

Elle looked at Julie, who was suddenly by her side. Still stretching, posture casual, voice low. Even now, days after the kiss, Elle caught herself shivering whenever Julie stood this close, unable to stop forgetting what it'd felt like to have their bodies fully aligned, Julie's lips open against hers.

Julie hadn't mentioned it since. They had texted here and there, but mostly logistical things about the team, Elle checking in on Snoozles, plans for the holiday. Elle had no idea if Julie regretted it. If she wanted to do it again. Because shit, Elle did.

Except doing it again was probably an even worse idea than doing it once.

Elle pushed her inappropriate thoughts away and glanced toward Ngozi, who had gotten distracted, chatting with other Bobcats a few yards away.

Elle sighed, discreetly looking to where Vanessa had slumped against the wall next to Katelyn.

"I think she's stressed about Thanksgiving."

"Ah." Julie lifted an elbow over her head. "Is she going to get to see Karly?"

"Not until the end of the day." Elle stretched out a knee. "We're going to meet her at night for a couple hours, just the three of us at a neutral location. I invited her to spend the day with us at Tricia's, which Amber said she'd approve, but..." Elle shook her head. "She said no. We all want her there, but..."

Elle understood Karly's hesitance. Her embarrassment, her need to get through this on her own.

At the same time, Elle wished Karly would let them in. She didn't see how Karly or Vanessa could get through this, start on a better trajectory, *without* letting them in.

"That's tough."

"Yeah." Elle blew out a breath. "Thanks again for coming over tonight." As soon as this one-on-one was done, Elle was heading to another foster certification class. "I hope she's not too..." Elle trailed off, not wanting to talk badly of Vanessa here, in the middle of the court. "But she loves you, so. Maybe it'll be good."

"I'm sure it'll be fine. And if it's not..." Julie shrugged, caught Elle's eye. "Then we'll get through it."

A sharp blow from Ngozi's whistle broke the moment, and Elle was glad. Because thinking inappropriate thoughts about Julie Parker—practicing relationship things with her—was foolish enough. But the temptation to give in to the feeling Julie inspired with that *we*—*we'll get through it*—like she and Elle and Vanessa were a team...not like their CPS team was a team, but a call-me-in-the-middle-of-the-night-if-you-need-me team, like Elle didn't have to bear the responsibility for Vanessa's well-being on her own...

The temptation to believe in that felt downright reckless.

"Enough dillydallying!" Ngozi blew on the whistle, unnecessarily, one more time. "Let's go!"

"I regret telling her she could use the whistle," Julie muttered.

"I regret that, too," Elle agreed. She added, as the Bobcats settled themselves around the court, "You know you're going to kick my ass, right?"

Because Julie Parker might have ridden the bench at UT, but she'd been coaching the Bobcats for two years. Elle was still adjusting to even being on a court again. Eight years was a long time.

She was doing this for Ngozi, for the team. To hopefully get a laugh out of Vanessa.

But Elle did not harbor any illusions that this was going to go well for her.

"And you should know, Cochrane," Julie said, and Elle's gut gave a kick of delight, as it had at the restaurant, at Julie calling her *Cochrane*, "that if you go easy on me, I'll never talk to you again."

Elle huffed a laugh as they resumed their starting positions.

Basketball players.

Ngozi blew the whistle. Tossed the ball in the air.

Julie snatched it first. Because of course she did.

Elle ran back. Matched Julie's stance, her jabs to the right and the left, arms out but not too high. Waiting.

Julie played it cool.

Backed up, took it slow. Did a showy dribble between her legs that made the Bobcats howl.

And Elle thought she probably could've stopped her. Could've blocked her, or made a steal. If only Julie had stopped smiling at her. If she'd broken eye contact, even once. If she hadn't laughed, bolstered by the cheers from the team, as she hip-checked her way past Elle to a smooth layup.

Elle stood straight, blowing out her cheeks as she scooped up the ball beneath the basket.

Julie's competitive joy was the dirtiest trick Elle had ever encountered.

"All right, Coach," Elle said as she dribbled. "I see you."

"Or you don't," Julie countered, in her face immediately. "Seeing as you just let me walk right by you."

Elle shook her head.

Basketball players.

She managed to get the ball down the court without Julie stealing it, but the woman was aggressive. Elle turned, backing her ass into Julie as Julie tried to swipe away from behind.

The whole thing was at once immediately familiar and strangely foreign. Like she was having an out-of-body experience at the same time that she was maybe, actually, finally returning to it.

Just barely, she was able to get a jump shot off.

Which somehow swished through the net.

It felt good.

It felt real good.

A feeling that diminished, somewhat, with the next three baskets Elle soundly missed.

The last one bounced off the rim almost directly back into Elle's hands. Julie lunged for her while Elle tried to get a quick, better shot off. Except Julie must have overshot her reach.

She crumpled on her knees just past her.

"Oh shit," Elle whispered, resting the ball on her hip and sinking down to where Julie was hunched over an ankle. If something had happened—the worst injuries happened so easily, just one awkward landing, and if Julie had hurt herself over this dumb one-on-one—

"Julie." Elle reached a hand to Julie's shoulder. The gym had gone silent. "Julie, you okay?"

It happened too fast for Elle to process.

"I am now," Julie said, as she turned and plucked the ball away from Elle's loose hold. She grinned as she dribbled backward down the court.

"Never do that, kids!" she yelled as she turned and raced toward her basket. "Faking injury for benefit is bad!"

Ngozi was laughing so hard she doubled over.

"That was dirty, Coach," Bianchi said.

Blake's mouth hung open in shock.

Elle dropped to her butt, shaking her head and staring at Julie, who was taking a victory lap around center court.

Basketball players.

Ngozi let them take a breather after that. And twenty minutes of trying to keep up with Julie Parker after that, they broke for halftime, which soon devolved into a Bobcat dance party in the middle of the court. Elle and Julie watched from the bleachers, laughing occasionally at the dance moves, sucking down water and getting air back into their lungs.

And with each moment that they sat in comfortable quiet, Elle knew. That she was okay. That she was playing basketball again, and it was only okay because she was doing it with Julie.

Who believed in Elle so much, even in the blatant face of her failures, that Elle knew she'd likely still consider her the best baller who ever lived, whether Elle had fallen flat on her face today or not. However false the notion was, Elle had to admit it soothed.

And who—even with that—wasn't afraid to play Elle like an equal anyway.

Elle's own, specific pressure-less zone.

Vanessa and Katelyn sat at the opposite end of the bleachers, ignoring the music and staring intently at their manga instead. Elle tried her best to not glance over at them too many times.

Julie was in the middle of breaking up the dance party when the Doc strolled in.

"Oh!" Julie's eyes flashed with clear panic. "Hi, Dr. Jones. We were just—uh—" Julie glanced around the floor, still half-full of teenagers dancing possibly too provocatively to possibly inappropriate music. The Doc only crossed her arms and smiled.

"I heard about this," she said, raising a curious brow. Mosk rushed to her phone to turn down the volume. "Who's winning?"

"Coach," Ngozi said. The Doc's grin grew.

"Which one?"

"Parker," Bianchi chimed in, before leaning toward the principal. "But she's playing, like, surprisingly dirty? It's kind of amazing."

And poor Julie Parker's face, which had just returned to its normal color after sufficient rest, flushed red again. Elle stared at the floor, holding in a laugh.

"Well." The Doc's eyes flashed with amusement before they flicked over to the corner, where Vanessa and Katelyn still sat, away from the crowd. After a second, her gaze settled back on Elle and Julie. "I wish I could stay and watch, but I was just passing through. Thank you, both of you"—she caught Elle and Julie's eyes in turn—"for giving our Bobcats a space to let off some steam before break. All of you"—her voice rose as she addressed the group again—"stay safe this week, and we'll see you soon."

A chorus of "Bye, Doc!" followed her on her way out of the gym.

Julie visibly released a breath when she was gone.

And then she turned to Elle and said, as serious as could be, "Let's finish this."

Elle snorted and followed her back to center court.

She was able to get some of her pride back, at least a modicum of it, ten minutes later, when Julie tried to steal the ball from Elle's hands and only ended up slamming her forearm across Elle's wrist instead.

Ngozi blew her whistle. "Foul!"

"What!" Julie twirled. "Come on, Williams! It's one-on-one!"

Ngozi gave her a stone-cold stare before blowing the whistle again. "Two throws for Elle."

Julie threw up her hands.

"Sorry, Coach." Elle bounced the ball between her fingers. "You see, you're supposed to reach for the *ball*"—she held the ball in one palm and gestured to it like Vanna White—"not my hand."

Julie's eyes narrowed.

"I'll show *you*—" And as Julie lifted a hand toward Elle's face, Elle was certain she was about to be flipped the bird. Until Ngozi tilted her head, arching a brow. "How to...display great sportsmanship," Julie finished, stepping back with a scowl.

This time, it was Elle who had to double over, dropping the ball and resting her hands on her knees as the laughter stole her breath.

Elle couldn't remember the last time she had laughed this hard.

In the end, she still got her ass whooped anyway.

"And our victor!" Ngozi hollered, holding Julie's hand and shaking it in the air like a boxing coach, "is Coach Julie Parker! Defeating Elle Cochrane with a score of—"

"Let's not focus on the details," Elle said.

"Forty to twenty-eight!" Ngozi shouted.

And the crowd went wild.

Elle winced.

And then she laughed. Again.

"All right, all right, everyone." Julie clapped her hands. "Get your stuff and get out of here. Have a good holiday, if you're celebrating. And hey, I'm serious about the popcorn. Clean up your junk; the janitors deserve a nice vacation, too."

The team was still whooping it up, imitating Julie's and Elle's moves, as they gathered their backpacks and trash. Julie walked over to shake Elle's hand, like they were true opposing coaches.

"I am worried you went easy on me," Julie said.

"I assure you," Elle said, "I did not."

"If you say so." She released Elle's hand. "See you in a bit?"

And then she winked. Elle bit her lip.

"I know you said to hold off on the winking," Julie said, "but I thought I'd give it a whirl." And she winked again, hands on her hips. "I don't know, I think it could work."

"It's not bad," Elle said. "We'll workshop it."

And what she meant, in her heart of hearts, by *workshop it*, was really *make out*. Because the wink wasn't just not bad. The wink was great.

Julie walked away to a wall of teenage high fives.

Elle couldn't stop grinning as she walked toward Vanessa.

She knew when Ngozi had suggested this, it was really a test for Elle. So Ngozi could see if the old basketball star still had any chops.

She wasn't sure if Ngozi had gotten what she wanted. But the stunt *had* succeeded in securing Coach Parker as the true star of the Bob-cats' hearts. Not that there had been any doubt.

But if at the end of the season, that was all Elle helped contribute to this team, well.

That would be worth it.

CHAPTER EIGHTEEN

Julie paced in Elle's kitchen, chugging Elle's seltzer and listening to the bass of Vanessa's music through the ceiling.

She tried to stop pacing once she heard the front door open, so as to appear casual and normal, leaning against a counter like Elle herself did so well, but Julie's body had gotten into a rhythm.

"Hey." Elle dropped her bag on the kitchen island and stared at Julie walking from the fridge to the door frame and back. "Everything okay?"

"I maybe sort of did a thing," Julie blurted.

"Okay," Elle said calmly. She glanced toward the ceiling. "Is anybody hurt?"

"No, everyone's fine."

"How's Vanessa doing?"

"Okay. I mean, she's sad." Julie made herself stop moving, planting her feet by the island opposite Elle. "We played *Super Mario Brothers* and she talked about her feelings."

Elle slumped onto a stool, blinking. "Huh. Do you think that would work for me, if I learned how to play *Super Mario Brothers*?"

Julie waved a hand. "It's not you, Elle. I'm just...an outside party, you know? It's easier for her."

Elle nodded and examined a whorl in the wood with a fingertip.

"But also, playing *Super Mario Brothers* really isn't that hard.

Anyway, she was telling me how awkward she feels about hanging with Tricia's perfect family on Thanksgiving while everyone stares at her and thinks bad stuff about her mom."

Elle hung her head in her hands. "I know. I know she feels that way, but it won't be like that. Well, Rose might be thinking that stuff, internally, but she's been good so far around Vanessa."

"I know. But anyway, I sort of, maybe, invited you both to my parents' house instead?"

Elle dropped her hands, looking at Julie in surprise. "You did?"

"Yeah." Julie scratched her head, avoiding eye contact. "Which I know wasn't the right thing to do, without talking to you first, and maybe weird, and it's super last minute. I told her she'd still have to spend *some* time at Tricia's, but that if she needed a break...she could come to Charlotte and Tom's. I think I told you about our Sunday suppers, when my mom invites a bunch of neighbors and friends and stuff...well, Thanksgiving is that tenfold. She likes to keep Christmas just family, but she always talks about how Thanksgiving should be a time of gathering and blah-blah-blah. So you guys coming would be totally fine; my mom would love it. And Vanessa seemed pumped, actually, when I described it. I think being able to sort of...melt into a crowd of strangers sounded like the second-best option to her."

"What was the first-best option?"

"Staying in her room and not talking to anyone all day."

"Right."

"Anyway, I obviously won't be offended if you don't want to come; I wouldn't want to upset Rose or Tricia or anyone either. I'm just sorry I ran my trap without talking to you."

Julie took a breath. Followed by a long slug of seltzer.

"Julie." When Julie allowed herself to look across the island, she found Elle smiling. "I think it's a great idea."

"Yeah?"

"Yeah. Tricia and Rose *will* be a little sad, I think, but I'll make sure we spend the whole morning there. And some extended family of Akhil's are coming this year, so it'll still be a full house when we leave. I understand how Vanessa feels, that going to your house might be a fun distraction from whatever feelings the holidays are bringing up for her. An outside party, like you said."

"Right."

"Great."

Elle smiled again before she stood and walked to a cabinet behind Julie.

"Do you want to watch a movie?"

What?

Julie turned, resting her palms on the kitchen island as Elle retrieved a mug and filled a teapot with water. Julie had been so sure she'd overstepped, that Elle would be, if not mad, at the very least, weirded out about the idea of inviting them to Julie's childhood home for the holiday.

"What?"

"A movie." Elle smiled over her shoulder at her. "You don't have to. You've had a long day of kicking my ass. But." She pulled out a box of tea from a cabinet underneath the counter. "Watching a movie together is a definite relationship thing, if you wanted to keep practicing. Plus"—she pressed a few buttons on the stove before turning to face Julie—"I really do think you need to rewatch *You've Got Mail*."

Julie stared at her. "You're serious about this *You've Got Mail* thing."

"Of course I am." Elle plucked a packet of tea out of the box. "It's Nora Ephron, Julie. Would you like some tea?"

"Um. I'm okay. I've consumed three cans of your seltzer in the last hour, so I think my bladder needs a time-out. Wait. I didn't even ask how your class was. How was your class?"

"This one was particularly depressing. Thanks for asking. Want to get the movie queued up? Feel free to rent it from wherever if it's not streaming."

"Just so you know," Julie said five minutes later, as Elle sat on the opposite end of the couch, "I *have* watched movies with other people before. I excel at it, in fact. I'm not sure if I need practicing."

"Yes, but." Elle took a sip of tea, wincing at the temperature before placing it on a side table. "Watching a movie with someone you're dating typically also involves..." She picked up Julie's feet, which had been snuggled between cushions, and plopped them onto her lap. Julie's stomach swooped. "Canoodling."

"Canoodling," Julie repeated.

"It's a fun word," Elle asserted, a second before she pressed Play on the remote and commenced massaging the ball of Julie's right foot over her sock. "But let me know if you're not into it."

Julie stared at Elle's elegant hands on her foot before dragging her eyes toward the screen.

Julie was already rather good at canoodling, too, at least so she thought. Whenever she and Ben watched movies, they draped all over each other.

But as Elle's fingers idly traced around Julie's ankle, sending tingles all the way up Julie's legs, she admitted that maybe this was... different.

Just as holding Elle's hand at the vet, even though Julie had held hands with plenty of people before, had also felt...different.

"Have you ever been to New York?" Elle asked as the opening montages of Manhattan furled across the screen.

For a few seconds, Julie was too distracted by the leg tingles to respond. After mentally shaking herself a few times, she recovered.

"In high school, when we took that trip to Boston, we went to New York, too. I loved it. My parents know a bunch of people there.

But I haven't gone back since, other than a few travel games with UT where I only really saw our hotel."

"Yeah, I've only been there for games, too." Elle hit a particularly good spot on Julie's foot that almost made her moan out loud. "But this movie always makes me nostalgic for it. Even though I've never actually lived there."

"I get that."

"I did contemplate..." Elle trailed off for a moment before continuing. "When I woke up after my ACL surgery and decided I was leaving basketball. I thought about going somewhere, starting brand-new. New York felt like a romantic place to do that. Renting some little walk-up apartment in Queens or something, you know?"

"But you didn't," Julie filled in after a moment.

"No. In the end, I couldn't leave Rose."

They listened in silence to a few emails between Shopgirl and NY152. Julie allowed herself to fully admit that Elle's hands on her legs felt astoundingly good. After realizing long minutes had passed wherein she had no idea what had occurred on the screen, she pinched herself on the arm, willing her mind to focus.

And...she had forgotten how charming the beginning of this movie was. Dammit.

"So they're both cheating on their partners," she summarized. "How romantic."

Elle hit her knee with the back of her hand.

"They don't love their partners!"

"Does that make it better? Wait. Are you crying already?"

Elle sniffed, hugging her mug to her chest.

"They're playing the Cranberries. I'm a lesbian. It's required for me to cry. And look, they keep crossing paths. It's so—"

Elle rested a hand over her heart. Julie huffed out a laugh.

And while Julie had always known Elle was a lesbian, even before their discussion at the vet—Elle had never been shy about it with the media—a flash of something like jealousy still coursed through her. While she knew labels weren't a requirement for existing, people who knew which groups they belonged to seemed to have so much *fun* with their labels. She wanted to make self-deprecating jokes about her identity, too!

"Okay, but come on!" she shouted a minute later. "Look at that bookstore! It's the coziest thing I've ever seen in my *life*. And NY152 is going to take it away from her."

"I know," Elle said, resuming her massage of Julie's calf. "But"— she lifted a shoulder—"love is complicated."

Sounded like some bullshit to Julie. But she kept her mouth shut.

Several minutes later, Elle spoke again, gesturing to the TV.

"Look at this man being so wonderful with these children. And you want Meg to punch him in the face."

"Firstly, I retracted that. Second of all, plenty of men are kind to children who are related to them and monsters to the rest of the world."

"Oh, come on. He's not a monster."

Julie only grumbled. Elle squeezed her toes.

Julie let herself go quiet, studying the characters on-screen. Just as she'd been studying *The Good Place* more carefully at home. Trying to figure out why, out of all the gorgeous people in the cast, Manny always stood out most.

"Okay," she eventually said. "I've been trying to think about this stuff more seriously. And I think…the only person in this movie I'd maybe like to make out with is George."

She could appreciate that Meg Ryan and Tom Hanks were fine-looking people whom she would like to get a beer with. She could not picture anything further than that. Which, really, was how she felt about most people.

Except.

She thought about being a teenager, staring at posters of Elle on her wall. How carefully she watched every postgame interview. How she often had to scour the internet for sites that actually posted women's basketball postgame interviews.

And maybe she hadn't always consciously known it.

But she was pretty sure she'd never wanted to just get a beer with Elle Cochrane.

Elle made a sound in her throat that sounded distinctly amused, startling Julie out of her thoughts.

"What?" Julie shoved her toes in Elle's thigh, trying to get over the discordant feeling of thinking about the Elle Cochrane of her teenaged dreams and sitting next to the real Elle Cochrane now. Who, increasingly, whenever Julie wasn't thinking about it too hard, felt more and more like just...Elle. "Tell me what that sound was for."

"It's just that"—Elle grinned at the screen—"George is definitely the most lesbian character in this movie."

"Huh." Julie turned this over.

"It's Heather for me," Elle added. "She would inevitably make me feel so bad about myself."

She released another dreamy sigh. Julie gave her a bewildered look.

"Love is complicated," Elle said again, as if that explained anything.

They settled into watching in earnest, Elle never stopping her light massages. Julie never stopping enjoying them.

But for some unknown reason, more than halfway through the movie, Julie talked over Tom Hanks once more.

"You know my friend Ben?"

Elle glanced away from the TV to nod at her. Julie kept her gaze glued to the screen.

"He's moving. To Oregon, just after the New Year."

She swallowed as Meg Ryan hung ornaments on a Christmas tree.

"He's going to be with his boyfriend. Which is good; his boyfriend's great, and they both deserve to be happy. But even without Lex, it kind of feels like…" Julie moved her jaw back and forth. "It's what Ben's always wanted, you know? To get out, go explore somewhere new. Like you were talking about before, with your imaginary walk-up in Queens."

Julie hesitated.

"Sometimes it feels like…everyone I know has moved on to something bigger and better. But I'm still just…"

Elle leaned over to pick up the remote and pressed Pause.

"I've never been able to leave my Roses, either," Julie concluded.

And god, what had even prompted Julie to say all that? She blamed Nora Ephron.

"Where would you go, if you could?" Elle asked after a moment.

"Oh god, I don't even know. Anywhere other than my Vandy cubicle, probably. Nashville isn't necessarily the problem. Just…"

Julie shrugged into the couch cushions. She could feel Elle staring at her.

"I don't know. Can you press Play again? I'm being weird and it's embarrassing."

Elle finally dropped her gaze and did as Julie wished.

But when she squeezed Julie's ankle a minute later, Julie let herself breathe out.

They were quiet while Tom won Meg over, both online and in person. NY152, in Julie's opinion, still peaked in the first ten minutes of the movie, when he waxed poetic about school supplies and New York in the fall. When he told Shopgirl he'd like to send her a bouquet of pencils. It was pretty much downhill from there, but Elle was so enraptured it was hard to not feel a small tug of… something.

"Well?" Elle asked at the end.

Julie sighed dramatically, mostly because she knew it would make Elle smile.

"I suppose it was fine." And then she added, "You should visit New York in the fall, next year. I'd hide a bouquet of sharpened pencils in your suitcase."

Elle's hands stilled on her ankle. And Julie wondered if she had lost her mind.

She hadn't meant to make some romantic declaration. She hadn't even known she was capable of making a romantic declaration, but she knew how it sounded the moment it was out of her mouth. She just wanted Elle to be happy. She just—fuck.

After a moment, Elle resumed massaging Julie's heel, even though Julie's entire lower half had long ago gone boneless. Julie stared at the credits, not knowing how to transition from here. She wished she could simply disappear into the couch and then *poof!* show up in her own bed, no awkward goodbyes necessary in between.

"Karly and Vanessa never showed at Thanksgiving last year," Elle said.

Julie looked over, embarrassment forgotten.

"We've done Thanksgiving at Tricia's ever since Sanjana was born. Karly and Vanessa used to come to almost every holiday, even if we didn't talk much the rest of the year. But last Thanksgiving…they never showed. Missed Christmas, too."

Elle looked down, ran a finger along Julie's ankle.

"We should have known," she said. "Lulu, Karly's mom, was an addict, and Karly has a long history of dating shady men." She worried her lip. "We should have done something."

Julie sat up, finally pulling her feet away. She tucked them underneath herself as she leaned against the back of the couch.

"Mostly," Elle said slowly, "I wish this had all never happened. But lately, I just think…I'm so glad they were able to find her. That she came back. That Karly's still alive."

Julie inhaled slowly. "Yeah," she whispered.

"Anyway." Elle cleared her throat, forced a smile. "What can I expect at a Parker family Thanksgiving?"

Julie exhaled. She didn't want to move on, but sensed that Elle needed to.

"Lots of pretentious yet annoyingly delicious food, courtesy of my twin."

Elle's grin turned more genuine. "Sounds up my alley."

"Yeah, you'll love it. The whole vibe will really depend on which aunts and uncles and cousins and neighbors decide to show. Oh, and I should probably warn you that my parents are huge Vols fans. I've tried to tell them to stand down around you, but..."

"I can handle that," Elle said.

"Everyone loves Charlotte, my mom. My dad, Tom..." Julie shook her head with a small laugh. "Tom's funny. He went through a phase for a few years of being a complete asshole, mostly about my twin being nonbinary. But I'm pretty sure Charlotte threatened divorce unless he started going to PFLAG meetings, so. Now he's all aggressive in the opposite direction, maybe because he's actually had a change of heart, maybe because he knows Charlotte is a catch. He even bought this shirt this summer that says, 'I love my gender-nonconforming child.' London appreciated the effort, I think, but also asked him to never wear it with them in public."

"I'm looking forward to meeting all of them. Thanks again for inviting us. I think it will be easier for Vanessa."

"Sure. I hope it is." Julie disentangled her body from the couch. She had no idea what time it was. "I should get home."

"Of course."

Elle walked her to the door. Julie stuffed her feet into her sneakers and messed with the zipper of her coat.

"Thanks for staying this time," Elle said, voice soft. When Julie looked up, Elle felt too close, but Julie couldn't seem to make her feet move. "I'm sorry Ben's leaving, Julie."

Julie swallowed.

"I'm sorry Karly didn't show up to Thanksgiving last year," she said.

And she knew it wasn't the same, Ben choosing his own happiness and Karly choosing the opposite, but Elle nodded, the curve of her mouth so gentle and pretty.

And Julie thought she should probably go. But Elle wasn't moving either, and that thing was happening again, where the space between them seemed to get smaller, Julie's skin tighter, and—

"Why do you love elephants?"

Elle blinked, smile growing. Julie's heart beat in her ears.

"What?"

"*Elle loves elephants*," Julie said, and for some reason, it came out as a whisper.

Elle's cheeks flushed. Julie couldn't stop staring. Normally it was Julie who blushed nonsensically around Elle, not the other way around.

After a moment, Elle shook her head.

"You know how sometimes you decide you love something when you're six years old and your family never forgets it? We took a trip to the Memphis Zoo when I was a kid, and I guess I was enamored with them. And ever since, Rose and Tricia made it a thing." She shrugged, eyes going slightly hazy. "But...I've read a bit about them, you know, as an adult, and they *are* pretty incredible. They're so smart, and they care for each other so much." She bit her lip, staring at Julie's mouth. "They take care of each other," she finished, faintly.

Julie could barely breathe.

"I've been thinking," Julie made herself say, voice wobbly. "The definition of *practice*, like Merriam-Webster–wise, is all about repetition, to get better at something. So, like, if you wanted to—"

She didn't get to finish her sentence before Elle's mouth was on hers. Before Elle's hands were cupping her face, her body pushing Julie's the few final steps before Julie's back hit the door.

"This is what you meant, right?" Elle broke away minutes later to ask, voice breathless. "God, I hope this is what you meant."

"Yeah." Julie nodded, the air that was able to find its way out of her lungs equally ragged. "This is what I meant."

And then she was the one leaning forward, seeking Elle's mouth with her own, her hands fisted in Elle's sweater. And something about doing this a second time, here, in Elle's foyer, wrapped in the quiet and warm cedar smell of Elle's house, having it all feel just as good...

Julie knew it was only practice. But she *wanted* this. Which felt like a pretty big answer to...something, at least one of the questions Julie had never been able to articulate.

But it was still hard to know, when Elle's mouth was on hers, when Julie's senses were infused with pine cones and softness and *Elle*, whether the wanting meant *this*, kissing and physical touch in general, or *this*, kissing and physical touch with Elle.

Because what if Julie *did* try this with someone else after basketball season, and it wasn't the same? What if she could only ever feel right doing this with Elle? Elle, who massaged her feet, who gave Julie a private, crooked smile any time Julie said something she thought was funny. Who had taken Snoozles to the vet in the middle of the night. Elle, who always texted her back, who always backed her up on the court. Who wanted to protect those she loved. Elle, who loved elephants.

Julie knew she should probably figure it out. There was too much going on here, suddenly, to quite keep track of. But...she had spent so long feeling so uncertain about everything, and having something feel so irrevocably *right* made her only want to sink inside of it and give up questions forever.

So when they broke for air again, Julie tried to be bold, dragging her lips down Elle's jaw, as Elle had done to her at the restaurant. And she felt halfway silly doing it, the way she felt a bit like an imposter doing any of this, no matter how good and right it felt, but when Elle dropped her head to the side, giving Julie better access to her neck, when a small whimper left Elle's mouth when Julie licked her way over the skin there, she thought maybe she was doing a decent job. Maybe practicing was working.

Julie navigated a hand between them to pull at the collar of Elle's sweater, to move her tongue closer to Elle's collarbone, her shoulder, feeling liberated now to explore, and Elle's fingers found their way under Julie's shirt again, cold and ticklish against her belly until they weren't.

"Elle," Julie said, voice barely a whisper. She honestly wasn't sure what she was saying her name for—to tell her to stop, to tell her to keep going, to command her hands to move to where Julie was aching.

Before she could figure it out, Elle was pulling back, her hands out of Julie's shirt and on Julie's face instead, cradling her cheeks from a safe distance. Julie blinked at her, mouth still hanging open.

"Good night, Julie," Elle whispered, kissing Julie on the forehead. It was rare for Julie to be this close to someone who was as tall as her. To be on equal footing, to look across the space between them and see eye to eye.

When Elle stepped back and walked away, Julie watched her go, eyes lingering on Elle's hand, pressed against her neck where Julie's mouth had just been, sweater still halfway down her shoulder.

CHAPTER NINETEEN

Vanessa whistled, long and low.

"Who knew Coach was loaded."

"Her parents are, anyway." Elle glanced behind them at the horseshoe-shaped driveway, filled with cars, before looking back at the door. It was...certainly different from how she and Tricia had grown up. And while Elle truly had been fine with this plan from the moment Julie explained it, now that they were here, on the Parkers' enormous front porch, nerves fizzled from her stomach to her fingertips.

Almost like...like they weren't simply here as invited guests, as friends. To provide a safe haven for Vanessa. But like it was Elle this time, getting in practice at relationship things, one of the biggest of all: meeting the family of someone you cared about. Something Elle hadn't done in...oh, about a decade now.

Which was illogical, of course. The driveway made it clear Julie hadn't been lying, that anyone could walk on in. This wasn't special. Elle's body was blowing things out of proportion.

She rang the doorbell.

Not thirty seconds later, all hell broke loose.

"Yes!" A large man with dark hair, twinkling brown eyes, and an epically ugly Christmas sweater flung open the door and fist-pumped. "Told her I'd get here first!"

"Hank!" Julie slid to the door in her socks, hip-checking Hank and almost knocking him into Elle's chest. "Oh my god! Rude. Hi, Elle. Hey, Vanessa. This is Hank."

Her cheeks were rosy, like she actually had sprinted to the door to try to beat Hank, her ponytail slightly askew. She also wore a Christmas sweater, a bright green one that brought out the gold in her eyes, with *And why is the carpet all wet, Todd?* in glittery letters surrounded by snowflakes.

Elle was experiencing possibly concerning chest pains.

"We gathered that," Vanessa said. "Sweet sweater."

"Thank you." Hank beamed, throwing out his chest. "Genuine thrift store trash, no Target replica for me."

"She could've been complimenting *mine*." Julie hip-checked him again, albeit slightly less violently.

"Oh no," Vanessa said. "I was definitely complimenting his."

"Have I mentioned it's a pleasure to meet you?" Hank leaned forward to grasp Vanessa's hand in both of his. "And you!" He shifted his enthusiastic handshaking to Elle. "You must be the hot basketball star London was telling me Julie—"

Julie elbowed Hank in the side hard enough to cut off his handshake with Elle. And possibly his air supply.

"Hank is Dahlia's brother!" Julie shouted, an overly enthusiastic smile pasted on her face. "I am so glad he is visiting this year!"

Dahlia. Something about that tugged at Elle's mind. But she didn't get a chance to think further on it, as a loud crash emanated from somewhere inside the house.

"Is everything okay?"

"I'm sure it's fine." Julie waved an unconcerned hand. "Just an animal or kitchenware or small child."

A tall, older man who looked just like Julie appeared between Julie and Hank's heads, pushing them both to the side. He had a small metal rainbow pin attached to his sweater, the word *ally* printed underneath the arch.

"Elle Cochrane! What would you know. It really is you. Incredible. Just incredible." He shook his head and held out his hand. "Tom Parker. It's an honor. And you must be Vanessa! Here, here, come on in! Let me take your coats."

After their coats were taken, and another person Elle didn't know distracted Hank, and Tom said, "Oh! I have to check on Sparky," Julie led them into a wide hallway, where a red Persian rug ran along a rustic hardwood floor.

"How was Tricia's?" Julie asked as they walked, voices echoing from all corners of the house.

"It was okay," Vanessa answered, and Elle's heart lifted at this assertion that the morning had been *okay* and not *awful*. Or *whatever*. "Everyone cried a weird amount."

Julie came to an abrupt halt, almost making Elle crash right into her. Which Elle wouldn't have necessarily minded, any other day, but she was trying to get her wits about her here.

"People were crying?" Julie turned, brow creased.

"Me and Rose and Tricia really love the Macy's Thanksgiving Day Parade. It's emotional!" Elle protested at Vanessa's stare.

"It's a bunch of balloons," Vanessa said.

Elle shook her head. Crying over the parade with her mom and sister was perhaps her longest, most favorite holiday tradition. She'd tried to watch it by herself, or with teammates, the years she spent Thanksgiving in hotels, on the road with the Vols or the Wreckers—but it was never the same.

Julie threw a small smile at Elle over her shoulder as she turned back around.

"My dad wore his ally pin for you," she said. "We're all embarrassed about it."

Julie continued on into the kitchen before Elle could respond.

But Elle kind of liked that Tom had worn his ally pin for her.

"Hey, loser," Julie said as they entered the airy, window-filled space. "Say hi to Elle and Vanessa."

The person at the stove threw a towel over their shoulder and turned.

Elle's breath caught in her throat.

Wait. *Wait.*

Holy—

Elle was an idiot.

"Hi, Elle and Vanessa," London Parker said.

Everything clicked into place.

This was why Julie had looked vaguely familiar the first time Elle had seen her. She had been so sure, after learning Julie had played for UT, that that must have been it.

But Julie had seemed familiar because she was London Parker's *twin*.

And that meant—

Dahlia came around the corner and curved an arm around London's waist.

"Hi, Elle," she said.

Elle's hands fluttered around her neck.

"Oh," she said.

Julie had even mentioned London, like multiple times! What was wrong with her?

"Uh," Vanessa whispered, loudly. "Coach, why is Elle being super weird right now?"

Julie glanced her way and sighed.

"Elle, do you watch *Chef's Special*?"

It was only in Elle's top five very favorite shows.

Season eight, in her opinion—starring London Parker and Dahlia Woodson—had been the best season, with season five coming in as a close second.

"Season nine wasn't as good," she heard herself say.

London smirked.

And then, to Elle's slight surprise, they reached over and smacked Julie on the head.

"Nice to see I mean so much to you that you've clearly told your new friends *nothing about me*, dearest sister."

"I thought you didn't even like talking about the show, doofus!" Julie yelled, smacking them right back.

"Children," a calm but stern voice warned. Elle turned to see a short woman with a trim gray bob enter the kitchen.

"*Anyway.*" London stuck out their hand. "Good to meet you, Elle. I sort of can't believe Julie convinced her childhood hero to come to Thanksgiving, but I also totally can."

Elle shook their hand. Darted her eyes to Dahlia again. And, to her horror, released a small giggle.

Julie's eyes narrowed.

"This is amazing," Vanessa whispered.

Dahlia reached out her hand next, and *oh*, Dahlia's hand was very small and cute and soft, and they were both somehow even more attractive in real life. Elle needed a glass of cold water.

"How're you holding up, Dahls?" Julie asked.

Dahlia pasted a large smile on her face before grabbing an oversized wineglass from the counter.

"Great. Having my dad *and* my mom *and* her new boyfriend here in Nashville is not weird at all."

"It's actually going totally fine." London rolled their eyes, opening their mouth to say something else until Dahlia shot them a glare. "And by fine, what I mean to say is, I one hundred percent support Dahlia and every single one of her feelings, and I'm going to check on the risotto now."

Julie groaned, following London toward the stove.

"London. Who has risotto on Thanksgiving?"

"It's butternut squash risotto with browned butter and sage!" London protested. "Just a side dish, fully fits the autumnal theme."

"Oh, good! Elle, Vanessa, you're still here." Hank bounded into the room, wrapping his arm around Dahlia's shoulders.

"We literally just got here," Vanessa said.

Hank turned toward her with a smile.

"Vaness—can I call you that?—I'm hoping to pick your gorgeous teenaged brain. Here's the sitch: I recently decided to stop waiting for a good man and go ahead and adopt a bunch of babies on my own."

"This is a lot of information to tell someone you met five minutes ago." Vanessa's voice was deadpan but, Elle could tell, intrigued.

"I know. But I trust you. You have good energy. But listen, I was made for babies. Right? Except! Babies are apparently hard to come by. And expensive. So maybe—hear me out—I'll just take in a horde of teenagers instead."

"Really?" Julie twirled from the counter, blowing on a wooden spoon of steaming risotto. "That sounds awesome."

"Thank you!" Hank lifted his hands in the air. "I knew you'd agree, Jules."

"Julie." Dahlia rubbed her forehead. "Stop encouraging him."

"Can you help me convince my parents later?" Hank continued, ignoring Dahlia.

"Sure." Julie shrugged and shoved the risotto into her mouth. And let out a little moan.

Elle would take that glass of water now.

London was at Julie's side in a flash, raising an expectant eyebrow.

"That was"—Julie handed back the spoon, licking her fingertips—"the worst."

"Mm-hmm."

"Anyway…" Hank turned back to Vanessa. "I was hoping you could fill me in on what the teens are into these days. Are we still into the nineties? Still on Snapchat? I need the deets."

Vanessa smiled, slow and sweetly malicious.

"Uh-huh," she said. "Let's do it."

Elle was able to gather herself enough to catch Hank before he left the room.

"Just so you know," she said, "I am pretty positive she is about to seriously mess with you."

"Oh, I know," Hank whispered back. "I'm obsessed with her already."

A lightness rose in Elle's chest as they disappeared around the corner, knowing Vanessa was in good hands.

Another tall, freckled face careened into the room, eyes bright.

"Uncle Jamie just pulled in. And he brought Bucky."

"Oh, *hell* yeah," Julie said.

"Dahlia, you have to meet Bucky." London grabbed Dahlia's hand.

"I've been waiting for years," Dahlia answered.

And like that, the kitchen emptied out, leaving one Elle Cochrane alone with a woman who was possibly Julie's mother and a simmering pot of butternut squash risotto. Elle sucked in a breath, feeling as if she had entered the eye of a hurricane, unsure how long she had to recover until another storm blew through.

She also, irrationally, felt the tiniest bit hurt that Julie hadn't told her more about London and Dahlia, so Elle would have made the connection sooner. That Julie hadn't grabbed her hand, like London had grabbed Dahlia's, to go meet Bucky. Had she been supposed to follow?

"I apologize for my daughter."

Elle twisted toward the woman with the gray bob.

"Charlotte Parker." Charlotte held out a hand with a warm smile.

"Elle Cochrane."

"Yes, we are well acquainted with who you are in this household, dear. But lovely to officially meet you."

Charlotte Parker was a good foot shorter than her, but she carried herself with a level of grace and control that immediately made Elle feel both intimidated and comforted. As with all of her favorite coaches, as with Dr. Jones, Elle was overtaken with the need for this woman to approve of her.

It was a feeling she understood. A welcome distraction from... whatever else it was she was feeling just then.

"Julie always has suffered from a lack of impulse control. I'm sure she meant to invite you to meet Bucky. You can go join them if you'd like."

"And Bucky is..." Elle ventured, hoping she didn't appear like the completely inept friend she so clearly was.

Charlotte rolled her eyes.

"My brother-in-law's ancient pot-bellied pig. Which he insists on bringing everywhere, even when we ask him not to. He's a special one, Jamie."

"Right." Elle nodded slowly.

"Or"—Charlotte tilted her head—"you can stay in here with me, and get a little break from the onslaught of new people? And pot-bellied pigs?"

"That... sounds nice."

"Come." Charlotte waved an arm toward a table in the corner before stepping toward the stove to give the risotto a stir. "Sit. Can I get you anything to drink? Coffee? Tea? Dahlia brought some fancy juice thing. Hibiscus something?"

"I'll try that." Elle settled into a chair at the table. Yes, she would most definitely drink a fancy juice thing of Dahlia Woodson's.

"I take it," Charlotte said as she poured a mug of coffee for herself, "that this is the first time you've seen my Julie and London in action together?"

"Yes." Elle looked out the window to her right, at the large array of cars out front. "She had mentioned her twin... but I didn't know... I'm sorry. I'm afraid we're still getting to know each other."

Charlotte let out a small snort that somehow still sounded elegant.

"Tom and I have been married over forty years." She pushed Elle's glass into her hands and sat on the opposite side of the table. "And I'm afraid we're still getting to know each other, too. The only person who should be apologizing is me, for not getting to warn you that my lovely twins act like twelve-year-olds in each other's presence. I wonder, in fact..." Charlotte blew on the mug cupped in her hands. "If Julie didn't keep you in the dark about London at least a little bit on purpose."

Charlotte smiled over her mug.

"It's no fault of London's, but I worry Julie's always felt a bit in their shadow. They've had quite a bit of attention, in particular, these last couple years. I would imagine that once Julie found you, she wanted to keep you to herself, for a little while."

"Huh."

Elle took a noisy gulp of her drink, embarrassed at her lack of eloquence in front of this woman. But she was unsure what Charlotte was saying here. The idea of Julie living in anyone's shadow was preposterous.

Yet. Elle remembered every uncertain look Julie had ever thrown her, the shrugging off of compliments, the nervous twisting of fingers. A feeling rose in her chest, one that had been living quietly there for weeks now, solidified a bit more each day. A need to hold Julie Parker and never let her go.

Charlotte leaned back in her chair.

"Although your surprise at meeting London here probably matched *my* surprise when Julie told me you were her assistant coach. And that she'd be bringing you today."

At this, Elle released a small laugh.

"For what it's worth, I found myself rather surprised about the coaching, too. But in terms of today, I hope we didn't impose—"

"Oh, no, no." Charlotte flapped a hand. "Please. You and Vanessa are welcome here anytime. I only..." She tilted her head, drumming her fingers on the table. They bore the most beautiful vintage rings: gold and garnet, silver and onyx. "I always wondered about Julie, of course. I try not to pry, but...I had begun to wonder if Julie would ever want a romantic relationship in her life. She's always been a spitfire, independent. I did worry about her being lonely, of course, but it would track, in a way."

Elle's heart thudded, a flush running up her neck.

"Oh, um, we're not—"

Charlotte barreled on, ignoring this.

"But of course, now that I see you here, it all makes sense."

"It does?"

Elle snapped her mouth closed as quickly as the two words had tumbled out of it. Probably not a good idea, when one was only practice-kissing one's daughter in secret, to appear so eager about... whatever Charlotte was implying.

"Of course." Charlotte's smile sparkled in her eyes now. And while Julie clearly took after her father in almost all physical aspects, she must have inherited this eye-sparkle directly from Charlotte. "Julie's always been competitive. Always believed she and those she loves deserve only the very best. She's loved you since she was fourteen." Charlotte lifted her mug once more. "Of course she waited to date until she met you. You're her own very best."

Something complicated—something mostly shaped like shame—hit Elle in the gut, as deep as the warmth on Charlotte Parker's face.

Elle was overwhelmingly inclined to agree. Julie *did* deserve the very best. And whatever she and Elle were doing now—stealing secret kisses in Elle's foyer—wasn't it. It wasn't it at all.

"I'm—" She swallowed. "I'm so sorry, Charlotte. Julie and I aren't dating."

"Of course you're not, dear," Charlotte said with a pat to Elle's hand. "Anyway," she went on, as if the topic was done, "I'm not

going to grill you about basketball, as much as I want to. Tell me"—
she patted Elle's hand again, turning it into a squeeze this time—
"about Vanessa."

Elle stared at Charlotte's hand, soft and smooth on top of her
own—she imagined Charlotte only used the finest hand cream—
until Charlotte withdrew a moment later.

"Julie's filled me in on the basics. But as someone who's raised
four teenagers myself..." Charlotte took another sip of coffee before
looking Elle directly in the eye. "How are you doing, Elle?"

Elle told herself it was the emotion of the day—holidays, family,
meeting new people—that made the threat of tears burn at the back
of her throat at this simplest of questions.

"I..." Elle gripped her glass between her hands. "I've never felt so
old. And so utterly incompetent, all at once."

Charlotte laughed.

"Sounds like you've got a solid handle on parenting, then."

"She's only been living with me for a little over a month, and I
can't seem to remember what my life was like before. Like, what did
I even *do* with myself?"

"Believe me, whenever you *do* have your house to yourself again,
you'll still have no idea. But you'll find ways to fill the time."

Elle took another sip of Dahlia's light, refreshing drink. Accord-
ing to Amber, Karly was following her case plan, attending all of
her appointments. Staying sober. Even if no one had given Elle any
implication about when it might happen, Elle assumed she would, at
some point, have her house to herself again.

It was simply becoming more and more difficult to picture it.

"I think we're doing okay," she eventually said. "I wish she would
talk to me more, but I understand that she might not ever want to.
I just wish I felt more...natural at it, you know? At being someone
she could trust."

The words poured out of Elle now that she had started, like water rushing toward a drain.

"I always remember my mom, my coaches, my favorite teachers having this aura of like...this was what they were born to do. They were adults who knew how to talk to kids, how to lead them. Julie has that, with the team. And it's not like I want to be Vanessa's mom, because I'm not. But it's like...I don't even know how to be a cool aunt to her, sometimes. Like I'm missing some inherent how-to-take-care-of-someone gene."

And oh god. Okay. Maybe it was past time for Elle to contact her therapist again.

Charlotte reached for Elle's hand once more. She held on a bit longer, a bit tighter this time.

"It's true. Some folks are born with that gene. And sometimes, it just looks different for different people. Some folks might be more natural at parts of this than others, but nobody's natural at all of it, honey. Nobody."

Elle didn't say anything, even though she knew she should. Charlotte was being incredibly kind.

But Rose had seemed natural at all of it. Charlotte sure as hell did, too.

"Comparison," Charlotte continued after a moment, "is as dangerous in parenting as it is in all other facets of life. And maybe you're not her mom. But you *are* parenting right now. You can give yourself credit for that, Elle."

Elle took another moment.

And then she squeezed Charlotte's hand back.

It felt like slipping into a warm bath after a long practice, letting Charlotte Parker soothe her bones.

At least, it was soothing for thirty more seconds.

Until Julie came roaring back into the room with a squealing pig, to which Charlotte immediately stood and objected, followed by London, who cursed and ran back to their risotto, and Vanessa, who ran to Elle to say, "Coach's family is *amazing*."

After that, Elle didn't quite have enough time to focus on tears, or guilt, or anything other than the slightly chaotic pulse of the Parker household and the fluttering of joy it brought to her heart.

CHAPTER TWENTY

Iris Caravalho shoved a bowl of caramel apple crisp into Julie's hands almost as soon as Julie walked through the door. "Scoop of ice cream on top?" Iris asked in lieu of a hello, as if Julie had been there for hours. She stood on her tippy-toes to give Julie a kiss on the cheek.

Julie took the bowl from Iris's hands—the bottom was still warm; it must have just come out of the oven—and shook her head.

"No, thank you. This is good."

"You sure?" Iris raised her eyebrows.

"I'm sure."

Even though Julie always had a scoop of ice cream on top. French vanilla was made for Iris Caravalho's caramel apple crisp.

But looking down at the gloopy goodness in her hands, Julie's stomach felt tight. Like her brain, overfull already from the day.

"Jules!"

Tiago swung an arm around Julie's neck, his voice a decibel or two too loud, as it always was on Thanksgiving night, when he'd had a little too much whiskey. Part of the reason Julie loved escaping to the Caravalhos' every Thanksgiving evening was that by the time she arrived, the entire family was "a bit in their cups," as Iris called it. Even Ben's dad, Luiz, who was kind but quiet as a mouse, tended to be extra jovial. The entire house was warm and loud, but less chaotic than the Parkers', full of an easy, loose energy Julie loved sinking into like a blanket.

Although, as Tiago clung to her a little too close, his smile a little too loopy, Julie was suddenly grateful beyond measure that she hadn't brought Elle and Vanessa here, even if that had never been part of the plan. They were probably already with Karly at the IHOP where they'd decided to meet. Julie hoped it was going okay.

It was just clear to her now, in a blink, that what had always seemed fun and inviting to her would be a nightmare for Vanessa.

"Listen. Jules." Tiago was still hanging around her neck. "I know we talked about this already, but I have to tell you, people are buzzing about Elle Cochrane coaching with you at East."

Julie froze.

"If I could just get *one* interview, Jules. It's such a good story! The entire state loved her for *years*, Jules! And then she disappeared! And now she shows up again almost a decade later in a Nashville high school gym?" Tiago shook his head. "That's a story, Jules. People want that story."

Julie extricated herself from Tiago's arm.

"I mean, sure," Tiago went on, "her performance in the W *was* pretty lackluster, but still—"

"No story," Julie forced herself to say, jaw tight. She clutched her bowl so she wouldn't drop it. Or toss it at Tiago's head. "Let it go, Tiago."

Tiago pouted. Iris chucked him on the arm.

"Pare, filho. Julie's not Elle's PR person, and you're not on the clock." Her expression softened as she reached out to squeeze Julie's forearm. "You've been doing a *fabulous* job out there this season, Julie."

Julie managed a smile.

"Thanks again for encouraging me to take the position, Iris. It's been fun. A pain in the ass sometimes, but fun."

"That's exactly how I'd sum up my entire career at East. Except more emphasis on the pain in the ass part. Now tell me." Iris's eyes narrowed. "What do you think our chances are against Wilson on Saturday?"

"Amor, your ice cream is melting. Oh, Julie! Happy Thanksgiving." Luiz entered the room, wrapping an arm around Iris's shoulders.

"Happy Thanksgiving," Julie echoed.

"I imagine these two have been hassling you enough. The boys are out on the back porch."

Luiz motioned with his head. Julie moved to follow his directions, but Iris grabbed her wrist first.

"Julie, hon, I actually have something else to talk to you about. Find me before you leave, okay? Promise?"

Julie nodded and, after receiving a pat and a smile from Iris, escaped the living room, passing Ben's younger sister, Carolina, having a heated conversation with one of their various cousins in the kitchen. Finally, Julie made it out the sliding glass doors to the Caravalhos' covered back porch.

Covered, however, didn't mean heated.

"Shit," Julie said. "It's freezing. Why are you losers sitting out here?"

"Julie!" Ben crowed from the saggy couch that had lived on the Caravalhos' back porch for forever. His head was nestled in the crook of his boyfriend Alexei's shoulder, while Alexei played absently with Ben's long dark hair. "Come snuggle!"

Weirdly, Julie hesitated. Only for a moment, dipping her spoon in and out of her apple crisp, before she moved toward the couch.

But Julie had never hesitated at an invitation to snuggle with Ben. It shouldn't have bothered her that Alexei was here, that he got to be the main event of the snugglefest. Alexei had been here last Thanksgiving, too. He and Ben had been together for over a year.

Julie was just off. She'd been off ever since she'd walked in on Elle and her mom holding hands in Julie's childhood kitchen, a sheen to Elle's eyes, like they'd just had some deep conversation. The details of which Julie could not stop wondering about. She'd been off ever since dinner, when Elle had put her hand on Julie's knee under the table any time someone had told an embarrassing story about her.

"Lex needed a moment of peace and quiet away from my family," Ben answered Julie's question as she sat at the empty end of the couch. He immediately threw his feet into her lap, almost knocking the bowl out of her hand. "Can you believe that?"

"Hi, Alexei," she said.

"Hi, Julie," he said, polite as ever. Although Julie noticed his cheeks were flushed, the color creeping beneath his blond beard even more than normal. Because sometimes, in his own quiet and adorable way, Alexei got into his cups too around the Caravalhos. Or maybe his cheeks were only red because it was fucking cold out here. Or because he was in love with her best friend and they both always had that flushed cheeks look about them when they were around each other. "How was your Thanksgiving?"

"It was fine." Julie rearranged the blanket that had been tangled around Ben's feet to more fully cover her lap.

"Oh my god." Ben struggled to sit up, only succeeding in grinding his heel into Julie's thigh. "How did it go with Elle and Vanessa? I meant to text you earlier to check in."

"It went...good? I think."

Her mind flashed back to an hour earlier, when Elle and Vanessa had finally left the Parkers'. Vanessa had jogged to the car, but Elle had hesitated, grabbing Julie's hand before she walked away.

"Hey," she'd said, twining their fingers together. Julie, as ever, without thought, let her. "Julie. Thank you, for today. It was... wonderful."

And then Elle had looked at her, like...she was contemplating kissing Julie again, right there on the Parkers' front porch.

Julie hadn't known what to say. She broke Elle's stare to look down at their interlocked fingers instead.

"See you at the game on Saturday?" Elle had said eventually.

"See you at the game," Julie had agreed, forcing a small smile. The thought had made her even more tired—she wanted to spend the rest of this weekend napping with Snoozles and doing nothing else—but also a tiny bit reassured. That they still had this one thing—basketball—that made sense.

And then Elle had dropped Julie's hand and walked to her car.

Where, it occurred to Julie, Vanessa had been waiting, likely watching them stand there holding hands.

"How's the Elle situation in general?" Ben waggled his eyebrows. "The, uh, practicing?"

Julie stuffed apple crisp in her mouth. She had broken, after the whole *You've Got Mail* night, and shared some information with Ben. She still wanted it to be private, something just between her and Elle, but...she also had to tell *someone*.

Ben had first said, "Wait. And this is the person you've been texting with? That you already possibly have feelings for? Oh, *Jules*," and hung his head in his hands. Which had been...less than encouraging. But then, after a while, he'd said, "No, you know what? This could work for you."

"Ben is very invested in the Elle situation," Alexei said now. Ben turned and shushed him. Very loudly.

"I am also invested in the Elle situation," Alexei added after a moment.

"Lex!" Ben slapped Alexei's arm with a gasp, his reproving look turning to glee. Alexei smiled, a bit pleased with himself. "I knew you were!"

Julie contemplated how to answer. How was the Elle situation?

I don't know what's happening.

Sometimes, it felt clear. She and Elle were co-coaches and friends. Elle was particularly nice to her, because she'd learned Julie was particularly pathetic. But it was working out for Julie. The Bobcats were doing great, and she'd discovered she maybe didn't hate kissing. All in all, a productive season thus far.

And then sometimes, Elle kissed her, and massaged her feet, and looked at Julie like she wanted to keep kissing her, and Julie increasingly fell asleep remembering the feel of Elle's lips on her neck, of Elle's hands slipping underneath Julie's clothes.

Sometimes, Julie started to wonder...if maybe Elle wasn't only doing this for practice. If she'd want to do it for real, if Julie only asked.

It still seemed implausible, Elle still impossibly out of Julie's league, but...sometimes, her heart said, *maybe.*

But I'm afraid if I push, if I ask questions, if this is all just in my head...

I'll lose whatever this is that I've been lucky enough to have.

"Is it okay if I just want to hear about your guys's day?"

Ben turned back toward her, brows creased in concern. But Alexei nodded, like he understood.

"Yes," he answered. "The day started with Carolina getting into an argument with Uncle Jaco about gun control at nine a.m."

Ben groaned, slapping a hand over his face.

"Why would you even bring that up? I had been living inside the bliss of forgetting that ever happened."

"Julie wanted a report." Alexei shrugged. "But yes. It was extremely uncomfortable. Then Iris made her delicious egg pudding that I never remember the name of, but which is very sexy when Ben says it."

Okay, yeah, Alexei was definitely in his cups.

"Sericaia," Ben purred with a grin, and gross.

"And then—"

"Oh my god," Julie interrupted, spoon clattering into her bowl. "Sorry to interrupt, Alexei; your reporting is excellent so far. But—" She turned toward the two of them. "Ben." She swallowed past the lump in her throat. She was *not* going to end this day by crying at the Caravalhos'. "Ben, this is your last Thanksgiving here."

Ben blinked, staring at Julie before catapulting out of Alexei's embrace. He grabbed Julie's arm.

"No. No, Jules. Alexei and I have already talked about it. We'll fly back for Thanksgiving next year. And Christmas. Or we'll alternate, if we can't afford both. But no, Julie, our family's here. I'll always come back."

Julie picked up her spoon, dragged it around her mushy apples, unable to look Ben in the eye. She had spent every Thanksgiving night with Ben for the last fifteen years, right here, in this house.

I'll always come back.

"Okay," she said quietly.

Ben's answer should have been comforting. But for some reason, she only felt more sad.

You only said *I'll always come back* when you were already gone.

Maybe...today had been too much. She was still ending it at the Caravalhos'. She had still made fun of London for making their fancy, delicious food. But it had already felt different from all the Thanksgivings before, with Elle and Vanessa there, with Dahlia's entire family there, too, like...like everything was changing too quickly for her to hold on to.

Even if Ben flew back home, she couldn't help but feel that next Thanksgiving would feel different, too. Maybe he and Alexei would get married, just like London and Dahlia. Everyone would be even more secure and happy, and she'd be left alone in the backyard, petting Bucky and wondering what Elle and Vanessa were doing at Tricia's house.

She stood.

"I'm so sorry," she said, suddenly needing to be alone with Snoozles and no one else. "It's just been a really long day, and I...Can we catch up later? This weekend, maybe? You too, Alexei," she added, looking at him, wanting him to know she loved him, too. Because of course she did. She had from the start. "Are you still here this weekend?"

He nodded. "I leave on Sunday."

Ben stood, his brow still furrowed in concern. But he wrapped Julie in a hug without protest. "Of course, Jules," he said into her shoulder, holding her close. "Saturday. We'll get together Saturday."

"I have a game."

"We'll come. We'll come to the game and then take you out after?"

She managed to nod. "That sounds nice."

"Good," he said. "I love you."

"I love you, too."

She made it all the way home before she remembered Iris had wanted to talk to her.

Julie picked up Snoozles from the couch and turned off the living room light. She would call Iris tomorrow.

She'd call Iris, and then she'd focus on getting ready to face Wilson on Saturday. These were things Julie could do.

She stared at her phone before she turned off her bedside lamp. She wanted to text Elle and see how IHOP had gone.

She flipped it over instead, clicking off the light.

CHAPTER TWENTY-ONE

I was thinking," Elle said on Monday, once the team had trooped into the locker room after sprints. "It's been a while since our first practice date at Bella's."

Julie gathered the last errant basketball and placed it onto the rack at the side of the court.

The past weekend had gone much better, after Thanksgiving. The game against Wilson had gone south in the second half, but Ben had kept his promise about going out afterward. It ended up being a big group thing, Ben and Lex and London and Dahlia; Hank, who was still in town and delighted to be invited; and some other friends of Ben's he normally tried to get together any time Lex was in town: Khalil and Jesse, Laynie Rose and Reina. Julie had been more than happy to catch up with them all, a chance to get out of her own head.

They'd taken up a huge table in the back room of the restaurant, stayed for hours. It had been loud and easy and *fun*, and the melancholy that had seized her Thanksgiving night had disappeared into the ether.

And interacting with Elle had been relatively smooth, uncomplicated, during the game on Saturday and then practice today. Routine, free of touches or lingering looks. It sounded like IHOP with Karly on Thursday night had gone well, and Elle had been in an almost buoyant mood, full of easy smiles, laughs with the players.

But the mention of the practice date made tension rise to Julie's skin again, a vague, uneasy sensation, like goose bumps after hearing an unexpected noise.

"This is true," she said, trying to sound casual.

"And practice, by definition, is repetition," Elle said.

Julie smiled as she messed with the basketballs, a light heat dancing into her cheeks. "I've heard that."

"Vanessa's going over to Katelyn's tonight for a while to hang out."

Julie lifted her head. "She is? That's great."

"I know." Elle smiled, looking at the locker room doors. "Katelyn just got some comic-manga thing they're both excited about. I didn't understand most of the words Vanessa said when she asked me about it. Anyway." Elle picked up a ball from the rack and twirled it on a finger. "Want to come over and watch the Duke-UNC game with me? I know it might not sound like much, but coming from a lesbian, it's definitely a date."

Julie bit her lip. And grabbed the ball from Elle's braggy finger.

She had to stop being weird. Stop overthinking things. She didn't have to figure anything out, when it came to *actually* dating, whether that be with Elle or someone else or no one, until after the season anyway. Regardless of anything else, hanging out with Elle now, just the two of them, made her *happy*. She could be happy.

And she'd been planning on watching the game anyway.

"Can we get Cook Out?"

Elle made a face. Which she immediately attempted to smooth away. And failed.

"Um. Sure."

"How about I get Cook Out, and you can make some barley."

Elle rolled her eyes. And grabbed the basketball back before a grin returned to her mouth.

Which was how, an hour later, Julie found herself on Elle's couch, stomach full, feet back in Elle's lap, and college basketball on the TV.

If this was a date, it was one Julie could handle.

And she had to admit, with the absence of Vanessa from the house . . . it did feel date-ish. More intimate somehow than the times Julie had lounged on this couch before.

Or maybe Julie just became a bit more comfortable each time she found herself here.

"When you were a kid," Elle said midway through the second quarter, "tell me you at least had some posters of Candace, too."

Julie grinned into her favorite pillow. "Yeah. A small one."

"Chamique?"

"She was a little before my time."

Elle shook her head with a disappointed *tsk*.

"I got to play with Candace, once. It was probably the closest I ever came to a spiritual experience."

Part of Julie wanted to jump off the couch and shout. Her feet were currently cuddled in the lap of someone who had played with *Candace Parker*. That deserved a shout.

But more than anything, Julie wanted Elle to keep talking. About this previous life she tried to pretend, most of the time, had never happened, but which Julie knew was important. Not just to Julie, and to the state of Tennessee, but to Elle.

"Do you keep up with it?" Julie nodded her chin toward the TV. "College, the W, anything. I was already planning on watching this game tonight, but I have to admit I was a little surprised you were, too."

Elle tapped her fingers against Julie's shin. She exhaled long and slow before she answered.

"I always keep up with what's happening with Tennessee. College in general, although not super closely. I couldn't tell you the current rankings, but . . . damn. South Carolina."

Elle exhaled an almost disbelieving puff of air. Julie nodded in agreement.

And waited, sensing Elle had more to say.

"Mara keeps up more," Elle added after a minute. A rueful smile curved her lips. "Has not-so-secretly wanted me to keep up more, too, so we can gossip about everything together. Sometimes I feel like I've been withholding this important part of our friendship from her for a long time and it's..." She swallowed. "Not fair, probably. But I'm going to try to change that, I think."

Julie curled her toes against Elle's thigh. Which she hoped Elle took as a sign of encouragement.

"I don't watch the W." Elle shifted, leaning her temple against her fist. "Which I also feel guilty about. I have so many former friends and teammates..." She shook her head. "When I gave it up for myself, I didn't mean to give up my support for them. It's just hard for me. Puts my brain in a weird place."

Julie watched the game for another minute, debating what to say. Maybe she should let the conversation move on to another topic. Elle had already been generous in what she'd shared. But...fork, Julie had to know.

"Is it hard for you," she started slowly, "because of what happened with the Wreckers? Or because of Sophie?"

Elle stilled.

It was possible that, over the last week, Julie had spent too much time googling Sophie Holiday. A shooting guard who had transferred to Tennessee from Oklahoma the year Sophie and Elle were both seniors.

It had been widely known, back in the college basketball blogs and social media channels Julie used to follow, that the two had dated. But Julie had forgotten about it until Rose had reminded her last week.

Sophie Holiday was a star now. She'd played for the Boston Blizzards for the last ten years, had helped lead them to the playoffs the last five.

Julie couldn't stop wondering what that felt like for Elle. What, exactly, had happened between them.

But she hadn't been able to ask until now. Because even thinking about it had made Julie feel flustered. Jealous. A relationship thing she hadn't asked for, feelings she didn't want.

"Sophie," Elle repeated. Julie couldn't read her tone. Was she annoyed? Had Julie fucked up? Julie had probably fucked up.

"I'm sorry," she blurted. "I swear I'm not being like…weird and stalkery or anything; you don't have to tell me a thing; it's just… Rose said something to me the other day about her."

With a groan, Elle flopped her head onto the back of the couch.

"*Rose.* Of course she did."

Elle stayed like that, blinking up at the ceiling for a moment more, while Julie's stomach twisted into knots. Finally, Elle leaned forward to pick up the remote and pause the game.

"I started dating Sophie when she transferred to the Vols our senior year. Which you might already know, since we weren't necessarily quiet about it."

Julie nodded, afraid to say anything else out loud.

"As previously mentioned, I'd slept around a lot throughout college, but Sophie was different from the start. It was a real relationship. Until I went to the Wreckers."

Elle sighed, still staring at the TV. Julie scrambled her feet away, tucking herself into her end of the couch. After that kind of sigh, it felt right to give Elle space for this story.

"As also previously mentioned, I was a bit of a mess the whole time I was in Milwaukee. Sophie had fallen in love with the basketball star at the top of the world, and suddenly, she was dating a depressed, unsuccessful woman who was bad at picking up the phone or wanting to do anything when she visited. I honestly have no idea why or how we stayed together for so long. I suspect she'd already started seeing other people in Boston, or at least sleeping with other people. Which I wouldn't blame her for; my sex drive disappears whenever my depression ramps up, and I was super not fun in that arena those days. Our relationship made me feel guilty and awful, but I was so depressed I didn't know how to end it. Getting out of bed felt impossible most of the time; I was not equipped to navigate a breakup. Anyway, she finally decided to dump me when I woke up from my ACL surgery."

Julie had been tracking this story so far, but here her brain screeched to a halt.

"Like . . . literally? When you woke up?"

"Yeah. The funny part was"—Elle actually laughed a little—"we were playing the Blizzards when it happened. My injury, I mean. She saw the whole thing happen, up close and personal. So she was able to come to the hospital. And she stayed with me, held my hand, all the normal stuff. But when I woke up from surgery, still totally out of it, she was there, looking at me, and she just said, 'I can't do this anymore,' and she was gone. I thought I'd dreamed the whole thing at first. So yeah, Rose has never forgiven her."

Julie could only stare at her. Elle was somehow *smiling*.

"Elle," Julie said after a beat. "What the *fuck*."

And Elle laughed again. "Look, we were young, and it'd been a long time coming. I don't harbor any ill feelings toward her at all. It fucked me up for a while, but honestly, I probably fucked her up more, with what a shitty girlfriend I was at the end. I should've let her go a lot earlier, so she wouldn't have been forced to break up with me like that when she realized I was *really* never going to be the person I used to be."

"But that's—" Julie sputtered. "That's—"

Enraging. Sophie stopped loving her because she wasn't a star anymore? Because she was suffering through a depressive episode? Broke up with her because she tore her ACL?

What the *fuck*.

"Julie." Finally, Elle looked at her. "It's okay. It was a long time ago."

"Did you love her?"

And fuck, where the fuck had that question come from? Why did it matter?

Elle's smile faded, but she didn't look away.

"Yeah," she said. "I did. And I'm happy she's doing so well now, even if I can't watch it. It's what she always wanted, what she deserves."

"Fuck *deserves*," Julie spat out. "You deserved it, too." She hoped Sophie fucking Holiday never won a single fucking championship.

Elle reached out a hand. Wrapped it around Julie's ankle.

"It was a long time ago," she repeated, rubbing a thumb along Julie's calf, and why was Elle comforting Julie right now? Julie should be comforting *her*; she wanted to crawl into Elle's lap and—and—

"Have you dated other people? Since then?"

And Julie was blushing, and she didn't know why she was asking all these things; she was being so inappropriate, and Duke was going to win this fucking game, and she wanted to break something.

"Here and there." Elle shrugged, still rubbing Julie's leg, still looking at her with patience. "I had to focus on getting myself together first, on coming back here and recovering from the injury, taking care of the house and building a new life for myself. Eventually, I realized that most of my past relationships had been too wrapped around my basketball life, everything too close and insular and, ultimately, unhealthy. So I tried dating some non-basketball people."

The smile that ghosted Elle's lips was wry, her voice turning soft when she said, "It hasn't fully worked out so far."

And then she withdrew, the loss of her hands leaving Julie's ankles cold as Elle picked up the remote and pressed Play on the game.

Julie couldn't move, couldn't stop staring at the side of Elle's face.

She was hot and frozen all at once, at a loss of what to do, how to reach over and touch Elle like she wanted to.

Until eventually, Elle once more took charge, reaching over without glancing away from the TV to hook a hand around Julie's ankle again. She tugged this time, said "Come on" in a half whisper. "Come back." And Julie did, her legs unfurling toward Elle's hands, her back slumping until her head hit her favorite pillow again.

The Duke and UNC players were running back onto the court at Carmichael Arena from halftime. The Tar Heels were down by six, and Julie started to regret, more than ever, telling Elle about her dumb freshman-year kiss, telling Elle about anything. Elle had been in love, had experienced real heartache and loss, and she must think Julie was the biggest child to ever almost reach thirty years old.

Julie was growing lost in her thoughts, barely able to follow the game, able to focus only on the feeling of Elle's fingers tracking all the way up to Julie's knee and back down again, a tickling sensation Julie somehow felt in her skull, a low, pleasant buzzing along her scalp. When Elle spoke again, Julie had to blink, as if shaking her way out of a fog. She was pretty sure Elle had said, "Can I ask you something now?"

Julie nodded against the pillow. "Yeah."

Elle traced a pattern along Julie's calf that tickled so much Julie's leg accidentally kicked out, smacking the arm of the couch, and Elle murmured an apology over a small laugh.

"I've just been thinking about London being your twin."

And Julie froze again, remembering Elle's reaction to London and Dahlia on Thanksgiving, the jealousy that had washed over her.

"I'm sorry, by the way, that I didn't make the connection sooner," Elle said. Julie almost interrupted her, almost confessed to purposely never bringing up *Chef's Special*, to never acknowledging out loud to Elle that everyone in Julie's life was so much more impressive than Julie was. "Although I have to confess," Elle went on, "that I have a million questions I want to ask them now. Like when, exactly, *did* they and Dahlia start hooking up during filming? Because fans have a lot of theories."

Julie groaned and covered her eyes. "Please don't ever ask them that."

Elle squeezed her ankle. "I won't. Sorry." The squeeze turned into a massage as Elle continued. "What I meant to say is that it was clear to anyone who watched the show that London has gone through a lot of identity searching. Is confident talking about it. And if you're close . . . I'm just wondering about the questions you have about yourself. If you've ever talked to them about it, if you could've worked through stuff together."

Julie lowered her hands from her face. Stared steadfastly at the screen.

"London never included me in any of that stuff. Which is fair; it's personal. I mean, a lot of their journey was obvious; I always knew they felt different, but they just kind of . . . took it all inward."

Julie tried to keep her voice casual, chest tight, knowing it was selfish to be hurt by any of it.

"And when they did figure it all out . . . honestly, I think being on the show helped them a lot. They weren't always as confident in talking about being nonbinary or pansexual until the show. So." Julie shrugged the shoulder that wasn't smooshed into the couch. "I guess . . . I wasn't really part of that, either."

Elle squeezed Julie's calf. "Hey. Julie. I'm sorry; I didn't mean to make you upset."

"I'm not," Julie lied.

"And you know," Elle said after a pause, "Julie . . . I'm sure you were a bigger part of London accepting themself than you even know."

Duke got a three-pointer.

"Sure," she said.

She could feel Elle watching her, saw, out of the corner of her eye, how Elle was biting her lip.

"Although," Elle said after a long moment, slow and careful, "I was mainly curious why *you* hadn't talked to them. About yourself. Which, even if London kept their own journey private...you can still do, you know."

Julie remembered London's words from the studio that night.

You know you can talk to me about anything anytime, too, right?

Had they and Elle talked on Thanksgiving or something? Conspired to bully Julie into talking about her feelings?

Julie curled her hand, hiding underneath her chest, into a fist.

"I don't know," she said at length. "I don't know why I've never talked to London. Why I can't be all easy-peasy casual about choosing labels for myself. Why I'm always a million years behind everyone else. I don't fucking know."

"Julie."

Elle didn't say anything else. Just stared at her, rubbing her thumb over Julie's knee.

After a minute, Julie exhaled.

"Sorry," she mumbled.

"You don't have anything to be sorry about," Elle said, voice almost a whisper. "I'm sorry I pushed."

"You didn't—"

"No, I did. And I'm sorry."

Duke got called for a foul. The Heels missed a free throw.

"There's nothing wrong with you, Julie," Elle said in that same half whisper that was slowly going to kill her. "You're not behind on anything. There's nothing for you to be behind *on*. There's nothing, and no one, you have to track your own life by."

Julie inhaled. Held the breath in her lungs before letting it out.

"Okay," she said, wanting to drop it, knowing she was being petulant. Wanting to be able to believe her.

Wanting, suddenly, *Elle*.

Not that Julie didn't normally, if she was honest, want Elle, but her fingers all over Julie's legs, *again*, that rasp in her voice as she showered Julie with kindness, the fact that she trusted Julie with her past...

Julie moved her foot. Rubbed it against Elle's thigh. Once, twice. She didn't know how else to say it.

But Elle must have heard the message. Because after a moment, Elle's hand traveled back to Julie's knee.

Where it paused, just for a second, before continuing on, underneath Julie's basketball shorts. Up the side of Julie's thigh.

Julie kept her eyes glued to the game. Her breath caught in her throat. She thought, *please*.

She was twisted in an odd direction, cheek smashed into the pillow, halfway on her stomach. Elle's fingers kept moving, pausing every inch or two to ghost a circle over her skin, until they reached Julie's ass.

Elle paused. Her other hand wrapped more firmly around Julie's ankle, pinning her there, while Elle shifted, leaning over to have better access to Julie's backside. Julie was trying to keep it cool here, hoping Elle couldn't hear the pounding of her heart, the hitches of her breath, but when Elle squeezed her ass over her underwear, a small sigh escaped her lips, followed by a barely audible "That feels good." Because it *did*. Elle squeezed harder in response, so it almost hurt, gave the other cheek the same treatment, and Julie closed her eyes briefly in wonder at this new knowledge, that she liked when Elle Cochrane squeezed her ass.

And when Elle moved her palm toward Julie's hip, pressing, Julie understood. Made herself turn, finally tearing her eyes away from the screen, lying on her back and looking up at Elle even though her body felt like it was made of lead, even though looking at Elle terrified her.

Elle released her ankle as she shifted more fully over Julie, fingers trailing up Julie's side.

"You okay?" she whispered, those iceberg-blue eyes tracing over Julie's face, and Julie hoped whatever she saw there was okay, that she wasn't somehow embarrassing herself.

Julie licked her lips while staring at Elle's. "Practice, right?"

She didn't know if she said it to reassure herself. To give herself the space to relax, to let herself feel safe and able to have this.

Or if she said it because she wanted Elle to object. Because she wanted Elle to tell her that this was real. That she wanted her, too.

But Elle only looked back at her, running a finger over Julie's brow.

"Whatever you need it to be, Julie," she eventually said.

And Julie was too turned on to interpret that, so she only whispered, "Okay. Yeah. I'm okay."

Elle leaned down, and when her lips met Julie's, Julie sighed again, opening her mouth to Elle immediately, because she had *missed* this. She knew it had only been a few days, technically, since the last time she'd gotten to kiss Elle, but now that she was more used to it, being this close, the feel of Elle's mouth against hers, Julie craved it. She craved it more than she thought she could.

Before Julie was ready for it, Elle was breaking away, leaning back, but it turned out she was only leaving Julie's body cold so she could take off her sweatshirt. And thank whatever spirits existed for that. Because Elle was wearing a tight-fitting gray T-shirt underneath that sweatshirt. And while Julie hadn't quite known what to do with her hands until this point, she reached out now and finally ran her fingers over that rose tattoo on Elle's forearm. Because she was practicing, and she could.

Elle sank back down, returning her mouth to Julie's, trailing her lips to Julie's neck. Julie moved her hands to Elle's hair, and Elle made a low sound in her throat that made Julie prouder than she had perhaps ever been. Elle's hands were underneath Julie's shirt, and Julie's blood was thumping in her veins, in between her legs, where Elle eventually moved a hand, pressing over Julie's shorts.

Julie inhaled sharply.

"Oh god."

The words were out of her mouth before she could take them back. Elle pushed away, looking down at Julie's face, hand now only hovering where Julie ached.

"Is that a good 'oh god' or a bad 'oh god'?" Elle rubbed a thumb over Julie's inner thigh.

"I..." Julie swallowed. "I don't know."

Because it had felt incredible. She knew it had. Part of Julie wanted Elle's hand back there immediately.

But also...oh *god*.

Elle watched her a moment more, brow slightly creased, before she leaned down to kiss Julie on the forehead. "Okay," she said softly. "That's okay."

And she retreated back to her side of the couch. Picked up Julie's feet again and took a sip of her water, eyes focused on the Blue Devils and the Heels.

Julie lay there, knees still too far apart, still breathing a bit too heavily, before she got ahold of herself and flopped over onto her side again, legs firmly clamped together.

"You okay?" Elle ran a finger along the arch of Julie's foot. "I'm sorry if I got carried away. I didn't mean to...We can just watch the game, Julie."

Julie tried to get her thoughts in order, except it was hard to think when all the nerve endings in her body were still vibrating.

Had it been embarrassing to be touched there because she didn't want it? Or simply because she wasn't used to it? Because she was still learning how to show her desire to another person? To trust herself enough to?

"No," Julie heard herself say. "I don't want to watch the game."

Well, that was an untruth; Julie absolutely wanted to watch this game, but events were superseding that right now.

She could do this. This was exactly what she had wanted, a chance to try. Elle was giving her a chance. Why was Julie being such a freak about this?

"You're not being a freak about this," Elle said. Because Julie was now so discombobulated that she was apparently saying things out loud without even realizing it.

"I said that out loud, huh?"

"You did." Elle ran her hand over Julie's calf again. "But I promise. You're just fine. You only ever have to do what you're comfortable with."

"But we're just practicing, right? And I want to practice. You're not going to judge me if I'm bad at this, or weird about this."

Elle looked at her for a long, serious-feeling moment before she affirmed, "I'm not going to judge you, Julie."

Julie nodded. Took a deep breath. And said, "Come back."

Elle kept looking at her, waiting, maybe, for Julie to change her mind. But Julie didn't want to carry this ache between her legs like a secret until she could get home and touch herself. Julie didn't know if she had a sex drive exactly like other people's, but she had one *now*.

"Please," she said. "Come back."

Elle leaned down then, to kiss the side of Julie's calf, the inside of her knee. When her tongue made its way up Julie's thigh, Julie tensed, uncertain if she was ready for *that*. But then Elle moved, crawling over her, pushing Julie's knees to the side as she made way for her body, like her lips on Julie's thigh had just been a stepping stone to getting them back to Julie's mouth.

Elle kissed her softly, that series of gentle kisses around Julie's mouth Elle liked to do, that let Julie relax back into the cushions, like she could lie there forever, inside the heat of Elle's body and the dim light of the room.

Elle's fingers inched back under Julie's shirt, her thumb swiping across the skin above Julie's hip, and Julie loved it just as much this time as the other times, a gust of breath escaping her mouth. Elle's lips were at her jaw now, and then, as her fingers began to travel across Julie's stomach, at her earlobe, sucking it into her mouth at the same time her hand navigated underneath the waistband of Julie's shorts.

"Still okay?" Elle released her ear to whisper, fingers grazing over Julie's underwear.

"Fuck," Julie said, a little more loudly than she had intended. "I mean..." She swallowed. "Yeah."

Elle huffed a small laugh into Julie's neck before she started moving her fingers with purpose, tracing a line up and down Julie's slit, and Julie knew, she could tell, that Elle's fingers were getting slick, even through her underwear, and she hoped Elle only found that hot, a compliment, instead of an embarrassment. Because it felt a little embarrassing to Julie, even though she knew it shouldn't, that it was just—

Elle's fingers pressed in a circle around Julie's clit, and Julie's head fell back, her mouth dropping open.

"This is how I like to start touching myself too," she said after a beat, and she couldn't quite believe she had said that, but she couldn't take it back now. "Over my underwear."

Elle's forehead was pressed against Julie's neck, and she paused, taking a deep breath before her fingers kept moving. "Yeah?" she whispered. "Tell me how you touch yourself, Julie."

She was moving her fingers in a wide circle now, a tease around where Julie really needed it, before moving in and circling just right, making Julie gasp before retreating again, and it was driving Julie wild.

"Um." Julie tried to find her breath, her words. "It depends. On how much I want it. Sometimes just using my hand is enough."

"And if it's not?"

"I have a toy."

"Just one?"

"Well," Julie said. "It works."

Elle bit her neck. It wasn't hard enough to truly hurt, but sharp enough to be a surprise, to make Julie's eyes wide as Elle moved her mouth back to Julie's, her lips and her tongue hungry this time. She was still kissing her as she slid her hand underneath Julie's underwear, and when she touched her skin to sensitive skin Julie moaned into Elle's mouth.

Elle moved back an inch, so their lips were only brushing as she moved her fingers down to Julie's center.

And Julie almost said something, not because she was against it, but because when she did use her toy, she often had a hard time navigating it inside herself. Typically, she just held it against her clit until she was done.

But apparently, she was so turned on at this moment, or Elle was more adept with her hands than Julie was with her own body, that she slid a finger in easily, followed by another, and it hardly even pinched, only felt good.

"Fuck," Julie said again.

Elle shifted her fingers, pushed them in deeper, only uncomfortable for a moment until she was situated like she wanted, so she could rub her palm against Julie's clit. It was less precise than her fingers, but Julie didn't particularly care. Julie was too busy fraying at the edges, grasping at the sides of the couch, to particularly care about any of the details anymore.

Elle whispered against her lips.

"You're so beautiful, Julie."

And it was the only moment, out of all the moments, that Julie wished she could snatch out of the air and take away.

Because she wasn't. Julie knew she looked like a kid. London had somehow been able to take their baby-face-and-freckles DNA and make it look cool, but Julie had never had the same level of skill. Had never tried as hard at making her appearance match how she wanted to look. Maybe because she didn't know how she wanted to look. A picture of Julie Parker at sixteen and a picture of her now would look nearly identical.

Elle, on the other hand, looked hotter than she had ever looked, her face half in shadow, her curls hanging over her forehead, whispering against Julie's eyelashes, the sharp lines of her face only more magical in the dark.

Just looking at her felt brave.

And even as unlikely as it felt, that someone as hot as her would be turned on by someone like Julie, Julie didn't doubt that Elle was enjoying this. She had never doubted, not really, that Elle had enjoyed all of their practicing. Her heavy breathing, the color that flushed the edges of her cheeks, weren't made-up.

But there was a difference between practicing and pretending. Between going along for the ride and acting. It was a difference Julie might not have been able to explain in exact detail, but it was a difference she felt in her bones. *Beautiful* pushed it too close to pretending for Julie. And Julie never wanted Elle to pretend.

But then Elle's mouth was moving, sucking at Julie's ear again, at her neck, and Julie was pushing against Elle's hand, and it was overwhelming, all of it, and she was—she was—

"*Elle.*"

She couldn't stop saying it, didn't know why; she *needed* to say it, felt so raw and open saying it, like just repeating Elle's name was the most honest and intimate thing she'd ever done, until she couldn't speak anymore, and Elle was maybe saying something back, but Julie couldn't hear. Julie had never been this gone yet so simultaneously present in every inch of her limbs.

And when she regained some sense of awareness, she discovered her own hand was there, over her underwear, holding Elle's fingers in place, keeping them still and pressed against her as she rode out the last of the waves. Until she said, "Okay, okay," and Elle retreated, giving her space.

Julie's toes were still tingling, her pulse still thudding in her ears, when Elle said, "I just need to—"

Julie blinked up at her, rapidly becoming conscious of what was happening. That Elle's hand was now lost underneath her own waistband, moving inside her sweatpants, just above Julie's still quivering body.

"Oh shit," Julie breathed.

"Yeah," Elle agreed. And then, "This won't take long."

Julie wanted to kiss her, badly, her mind suddenly overtaken by a whole litany of brazen things she wanted to do, but Elle's face was too far away to kiss, and Julie was still too boneless, one leg trapped between Elle's knees, while the other had fallen off the couch.

Her hands took over instead, reaching for the hem of that gray T-shirt without the apparent help of Julie's brain, and when her hands brushed the smooth softness of Elle's belly, Elle's head fell back, lips parting, and Julie's own mouth opened in wonder. This was...getting to touch Elle while she looked like this...this was even better than anything that had just happened, somehow. Julie could do *this* forever.

When she inched her hands upward, and Elle said, "My breasts are super sensitive," Julie almost came again right then.

Elle had small breasts, as opposed to Julie's, which had always felt slightly too large for her body. She'd tried touching them, in her masturbating experiments, but it had never done much for her. She normally kept them stuffed away in whatever sports bra she could find that was supportive but comfortable enough to not be confining.

It only surprised her a little that Elle was wearing something lacy, a barely there bralette thing, but as soon as Julie touched it she was obsessed with it. She was picturing Elle now, in every outfit she'd ever worn, every sweatshirt and blazer, every butch-adjacent button-down, with this intricate lace beneath, and she wanted to explode. She wanted to see it with nothing else. Just lace, bracketed by Elle's biceps.

When Julie ran her thumbs over Elle's nipples, hard pebbles beneath the delicate swirls of fabric, Elle shuddered and said, "Pinch them."

"Fuck," Julie muttered. It was a little awkward trying to reach both, as Elle's arm, still working away inside her sweatpants, was partially obstructing Julie's way. But she did what she could, rolling Elle's nipples between her thumb and forefinger, pinching lightly, afraid to apply too much pressure and hurt her.

"Oh god," Elle cried, eyes closed as her head fell forward. "*Julie.*"

Julie left one hand underneath Elle's shirt, still toying with Elle's breast, the other escaping so she could run her fingers through Elle's curls. So she could see Elle's face better as she came. Mouth open, brow creased, high-pitched breathy noises escaping her throat.

It felt almost as intense as her own orgasm, getting to watch this one. Made Julie feel more haywire than ever. It was so private, so honest; it almost felt wrong, that Julie was looking, that she was a part of this at all. A feeling akin to panic seized the back of her neck.

But if she allowed herself to sink into the moment—when Julie let herself forget herself completely, for just a moment, she knew—

This was beautiful.

Elle collapsed when she was done, face pressed into Julie's shoulder, and the panic that had clutched Julie's neck crescendoed into something different, something bittersweet. It had been too fast, and there was still so much Julie wanted to know. If there were other parts of Elle's body she liked to have touched. What it would feel like, how Elle would react, if Julie covered those nipples with her mouth. How she looked when she wasn't hunched over a couch in a mostly dark room. How Elle liked to touch herself when she was alone.

After a moment, hesitantly, Julie ran a hand over Elle's back.

The sounds of the TV came back into Julie's consciousness. She caught her breath, blinked at the ceiling. Her chest was tight underneath Elle's weight. And as the heat of the moment faded, Julie couldn't quite believe any of that had happened.

Elle pushed herself up. Leaned an elbow on the back of the couch, looked down at Julie. Julie had never felt so unprotected, like an errant wind could blow her away.

"How do you feel?" Elle asked.

"Really, really vulnerable."

A soft smile curved Elle's lips. "Thank you for trusting me with that."

Julie swallowed. Tried to hold on to the moment, even as she rapidly, by the second, returned to feeling ridiculous, not cut out for any of this.

"You were hot, though."

Elle's smile grew, her eyes hooded; lazy, punch-drunk. "So were you."

Julie didn't know what to say to that.

Elle stared at her a moment more. Her smile faded as she tucked a stray hair behind Julie's ear.

"Was it too much?"

And Julie answered, honestly, "I don't know."

She added, after a moment, in a whisper, "It felt really good." Because it had, and she didn't want to deny that.

Elle's eyes searched hers. "It can still be a lot."

"Yeah." Julie swallowed again. "I think...I need time to process it."

Elle swept a hand over Julie's temple, feather-light, barely there.

"Of course."

"I feel safe, with you." Julie probably didn't need to keep talking. But she wanted Elle to know she wasn't regretting it. Didn't want Elle looking at her in concern, like Julie was something she had to fix. This was Julie's thing to figure out. "I liked watching you."

Elle's smile returned, even gentler this time. "I liked you watching me." And then, "Will you stay? You can stay down here, if you're not comfortable moving to my bed. I just..." She trailed off before meeting Julie's eyes. "I want to make you pancakes."

Julie's heart thumped. She was so thoroughly tired, so warm and overwhelmed, that even contemplating leaving this couch, either in the next eight hours or ever, hadn't yet entered her brain. But being asked to stay in such a way still felt like a surprise.

"With chocolate chips," Elle added a minute later when Julie didn't respond, and Julie couldn't help herself. She smiled, the familiar movement of her facial muscles a relief to her system, like her body was returning to itself.

"You have chocolate chips in this household?"

Elle squeezed her side, made a half-heartedly affronted *mm* sound.

"I'm not a total killjoy, Julie Parker. I like chocolate chips."

Julie wanted to run her fingers up Elle's thigh, wanted to reach up and put her hands in Elle's hair again, press her thumb along Elle's cheeks to assure her Julie was okay. But the moment had passed, and she'd lost her courage again.

Suddenly, a thought occurred to her.

"Vanessa," she said.

Elle stilled, just for a small moment, before her eyes relaxed.

"Vanessa will be okay. We'll tell her we were watching a movie, that you got sleepy and didn't want to make the drive home. I really think it'll be okay. Although." Elle turned, stretching her neck to look at the clock in the kitchen. "It is getting late. She better be getting home soon."

Elle frowned, in that half-concerned, half-annoyed parental way, before turning back to Julie with that punch-drunk look again.

"Even if I am glad she didn't come home, say, fifteen minutes ago. And in case she happens to walk in the door now..." Her eyes flicked past Julie's head, to the hallway and the half bath and foyer beyond. "I'm going to go wash up. I'll run upstairs, so you can use the bathroom down here if you need to."

Julie did need to, even if leaving this couch was a difficulty. She tried not to look at herself too hard in the mirror, at the flush of her cheeks or the disarray of her hair. She'd told Elle she needed to process this, but that felt impossible to do while she was still in Elle's house, too close to what had just happened, a small part of her still running wild with it. Wanting to run upstairs and capture Elle behind the sink, kiss the back of her neck and say that, actually, she did want to sleep in Elle's bed. She wanted to watch Elle undress, and tuck her bare back against Julie's stomach, and—

Julie returned to the couch in the dark den posthaste. She was pulling a blanket she found in a basket over herself when suddenly Elle's hands were there, taking over, tucking Julie in.

And Julie, again, didn't know what to say.

"Do you want to keep this on?" Elle asked after the tucking was done, picking up the remote and motioning to the TV. The screen had long gone into postgame analysis. Julie was pretty sure the Blue Devils had won. She'd figure it out tomorrow.

She shook her head, and Elle clicked it off, leaving the room even darker than before. "Do you think Vanessa knows?" Julie asked. "That we're..."

"I don't know," Elle said, looking back at her. "I mean, she knows—" She cut herself off with a shake of her head. "I don't know. But I think...she'd be okay with it. If she did."

Julie nodded.

"I have to wake up really early. To get home and get to work."

God. She could not believe she had to *work* tomorrow. What a scam.

"Then I suppose we'll be having some early-morning pancakes."

Elle leaned down and kissed her on the forehead.

"Good night, Coach."

Julie couldn't wait for Elle to go back upstairs, so Julie could be alone and fall asleep while freaking out, privately.

Julie never wanted Elle to leave.

CHAPTER TWENTY-TWO

December, as always, was a blur from the start.

The Bobcats were on a winning streak, enough of one that Julie was starting to believe, seriously, in success at districts. Enough of one that she was nervous they were running too hot and it'd all go to hell any minute. Elle almost liked Julie on the knife's edge of adrenaline like this. Liked seeing the fire in her eyes when she believed. Liked being the one to remind her to breathe when she didn't. To assure her it would be okay, either way.

The weekend after the Duke-UNC game, Elle invited Julie over to help decorate the house for Christmas. She told her it was Vanessa's request, but really, Elle just thought it'd be more fun with her there. And it was. Everything was always more fun with Julie there.

Vanessa continued to have complicated feelings about spending the holidays at Elle's, and in fact had initially refused to partake in any decorating at all. Christmas, she said, was "capitalistic bullshit." Being as Elle couldn't remember the last time she'd stepped inside a church, she wasn't necessarily inclined to disagree.

But when Julie wrapped twinkle lights around Vanessa's shoulders, when Julie danced around the house to Vanessa's chosen Christmas music—because even if it was capitalistic bullshit, apparently Vanessa still had a Christmas playlist—when Julie laughed so hard at the creepy Victorian dolls Elle had inherited from her grandmother, which she felt required to display at Christmas, that Julie had literally cried—

All those things made Vanessa laugh, too.

Elle wasn't sure if her little house had ever heard as much laughter as it did that weekend.

The time Julie spent at Elle's house, in general, became blurred; it sometimes felt like Julie was there more often than she wasn't. There was always some reason Elle could think of to invite her over—practicing getting takeout together after a long day; working on the online dating profile for Julie they never seemed able to finish—and Julie always said yes.

And Elle might have secretly wished, every single time, for a repeat of that night when they'd watched the Duke-UNC game. An expansion of it.

Because Elle had been berating herself about the whole thing. That Julie's first sexual experience with another person had been a fast fingering on a couch, like Elle had turned into a horny teenager who couldn't help herself. Which was...well. How Elle felt most of the time these days. Because she also couldn't deny, any time she thought about it—which was often—that it had been the hottest thing she'd experienced in years.

Julie might be the one questioning the details of her relationship with sexuality. But while Elle's younger life had had its moments of recklessness, the last eight years had been about stability: a reliable life of antidepressants and the resulting low libido. Which hadn't overly bothered her much, until Julie Parker. Julie Parker had awakened things, and even though Elle knew, because she knew herself and her body by now, that it wouldn't be a forever sustainable kind of awakening, she was still filled with wonder that it was happening at all.

Elle couldn't stop thinking about when Julie had talked about touching herself. Elle wanted to watch her, spent her nights wondering if Julie was doing it right then, on the other side of town.

Elle was driving herself wild with all the things she couldn't stop thinking about.

Like how, while the night on the couch might have been hot, Julie deserved to be laid out on a bed, given space and time and decadence. To be teased and then rewarded. To be touched and kissed slowly, reverently, from wrist to wrist, shoulder to toe. If she wanted to be.

Elle dreamed, every night and sometimes half her days, about making it right.

She would've given up the dreams completely, or at least locked them away in a private, closed box, if Julie hadn't shown signs that she was still interested. Elle hadn't doubted that Julie had enjoyed that night, but she also hadn't doubted her uncertainty afterward. That maybe that night had been more than enough practice for Julie.

Except, even while they hadn't found the opportunity to be truly alone again, even if they had never explicitly talked about whether they should, Julie kept finding pockets where she initiated touch. Small spaces in the day to do aimless things like tracing Elle's tattoo with her finger when they were temporarily alone in Elle's kitchen. To squeeze Elle's hand whenever she thought Elle needed it.

There had even been the thrilling afternoon, early in December, when Julie had tugged Elle into her office inside the East High gym, after the team had trotted into the locker room, and shoved Elle against the wall, out of the view of the door, and kissed her thoroughly, breathlessly, hands roaming underneath Elle's shirt with abandon.

"Sorry," she had said, hugging her hands behind her neck when she'd pulled away, face flushed. "You just looked particularly hot today. And I've been thinking I should practice taking initiative more."

"Good," Elle had said, a bit dazed. "That was good."

And Julie had looked, for a moment, so pleased with herself, that

Elle almost demanded she go home with them and stay the night again. In Elle's bed, this time.

Except if this really was about Julie taking initiative, then Elle needed Julie to ask. She needed Julie to want it enough, to *trust* herself enough, to invite herself there.

But she'd only grabbed her bag, told Elle she'd see her tomorrow, and rushed away. Leaving Elle alone, overly aroused in an office that smelled of stale sweat and bleach.

On a Monday, while Vanessa was at school and Elle was catching up on errands before an away game, Elle received a text in the middle of Kroger.

> I assume you won't be coming to the annual Christmas party . . . but I have a present for you anyway. Can I drop it off at your house sometime? Miss you!

Elle came to a halt in the middle of the bread aisle.

The text was from Charlize, Elle's favorite coworker at Vandy.

Charlize, whom Elle hadn't thought about—just as she hadn't thought about anything, really, about the hospital—since she'd started her leave of absence weeks ago.

The realization made Elle blink.

For eight years, her job had given her life routine. Paid her bills, financed repairs and maintenance to her home. Helped support her mother, when Rose became overwhelmed with medical costs. Elle had liked that routine. That steadiness.

And then she'd simply . . . stopped.

And she hadn't thought about it since.

Her life had swiftly been consumed with taking care of Vanessa, daydreaming about Julie, and Bobcat basketball.

Which she was becoming increasingly invested in, although in a slightly different fashion than Julie. She also wanted the team to get to districts, of course, but with less fervor than Coach Parker. While she was glad Julie had that competitive fire for the team, the closer Elle edged to it, the more it only brought bad memories and anxiety: reminders of the things she had walked away from and didn't miss.

What she did find herself caring more and more about were the players. Not just Ngozi and their one-on-one sessions, although she continued to enjoy those. But all of them, their form and their practice, making sure they were healthy and safe on the court. She'd convinced Julie to let her integrate more strength training and targeted stretching into practices, the things her own athletic trainers had worked with her on throughout college and the pros. She'd met with East's weights guy and worked out times the team could use the weight room, had assured him that "the girls" could take care of his equipment, even as she'd had to grit her teeth through his condescension and false assumption that the players were all girls.

But such was the ingrained hierarchy and immovable binary of most sports, problems she and Julie often discussed at length—without finding many immediate solutions, other than the slow, steady persistence of queer existence.

Which, for Elle and Julie, had always included taking up space in the ostentatiously patriarchal world of sports. Making space for any player who wanted to put in the work, regardless of their identity.

It didn't feel like enough, but it was what they could do.

The Bobcats were more than game for the new strength training routines, which broke up the repetition of scrimmaging and drills. Elle did worry, at first, that it was overkill, that their bodies were still so young and healthy that they didn't need all the precautions her professional training had required. But maybe if the Bobcats properly prepared themselves now, if they kept their ankles and knees and shoulders strong, they'd be less likely to suffer stress fractures and torn ligaments later on.

Another Kroger customer jostled Elle's cart. Elle startled, staring again at the text from Charlize.

Shouldn't she have missed her real job, even a little bit?

Of course ❤, she texted back after a moment. Miss you, too.

Later that week, Vanessa requested a haircut. After getting permission from Amber, Elle took her to the nicest salon on the east side that took walk-ins.

The next day, Katelyn came over. And when she and Vanessa emerged from the upstairs bathroom, Vanessa's old lavender highlights were replaced with fresh, vibrant turquoise.

Elle attended parent-teacher conferences at the end of fall semester; Vanessa's teachers remarked how impressed they were at the strides she was making. She was caught up on back assignments, participating slightly more in class. She still wasn't a straight-A student, but she was trying.

Elle wanted to smother Vanessa in a hug in celebration.

She made a cake instead. A box one, full of things that humans shouldn't consume, that she let Vanessa pick out at Target.

Karly was continuing to show up to every appointment, attending therapy and AA meetings. She had finally gotten a job, working overnight stocking shelves at Kroger. The schedule obviously wasn't great, but she said she was getting used to it. That she liked it, the quiet of the store at night. She hadn't missed a single Bobcat home game. Every time Elle saw her, she swore her skin had a little more color, the bags underneath her eyes less pronounced.

There was so much color, in general, these days, in Elle's

life—Christmas lights in her windows, reflected in Julie's hazel eyes; the new shade of Vanessa's hair and Funfetti icing; red and silver pom-poms underneath bright gymnasium lights—that it took her by surprise, as it often did, when the darkness arrived again.

Julie turned on the TV, taking a bite of the Trader Joe's stir-fry she'd heated up for dinner. Snoozles strolled over, a loud purr vibrating through her throat at the scent of food. Julie scratched under her chin and lifted the bowl away from her nosy nose. Snoozles's incision was healing well, and her energy—measured in how aggressively she followed scents with that nosy nose—was back to normal, too.

"I know, girl," Julie said. "I've missed you, too."

It had been an objectively fine December Saturday. There were no Bobcat games or practices this weekend, so Julie had gotten some Christmas shopping done, along with two loads of laundry. She'd stopped at Trader Joe's and picked up this stir-fry and an irresponsible amount of seasonal snacks. She was grateful for the time to lounge with Snoozles, who she feared had started giving her dirty looks, each night she returned home too late from Elle's.

But as Julie scrolled to where she'd left off on *The Good Place*, an unshakable sense of *blah* hung over her anyway.

Maybe it was simply the season. There was always something melancholy to her about this time of year, even with it being the heart of basketball season. Too little daylight, too many acquaintances posting about the things they'd achieved this year, their lofty goals for the new one. While Julie kept spinning the wheels at her cubicle, eating Trader Joe's stir-fries alone on Saturday nights.

This melancholy had often been offset, in past years, by Christmas movie watches with London or Ben, but Ben was working an overnight tonight, and London and Dahlia were out of town. A cancellation had made a last-minute spot open up for London's top surgery, a week from now, just before Christmas. London had taken it, even if it meant they'd be recovering during the holiday. They'd arranged this weekend away at a cabin outside Gatlinburg soon after, which they had told the family at Sunday supper last week was for a chance to relax before the procedure.

But Julie was pretty sure it was so London could propose. Because of course London would propose at a cabin in Gatlinburg. It was so romantic Julie could puke.

She kept checking her phone for updates anyway.

And for texts from Elle, but none of those had come in today, either.

Snoozles nabbed a chunk of chicken between her teeth and jumped onto the carpet in triumph.

Dammit. Julie frowned, throwing her phone down on the couch.

She should just turn the damn thing off, to prove to herself her melancholy did *not* have anything to do with not hearing from Elle. It was a busy time of year. Julie didn't have to know where Elle was at every moment of the day.

A text lit up the screen.

Julie almost spilled the rest of her stir-fry in her haste to reach for it.

The text was from an unknown number.

hey coach

Julie frowned again, wondering which Bobcat would be texting her on a Saturday night. She always gave the team her number at the beginning of the season. Most of the time the texts she received were logistical ones, letting Julie know they were sick and would miss practice, questions about the schedule. But a few of her senior players from last year had used it to maintain contact, to talk about summer rec leagues, about playing on their new college teams.

One player in particular, Hailey, had confided in Julie about her disordered eating last year, and Julie occasionally checked in with her about how freshman year was going, a perilous time for someone who struggled with disordered eating. She'd texted Julie a photo of her favorite meal from the dining hall just last week, and Julie had been so excited she'd wanted to drive over to Lipscomb to high-five her.

But this wasn't Hailey, or any of the current Bobcats who had contacted her this season. Within a few seconds, though, it became clear.

> sorry to bother you
>
> but elle has been in her room all day and won't come out
>
> i know she gets migraines sometimes so she's probably just sleeping
>
> but i dunno it feels weird
>
> like
>
> i dunno
>
> i didn't know who else to text

Julie clicked off the TV and threw her bowl in the sink.

> Hey, Vanessa. Don't worry, okay? I'm on my way.

CHAPTER TWENTY-THREE

Vanessa was biting her fingernails when she let Julie inside.

"I'm probably overreacting. Sorry. It's just—sometimes, my mom, when she was—she'd go into her room and wouldn't come out and then sometimes she'd leave and—"

"Hey there, tiger." Julie grabbed Vanessa by the shoulders. "It's okay. Okay? Elle isn't leaving. I'm not leaving. I'll figure out what's going on. Have you eaten today?"

Vanessa exhaled.

"I ate some pizza rolls earlier. I can't believe Elle bought fucking pizza rolls. I could feel her stove judging me. Fuck. I curse a lot when I'm nervous. Sorry."

"Don't tell anyone, but I do, too. When did you have those fucking pizza rolls?"

A surprised laugh stuttered out of Vanessa's mouth, an ounce of tension easing from her face before she went back to biting her fingernails in thought.

"Um. I dunno. Like, a while ago?"

Julie turned her around and marched her toward the kitchen.

"Let's order something. For all of us. Do you like Thai food?"

She knew Elle liked Thai food, that pad see ew was her guilty pleasure, as she had called it, even though Julie objected to the term.

They had texted about it weeks ago. Julie had been eating perhaps a higher-than-normal amount of Thai food ever since.

Fifteen minutes later, Thai food ordered, Julie took a deep breath before knocking on Elle's closed bedroom door.

Silence.

Julie pushed it open anyway.

The back of Elle's head greeted her from the bed, barely sticking out from the covers. It was dark, the curtains pulled over the windows, the air in the room stale. The bed surprisingly neat, aside from the lump where Elle's body lay. She looked compact, somehow, under the covers. Folded up and small.

Julie stood a moment, contemplating what to do, before walking around the bed to kneel at the side of it. She rested her chin on the comforter and looked at Elle's sleeping face before nudging her shoulder.

"Hey," she said. "Hey, Elle."

Elle's face made an expression of displeasure. Julie almost laughed, it was so cute and pouty. So unlike fully conscious, in-control Elle.

"Elle." Julie kept pushing her shoulder until, by degrees, Elle woke, her eyelids fluttering open. Julie felt bad waking her. But for Vanessa's sake, she needed to get the lay of the land here.

"Julie?" Elle squinted, her voice gravelly.

"Hey. Vanessa texted me. I came over to make sure you were all right."

"Vanessa texted you?" Elle frowned, still squinting. "What time is it?"

Julie glanced at the clock on the bedside table.

"Nine o'clock."

"At night?" Elle's eyes widened, the confusion on her face turning to dread.

"Yeah. Are you having a migraine? How long have you been sleeping?"

Instead of answering, Elle struggled to sit up. She didn't get very far before she groaned, slumping back down.

"I don't know how long I've been sleeping," she answered, voice still scratchy but sounding more awake. "And yes, migraine. Except..."

She trailed off, staring at the ceiling. When she didn't continue, Julie said, "I ordered some Thai food. Pad see ew for you. Do you think you could come down in a little bit and eat with us?"

Elle made a face, turning her head away.

"That's kind of you, Julie, but...I'm so nauseous. I'm sorry."

"That's okay." God, Julie wanted to crawl onto the bed and wrap Elle in her arms. But she wasn't sure what Elle needed here. "I'll put it in the fridge. Save it for when you're feeling better."

And even though Elle was turned away, Julie saw her wince.

Almost like...she didn't quite believe she could feel better.

"Is Vanessa okay?" she whispered after a moment.

"I think..." Julie swallowed. Clearly Elle wasn't in a good space, and it was killing Julie, but...she also thought Elle should know. "I think you disappearing all day has spooked her a little. Triggered something about her mom doing drugs in her room or something. I don't know."

"Fuck," Elle muttered. And then, louder, angry: "*Fuck.*" She forced herself up as she said it, even as it obviously brought her pain; she pressed her palms to her eyelids as soon as she was upright. Julie finally joined her, rubbing a hand along her thigh underneath the covers.

Julie had spent the majority of the last month dreaming about being in this bedroom, in this bed, under the covers with Elle, in a much different scenario. Part of her melancholy today might have been a result of her frustration with herself that she hadn't yet been able to initiate anything that would have led her here, even after she'd decided she definitely wanted to.

But none of that seemed very important right now.

"They asked me about this," Elle said into her wrists. "When they were doing the home study, to make sure my house was safe for Vanessa, they asked about my mental health history, and I told them..." Elle sighed, a big, heaving thing that looked like it hurt, and dropped her hands, staring bleakly forward. "Sometimes, my migraines are just migraines. Painful, exhausting. Sometimes I go months without one, especially since I've been on preventive medication. But sometimes..." She shook her head. "Sometimes, they coincide with depressive episodes. Today, before my head started to hurt...I was just *sad*, first."

Julie reached for one of her fallen hands, lying open on top of the comforter. Elle let her twine her fingers through, but didn't squeeze back.

"Did anything happen?" Julie asked tentatively. "To make you sad?"

Elle shook her head again, lower lip trembling. "No. That's always the fucking—" She bunched the comforter in her other fist, knuckles white. "Sometimes something triggers it, when I'm overwhelmed or stressed about something. But I hate when it's just...when it's just because my brain's bad."

"It's a hard time of year," Julie offered softly, "for depression. Your brain's not bad."

"Well, it is. But that's still not an excuse—" Elle turned her face away again, wiping at her eyes with her free hand. "It's not an excuse when Vanessa's here. I told CPS it wouldn't affect my ability to care for her. That I had it managed. Because I *do*. I do!" She ripped her hand away from Julie's to wipe at her other cheek. "I take my pills, and I feel nice and steady and okay, maybe half-alive sometimes, but I get out of bed. I should have made myself get out of bed today."

"Hey." Julie shifted, so she was facing Elle's side. "Elle. Sometimes even people without diagnosed depression want to stay in bed all day. And it's not your fault Karly did things that made this trigger something for Vanessa. Which I say with all respect for Karly and the progress it sounds like she's making now. But I think all Vanessa needs to know is that you're okay, that you're not in here because of *her* or because of something dangerous you're choosing over her. Which I'll tell her, if you're not able to come down tonight, okay?"

Elle's eyes scrunched closed again.

"But I do think," Julie said gently, after a minute, "that if you're able to come down for even a little bit, it might be good for her. And for you."

"What if I can't get out of bed again tomorrow?" Elle's voice broke on a sob. Even with knowing Elle's mental health history, it was a shock—gut-wrenching, surreal—seeing her like this. Julie's heart lurched into her throat. "Sometimes it lasts a while, and—"

"Then I'll be here tomorrow, too. I'll stay the night. You just have to tell me what you need."

Elle still wouldn't make eye contact. But she didn't protest, either, which Julie took as a good sign.

The doorbell rang. Julie heard Vanessa shuffling downstairs.

"That must be the food. I'm going to go eat with Vanessa. We'll hang out and play *Mario Kart* or something. Come down if you can. But it'll be okay, okay?"

Julie only hesitated a moment before she leaned forward and pressed a kiss to Elle's temple. Rubbed a hand over her back. Julie wanted a magic cloak she could wrap around Elle's shoulders, one that would capture all of her sadness and whisk it away. She wanted to rest at Elle's side for hours, listening to nothing but the wind outside, counting the freckles on Elle's collarbone, until Elle felt better. She wanted Elle to sink into her, to turn her face into Julie's neck. Ask her to hold her. Let Julie shoulder some of it.

But Elle only remained still, silent, until Julie dropped her hand away.

Julie blinked when she stepped into the bright light of the kitchen.

Vanessa was already getting out plates, organizing the tidy white takeout boxes. Julie glanced back up the stairs before she joined her.

Even without a migraine, even without diagnosed depression, Julie could see how easy it would be to sink into the darkness of that bedroom. To get lost, lose time. The kitchen felt like a different world. Like even Julie had forgotten, in the last fifteen minutes, what it felt like to breathe.

She knew coming downstairs wouldn't fix what was happening in Elle's brain.

But she hoped Elle came downstairs soon anyway.

"Hey." Julie picked up the plate and fork Vanessa had gotten out for her. "It is a migraine. I think she just conked out hard. She seemed surprised at what time it was."

"Yeah." Vanessa twirled pad Thai around her fork. "Told you I overreacted."

She seemed calmer, eyes dry. If anything, her face now only betrayed embarrassment.

Julie borrowed a bit of Vanessa's strength.

"No," she said. "You didn't. I hadn't heard from her all day either, and I'd been a little concerned, too."

Vanessa cut her a look over the kitchen island. A smirk kicked up the side of her face.

"It *is* you, isn't it? That she texts all the time."

Julie turned to hide in the fridge as she grabbed a seltzer.

"We're friends," she told the cheese drawer.

"Suuuuure," Vanessa drawled.

"Anyway." Julie stood and popped the tab. "I'll hang out tonight, and tomorrow if y'all need me, until she's feeling better."

Vanessa groaned. "I seriously didn't text you to come babysit me, Coach."

"Please." Julie scoffed as if in offense. "I've been dying for another chance to beat you at *Mario Kart* anyway."

And beat Vanessa she did, after they'd finished their dinner, after she'd let Vanessa beat *her* a couple times. Julie was in the middle of cackling in triumph, in fact, while Vanessa mumbled, "This is such bullshorts," when Elle appeared in the den.

"Hey," she said, sinking into the armchair next to the couch. "Is Coach beating you again?"

"It's not right," Vanessa muttered. "You're *old*."

Julie looked at Elle, chest warm with pride. That she had come down. That she was going for normalcy, for Vanessa, however much she was still hurting. Which Julie could tell she was, from the way she carried herself: stiff and careful, face pale. Eyes still squinted, as if opening them all the way was impossible.

And Julie was proud, too, when after a few minutes, Elle admitted it.

"I'm so sorry," she said, eyes fully closed now, "but can we maybe watch something else? Something about the video game; it's too fast, and—"

And Elle looked like she was a second away from throwing up. Vanessa seemed to sense it too, clicking out of the game first.

"Of course." Vanessa picked up the remote to return to cable, muting the sound along the way. "Is there, uh, anything we can do?"

Elle glanced at Vanessa, the barest of smiles on her lips before she said, "You can not laugh at me when I do this."

She pulled out a pair of gargantuan sunglasses from the pocket of her sweatshirt, slipping them over her eyes and resting her head on the chair with a sigh of relief.

Vanessa snorted. "Yeah, I am definitely going to laugh at those."

The smile on Elle's face stretched the tiniest bit.

"You can still watch something," she said after a minute of silence had stretched through the den.

"Can we actually..." Vanessa shifted on the couch. "Uh. Watch *The Great British Bake Off*?"

"Fork yeah we can," Julie said, reaching for the remote before Vanessa had even finished the sentence.

"That sounds nice," Elle said quietly.

Julie scrolled on Netflix. It felt a bit surprising, an un-Vanessa ask.

But it made sense, halfway through the episode, when Vanessa spoke.

"This is my mom's favorite show."

She said it so quietly Julie wasn't sure if she would have heard her if they hadn't turned the volume so low for Elle.

"We always watched it whenever she was doing good. Whenever she wasn't out with *Jake*—" Vanessa said the name with such derision that the hairs on the back of Julie's neck stood on end. She sensed, more than saw, Elle turn her head toward the couch. Neither of them dared speak, lest Vanessa stop sharing information she'd never shared before. "Or Aaron or whoever or...whatever. We watched lots of cooking shows, but she always wanted to watch this one when she was feeling sentimental. She always said...she always said she wished life could be as pure and simple as a good bake."

Quiet settled again. Julie sensed both she and Elle were waiting, making sure Vanessa didn't have anything else to say. Until eventually Julie said, "I feel that."

And Elle whispered, "Me too."

Elle lasted until the end of the episode. She pushed herself up with a wince.

"I have to lie down again."

"Can I bring you anything?" Julie asked. "A warm washcloth or anything?"

Elle forced a smile. "No, that's okay. Thank you, though." She was still wearing her sunglasses. She turned toward Vanessa. "I'll see you in the morning, okay? I can still drive you to Katelyn's in the afternoon. Or...I'll make sure you get there."

Vanessa nodded and said, "Okay," sounding bored. Kept staring at the TV as the next episode started.

But Julie kept her eyes on Elle as she walked out of the room. As she paused at the kitchen doorway and looked back. Julie smiled, gave her a reassuring nod. Elle managed one in return before she disappeared up the stairs.

But Julie could see it. The pain still written in every line on her face.

Vanessa lasted another episode and a half before she started snoring on the other end of the couch. It was past midnight now. "Hey." Julie nudged Vanessa's shoulder, similarly to how she'd nudged Elle's a few hours before. "Hey, kid. Time to go to sleep."

Vanessa looked at her from hooded eyelids and rolled off the couch with a grunt.

"Night, Coach," she mumbled, before she too stumbled up the stairs. Julie made sure the front door and the door to the deck were locked. Walked around the house, turning off Christmas lights. Elle's holiday decorations were classy, which Julie had expected— white lights and one of those detailed Christmas villages, set up in the bookshelves in the sitting room; a wreath of real evergreens on the front door and Spode glassware in the kitchen—but there were surprising bits of kitsch here and there. Half-broken childhood ornaments on the small artificial tree Elle kept in the corner of the den. Those terrifying dolls. The same ceramic tree with colored lights Julie's grandparents had had, sitting on a side table. A sparkly, rainbow-colored stretch of garland draped above the mirror in the downstairs bathroom, a touch of jingle bell pride.

She paused by the cross-stitch in the den for a long time. Traced a finger down the frame. *Elle Loves Elephants*. Thought of Elle saying *They take care of each other*, while something both bitter and sweet wrapped around her heart.

She clicked off the light.

When everything was done, the dishes in the sink cleaned and placed in the drying rack, Julie padded upstairs, down the hall once more to Elle's room.

The bed was messier this time, like Elle had tossed and turned before finally finding rest, as she had before, all curled up, back facing the world.

Julie shut the door slowly. Took off her sweatshirt, her sports bra. Left them in a neat pile by the side of the bed.

She knew, as she climbed under the covers, that she hadn't explicitly asked permission to do this. That maybe she had been expected to sleep on the couch again. But somehow, just as it had felt turning off the Christmas lights and double-checking the locks, positioning herself behind Elle's back, resting her head on Elle's pillows, hugging an arm around Elle's side, not too tightly, in case her stomach was still hurting—it all only felt natural. Something, for once, that Julie didn't second-guess.

Elle shifted her body closer. Made a small noise in her throat before she fell back asleep.

It only took a few minutes for Julie to do the same.

When Elle woke, her brain remembered all the right things.

She woke because she needed to pee, and as she made her way to the bathroom and back, she could tell the worst of the migraine was over. Her entire body still ached, but the nausea was mostly gone. She could open her eyes. She could breathe.

She risked opening the curtains, just an inch, before climbing back into bed. Just enough to reveal that it was early, pale morning light barely cracking the horizon, sliding through the gaps in the trees that bordered the back of her property.

It had only taken half a second when she'd awoken to know, to remember, to feel Julie behind her. It took almost as little time now to sink back against her.

And even though Elle hadn't shared her bed with anyone in years, even though she should have felt concerned that Julie had seen her at her worst, that they were getting in too deep—the warmth of her, the weight of her body at Elle's back, only felt right, too.

Elle never knew why or how this happened, when she woke up and suddenly her brain worked right. She didn't think it had to do with her medication, which never made her feel good, necessarily, but only kept her from feeling too bad. Kept her functioning. For which she was appreciative. But it didn't make her brain fully clear, like it was now.

It happened, sometimes, when she felt particularly sad. Sometimes the sadness dragged on for weeks, months. And then sometimes, she woke up the next day and it was like a switch had been flipped in the opposite direction.

The sadness normally creeped back in again, later in the day or the next, until she eventually evened out again. But for a few hours, her brain remembered the right things.

Elle remembered, this morning, how glad she was to live in this house. How much she loved the exact shade of navy blue she'd chosen for the walls in this bedroom. How much she loved the black-and-white photographs Akhil, a photography enthusiast, had given her as a housewarming present, how crisp and clean they looked in their frames.

She remembered how it always felt, coming back home to Nashville during a break when she was at UT, when she was with the Wreckers. Rose's dog, Holly, would greet her, slobbery as ever, and Rose would give her a hug, and she'd always feel so grateful, to have a place to land. She remembered how good it had felt, making her own space in Nashville again these last few years, a thing that felt new and familiar all at once, specific to her and her alone.

She remembered how much she liked early mornings, when everything felt hushed and fragile. When the possibilities of the day were still wide open.

In these rare moments when the chemicals and synapses in Elle's brain fired like they were supposed to, everything always felt right. Even the mistakes, the hard things and the heartaches, felt easier to handle. Everything was brighter, crisper, like Elle spent the rest of her days living in fuzzy darkness, and suddenly blinked and was able to see how colorful everything was, how reassuring, that the world existed. That Elle was able to survive within it.

Julie shifted, making a low, half-asleep noise, throwing an arm over Elle's side. Her breasts and her belly sidled closer to Elle's back, separated only by the cotton of their T-shirts, Julie's hand tucking underneath Elle's ribs.

"Good morning," Elle whispered.

Several quiet moments went by. Elle thought Julie had likely fallen back asleep, if she had woken at all.

But then Julie said, "Elle?"

"Yeah?"

"This is my favorite relationship thing."

Elle's throat grew tight.

"Me too," she whispered, at length.

A minute later, Julie mumbled, "I wish your trophies weren't in a box."

And then she did fall back asleep, her breathing even against Elle's neck.

Elle's own breath hitched in her throat. She wondered when Julie had seen the box. How long she'd been wanting to say something about it.

In the clarity of her fully functioning brain, Elle could also let herself remember, at least for a moment, how much receiving those trophies had meant at the time. And how much it had hurt to look at them after her injury.

Now, she mostly felt neutral. They were a memento of things she had done, once. They weren't who she was.

Julie might be right, though. Maybe she should finally do something about that box.

Elle stayed awake to watch the sun rise. To keep remembering. To think about all the things she wanted to do next. She wanted to take Vanessa to Opryland for Christmas. She wanted to drive to Knoxville and have Mara take her to all the new restaurants that had inevitably opened since the last time she'd been there. She wanted to get Julie back in this bed, when Elle's head wasn't hurting, when she could treat her right. She wanted to call a contractor and get a quote about installing a small court in her backyard, a dream she thought about, sometimes, when she let herself. She wanted to cook for Julie, not just pancakes in the middle of the night when Julie was still half-asleep. She wanted to see Charlotte again. She wanted to officially meet Ben.

The sun rose, and Elle held on to all the things she wanted to keep, all the tiny dreams, before it all grew blurry again.

CHAPTER TWENTY-FOUR

On the Thursday before Christmas, Julie descended the stairs to the Caravalhos' basement and tried to not appear too alarmed.

"I know. I know." Ben ran both hands through his hair. "Finally move out of your parents' basement, they said. It'll be easy, they said."

Julie searched for an empty spot to place Ben's Christmas present.

"Ben. This is rough. How can I help?"

"Told me I should've started packing weeks ago?"

"How much are you actually packing? I thought you wanted to pack light."

"I do! I did! I told myself I'd only pack two suitcases, mail myself a few boxes. There'll barely be room for the suitcases in the Jeep, with me and Delilah in it, too. But...I don't know how I have so much shit in this basement." He picked up something by his feet. "Do you want my *Fast and Furious* box set?"

Julie gasped.

"Ben, you're *moving*, not *dying*."

"You're right." Ben sighed, throwing it in a box that was already overflowing. "I need it. Anyway." He shoved a small mountain of clothes off the bed. "More important things. Presents!"

"Presents," Julie agreed. She plopped by Ben's pillows, while Ben grabbed a flat box from underneath the bed and sat cross-legged at the foot of it. Ben's dog, Delilah, sat on the floor next to them with a big rottie whine at being left out of the party.

Christmas was still four days away, but the Caravalhos were hosting a bunch of extended family this year to celebrate Ben's last Christmas living in Nashville, so she and Ben were squeezing in their gift exchange before their arrival.

Elle had been recovering since the episode that had hit her last weekend. She had been able to get out of bed on Sunday, even if her head had still been hurting; she had shown up to every practice and game all week. She was surviving, but Julie could tell she was still struggling, possibly not sleeping well. Her smiles never quite reached her eyes.

She let her exhaustion show more at home. She had admitted she normally had a hard time cooking or eating regularly when she felt like this, so Julie had taken to coming over most nights after practice to make sure everyone had dinner. Elle sometimes sat at the kitchen island, watching Julie quietly as she cooked—that is, heated up a frozen dinner or something London or Dahlia had made; sometimes she lay on the couch while Vanessa watched TV.

Julie hadn't stayed overnight again. Elle had told her she didn't need to, and Julie had respected that. Which was okay, because Snoozles would have started to get lonely.

But she still remembered, every night, what it had felt like to fall asleep next to Elle.

"Me first!" Julie shouted, grabbing the present out of Ben's hands.

Ben only scratched his head as she ripped the wrapping, a pensive look on his face. Which should have been her first clue. Ben had always been an enthusiastic gift-opening spectator.

Julie opened the box, pushed aside the tissue paper, and discovered a book.

A photo book, with a picture of her and Ben on the cover. *Ben & Jules*, it said.

She opened to the first page and burst into tears.

"Oh no." She ran her fingers over the pictures: Ben and Julie on a Slip 'N Slide in Ben's backyard; Ben and Julie with birthday hats strapped around their chins and frosting smothered on their cheeks. She estimated they were eight years old.

"Okay, so," Ben started, "it did occur to me, after I'd already ordered it, or rather, Lex pointed out to me, that it might seem—"

Julie laughed through her tears as she turned to the next page.

"Like a goodbye forever gift?" she supplied. "Something you make when someone has died? Oh my god. I don't even remember who half these other kids are." She held up the book to point at a picture of Ben and Julie at someone's roller rink party.

Ben exhaled. "Yes. I'm sorry."

Julie gasped at the next spread. "Where did you even *get* these pictures?"

"Iris. And Charlotte."

Julie looked up from the book to gape at him. Iris made sense, but—"You contacted *my mom* for this?"

Ben blushed, shoving his fingers into the comforter.

"Oh my *god*." Julie closed the book temporarily to smack Ben on the shoulder with it. "Why are you so thoughtful? And, Ben. Fuck. My present to you is the *worst*."

"Can I open it now?"

Julie sighed. "If you must."

And of course, because he was Ben, his face lit with genuine joy when he unearthed the dumb mug.

He held it up next to his face, mouth open wide. "Sasquatch!"

The mug had a picture of the big furry monster on it, crossing a forested road. *Sasquatch Crossing*, it said. It was the one thing she'd had to order online this year, when she'd googled *pacific northwest shit*.

"I'm going to be a Sasquatch guy now!" Ben stared at the mug as if it was the best thing he'd ever seen.

"Ben." Julie shook her head, wiping at her eyes. "That mug is so dumb. This is the worst."

"It is not!" Ben curled the mug protectively into his chest as he knee-walked to Julie, shoving her onto the pillows as he hugged her side. Delilah jumped onto the bed, lying at their feet with a sigh. "I *love* it. It's my first Portland mug. And it's from *you*. It's perfect."

"Well." Julie snuggled into a more comfortable position, soothed by the familiar feeling of Ben's arm around her, by the laundry detergent smell of the Caravalhos' basement. "Just know, any time you use it, that I'm over here quietly judging it. Because that dude is totally just Bigfoot."

Ben laughed. "I will." And then, "You're not upset? I was worried it might make you upset."

Julie picked up the book again.

"No," she said softly. "I love it."

Ben's instinct had not been wrong. Julie could picture Ben's gift sending her into a genuine tailspin a few months ago, a few weeks ago even. It was hard evidence of the friendship they'd built together in Nashville. It *was*, even if Ben hadn't intended it to be, a sort of forever goodbye.

And Julie's chest did ache, thinking about that. Her body had reacted immediately with tears for a reason. But as Ben's departure date had gotten closer, she only felt happy for him. Sad, but happy. Ben was the most loyal person she'd ever met. Their lives would be different now. But she knew he'd never disappear.

They spent a while looking through the book together, laughing at the outfits from all the middle and high school dances they'd gone to together. Julie's heart gave a particularly nostalgic pang at the few photos from the East High gym, Ben's arm slung over Julie's shoulder, Julie in her Bobcat uniform after a big win.

Julie rested her head on Ben's arm when they were done.

"How are you feeling about being done with Lakeview?" Ben had worked his last shift yesterday at Lakeview Hills, the nursing home and rehabilitation facility where he'd been working on his nursing residency over the last year.

"Well, I picked up a couple of New Year's shifts," Ben said, and Julie laughed.

"Of course you did."

"They needed someone! But..." Ben adjusted the pillow behind his head. "I feel okay. Sad, and a little disappointed I couldn't give Ted more time. I'll miss it. But I think mostly, I just feel excited. And scared. But mostly excited."

Julie rotated her head toward him. "You're scared?"

Ben gusted out a breath. "Fuck yeah, I'm scared."

"But... for this whole past year, you've been so happy, Ben. Looking forward to this."

"I have been. But... I don't know. You can be happy and still feel like you don't really know what the fuck you're doing."

Julie absorbed this, feeling a bit stunned. *Happy* and *don't really know what the fuck I'm doing* seemed to summarize the last few months of her life... well, perfectly.

"I mean, Julie," Ben's voice turned soft as he met her gaze. "I'm leaving Tennessee. The only place I've ever lived. And it's not like I'm just moving to, you know, Louisville, or Asheville or Atlanta or something. I'm moving to the West Coast. Like, a whole different country practically! Away from my family. Away from you."

"Yeah," Julie said with a small smile. "Why are you doing that, again?"

"I don't know," Ben replied, his own eyes glittering. "I guess I fell in love or something."

Julie let out a long breath. "Sounds dumb," she said.

"Yeah." Ben looked down, rubbing his thumb over Julie's

knuckles. "No, it's the best. But..." Ben shifted onto his back. "I don't know, sometimes I feel nervous about that, too."

Julie's forehead knitted in confusion.

"You're nervous about *Alexei*? Are you kidding me? I've never seen such a love-drunk fool. He's almost worse than London. Wait." She leaned up on her elbows, eyes going wide. "Did something happen? Do I have to hurt someone?"

"No, no, no." Ben smiled, pushing her back down by the shoulder. But his smile melted away again, too quick for Julie's liking. "It's just...he's been in the closet most of his life, and I think I was maybe the first good gay he happened to come across. You know? Like, what if one day he discovers that there are so many other good gays? And he gets FOMO?"

"Ben." Julie rolled her eyes.

"Plus, he lives in *Portland*. Every time I go out there to visit, it's like..." Ben threw his hands toward the ceiling. "The land of the gays! So many good gays to get FOMO for!"

"Hasn't Alexei lived in the land of the gays for like, a long time?"

Ben's arms fell back to his sides. "Yeah."

"And he's only ever wanted you? This whole time? Even long distance?"

Ben picked at a thread on his T-shirt. "Yeah. Okay. So I'm pretty sure Lex is super in love with me." Julie smirked. "But...it's still starting to feel kind of scary. We had gotten so good at long distance, and now we're just jumping to living together." Ben sighed. "I'm going to annoy the shit out of him."

Julie scooted her head to rest on his shoulder.

"You won't," she said. "I promise."

"And what if I can't find a good job out there? I should be applying for jobs right now. I should have started the process like...months ago, if I'm being honest. But I've been wussing out. Thinking about starting over at someplace brand-new where no one knows me is so stressful. I just...want to focus on my time left here, and on Lex, making sure he's sure about everything. But..." Ben sighed again. "Realistically, I know I'm already behind."

"Doesn't Alexei make a decent amount of money?"

"Yeah. He can afford his apartment. Our apartment? But he keeps talking about wanting to buy a house together."

With a squeeze of her heart, Julie thought about Elle's house. How...sometimes, she could picture herself living there for the rest of her days.

Which was...

She'd get to that, in a minute.

"A house can wait, Ben. I'm sure he's just excited, you know? To start living your life together. But he's not going to be disappointed if you need to take a month, or a few months, after you get out there to find a job. Even though I really don't think it will take you that long. You're an employer's dream. But the move itself will be a lot for you two to adjust to, like you said. You're allowed to take some time to breathe once you get there, Ben. Seriously. You've been working your ass off. The rest can wait."

She felt Ben's shoulders relax underneath her.

"Yeah," he said. "Thanks for saying that, Jules. I think I needed to hear that."

She smiled, her chest, once more, full of bittersweet things.

"I'm excited to get to Lex, obviously," Ben said a minute later, the smile returned to his face. "But, Julie, I am so jazzed for the ride. I'm going to get to see Colorado. And Utah! I'm so excited for Utah." Delilah had inched up the bed next to his side. Julie reached over and scratched her back.

"You'll text me every night? To let me know you're safe?"

"Of course."

"And text me pictures of weird roadside attractions?"

"Always."

After a moment, Julie said, "Okay."

And she meant it.

"All right, enough about me!" Ben said brightly, after a time. He flipped onto his side, smiling. "You said you had something you wanted to talk about. Am I hoping it's about Elle? Of course I am. But I'm playing it very cool."

Julie rolled her eyes again.

And then she took a deep breath.

She'd been thinking a lot, on her dark drives home from Elle's. About the things that she knew.

Maybe they were things she'd known for a long time.

Or maybe she only truly knew when she stood in the checkout line of a natural foods store two days ago. In a bit of a panic, she'd grabbed every random grain she could find. She hadn't known what to get Elle for Christmas, knew a bunch of bags of sand-looking food didn't exactly shout the holiday spirit. But as the cashier scanned in their codes and their names popped up on the screen, she knew Elle would be able to tell her the nutritional values of each one. It had made her laugh, at first. And then it had changed to something else, expansive and persistent in Julie's gut, that still made her laugh any time she pressed it.

Maybe she knew every night this week, when she'd stood in Elle's foyer. When she'd pulled Elle into a hug before they said good night. Elle was always listless, at the start, her strong body too limp under Julie's arms. But Julie always held on. Until, eventually, Elle hugged her back. Hands clutching Julie's jacket, quietly desperate.

Julie knew Elle would get through this.

And she knew, as hard as it was to see Elle like this, that she couldn't imagine not being the one to be there, every day in the future that Elle needed someone to convince her to hug back.

"So," Julie made herself say to Ben, before she lost her nerve. "The thing is. I'm sort of in love with her."

Ben, as she had predicted, screamed.

"Julie!" He stood on his knees, shaking Julie's shoulders. "Julie Parker! You are in *love*!"

Delilah whined and jumped off the bed.

"Ben." Julie laughed. "Stop."

"Okay. Okay." He released her shoulders, bracketing his forehead with his hands. "I need to know everything. When did you decide this? Does she know? Does she love *you*? Of course she loves you. Who wouldn't love you. But has she told you?"

"No, she doesn't know. And I have no idea if she loves me. That's sort of the, uh, big question. You're the first person I've told."

Ben gasped, holding a hand to his chest. "Even before London?"

"Yes, but don't ever tell them that in case it hurts their feelings. I just…"

"Didn't want to take away from their engagement glow?"

The cabin in Gatlinburg had indeed been for the proposal. London had assured Julie they hadn't gotten down on one knee. That they'd been ready to just talk, to accept Dahlia's feelings, whatever they were.

Dahlia's feelings, of course, had been an enthusiastic *yes*.

"Yeah, exactly. I will talk to them about it eventually, but…" Julie bit her lip. "It might not even work out anyway, so."

"Julie." Ben nudged her knee. "The woman offered to practice-date you. She took a leave of absence to coach with you. It will work out."

Julie stared at the ceiling. "But what if it doesn't? I…" Julie shook her head. "You're a little nervous about stuff with Lex? I've never done any of this before. I am all the way nervous."

Ben fell back down next to her. "Of course you are, Jules. It's fucking terrifying. But you're sure? About how you feel? I know you had…questions."

"Yeah." Julie breathed out. "I know it probably sounds ridiculous. Considering—"

"It's not ridiculous." Ben cut her off before she could list all the things she'd spent her whole life considering. For which she was grateful. She was, frankly, exhausted of feeling ridiculous.

"I just..."

"You just know," Ben said with a gentle smile, and Julie exhaled.

"Yeah."

And Julie knew the timing wasn't great. Elle was still in the middle of a depressive episode, and even if it seemed like Elle was feeling a bit better each day—her hugs back coming a bit quicker—Vanessa wasn't in a great spot, either, with the emotional stress of the holidays. Julie should wait until the end of the season to tell Elle that she didn't want any of it to be practice anymore. That *Elle* was the one she wanted to ask out on a real date.

But she had to know. If Elle felt it, too.

"*Julie.*" Ben hugged her side. "You've made your childhood hero into your modern-day lover. I can't get over it."

Julie wrinkled her nose. "Ew. Only you would refer to her as my *lover.*"

"Well." Ben tapped her nose. "Is she? Have you...made the love?"

Julie rolled her eyes once more before releasing another deep breath.

"A few weeks ago, we..." Julie's face heated. "Fooled around? Did sex stuff? I don't know." She covered her face with her hands.

"Did one or both of you come?" Ben asked, propping his head on a fist. He asked it so matter-of-factly, without embarrassment. Julie could not picture ever being able to talk so casually about this, but the fact that Ben could made her braver.

She dropped her hands. "Yes."

"Well, I know the straights sometimes have their own weird rules about this, but in my book, if someone comes—or comes close to coming, if orgasm is hard for them—that counts as sex."

"Yeah." Julie breathed out. "It felt like sex."

Ben nodded, studying her. "But nothing else has happened, since then?"

"We've kissed a few times." She rubbed her palms, suddenly clammy, down her thighs. "But no. It's hard to find times Vanessa isn't around, for one, and Elle's in kind of a rough spot right now, mentally. But I also think she's been…waiting for me. To show a sign that I want to keep doing it. Because I might have said something. After that time a few weeks ago. That I wasn't totally sure about it all."

When Ben was silent, Julie was forced to look over and make eye contact. He was holding a hand over his mouth, eyes shiny.

"Oh my god." She scrunched up her nose again. "Are you *crying*? Stop it."

"It's just!" Ben dropped his hand to burst out. "You expressed what you were feeling! And she's respecting you! I'm just—" Oh my god, he *was* crying. Which made *Julie* want to cry again. What the hell. This was the worst.

"This is so good, Julie. I'm just really happy about this."

Julie sniffed as she looked away.

"Yeah. Well."

"So," Ben said with a sniffle of his own as he pushed himself up, sitting cross-legged at her side. "Have you decided you *do* want to keep doing sexy stuff?"

"Yeah." Julie nodded. "I do. I think…I might be demi? I don't know. Every single label I research still feels weird."

"That would make sense to me," Ben said. "You being demi. But you also don't *need* a label, Julie. Like." He lifted his shoulders, let them drop. "Whatever."

A small laugh escaped Julie's mouth. Mostly because the more she thought about it, *whatever* was, in fact, *exactly* how Julie felt.

But Ben must have taken the laugh as dismissive, because he kept going, waving his arms as he did.

"Seriously! If you're happy doing what you're doing with Elle, just be happy! Don't stress about whether it means you're a lesbian or bi or whatever. If you like sex with Elle, even if you never have sex with anyone else, don't stress about where that puts you, or doesn't put you, on the ace spectrum, if you don't want to stress about it. Labels can definitely be helpful, but if you're happy where you're at, then just—whatever!"

"Whatever," Julie agreed with a smile.

"Whatever!" Ben echoed, throwing his arms in the air again.

"Whatever!" Julie shouted it, mimicking his arm motions. And then they kept shouting it, throwing their arms around, until they were laughing so hard Ben collapsed back onto the bed, and Julie had to stop to get a breath.

"You are such a dork," she said. "And I love you so much."

"Same, Jules. Same."

"I'm going to miss you so much."

"I don't even want to think about how much I'm going to miss you."

"Yeah." Julie smiled. "So let's not."

"Agreed. Let's not." Ben ruffled Julie's hair. "So what's the plan? When are you going to tell her?"

"Christmas," she said. "At least, if it feels right. We'll each be with our families during the day, but I was thinking I could go over there at night. And considering I'm not even one hundred percent sure that she *likes* me, I'm not going to declare my love or anything. But I'll tell her I don't want to practice anymore. That I want it to be real."

Ben stared at her for a long moment.

"From what you've told me," he said slowly, "it feels like it's probably been real this whole time. And for what it's worth..." He tapped her nose again. "Lord knows I've been guilty of popping the L-word too early before, to guys who never deserved it, but... if you really love someone? Life's short, Julie. Sometimes it's worth it to just tell them."

Julie took one last deep breath. Maybe Ben was right. Maybe it had always been real, and Julie simply hadn't been brave enough to believe it.

Either way, it was Christmas. The season of hope. Of preparing for a new year.

Maybe sometimes leaps of faith were worth it.

Julie was almost out the door when Iris called from the kitchen.

"Julie! Julie Parker! Don't you leave this house yet, young lady!"

Julie paused, car keys in hand, as Iris hustled over. Clad in a flour-dusted apron, she dragged Julie by the wrist into the kitchen.

"You never talked to me at Thanksgiving, you know."

Julie blinked. Dropped her keys on the counter. *Shit.* She had totally forgotten.

"I'm sorry, Iris. I kept meaning to check in, but—"

"Ach, it's fine." Iris bent to check something in the stove. "You want a slice of queen's cake, love?"

"No, that's okay."

"Arroz doce?"

"No thank you."

Iris turned. "Sugar cookie?"

And because Julie knew Iris would in fact keep listing desserts until Julie accepted one, she said, "Sure."

With a satisfied smile, Iris plopped some cookies on a paper towel in front of Julie before seating herself on a stool next to her.

"It's okay you forgot to talk to me," she said, "because it wasn't a sure thing yet anyway. I would've tracked you down, otherwise. But I was at the East office before break and found out for sure."

Julie broke off a snowman's head, eyeing Iris warily.

"Found out what for sure?"

"Hiram's retiring."

Iris snapped into her own cookie.

"And Hiram is…"

"A counselor. He handles sophomores and seniors, currently."

Julie stared at her. "I'm…glad for him?"

Iris gave her one of her focused looks, like she was disappointed Julie hadn't figured it out yet.

"Me and the Doc want you to take his place."

Julie continued to stare. "Excuse me?"

"Tell me, Julie, does alumni relations make you content? Don't mind me if it does, but from what Bento says, that's not quite the case."

"Iris." Julie spluttered an incredulous laugh. "I understood you convincing me to take the coaching position; I have basketball experience, but—"

"The Doc wants you."

Julie spluttered some more. "But I don't—What? Why?"

"She likes what you're doing with the team. I mentioned your name when they were talking about filling Hiram's position. I did"—Iris held out a hand when Julie made another unintelligible noise—"say that you'd probably have to go back to school, get your education credentials. But when I said you had a psych degree already, Doc's eyes lit up. I believe her exact words were 'We have to lock that girl in.'"

Julie looked away.

"She hasn't said anything to me about it."

"I told her I'd talk to you first, give you some space to get used to the idea. Hiram is finishing out the year, so the position likely won't even post until the spring sometime, but that'll give you time to do some research about what you'll have to do. The Doc said you could be hired on a provisional basis, start work at the same time you go back to school, as long as you commit to finishing your coursework within a certain time period."

Julie rubbed her hands along her temples.

"Iris. I don't...I love you, but it feels weird that you keep... directing my life for me."

As soon as she said it, she felt a little guilty. It wasn't Iris's fault Julie couldn't figure out what to do with her life on her own.

"Bah." Iris dismissed this with a wave of her hand. "I'm doing no such thing, Julie. You could have said no to the coaching position; you can say no to this. To be honest, I could be handing you a raw deal here. Being a counselor is a time-consuming, thankless job where students and parents only come to you with their problems, hardly ever their own compassion. And counselors juggle a whole heck of a lot these days, more than is fair. But, Julie."

Iris leaned forward, rested a hand on Julie's arm.

"I've been to a couple games this season, seen how the team responds to you. It can be a tall order, earning teenagers' respect, but you got it. And I know balancing Vandy and the team during the season is tough for you. Might as well join the whole system, eh?"

This was undeniably true, at least. Working at East would make the logistics of coaching far simpler, but...

God. Could she tackle one thing at a time, here? Her mind was already spinning from everything she'd just discussed with Ben. Why couldn't a life-altering career change smack her in the face, you know, after basketball season, at least? After she'd survived declaring her love for Elle?

Elle.

Suddenly, all Julie wanted to do was discuss this with Elle. She was so smart and logical, and she'd always...

Julie took a shaky breath as the truth of it hit her.

Even when Julie hadn't been able to do so herself...Elle had always taken Julie seriously.

She'd be able to help Julie work through her thoughts.

But first, Julie should actually do that research. About what the job did, in fact, entail, if it was something she felt she could handle, and god, did Julie really want to go back to school?

"Could I talk to Hiram? So I could know what I'd be walking into here?"

Iris's mouth curved into a smile, almost mischievous, so like Ben. Like Julie had said exactly what she'd been waiting to hear. Like Julie had just accepted the job.

"Absolutely you can," she said. "I can set it up for you myself."

Julie laughed a little. "I thought *you* were retired, too, Iris?"

While Iris used to run the front office at East, she'd "retired" last school year. She still substituted now, when they needed her, and it didn't surprise Julie a bit when Iris tipped her head, grin deepening as she said, "Eh. I've earned the right to still do what I want over there, and they know it."

Julie shook her head, her laughter fading.

"Iris," she said. "I know you believe Dr. Jones wants me for this, but...I assume HR will still have to interview multiple candidates, right? People who already have the qualifications, who have more experience with the district? What if..." Julie spread her hands open on the counter. "What if I start to really want it? And then it's all for nothing anyway?"

Iris's smile changed, eyes softening.

"I wish I could tell you that wouldn't happen. Seeing some of the things this district has done over the years?" Iris's shoulders rose and fell. "I can't guarantee it. But, love. If you're not happy doing what you're doing now? Life's too short to not take some risks every now and then."

With another pat of Julie's arm, Iris stood, checking the temperature of her queen's cake with a pleased hum.

Julie wondered if there actually was magic in the Caravalho connection. If Iris knew that not thirty minutes ago her son had said almost the same exact words to her, a floor below.

She stared at her half-eaten snowman and let a small laugh escape.

If you took enough leaps of faith at once, at least one of them had to stick, right?

Julie kissed Iris on the cheek. Told her she'd be in touch. And when she finally headed home to Snoozles, every landmark she passed on the way seemed somehow brighter than before.

CHAPTER TWENTY-FIVE

Elle was taking Christmas cookies out of the oven when her phone rang.

She still wasn't completely okay; she hadn't yet been able to return to the clarity of that quiet morning in her bed. But Elle would likely never be completely okay, and what was important was that she was feeling okay enough. Okay enough to use her own kitchen for the first time in more than a week. And maybe it was a little late in the season to finally be making Christmas cookies, on the day before Christmas Eve. But oh well. They would still taste good. She was still proud of making them.

She couldn't wait to show them to Julie.

Elle pulled off her oven mitt and picked up the phone. She frowned when she saw the caller ID; Vanessa didn't have any scheduled CPS visits this week.

"Hi, Amber," she said. "How are you?"

"Good!" Amber chirped. "Good. I'm so glad I got ahold of you. I have some news."

It was almost funny. Elle would have sworn she'd never feel as taken by surprise, as thrown off guard, as when she had received that very first call from CPS, back in October. But as Amber talked about how a judge had just approved Karly's reunification plan— apparently she and her lawyer had put in a special request that she and Vanessa be reunited for Christmas—"Courts are always waiting until the last minute around here!" Amber said with a chuckle, "but I'm so glad for you all. Karly has been doing so well, and I'm sure Vanessa will be glad to be home for the holiday"—as Amber's cheery voice explained how she couldn't get there today for the transfer, but she could come tomorrow, if that worked for Elle and Vanessa?

Elle stared at the shapes she'd cut out of dough—snowmen, candy canes, evergreen trees, crisp and ready for icing—and as she listened, and nodded, and said "Yes, of course" and "Right, I will" and "Okay," she knew that this call, this moment of surprise two months after the first, was somehow worse.

She placed the phone on the counter. Stared across the kitchen at the lights on the Christmas tree.

And she wondered why. Why she hadn't prepared herself more for this. Why she hadn't known that Karly had put in a special request to be reunified by Christmas. Why Amber, why Camryn, why no one else at CPS had told her, had *warned* her. She had known Karly was doing well with her case plan, but no one had ever given Elle even an estimated timeline. No one had told her.

Except, no. She had talked to other foster parents, in the classes she'd been going to, in the Nashville Foster Parents Facebook group she'd joined, about how this was a system where everything happened either too slow or too fast. How you waited too long for the courts, too long to hear back from CPS, to get the answers you needed.

And how suddenly, then, you took a child into your care that hadn't been there before.

And how suddenly, one day, they could be gone.

"Hey, Elle. Did you make *cookies*?"

Elle jerked at Vanessa's voice.

Vanessa poked a finger at the sugar cookies. "Sweet."

Elle stared at her, and she thought—*no*.

Elle had been on Karly's side this whole time, rooting for her, but she had left Vanessa home alone for *weeks* without an explanation, had chosen her addiction over Vanessa's well-being, and Vanessa must have been so *scared*. Didn't it take longer than this, longer than a couple of measly months, to detox? To recover from addiction? Except no, Elle had learned in her classes about how there *wasn't* a foolproof recovery from addiction; you could only maintain your sobriety; you could only ever manage it. You couldn't make it go away. Was Karly really ready for that? What if she relapsed, met a new guy, a few weeks into January, and Vanessa would have to go through this all over again?

And maybe this was a broken system, full of imperfect choices and poor communication and last-minute decisions, but *Karly* should have kept Elle in the loop. She should have told Elle about the request. Karly and Elle weren't part of the system. They were Karly and Elle, cousins, family, Vanessa's team, and Elle had been so open with Karly, had told her she could talk to them anytime. And suddenly, Elle was filled with rage. If Karly wanted to take responsibility for Vanessa, if she wanted to make a safe home for her, she had to *talk* to them. Wouldn't Karly have known that Elle might have had Christmas plans, too?

And *god*, she had spent the last week wasting so much time! She hadn't even taken Vanessa to Opryland yet.

"Elle…are you okay?"

Vanessa was staring at her, head tilted. She frowned as she got closer. Elle didn't know what to do, how to hold her face.

The frown on Vanessa's face turned into a wide-eyed look of panic.

"Elle. Elle, what's going on?"

Elle had to get it together. This had always been the plan, right? This was what Elle had wanted.

What Vanessa wanted.

"Fuck. Fuck, Elle, is it my mom? Did she—"

"Vanessa." Elle took Vanessa's hands in her own. Used every ounce of control she had to smile and look Vanessa in the eye. "No. Everything's good. Your mom is fine. Vanessa—" Elle swallowed, told herself it didn't feel wrong to say it, that Elle's house had only ever been temporary for her. "You're going home."

Vanessa stared, eyes still wide, for one beat, two.

Finally, she took a deep, heaving breath—the most animated show of emotion she had ever shown Elle directly—and said, in a small voice, "Really?"

"Yeah." Elle squeezed Vanessa's hands. Vanessa's face blurred as Elle's eyes filled with tears she couldn't repress. "They just called. You're going back to your mom's—your house—tomorrow. You'll be there for Christmas."

Vanessa kept staring. Until she repeated, "Really?"

"Really." Elle squeezed Vanessa's hands even tighter, even though she knew Vanessa didn't like physical contact, even though she knew she should let go, that she was squeezing too hard. When Vanessa still didn't say anything else, when Elle could tell she needed something, some reassurance that this was happening, Elle whispered, "Your mom's doing so good, Vanessa."

Vanessa's lower lip trembled.

And then she hurled herself into Elle's arms, and Elle grabbed her tight around the shoulders. They cried, big and ugly, and they laughed at how big and ugly they were crying.

When Vanessa stepped back, Elle realized it was the first time Vanessa had hugged her since she'd shown up at her door two months ago.

"I can still come back here sometimes, right? To visit?"

"Yes. Vanessa, of course." Elle wiped at her face before she took Vanessa's hands again. "Vanessa, I mean it. You have the key I gave you, right?" Vanessa nodded, mascara running down her cheeks.

Elle tried to smile at her. This part was important. "You use that key anytime you need to. All right? I'm serious. For anything, anytime. Mi casa es tu casa, siempre."

"I'll miss you helping me with my Spanish homework."

Elle laughed. Vanessa had barely ever let her help her, even though Elle had minored in it at UT.

"FaceTime me anytime you need help, okay?"

Vanessa nodded. And finally, Elle released Vanessa's hands. Elle took a deep breath, straightening her spine. She picked up a snowman cookie and bit its head off.

"These are better with icing," she said.

Vanessa picked up another snowman and did the same. "Yeah," she said.

And then they both laughed again.

"Okay." Vanessa hugged her elbows. "I guess I should pack."

Elle put down her half-eaten cookie. "Yeah," she said, and her smile felt easier. "You should."

"This is weird," Vanessa said after a minute.

"I know. How are you feeling?"

Vanessa looked around the kitchen, stared into the den.

"Happy," she said. "But weird."

"Yeah," Elle said on a half laugh. "Me too."

"Okay," Vanessa said again. And finally, she turned and headed toward the stairs. She stopped at the bottom, staring up.

"Hey, Elle?" She turned again, still holding her elbows.

"Yeah?" Elle leaned against the kitchen island, her body heavy and light all at once.

"Thank you."

And there was so much in those two words, so much that a part of Elle had always wanted to hear. Even though now that she heard them, she realized she didn't truly need them. She only wanted Vanessa to be okay.

Elle swallowed around the lump in her throat. "Anytime."

Vanessa bit her lip. Took a deep breath through her nose.

And went upstairs to pack her room.

Elle wanted to text Julie, to let her know what was happening.

Her instinct, these days, was to always tell Julie. She had been able to tell Julie, that night when Julie had shown up and ordered Thai food and taken care of them, more about how her depression worked than she had ever been able to put into words for Sophie.

But these words were hard to type, because Elle was still processing these words, still putting them in order and making sense of them, and she knew... she knew Julie would come over, and help, like she had been helping for the entire last week. While Elle had lain on the couch, useless and sad, for no fucking reason.

Like Julie had been helping them, from the start, this entire time.

And if this was Elle's last night as a foster parent, she needed to do it right, for once. For herself and for her family. Help Vanessa pack. Be here, *present*, for Vanessa. Maybe, finally, ask her how to play *Super Mario Brothers*.

Be in control again.

And then, somehow, time went by in a blur.

Amber showed up before noon on Christmas Eve. It felt so strange, watching Vanessa tumble into Amber's car, the same backpack and gym bag she'd had when she'd first shown up at Elle's door, so angry and blank. She wasn't blank on Christmas Eve—she was full of smiles, and nerves, and hugs, a child Elle had barely met before—and she had more now than what she'd been able to fit in two bags.

Elle had almost given her one of her own suitcases, to accommodate the extra stuff Vanessa had accumulated over the time she had been living with her.

Instead, she'd told Vanessa she could get the rest next time. Whenever she wanted to come back to visit. Or Elle would bring it herself, when she visited them at Karly's. Which she was determined to do, on a regular basis. This wasn't an ending, she told herself. And if Karly faltered again—because it was likely, as much as Elle wanted to believe in her, that she would falter again—Elle would be there this time.

With a whisper of Amber's tires as she backed out of Elle's driveway, they were gone, the sunlight thin in the winter sky.

And then it was time to go to Rose's house, where Elle always spent Christmas Eve, and Rose clutched her hands when she walked in, Holly running around their feet, and said, voice as soft as Rose ever made it, "Hey, Elle Belle. Let's go have a sit."

And so they did.

And Elle wanted to call Julie then, when she got home. Julie had texted her a few things, the last two days, each one making Elle smile, each a tiny miracle.

But it was late, and it was all feeling so hard, fighting off the sadness. Hard to imagine spending the day at Tricia's tomorrow, full of children's excitement over presents. And Elle *loved* watching Tricia's kids open presents. At least, she knew she did, that she had in the past; her old therapist always told her to remind herself of things she knew were true, when her brain was telling her that nothing was.

Her house was too dark and quiet. The sugar cookies still sat on the counter, never moved from the baking sheet; the bowls of icing she'd made turned hard and ruined. She felt so far away, so removed from everything. Incapable of even sending a text. Her head was a hollow rubber ball that only wanted to sleep.

But her body wouldn't let her sleep. It never did, whenever she needed it most.

The clock crept closer toward Christmas, and Elle sat alone in her sitting room, staring at her little Christmas village, wondering what the hell had happened these last few months.

She wasn't working. Didn't know, really, if she actually wanted to return to the job where she had spent so much of the last decade. But she knew, even if it was hard to think about just then, that she would have to, and soon. She'd been ignoring it, but her savings had started to run thin. And there was no reason to continue the leave of absence now, when there were no more appointments to run Vanessa to.

She had been a temporary parent.

A practice girlfriend.

And maybe that one wasn't quite true. Maybe she was more than that to Julie, as Julie had always been more than that to her. Elle had been planning, in fact, on making a big declaration to Julie about it on Christmas. Which, looking at the clock, was…today.

But perhaps even that was foolish, another mirage Elle had tricked herself into believing. It had been Julie, after all, who always reminded them that this was all practice for her. Julie who had never made any true signs, even after the last month, even after they'd had sex, that she wanted to change that.

Even Elle's house, which had always been Elle's safe space, felt wrong without Vanessa or Julie there.

She had worked so hard, these last eight years, to build a life that was steady, reliable. Hers.

But as the morning hours marched on, and Elle attempted to prepare herself for Tricia's, as she dumped the cookies and the icing in the trash—

Elle only felt like a shadow.

CHAPTER TWENTY-SIX

You doing okay, Jules?"

Julie put her phone down as Charlotte sat next to her on the couch.

"Yeah," Julie lied. "Sorry. I know I haven't been very present today."

To be more to the point: she couldn't stop looking at her damn phone. On Christmas. She was annoying to herself.

"That's okay, dear." Charlotte patted her knee. "Just wanted to make sure you're okay."

"Thanks, Mom."

It had been a different and relatively quiet Christmas, in Parker family terms.

They'd gone to visit London and Dahlia in the morning, just Julie and Charlotte and Tom. London was still tired and mostly bedbound from their surgery a few days ago, but didn't seem to be in too much pain. Hank had sent them a special pillow, along with advice from his own top surgery, that seemed to be serving London well. They had been able to stay awake for presents, and to briefly discuss wedding plans—they had a few venues they were interested in; they were thinking next fall—before falling soundly back asleep.

Charlotte and Tom had gone for a walk, and Julie had sat on the kitchen counter while Dahlia packed up the ridiculous amount of food she had prepared for them to take back to the Parker house.

"I cleared my calendar, am in full caretaking mode," Dahlia said, "and they just sleep. Which is good, but I can't stop making things. Our freezer's running out of room. Please help me."

As odd of a Christmas morning as it was, it had been nice getting to talk to Dahlia, just the two of them, like they used to talk during those after-work drinks. Dahlia was so excited about the wedding that she was practically glowing. No, not practically; she was just glowing.

"It feels so good, to get a second chance, you know? The first time around, I hardly even knew myself. I just planned everything how all the bridal blogs told me I should, whatever I thought would make David and our families happy, that would look prettiest in pictures. But now...London and I can both do what we *want*."

And then Dahlia's eyes had gotten wet, and she'd turned away to put a lid on the rugelach. Julie hopped off the counter to hug her from behind.

"You'll help us figure everything out?" Dahlia asked through her sniffles. "You'll tell us if we're getting annoying?"

"You know I will," Julie said, her cheek on Dahlia's hair.

It was the longest stretch of time, those couple of hours, that Julie had been able to stop staring at her phone in the last three days.

Back at the Parkers', a few aunts and uncles and cousins stopped by, a neighbor who always had an automatic invite. But neither Sara nor Jackie, Julie and London's older sisters, had come home; there had been no Uncle Jamie and Bucky. It hadn't been quiet, really; the food Dahlia sent them with was still consumed, the house still full of laughter and warmth. But it was still quiet for the Parkers, and quiet enough that Julie had plenty of time and space to stare at her phone and wonder, again, what the hell was going on with Elle.

She had their last few texts memorized at this point. She'd texted on Friday morning to report that London was out of surgery and then when they were safely home.

Good, I'm so glad, Elle had responded.

But the next few days had been all Julie.

> **Julie:** This is the worst. The one thing you're supposed to be able to do when someone's recovering from surgery is bring them food, but London had to go fall in love with Dahlia, who cooks any time she has a feeling! I am useless!

> **Julie:** Happy Christmas Eve, Elle. Christmas Eve > Christmas, amiright

> **Julie:** [A photoshopped photo of Snoozles's face transposed onto Santa's body]

> **Julie:** It feels weird not spending Christmas Eve with London.

> **Julie:** I hope you're doing okay.

> **Julie:** Tell Rose I said hi.

By the time Julie had sent the Rose one last night, she had never felt so pathetic in her life.

She had also started to worry that something was seriously wrong. She'd tried calling, then, but Elle hadn't picked up. Julie had talked herself out of driving over there, because it had been late, and maybe Julie was, in fact, being hyper-annoying and needed to chill the fuck out.

And then this morning, there had been a sign of life.

Elle: Merry Christmas, Julie.

Elle: I hope it's merry and bright.

The messages had been sent at 3:16 a.m., and Julie could not decipher them at all.

Ostensibly, there was not much to decipher; it was simply Elle saying merry Christmas. But sometimes when Julie read it in her head, it felt warm, personal—the inclusion of Julie's name, the period, making it somehow sound like *I love you*—and then other times, it only sounded oddly cold and impersonal. Especially since she hadn't responded to any of the earlier texts from Julie. Like a generic message you'd send to your entire contact list.

Charlotte rested her head on Julie's shoulder.

"What is Elle up to today?" she asked. As if she could read Julie's mind. As if she'd been reading Julie's mind all day.

Julie almost answered, *I don't know*, but worried it'd come out bitter. So she said, trying to keep her voice neutral, "She's at her sister Tricia's house."

Charlotte made a small *hmm* noise. She and Julie resumed staring quietly at the tree. They were alone in the living room; the rest of the guests who were still around congregated in the kitchen.

"This song always makes me feel sad," Charlotte said after a moment. John Lennon's "Happy Xmas (War Is Over)" was playing over the house's stereo system. "Even though it's called 'Happy Christmas.'"

"Yeah," Julie managed to croak out. "Me too."

"But." Charlotte put a hand on Julie's knee again before lifting her head. "Life is like that, sometimes."

After another few moments of silence, Charlotte said, "Shall we do it?"

And Julie sighed. "Yeah. Let's do it."

"I'll get the hot chocolate."

And they tucked into their annual Christmas rewatch of *It's a Wonderful Life*.

Julie cried the whole way through.

At her apartment later that night, Julie stared at the bag of oddly shaped lumps of grain on the coffee table. She'd ended up wrapping all the various things she'd bought at the health food store, even if most of it was just stuff purchased in bulk plastic bags, resulting in a pile of Christmas-wrapped squishy blobs. But she had thought it was funny, at the time, each increasingly horribly wrapped item making her giggle, and she had hoped they would make Elle do the same.

But now, she didn't know what to do. She was probably overreacting to Elle's lack of text messages. It felt like such a silly thing to be upset about: *my friend hasn't texted me enough.*

But she hadn't even reacted to the Snoozles Santa Photoshop. And Julie had worked hard on that.

Yet. Julie had planned to go over and make her big declaration tonight, and there was no *real* reason to change the plan. It was Christmas. Julie worried that if she waited too long, if the temporary bravery that an entire oeuvre of Hallmark movies had made her believe existed on this day passed, then she'd never get the nerve at all.

"Well, Snoozles," she said. "Here goes nothing."

She picked up her bag of lumps and headed once more to East Nashville.

CHAPTER TWENTY-SEVEN

When Elle opened the door and saw Julie's face, something inside her immediately thawed.

"Julie," she said, voice wavering in the middle. God, it felt good to see her. Julie hugged her elbows, a grocery bag in her hand hitting her side. She looked down at her feet before glancing, uncertainly, at Elle.

And then she froze. Just for a moment. Before she stepped inside the foyer and reached a hand toward Elle's face.

Elle's heart thudded.

But before her hand reached her, Julie dropped it.

"Glasses," she said. She cleared her throat. "I didn't know you wear glasses."

"Oh." Elle touched the frames. "They're just blue light glasses, for when I'm working on the computer. I forgot I had them on."

"They're hot," Julie blurted, and then blushed, and Elle smiled. It felt like the first real smile her face had made in a long time.

"Come on in." She stepped back, giving Julie space to take off her shoes before they walked into the kitchen. Elle took off the glasses and set them next to her laptop, where she'd been working at the kitchen island.

"Where's Vanessa?" Julie asked. She placed the grocery bag on a stool. "Upstairs? How was Tricia's?"

Elle paused by the sink.

And she knew, with sudden, sickening clarity, how much she had messed up.

"Vanessa's not here. She…" Elle made herself look at Julie. "She's back at Karly's."

Julie stuck her hands into the back pockets of her jeans. Her forehead creased in confusion.

"Back at Karly's… to visit? Is that allowed now?"

Elle only shook her head. Julie stared at her for another moment.

"She's back at Karly's, for good," Julie eventually summarized, all expression draining from her face. "Like, she doesn't live here anymore."

Elle nodded. "Yeah."

Julie broke eye contact to stare at the fridge. "When did you find out that was happening?"

Elle looked at the floor. "Saturday. Her caseworker came and got her yesterday."

Julie was quiet then. And Elle knew, from that quiet, without even looking at her, how much she had hurt her.

But Julie didn't ask, *Why didn't you tell me?* Because she was Julie, and she was kind, and she only said, "How are you doing? The house must feel so quiet."

Elle lifted her eyes. Julie was smiling at her, except the smile didn't reach her eyes. Elle had never seen a smile not reach Julie's eyes before.

"Julie," she said, feeling her seams slowly coming unraveled. "I was planning on telling you, tomorrow. I've been in a kind of bad space, and I just…wanted to get through Christmas, wanted to be better, before I saw you."

"You don't…" Julie shook her head, breaking eye contact and shifting on her feet. "You don't have to be in a good headspace to tell me things, Elle. I'm not Sophie. I don't care."

Elle took in a shaky breath. Part of her wanted to tell Julie that it was the bad headspace that made it impossible for Elle to tell people things. That if she *could* talk to people when she wasn't in a good headspace, she would.

But maybe Julie was right. Of course Julie was right. And suddenly, this felt *exactly* like Sophie, all over again. Elle fucking up, not treating someone she cared about right enough, forcing them to slip away at the time she actually needed them the most.

"I know," she whispered. "I'm sorry."

A strained silence stretched before Julie said, "What are you working on?" She motioned with her head to the open laptop.

"Oh." Elle brought a hand to her neck. She'd planned to draft some emails to her boss and HR tonight, letting them know she could come back earlier than expected from her leave of absence. But when she'd logged into her Vandy email, she'd gotten distracted by the hundreds of emails she'd missed since the last time she'd logged in. Strangely, it had ended up being the one thing she'd done in the last three days that had started to make her feel better. She'd forgotten how satisfying it was, deleting emails she didn't need. "Just work stuff."

"Work stuff?" Julie jerked her head toward her, that crease back in her forehead. "For Vandy? But—" And then she cut herself off, eyes going blank.

"Yeah. Since Vanessa's gone, I figured..."

"Time to go back to work." Julie swallowed again, nodding, except it felt all wrong. Her face was so vacant, like she had disappeared completely. "So you'll probably have to cut short the coaching gig. I know you had a work conflict, before."

"Oh," Elle said, panic rising in her veins, moving toward her, but when Julie took a step back, she stopped herself. "Actually—"

"No, no," Julie cut her off. "It's okay. I understand. You've already helped so much. Maybe you could come see a game, sometime, if we make it to districts."

She gave Elle a sad smile, and Elle's heart broke in two.

It had actually been a big part of the emails she'd planned on drafting, that she could come back, but she'd need an adjusted schedule, so she could still make it to practices and games. And now Elle's heart ached for a different reason. That Julie apparently thought so little of Elle, thought Elle was a person who would walk away from a commitment—from the Bobcats—so easily.

"No, Julie," she managed to say, even as tears burned behind her eyes. "I'm still all in on the Bobcats. So is Vanessa." She'd made sure to ask, before Vanessa left, if she planned on still playing for the team, since getting to see her mom had been a big part of her agreeing to the team at all. But Vanessa had only given her a funny look and said, "Uh, yeah."

"Yeah," Julie said now, taking another step away. Not even listening. "Bobcats forever, right?"

"Julie."

"That's, uh, for you." Julie motioned toward the bag, cheeks pinkening. "Kind of dumb. Sorry."

"Julie," Elle said again. "I got something for you, too, but I had to special order it and it hasn't come yet." Because of fucking course it hadn't. It sounded like such a lie, coming out of her mouth now, only adding to the awkwardness of this entire conversation, but she had ordered it weeks ago. At the beginning of December. It had been a risk, but she had thought, by Christmas, maybe she'd be ready to give it to her. Maybe by Christmas, Julie would be open to receiving it. But then she'd gotten an email last week that shipping was delayed, and of course, she hadn't even been able to do this one thing right.

"That's okay," Julie said. "Don't worry about it. Anyway, I should go."

And she was turning, walking out of Elle's kitchen, and by the time Elle got enough breath in her lungs to follow her, Julie already had her shoes on, hand on the doorknob. She must have heard Elle coming, because she paused.

"Thank you," Julie said to the door, "for everything you've done for me this season."

"Julie," Elle breathed, wanting to run to her, to hold her, but Julie's body language was making it so clear that she didn't want that. That she was saying goodbye. "Please stay."

"I should go," Julie echoed herself as she opened the door. A gust of chilly December air blew into the foyer. "Merry Christmas, Elle," she said over her shoulder as she closed the door behind her and walked away.

When Elle heard the front door open and shut again ten minutes later, she leaped off the kitchen stool where she'd been staring into space.

She had come back. She'd realized that she hadn't even given Elle a chance to talk. Maybe she'd forgive Elle for—

Vanessa walked into the kitchen.

"Hey, Elle," she said. "Me and Mom were just out for a 7-Eleven run, so we thought we'd stop by and I could get some more of my... Are you okay?" Vanessa frowned. "You look super weird."

Elle huffed out a small, sad laugh. She was going to miss Vanessa's astute assessments of her appearance. And of course it was Vanessa, who had a key. She should have given Julie a key a month ago.

"Is your mom coming in?"

"Nah, she said she'd wait in the car."

Elle pressed her lips together as she nodded, trying to keep her face neutral. Of course. Elle had only taken care of her child for two months, but Karly couldn't even muster the energy to come in and say hello.

Elle sat back on her stool. She'd have to get over these spikes of anger she kept having if she wanted to navigate a better way forward for everyone. Maybe Karly just needed time. Maybe seeing the house where her daughter had lived for two months without her would be difficult. Maybe everyone just needed time.

"How was your Christmas?" Elle asked.

"Good. I mean. Kind of weird, but good. How was yours?"

"It was okay." Elle looked at Vanessa with a soft smile. "I missed you."

"You did?" Vanessa asked with surprise, an embarrassed look taking over her face a second later, like she hadn't meant to say it. Elle laughed.

"Of course I did, Vanessa," she said. "I love you."

And Elle's heart broke, again, when that look of surprise returned to Vanessa's face.

"Oh," she said, scratching her head uncomfortably while looking away. "I, uh. Love you, too."

Elle stared at her, feeling stunned.

Had Elle really never said those words, the whole time Vanessa had lived with her?

"I kind of thought you'd be, like"—Vanessa gestured around the kitchen—"celebrating your freedom."

Elle's shoulders crumpled. "No, Vanessa," she said. "No. Hey. Look at me. It wasn't like that at all, okay? I promise. I will *always* want you around."

Vanessa nodded, making eye contact for a second before she looked away, but Elle was proud of her for that second. She'd take it.

"What's this?" Vanessa prodded the bag Julie had left, clearly ready to change topics.

"Oh." Elle swallowed. "Just some presents Coach left."

"For you?" And when Elle nodded, Vanessa said, incredulous, "And you haven't opened them yet?"

"Want to help me open them?" Elle was pretty sure Julie wouldn't have gifted her anything inappropriate. At least, she sincerely hoped she hadn't, now, although she also would've been proud of her, if she had. Either way, Elle worried she'd never be strong enough to open them on her own.

"Fork yeah, I do." Vanessa was already lifting the first package and ripping into it. "Man, Coach could seriously invest in some better gift-wrapping skills."

Elle laughed as she picked up the next one. They really were horribly wrapped, but they were also soft and oddly shaped, so she imagined they had been difficult to wrap well. She loved them.

"Coach got you..." Vanessa stared dubiously at the bag in her hand. "Millet?"

Elle laughed again, louder, brighter this time. "She did?"

She finished unwrapping the lumpy gift in her own hands. "Oh, I love farro!"

Vanessa gave her a look, but reached for the next one. Soon, they were racing through them, throwing the wrapping all over Elle's floor, tossing each grain and nutrient supplement onto the island, Elle laughing the entire time, until she got to the last one.

Barley.

Elle smiled at it, before hugging it lovingly to her chest.

Vanessa stared at her.

"What did you get *her*?" she asked.

"Pencils," Elle said.

Vanessa stared a second more before she shook her head. "You two need help."

"They're supposed to be pencils that show her I love her," Elle went on, the adrenaline of the presents spurring on honesty. She wasn't sure when, exactly, she knew for sure that she loved Julie Parker. At some point before she'd ordered those pencils, at least. Maybe it had been when she'd laughed at Elle's creepy Christmas dolls. Maybe it had been their one-on-one in the East High gym. Maybe it had been at Bella's Italian Eatery.

When she thought about it now, she thought maybe it had been the first time she'd heard Julie tell her players they had to be nice to their bus drivers.

Regardless, there was no use keeping it from Vanessa, who had been able to see through Elle from the start. "But they haven't come yet."

Vanessa shrugged. "I mean, she already knows you love her, so."

Elle placed the bag of barley on the counter, shaking her head.

"I don't think she does."

"Have you told her?"

"I want to, but…" Elle sighed. "I think I hurt her feelings."

Vanessa leaned forward, face turning serious.

"Are you and Coach fighting? Is that why you're sitting here all sad on Christmas?"

Elle didn't say anything.

"Listen," Vanessa went on. "You have to fix this. If you and Coach don't get married by the end of the season, the entire team is going to be disappointed."

A wobbly laugh escaped Elle's throat. "The team?"

Vanessa straightened. "Yeah. Everyone's invested."

Elle wasn't sure how she felt about a squad of teenagers gossiping about her. "That feels…kind of invasive."

"Elle, it truly is. You don't even know. Makes me feel pretty weird, to be honest. But seriously, if you've messed up with Coach, you better make it up to her."

Elle sighed, staring at the shreds of wrapping paper around them.

"She deserves better than me," she said quietly.

It sounded pathetic, as soon as it came out of her mouth, even if it was true. And she shouldn't be seeking counsel from Vanessa, anyway. She cleared her throat and stood, starting to organize the mess.

"You should go get your stuff. I bet your mom's wondering where you are."

"Shorts, yeah." Vanessa walked to the foot of the stairs before she turned back. "You should do something big for Coach," she said. "If you really think she doesn't know."

Elle stood by the sink, a ball of crumpled wrapping paper in her hand.

"You're right," she said. "I just . . . don't know what that something big should be."

Vanessa shrugged. "Just think about what she does deserve. You'll figure it out."

Vanessa sprinted to her room. Elle had already decided she wouldn't convert it back to an office; it would always be Vanessa's room, for whenever she needed it. She sprinted back down ten minutes later, yelling a goodbye as she slammed the front door.

Elle followed after her, made sure the door was locked. Stared out the window as Karly drove away, the muffler of her old car loud as it rumbled down Elle's street.

She returned to the kitchen, finished cleaning up the wrapping paper. Pushed all of Julie's gifts into a pile in the middle of the island. Stared at them awhile.

And then she picked up her phone and brought up Mara's number.

Elle: Can I come see you?

It took Mara a few minutes to respond, and Elle remembered—because she kept forgetting—that it was Christmas. That Mara was probably busy with family. But when she did respond, she said, Literally any time.

Elle only hesitated a second. She could wait until tomorrow, get some sleep. Not interrupt Mara's holiday. But sleep, or more accurately, the thoughts that invaded her brain when she tried to sleep, had not been kind to her this week. She didn't want to be in her empty house anymore. She wanted to be on I-40, driving in the quiet dark, toward Knoxville. Can I come now?

Mara: Girl. I'll be waiting.

CHAPTER TWENTY-EIGHT

Julie received the email the day before New Year's Eve.

The week between Christmas and New Year's always sucked, but this year sucked particularly hard. The next Bobcat game wasn't until January 3, and it was against McDougall, and Julie would be coaching alone, so she wasn't even looking forward to it.

London was still recovering from surgery, and increasingly grumpy about the fact that they were yet unable to tap-dance away from the couch. Dahlia was still cooking too much, assuring Julie they didn't need anything. Ben had finally finished packing, and was now anxiously ready to go. Julie would be at the Caravalhos' on January 2 to help see him off. But until then, he was busy working his final shifts at Lakeview.

And Vanessa was no longer living with Elle, so Julie wasn't needed for babysitting, or anything else.

Julie, in short, was no longer needed. By anyone.

Well, except for Snoozles, with whom Julie had been spending lots of time this week whilst feeling sorry for herself.

And possibly tussling with some feelings of regret.

She picked up her phone and stared, once again, at the text she'd received from Elle three days ago.

I'm out of town for a few days, it said. But can I see you when I get back?

And when Julie hadn't responded right away, Elle had added, I'd really love to see you.

Julie kept thinking about the day Vanessa texted to tell her Elle hadn't come out of her room. How Elle herself hadn't been able to let Julie, or Vanessa, or anyone know something was wrong, until Vanessa had stepped in.

Maybe Elle really had wanted to tell Julie that Vanessa was gone but had been too depressed to do it.

But Julie also thought about how, if it had been anything else, it wouldn't have hurt Julie so much. She would have been able to get over it faster. Except... Julie had started to feel, rationally or not, that in a little way, she was partly Vanessa's foster parent, too.

And being left in the dark while Vanessa was being reunified with Karly—it was like she hadn't even had a chance to grieve, or... to celebrate, or to feel whatever it was she was supposed to feel. She still couldn't quite land on what the correct emotion was. Either way, she had always thought, if Vanessa did go back to live with her mom, that Elle would want her there. That they'd work through it, together.

It stung, that she'd been wrong.

Even so. Julie didn't want to be Sophie. She had said she wasn't, that night, which was probably a ridiculous enough statement on its own. As if she was on the same level as someone who had dated Elle, officially, for years. Who just happened to be a leading star of the WNBA. Which did not give Julie an inferiority complex at all.

But maybe Julie had, in fact, been exactly like Sophie, in the worst way. Maybe she had walked away from Elle when Elle might have really needed her. Julie had seen with her own two eyes how Elle's depression worked, but she'd been thrown so off guard, had felt so *silly* that she'd been about to tell Elle she *loved* her when clearly she wasn't even important enough in Elle's life to share major events with. It had been like a survival instinct had kicked in, a need to protect her own clearly misguided heart, before she was able to investigate what was really going on with Elle. Before she could see what Elle needed.

And maybe it wasn't okay that Elle hadn't told her, valid depression reasons or not. Maybe Julie's reaction hadn't been illogical. Maybe Julie deserved to protect her heart.

Either way, whether Elle had done the wrong thing, or Julie had, or neither of them had, the fact was... Julie was still in love with Elle.

Still wanted to know where Elle was, why she was out of town. How she was feeling. Julie wanted to know what Elle's nieces and nephews had gotten for Christmas. If she needed help taking down decorations. If she was excited to go back to work, or not. How things had been going so far at Karly's, if she had heard from Vanessa. If the house felt lonely now. If she ever wanted to play another game of one-on-one, sometime.

If she wanted to kiss Julie again, one day.

And so Julie had eventually texted Elle back: Okay.

Elle hadn't said anything else since then, and Julie had been staring at her own Okay for the last seventy-two hours, wondering if not saying anything more effusive had made her sound like a bitch. She wanted to text, *where are you?* And *I miss you*, and *I want you to still coach the Bobcats with me, even if you can't make it to every practice.* And *I can't believe you didn't laugh at Snoozles Santa.* And *This week sucks and I wish you could help me feel less sad.*

To distract herself, she'd been taking occasional breaks from her pity party to think about the New Year. She'd clicked on the link to the graduate program Iris had emailed her. Studied the requirements and the timeline. She was pretty sure some of her classes from her psych major would indeed count toward the prerequisites, which for some reason made her want to laugh. That her degree apparently hadn't been useless, after all. Maybe.

It was still a lot to think about, applying for the counseling position.

But when Julie let herself believe it could all work out...when she let herself believe she could be good at it...

Snoozles jumped up on the couch. Julie scratched underneath her chin and looked away from her computer, staring out the window.

Maybe spending eight hours a day inside a building where Julie wasn't fully herself, where she only ever felt tired, year after year... maybe Julie needed to give more credence to the effects of that on her mental health. On what she believed she deserved.

Maybe coaching the Bobcats really wasn't a small thing at all.

Maybe what she needed was to spend *more* time chasing the feeling being Coach Parker gave her. It wasn't always easy, being Coach Parker, or even natural; she still often felt like a fraud.

But at the end of the day, she still always felt better, after a few hours of being Coach, than she did the rest of the year, when she retreated back to being just Julie.

It had occurred to her, over the years, that she was perhaps not the best at change.

But maybe, next year, she could try.

She was checking her email to bring up her UT transcripts again when she saw the new message in her inbox.

Hello Coach Parker, it started.

Julie's mouth hung open as she kept reading.

When she finished, she read it again.

And again.

None of it made sense. Even after reading it ten times, she struggled to make heads or tails of it.

Phrases leapt out at her. Internship with our coaching staff and heard such great things about your skill and passion and wonderful opportunity and excited to meet you.

What she stared at most, though, was the signature.

Tony McCombs
Director of Athletics
The University of Tennessee

Julie stood abruptly, almost knocking her laptop to the floor.

She stalked to the other side of the room and paced back and forth, glaring suspiciously at it.

UT. UT wanted her, Julie Parker, to apply for a coaching internship. Were coaching internships even a thing? Even if they were, there was no way in *hell* Julie Parker, East Nashville High basketball coach for a season and a half, was qualified.

There was only one way this had happened. Only one reason that email had landed in her inbox.

And Julie didn't know whether she was hurt or angry. Actually, she was hungry, too. Hangry squared.

She paused to chew on a fingernail.

It was possible she was overreacting.

And Elle might still be out of town.

But fuck it. Julie threw on a sweatshirt, grabbed her car keys, and drove herself to East Nashville anyway.

She stopped at Cook Out on the way and shoved a burger in her face, to help herself calm down. She wanted to invest more time in self-care next year, was proud of herself for getting a head start.

And then she drove to the house she loved so much, and beat the hell out of its front door.

Elle had one second of being thrilled she wasn't being murdered. Or burgled. Or that the tree in the front yard hadn't fallen and smashed directly into her front door. From the sound that had startled her from the kitchen, any of those things could have been possibilities.

But Julie Parker standing on her porch was the most breath-stealing of them all.

Her face was like a thunderstorm. And wonderful. It had only been a few days, Elle knew, since she had last seen it, but god, Elle loved that face.

Julie barged past her into the house. Elle stumbled back, trying to calm her heart. With unsteady hands, she closed the door and followed in Julie's wake. It wasn't until Julie reached the kitchen island and whirled around that Elle fully processed that Julie was very, very angry.

"You want me to go to Knoxville?" she asked, before Elle could get a word in.

And... oh. They must have contacted Julie already.

Elle ran a hand through her hair, opening her mouth to explain. But Julie kept going before she could.

"You talked to Tony McCombs about me?" Her chin wobbled, just a little, as she said it, and oh no. Maybe Julie wasn't angry. Maybe Julie was only aggressively sad. "Asked him to give me some..." She threw a hand out to the side. "I don't even know. Pity internship?"

"What?" Elle's head jerked back, as if Julie had slapped her. "No, Julie. It wasn't pity anything. I just—I was already at UT, talking to some people in the program about something else, and I'd been thinking about you, the whole drive to Knoxville, and..." Elle swallowed, crossing her arms close to herself so she wouldn't reach for Julie. She had to get this right this time, had to make sure Julie listened before walking away. "And I'd been thinking about what you deserve. I know you're not happy at your job, and you deserve to be happy, Julie. And you are *good* at coaching—"

"I coach a barely competitive high school team, Elle!"

"You are *good* at coaching," Elle repeated, her own temper flaring.

She was goddamn *tired* of Julie Parker not giving herself enough credit. "Real fucking good at it. And I know you love UT. I just thought it could be a good opportunity for you. That was all. I'm sorry..." She sighed, her temper cooling as fast as it had spiked. "I'm sorry if I overstepped. I wasn't even sure if they'd contact you. I swear I didn't mean any harm."

Julie breathed out and turned away, hands on her hips.

"For the record," Elle couldn't stop herself from adding, "I think UT would be lucky to have you."

"I don't *want* UT, Elle!"

Julie twirled back around as she shouted it. Elle's shoulders tensed.

"Okay," Elle said, sounding weirdly winded. "Okay, I'm getting that." She licked her lips, trying to acquire more air in her lungs before she asked the question she'd been wanting to ask for weeks now. "What *do* you want, Julie?"

Julie stared at her. Slowly, through a long moment of silence, her body language shifted. Like her anger-sadness had been replaced with uncertainty, her arms jangly at her sides.

"I don't want Knoxville," she repeated.

And then, finally, she stopped fidgeting and looked Elle in the eye.

Something akin to hope started to build in Elle's gut, light and fluttering and terrifying.

"I want Nashville," Julie said, voice steady. "I want the Bobcats. I want my life, with my people, here." She paused, face red as her breath grew quicker. "I want this house. With you."

Elle put a hand over her mouth.

"I mean, not that—" Julie faltered, shaking out a wrist. "Not that I'm implying you should want me and Snoozles to move in with you; that is...a lot, I just mean—I want *you*, Elle. And not just for practice. I know I'm new at this, that I don't know all the ins and outs of..." She swallowed, and Elle could *see* her gathering her courage in that freckled, beautiful face that was incapable of hiding a damn thing, and Elle was dying, the hope beating its wings like all hell against her veins. "Of being a good girlfriend," Julie continued, "and maybe you don't feel the same way, but I think maybe you do, and I think maybe we could try."

Elle took a step forward. Julie took a step back. And kept talking. And Elle loved her so, so much for it.

"I think...I haven't been comfortable enough with anyone else, to try, before you. And you...you've been really patient with me, and that makes me feel so..." Elle took another step. Julie swallowed once more as she followed the dance, stepping back again. "Cared for. And special. *Fuck*, you make me feel so special, Elle. And I think...I think maybe we're both a little sad, sometimes. But I think we're a little less sad when we're together."

And then Julie's back hit the counter.

"I think I'm always going to be a little sad," Elle whispered. "It's just the way my brain works."

"Okay," Julie said, voice quieting. "That's okay."

"Julie." Elle took the final step to meet her. "I have to tell you something."

She rested a hand on Julie's side. Rubbed a thumb over her sweat-shirt. Julie's breath hitched and her pulse jumped in her neck, and Elle had to tell herself to wait, to not lean forward and bite it.

"I'm allergic to cats," Elle finished.

Julie blinked, her face morphing to confusion.

"But Snoozles is welcome," Elle said. "I could stock up on Benadryl."

Julie froze. Stared at her.

"You can't be a lesbian and be allergic to cats," she eventually said, voice strained. "There should be a rule about that."

A small laugh fell out of Elle's mouth. There was her Julie. "I know."

"And would Benadryl really be enough? Because let me tell you, Snoozles's hair gets *everywhere*, like everywhere; my bras can tell you—"

"Julie," Elle said. "I'm sorry I didn't tell you about Vanessa." She talked quickly, so Julie couldn't interrupt. "It all happened so fast. I had hardly any warning, and then she was gone. I was in shock, and sad, and angry, and I thought about calling you, so many times, but I wanted to be able to handle it myself first, be less of a mess. Which is partly my depression, telling my brain dumb things, and partly because I spent eight years, before all this, learning to rely only on myself. Basketball had been in charge of my life for so long. It's been so important to me to be in control of everything now, and it might take a while to deprogram that out of myself. But none of that is an excuse. You were more of a parent to Vanessa than I was, half the time, and I'm so sorry I didn't tell you immediately. Lastly—"

Elle took a deep breath, worried she had meandered a bit too much in the middle there. Julie's chin had started to wobble, and Elle could hardly take it, but she was almost there. Almost done.

"I'm not quitting the Bobcats. It hurt my feelings that you thought I would. I'm going to make Vandy work around it. If they don't like it, I have other plans, anyway."

Elle reached up a hand to wipe away Julie's tears.

"I was actually just about to go over to your apartment," Elle said, voice soft, "to tell you all that. And to give you your Christmas present. I'm so sorry it's late."

"Elle," Julie said, voice thick. "I don't care about the present. Well, actually, I do; I love presents, but—can I kiss you first?"

"Julie." Elle smiled at her, caressing her cheek. "*Please.*"

Julie grabbed the back of Elle's neck. And then—

"I'm so sorry. I just—I seriously need a tissue. I can't kiss you while I'm snotting."

And Julie pushed Elle away, running out of the kitchen to the bathroom, running back a minute later saying, "Okay, I'm better now," and Elle was laughing, and Julie pushed Elle back against the sink and kissed her with a fierceness that took Elle's breath away, that made the laughter die in her throat. That kicked Elle's libido awake, made every hopeful nerve flutter right out of Elle's skin until they danced above their heads, lighting up the kitchen like fireflies.

"I missed you so much," Elle said in a rush into Julie's jaw, minutes later, as she kissed her way to Julie's neck. "God, Julie."

"Yeah?" Julie's voice was breathless, and the sound of it only drove Elle's need higher.

"Yes. *Julie*. Yes."

Elle had missed getting to put her mouth on Julie's jaw. She had missed her honesty, her laugh. The way she rolled her eyes, the way her breath wavered when Elle sucked her earlobe into her mouth. The color of her hair, the freckles on her arms, the spark that lived inside her eyes.

"Elle." Julie took a step back, and Elle groaned out loud. Julie laughed a little as she said, "I think I want my present now."

Elle took a few deep breaths. She only wanted to drag Julie upstairs, but—yes. The present. Elle very much wanted to give Julie the present.

Forcing her mind to clear, she walked to her bag on the counter, where she had been getting it ready to go to Julie's. She plucked out the rectangular box and handed it over.

When Julie started to unwrap it, some of the fireflies returned to Elle's belly.

Julie smiled when she saw the top of the box. "From the desk of Coach Parker," she read.

"Picture"—Elle cleared her throat—"that it's from the whole team. I wanted to arrange them in a bouquet, but...the box was so nice."

Julie opened the lid and began lifting the red and orange pencils, examining the inscriptions on each one.

What the fork, Coach
The good shorts
Bobcats Forever
Every minute counts

Julie finally looked up at her, wonder on her face.

"Everyone's outgifting me this year," she said, barely audible, as if talking to herself.

Elle cleared her throat again. "There's a card, on the bottom."

Julie dropped the box to the kitchen island, digging through pencils until she found the tiny card.

"That's just from me," Elle said.

Julie stared at it before looking back at her, mouth open.

For Julie, the only girl in the world
I love you.

"When did you order these?" she whispered.

"Four weeks ago."

Julie glanced again at the pencils, running a finger over the words on the card.

"Will you go with me, next year?" Elle asked, just as quietly. "When I visit New York in the fall?"

"Yes," Julie said. "Elle. I love you too." She looked at Elle again, chin on the wobble path once more. "I came over here on Christmas to tell you that. I wish I had stayed. I wish—"

"Julie." Elle pulled her into her, rubbing her hands up Julie's back, letting Julie bury her head on her shoulder. "Shh," she whispered into her ponytail. "It's okay."

And as she said the two words, she knew she was saying it for herself. That both she and Julie maybe needed a moment to breathe. To let themselves finally have a moment of true honesty. Of settling into this, just the two of them, here in this house. Not just because of Vanessa. Not just because of basketball. Even though both of those things would always be part of their story.

With one hand still firmly on Julie's back, Elle retrieved her phone with the other. Swiping the screen behind Julie's shoulder, she chose her gentlest playlist, connecting to the house's stereo system.

"Hey," she said softly as Sade filled the kitchen. "Dance with me."

"Elle," Julie groaned into Elle's neck as they began to sway. That groan vibrated inside of Elle's sternum, stretched its fingers lower. "This song. You're trying to kill me. Death by lesbian."

Elle chuckled and held her tighter. "I love you, Julie."

"It might take a while for that to really sink in," Julie said after a moment.

"I know," Elle said. "That's okay. I'll keep saying it." She'd keep saying it, to everyone, so much more.

"Thanks," Julie whispered, her arms now wrapped around Elle's neck, fingers curling into Elle's hair.

Sade changed to Chris Stapleton to Leon Bridges, until Elle felt Julie truly relax. Because after months of standing by Julie's side on the court, sitting next to her on school buses, holding her feet on the couch, Elle understood Julie's body language now. The way she tensed, the way she let go. So Elle waited, until the moment Julie let herself simply dance. Body to body, quiet beat to quiet beat.

And only then did Elle kiss her again.

Elle kissed her until Julie tugged at her shirt. Elle raised her arms, helped Julie yank it off. She had missed the way Julie's fingers felt on her skin, the way her lips looked when they were overly kissed. She'd only been able to experience those things a few times, but they had been enough: enough to remember, to want. She'd missed the way she felt freer whenever Julie was near.

Elle brought her mouth to Julie's neck as Julie's hands drifted toward her bra.

When Julie's fingers pinched her nipple, Elle gasped and immediately began stumbling them toward the stairs. She let the music play.

"Bedroom," she breathed into Julie's neck. "I've been wanting you in my bed for so long." Her heel hit the first step.

"I want to be there, too." Julie threw off her sweatshirt, left it at the foot of the stairs as they made their clumsy way upward. "Thank you for waiting for me."

"Anytime." Elle sucked Julie's earlobe into her mouth, hand underneath Julie's T-shirt, and Julie grabbed the railing. A second later, she jerked her head so she could take Elle's lower lip between her teeth, and Elle paused at the next step to yank off Julie's T-shirt.

"Stairs are hard," Julie observed.

"I don't know," Elle said. "I think I have a newfound appreciation for them."

She scratched her fingernails across Julie's shoulders, down her back, and Julie leaned down to suck Elle's nipple through her bra.

Elle gasped, her own hand gripping the railing now. "Parker," she breathed. "You play dirty."

Julie glanced up at her with a look Elle hadn't seen since one-on-one. "You know I do."

"Shit." Elle made herself stumble up a step, away from Julie's mouth. "Coach, I think you were made for dirty talk."

Julie followed, the light from the upstairs hallway just reaching them, glowing on her pinkening cheeks.

"Only for you," she said, shy again, and Elle yanked her up the last few steps until they were on solid ground, until she could shove Julie against the nearest wall and kiss her properly, tongue searching Julie's mouth as her hands traveled to that beautiful ass.

"Bedroom," Julie broke away to say. "Please."

When they finally got there, Elle nudged Julie toward the bed, aiming to push her onto it, but Julie pulled back at the last second. Elle waited as they paused there, a foot apart, chests heaving.

"I want to do things to you," Julie blurted. "I want to do all the things you did to me, and kiss you everywhere, and anything else you want me to do, even if I'm not good at it at first. That's—" She licked her lips. "That's what I want most."

Elle's heart almost overflowed with affection.

"I can't complain about that." She took Julie's hand, placed it on her breast. "But we do have time, okay? This doesn't start being a race, now that we're dating for real. We have all the time in the world, to do or not do whatever we want."

Julie watched her hand massage Elle's breast.

"I'm dating you," she said, quiet. "You're dating me."

"I am," Elle affirmed. "For as long as you'll have me, Coach Parker."

Julie glanced at her for a quick moment before she dropped her hand and took a step back.

"Take off your pants." Elle shivered at the directive. Did as she was told. "Get on the bed," Julie said next, voice soft, as if she was starting to doubt herself. Elle wanted to encourage her, but she also wanted Julie to feel it out herself, figure out what she was comfortable with.

Elle took her time arranging herself, propping her pillows behind her, even as her legs shook from Julie watching her. She opened them, the vulnerability of the position and the shock of air hitting between her thighs making her bite her lip.

Julie watched her for another torturous minute before she took off her own pants, revealing a pair of boy shorts with foxes running across them; stripped off her sports bra. Elle sighed out loud when Julie crawled onto the bed, fox underwear still on, and made her way over Elle's body.

With her fingertips, Elle explored the freckles on Julie's shoulders that Elle hadn't been able to examine before. Cupped the sides of her soft, full breasts. Julie only looked down at her, hands planted at Elle's sides, eyes serious.

And then, slowly at first, but soon growing more confident—Julie kissed her.

She started at Elle's collarbones. Her shoulders, the crook of her elbows, her wrists. She kissed the tops of Elle's breasts. She kissed Elle's sternum, her stomach. Her hips and her thighs. Her knees, the sides of her calves.

And then she leaned in, kissing Elle's center through her underwear, her nose nudging Elle's clit, gentle but so perfect that Elle gasped, grasping at the comforter with both hands. Julie's careful attentions, her slow adoration of Elle's body had every nerve on edge, her head dizzy and slightly desperate.

"Julie," she breathed. "Right there. That feels so good. Please. Lick me there."

And Julie did, a long, heavy drag of her tongue, so warm through the fabric, the pressure just right, that Elle needed her to do that again, exactly that, with her underwear gone, immediately.

Luckily, Julie was on the same page, leaning back to tuck her fingers under the fabric. But before Julie returned to where Elle was throbbing, she tugged on Elle's bra, too. Elle gladly obliged, and Julie's mouth was covering her nipple before the fabric had even left Elle's fingers.

"Julie," Elle breathed again, her fingers in Julie's hair while Julie's tongue swirled and sucked. Elle writhed beneath her, high-pitched sounds escaping her mouth, almost embarrassing, but it just felt so *good*, so incredibly good that it was Julie, doing this for her.

Julie paused her ministrations to rest her forehead on Elle's stomach, her back rising and falling with her breath.

"Making you make sounds like that...getting to touch you..."

And Elle remembered how Julie had looked, after the first time they'd done this, the wonder but also the slight fear, the uncertainty. While Julie *sounded* certain now, maybe Elle was only hearing it as certainty because she was so turned on. Maybe Julie was actually only overwhelmed.

So Elle tried to calm herself, cool the blood boiling in her veins, make sure she was accurately monitoring what Julie was feeling—

And then Julie moved down, her tongue doing that flat, warm sweep again, unobstructed by fabric, and Elle short-circuited.

"Julie." Her hips tilted into Julie's face, helpless as Julie's tongue swirled around her clit. "God, you feel good." And when Julie first slid a finger inside, Julie whispered, "Is this okay? This feels all right?" followed by a quiet, awe-filled, "*Fuck*," and Elle said, "Yes, it feels good, do another—*yes*, Julie. Yes."

And when Julie's mouth returned to her clit, it was a bit sloppy, her fingers pumping a bit too fast as she struggled to find a rhythm. But it all felt good anyway. Until Elle worried she maybe wasn't going to get there, and she could feel Julie's frustration, her worry that she was doing something wrong.

"Julie." She reached a hand down to grasp Julie's wrist. "Julie, it feels so good, but let's break for a second. Is your wrist hurting?"

Julie kept her face turned away, toward Elle's thigh. Eventually, quietly, she said, "Yeah."

"Okay." Elle rubbed a thumb over the pulse point in Julie's wrist, her fingers still buried inside her. "That's okay." Elle licked her lips, gathering her breath. "It feels good sometimes to have breaks in the stimulation, helps the tension build. Especially if you need a break, too. You can pull back and—" She tapped the inside of her thigh. "Kiss here instead. Or here." She rubbed her belly. "Here." She touched her lips. "Anywhere, really. I also like when you moan against my clit—the vibration of it, you know? And sometimes, when I'm close, it feels good if you..." Elle dug her teeth into her lower lip. "Pinch it."

Julie finally looked at her. "Pinch your clit?"

"Yeah. But not too hard." And she couldn't help but ask, when Julie kept looking at her, "You doing okay? It's not too much?"

Julie blinked. As if contemplating. And then a smile curved her lips, and she said, "Yeah. I'm doing okay. You promise I'm making you feel good?"

"Promise."

Slowly, Julie withdrew her fingers. Elle whimpered. Sighed when Julie kissed her again, in all the places Elle had suggested. Wrapped her legs around Julie's hips when Julie returned to her mouth, scraping her fingernails down Julie's back, kissing until she felt ready, burning again, and she dropped her legs, opened her knees, pushed her pelvis into Julie's.

When Julie dropped back down this time, she sank her fingers in slow, left Elle's clit alone until Elle was panting for it, begging for it. Until finally, Julie hovered her mouth over her, just barely there, until Elle was writhing again, until Julie reached up her other hand and pinched her, just right, not too light and not too hard and Elle *yelled* until the yell turned to whimpers as she clamped around Julie's fingers. The waves crashed through her so deeply, so thoroughly, that by the time they subsided, she wanted to laugh, too. "Julie," she said. "Baby."

And she was pulling Julie up, kissing her forehead, her cheeks, her nose. And Julie was quiet, quiet, while Elle was a pulled-apart mess, and it took her a moment to realize Julie was moving, rubbing herself slowly, silently against Elle's thigh.

"Yes, baby," she breathed, tilting her leg so Julie could use her better. She brought her hands around to squeeze those foxes on Julie's ass. Let Julie hump her for a while longer until Julie's breath grew heavier, until she could feel the wetness seeping through the fabric onto her skin. "Julie," she whispered, sliding her hands underneath the waistband. "Baby, get these off now."

And Julie huffed a breath as she made herself pause, equal measures annoyed and turned on, and Elle smiled as she complied.

The annoyance must have been worth it, though, because when Julie returned to her position, skin to skin, she made a low sound in her throat, eyes shuttering, neck stretching toward the ceiling as she arched her back.

It was *sexy*. Elle needed Julie to know.

"Julie." She ran her palms up Julie's chest, Julie's neck. Ran them down Julie's back, cupping her ass again as Julie rubbed against her over and over. "You are so sexy. God, Julie. You have to believe me."

"Feel sexy," Julie breathed, eyes still closed, "with you."

And then Julie was coming, mouth open, a small, vulnerable sound escaping her throat that made Elle want to burst into a million pieces. And for a moment Elle only watched. But then she leaned up and sucked at Julie's neck, and Julie was collapsing on top of her, and Elle was wrapping her legs around her again, never wanting to let go, but Julie was pushing away—"Fuck, can't breathe, fuck"—and Elle let her roll away. But she found her hand, wrapped their fingers together, held on how she could.

Eventually, they situated themselves. Julie's cheek rested on Elle's shoulder, an arm across Elle's stomach. A leg across Elle's thighs.

Elle couldn't stop caressing Julie's forearm, kissing Julie's hair.

"So you're a 'baby' person, huh?" Julie said at length, and Elle laughed.

"You know, not usually? It just kind of happened. Felt right, in the moment."

"I didn't hate it," Julie admitted. And then, after a moment, she added, "I'm going to get better at that."

Elle's heart sank. "Julie—"

"Shh." Julie brought a hand to Elle's lips. "Elle. I don't know if you're aware, but I'm a bit of a competitive person. I like having something I can get better at. And you were an excellent teacher, back there. This is good."

Elle smiled. "As long as you keep believing me when I tell you it feels good."

"I will. I do."

"And that you're sexy."

A grunt.

"And that I love you."

"Elle."

"Okay, okay." Elle laughed again. "I'll stop."

A few quiet moments passed. Elle comprehended, slowly, that it was still the middle of the day. That she had just had the best sex she'd had in a decade at two o'clock in the afternoon.

They still had the rest of the day. Assuming Julie didn't have any other pressing plans, they still had New Year's Eve, too.

Maybe Elle had messed up Christmas.

But maybe they could still have New Year's.

Maybe they could still have all the days after that.

"What did you mean, earlier?" Julie asked into Elle's shoulder. "When you were talking about Vandy, going back to work. About having other plans."

"Oh." Elle shifted underneath her, remembering life beyond this room. Their conversation in the kitchen already felt so long ago. "I'm thinking of going back to school."

Julie moved onto an elbow, looking down at her. "Seriously?"

Elle gave an uncertain smile. "Yeah. I went to see Mara, and—"

"Just," Julie interrupted with a shake of her head, that look of wonder creeping into her smile again. "Same fucking trajectory."

"What?" Elle tilted her head, smiling back, even though she didn't know why. She was still a little sex-drunk.

"Sorry." Julie rubbed Elle's stomach. "Continue. You went to see Mara."

"Yeah. This week. That's where I was. And we started talking about…the things you talk about with your best friend when you haven't seen them in too long. Life. The things we want to do next."

Elle turned her head to look out the window.

"My job at Vandy was comfortable for so long, but…I've always been interested in medicine. And this idea has been kind of percolating, while I've been helping with the Bobcats."

Julie rested her chin on Elle's shoulder, encouraging her to go on.

"I don't think I'm destined to be a coach. You'll probably have to find a real assistant, next year." She ran a hand down Julie's shoulder as she said it, in apology. Julie frowned, but only for a moment.

"I'll miss you. But I understand."

Elle smiled at her before turning back toward the window.

"I like working with the players, though. Being closer to the game again, in a different way. I think…I want to be an athletic trainer."

Julie rubbed a hand over Elle's stomach again. Elle kept talking before Julie could say anything. Saying it all out loud to Julie made it feel real, realer than when she'd been in Knoxville, half-delirious with happiness at being with Mara and sadness about everything else. A strange state of both grief and possibility.

"That's why I was at UT. Mara made, like, two phone calls, and all of a sudden I was back on campus, talking to trainers. Some of our old coaches were there, too. That's how I got to talking about you, when they were asking me what I'd been up to." Elle smiled at her again, ruffling the end of her ponytail. "I couldn't quite shut up about you, actually. But anyway. They all told me one of the best grad programs in the state for athletic training is at UT-Chattanooga, which…" Elle blew out a breath. "I don't know if I want to spend two years in Chattanooga, especially if…"

"Me and Snoozles can hold down the fort," Julie said, the smile on her lips so gentle Elle almost cried. "If that's what's best for you. Chattanooga isn't so far away."

"I don't know," Elle whispered. "We'll see. There are other options around the state, too. Middle Tennessee, Cumberland...I'm still thinking on it."

"I think that sounds amazing, Elle. Wherever you choose." After a moment, Julie added, "I bet your degree in biology will help with whatever, like, medical prerequisites you might need."

Elle gave her a puzzled look. She was right; they would. But Elle couldn't remember ever talking about her bio degree with Julie.

"Oh, right." Julie's smile grew. "Did you forget I've been obsessed with you my whole life? Because yeah, that's still a thing."

Elle let out a small laugh as she lay her head back on the pillow.

A minute passed. Elle could feel Julie's smile fade, her stare turn pensive.

"Were you serious, before?" she asked. "About me and Snoozles?"

"Moving in, you mean?" Elle painted another pattern around Julie's shoulder with a finger. "Absolutely."

"Even though we've only known each other for two months?"

Elle squinted at the ceiling, calculating. "By lesbian standards, that puts us about...a month behind, I'd say."

Julie smiled, one of her small, private ones. "I would love to live here," she said, quiet. "Even if I don't know if I'm a lesbian."

"That's okay, Julie." Elle ran her finger down Julie's cheek. "I'll love you whatever label you land on. Or maybe you never choose one, and that's okay, too."

Another moment passed before Julie said, "I'm serious about Snoozles's hair. I don't want to make you sick."

"I'll talk to my doctor about it."

"Wait, what about when you brought Snoozles to the vet with me? I don't remember you having trouble."

"I took a Benadryl before I left. And chugged some of Vanessa's soda, so I wouldn't fall asleep. It was gross."

Julie smiled before her face fell. "Oh *no*. Elle. She'll scratch all your nice furniture to hell."

Elle laughed. "I think I can handle it."

"No way. Your stuff is so *nice*. Elle. Are you kidding me? And I know I'm related to London, but I have to tell you now, I can't cook for shit. Which... you might already know, considering most of the stuff I fed you recently was actually made by Dahlia."

Elle only smiled at her, booping her nose. "S'okay. I'll cook you so much barley."

Julie looked at her for a long moment. And then she rested her head on the pillow and said, "I've been making plans, too."

"Yeah?" Elle shifted until she was on her side, an arm curled around Julie's back. "Tell me."

"I think I'm going back to school, too."

Elle grinned. "Tell me," she said again, softer this time.

And Julie talked about a counselor at East who was up for retirement. An accelerated grad program at Vandy she could start in the summer.

Julie shrugged a shoulder.

"I've talked to him, the counselor who's retiring, and he told me that a lot of the job is just, like, handling scheduling issues and coordinating with social services and filling out paperwork. That it's not always about actually connecting with kids. But... I don't know. I think I might want this. And it would make getting to practice a hell of a lot easier during the season, so."

Julie frowned.

"Elle, are you crying?"

Was she?

Elle put a hand to her cheek and found it wet. Well. She supposed it was her turn.

"That sounds wonderful, Julie," she managed to say. "You would be an *incredible* school counselor."

"I mean, maybe. Hiram keeps trying to tell me that most of the job is frustrating, or depressing, and stressful, but...yeah." Another shy smile. "Maybe."

"Oh my god," Elle said. "The Doc is going to be your *boss*. Like, full time." She grinned. "That's hot."

"*Maybe* she will be my boss," Julie emphasized. "And you can find it hot. I only find it terrifying."

"She'll love you. She already does."

"If you say so."

"She does. Julie, East would be lucky to have you, just like UT would be lucky to have you. *Anyone* would be lucky to have you. Julie, you are...You deserve the world."

"Shit." Slowly, the uncertainty on Julie's face faded away. "You really love me."

"I really, really do."

"We're going to go into student debt again together," Julie said after a moment.

Elle caressed Julie's face.

"There's no one I'd rather FAFSA with."

And Julie laughed into the pillow, until silence settled over them like the afternoon light shining in the window: golden and gentle and good.

Until eventually, Elle spoke again.

"You know what else I've been thinking about?"

"Hm?" Sleepily, Julie blinked open her eyes.

Elle played with the corner of the comforter.

"I want to keep going to those foster classes. Even though Vanessa's gone."

Julie inched herself closer. Waited for Elle to continue.

"They talk a lot in the classes about the most at-risk kids, who need help the most."

Julie's eyes were dark, the gold turned into caramel. She nodded.

"One of the groups is LGBTQ+ teens. And I know"—Elle's breath sped up—"that taking in total strangers is a whole other thing, and that I wasn't necessarily good at it even with Vanessa, but—"

Julie reached across Elle's stomach. Hugged her.

"You were good with Vanessa, Elle," she whispered. "You were so good. Exactly what she needed. You have to believe me."

Elle smiled faintly at the echo of her own words. Allowed herself to believe it for at least a small, kind moment before she pushed on.

"When you asked me if I wanted kids...I've never really had a desire to have kids in the traditional sense. But maybe, in a few years, after I finish going back to school and starting a new career, if things have settled down...I think giving queer teens a safe space here could be something I'd want to at least try."

Julie grabbed Elle's hand. Brought it to her lips. Kissed her knuckles.

"Elle. I am so fucking in love with you."

"Does that mean you don't think it's the worst idea in the world?"

"Not at all. Oh my god, Elle. Can I help?"

"Again, it's down the road, but...well, you'd have to take the classes, too. If you and Snoozles are going to be living here. So we can be certified together as a home."

"Yes," Julie said softly. "I would love to."

And after a moment of continuing to kiss Elle's knuckles, her wrist, her palm—Julie sucked Elle's thumb into her mouth.

"Julie," Elle said after a moment. "If you keep doing that—" Julie had moved on to Elle's pointer finger, and the next, and the next— "I'm going to be ready to go again in like, thirty seconds." That was a lie. Elle was ready to go again right now.

Julie swirled her tongue around Elle's pinky before releasing it. Resumed her path of kisses around Elle's hand before she glanced at Elle's face, that mixture of shy and bold warring within her eyes.

"I'd love to watch you touch yourself again."

Elle smiled. "I think that can be arranged, Coach Parker."

But as she watched Julie trail her mouth down her forearm, a cloud outside the window shifted, a ray of light landing on Julie's hair, the soft curve of her cheek. And Elle's tone changed when she whispered, "Kiss me, baby."

And when Julie said her name, some minutes later, soft and reverent as Elle was beginning to lose herself again, she heard more in that single syllable than she had let herself dream of wanting for a long time. Better than any trophy.

A relationship thing that was unnameable. A possibility specifically Julie-and-Elle-shaped, belonging only to them.

FORMER LADY VOLS STAR FINDS HER WAY FORWARD—FROM THE SIDELINES

By Tiago Caravalho

For ESPN.com

Originally published in *The Nashville Source*, March 27

Every Tennessee Volunteer fan of a certain age remembers where they were when Elle Cochrane led the Lady Vols to a national championship win over UConn. Or when her buzzer beater three against Notre Dame brought the Vols back to the Final Four the following year. Or when, for all four years of her reign, assisted by the equally impressive Mara Daniels, the Vols simply dominated the SEC.

They might also remember her first-round draft pick that secured her a spot on the Milwaukee Shipwrecks. Cochrane spent two years in the WNBA, with surprisingly limited playing time, before she exited the game for good after an ACL injury.

And no one heard from her again.

Until this month, that is, when Cochrane and Daniels announced they would be spearheading an alumni charity game, to be held at Thompson-Boling Arena next month. The duo have recruited over thirty former Lady Vols for the event, the proceeds of which will be split between QueerOut, a summer camp for LGBTQ+ youth, and the You Can Play Project, which supports LGBTQ+ athletes nationwide.

For certain East Nashville residents, however, the announcement of the much-anticipated charity game wasn't the only sighting of Cochrane in recent months. She first reentered the world of basketball this winter as a coach for the girls' team at East High, assisting head coach Julie Parker, where she helped lead the Bobcats to district finals for the first time in seven years. While the Bobcats ultimately fell in the championship against the fearsome McDougall Raccoons, they played a remarkable season, and the reappearance of Cochrane on a high school court was certainly intriguing.

Still, Cochrane refused an interview, as she had refused all interviews since her first season with the Wreckers a decade ago.

Only when the charity game was announced did Cochrane finally agree to sit down with the *Source* and allow us to catch up on that mysterious disappearance from the Wreckers, where she's been since, and what the future holds for her.

Caravalho: Thank you so much for meeting with us today.

Cochrane: Thank you for waiting for me.

Caravalho: First, why don't you tell us more about this charity event.

Cochrane: It was mostly Mara's idea. We were discussing the most recent wave of bills targeting trans youth and trans athletes. I know from my own experience, as a queer woman who has always struggled with mental health, how much sports saved me when I was young. Basketball gave me a place to excel and stand out because of my skills and hard work, instead of being ostracized for who I was. Queer and trans youth have as much right to have that same experience as anyone else.

And on a lighter note, well, we all miss playing at Thompson-Boling. I especially have spent too much time away from UT since graduation, and it's been great reconnecting with old teammates and other alums. I hope it ends up being a fun time for everyone, while raising funds for these important organizations.

Caravalho: I understand it's also the first time you'll be stepping onto the court as a player in over eight years.

Cochrane: [with a grimace] Yes. I can't promise it will be pretty. [Laughs] I'm nervous as hell. But I'm also trying to let myself be excited.

Caravalho: Can you say a little more about why it's been so long? Was your departure from the Wreckers about more than the ACL tear?

Cochrane: No, it wasn't just the ACL tear, although it was a doozy of one, and my recovery was long and slow. I couldn't get my rhythm in the WNBA; I felt constantly out of sync, hoping one day my game would come back to me, but...it never did. I was also severely depressed during my time in Milwaukee, and it's very likely that affected my play. It's possible that, with time, I could have recovered from both the injury and the depression and gotten my game back, but it simply felt like my time to go.

Caravalho: I appreciate your candor in discussing how your mental health played into it.

Cochrane: The discussion around athletes and mental health has improved by leaps and bounds over the years, but there's still a long way to go. Athletes in our culture do experience a lot of privileges—well, if you're a man, mostly—but the pressure that's put especially on young athletes can take such a toll. Even when the public eye isn't trained on you, many people are drawn to sports as a way to escape other things in their lives. And when the sports disappear as an option—the season ends; you flop in the big leagues—you no longer have that mechanism you'd relied on for so long to deal with your life.

Caravalho: So did quitting the Wreckers help your mental health?

Cochrane: Ultimately, yes. I don't regret my decision. But I've recently started to go back to therapy and have realized I likely didn't go about things perfectly. Even though I'd already gone through therapy after the Wreckers, already thought I'd put it all behind me. But it turns out that grief, mental health, dealing with failure—all of it—is always cyclical, never something you can fully put behind you at all.

There's this idea embedded in our culture of *getting over* things. For a long time, I thought if I could just keep my head down, start a new life outside of basketball, I would eventually get over my failure in the WNBA. But the fact was, it forking sucked. [Laughs]

For the last eight years, I've kept every trophy and plaque, my ESPY, in this cardboard box in my closet. Looking at them while I was recovering from the ACL, it just felt like this vivid reminder of my failure. I still don't necessarily want my house to be a shrine to my past, because I know now that I'm more than just my basketball record. But I recently experimented with putting a couple things out on a bookshelf. Because even if what happened afterward wasn't how I envisioned it, that was still an important stage of my life, and I can still be proud of it.

Caravalho: Heck yeah, you can still be proud of it.

Cochrane: I know! [Laughs] I know. Mara, Julie, my family, all the most important people in my life have been trying to get me to see that for a long time. But it's been hard to reconcile sometimes. Still is. But I'm working on it. Working on acknowledging that I've had triumphs, and I've had failures, and both will always give me a lot of feelings, but both are a part of me.

Caravalho: You just mentioned Julie. If you don't mind pivoting for a moment, let's talk about Julie Parker and East High.

Cochrane: [Grins] Let's.

Caravalho: For full disclosure to readers, Julie Parker is one of my oldest friends, and also happens to be your girlfriend.

Cochrane: *And* she is another Vols alum, who will also be playing in the charity game next month.

Caravalho: I have to know—are you going to be playing on the same team, or on opposite sides?

Cochrane: Opposite. I am very much looking forward to Julie kicking my ass. She's done it before. Although Mara will be on my side this time, so that might even the score a bit.

Caravalho: How did you come to coach a high school team with Julie Parker this season? And will you be continuing to do so in the future?

Cochrane: First, no, I will not. But I did learn that I liked being part of the sport again from the sidelines, that I liked working with young people, encouraging them to engage with the sport in a healthy, positive way. It's actually inspired me to work toward getting my degree in athletic training, so I can keep working to ensure that players are safe and healthy on the court.

Caravalho: And it doesn't feel strange, being behind the scenes?

Cochrane: No. It feels right, a positive path forward where I can still have my own life but maintain a connection to the sport in a meaningful way.

And the idea of helping young people feel like they're in control of their bodies—not just helping them when they're injured, but training them to feel strong, to know their limits and prevent those injuries in the first place, if we can—that's a powerful thing to me.

Caravalho: I'm sure the Bobcats will miss you next year.

Cochrane: And I'll miss them. But I'll still be in the stands, cheering them on, when I can.

To answer your earlier question, I first got involved with the Bobcats because my cousin's daughter was on the team, and because Julie needed help. I think Julie was a bit bewildered, at first, that I would be assisting her, because of my history with the game, like I was somehow more important than what she was already doing.

But the truth is—and this isn't downplaying my own accomplishments at all—I just have some trophies. What Julie does? Who Julie is? The way she makes her players feel part of the team, making a safe space for them there, no matter who they are. The way she's able to infuse her passion for the sport while still remembering the joy in it. The way she always shows up for every single person in her life. The way she makes them laugh. [Smiles] That's the most important thing in the world.

EPILOGUE

Early October

J ulie lifted an arm and shoved it in Elle's face.

"Pit check."

Elle pulled Julie's arm back down. "You're fine."

"God, you are such a liar. I am a sweaty, stress-soaked monster. Where's Hank?" Julie stretched on tippy-toes, looking over Elle's shoulder. "He'll be real with me."

"Julie." Elle placed her palms on Julie's cheeks. "Don't be a stress-soaked monster. You are already killing it at being Julie of Honor."

"Am I? I could barely keep it together up there!"

Julie gestured toward the sun-dappled glen in the distance where, approximately an hour ago, London Parker and Dahlia Woodson had gotten married. Peach-colored rose petals littered the grass.

In planning their wedding, London and Dahlia had strived to keep everything gender-neutral. And while Julie had stood behind London underneath the sycamore tree where they took their vows, and Hank had stood behind Dahlia, London and Dahlia were adamant that Julie and Hank were there to support both of them. They told them to choose their own titles.

Julie had settled on Julie of Honor.

Hank had chosen The Most Honorable Hank.

London and Dahlia had landed on Two People Getting Married.

Barbara, their friend from *Chef's Special* who married them, stuck with Barbara.

"Julie, no one could keep it together during that. Deep breaths."

Julie closed her eyes and breathed in, focused on what she could hear and smell and feel.

When she opened them, Elle still had her hands on Julie's face. But her eyes were focused on something in the distance.

Julie craned her neck to see. And twirled back to shove Elle in the shoulder.

"Elle. Stop creeping on Dahlia. *I* am your in-distress girlfriend here."

"Sorry." Elle blinked. "She is just...remarkably pretty."

Dahlia was, indeed, remarkably pretty in her champagne gown with its delicate beadwork and voluminous tulle, daisies strung through her equally voluminous dark hair. It was practically impossible to look away from her.

Still. Julie was in a stress sweat emergency.

"You're pretty, too," Elle added, a guilty beat too late. She took a step closer, placed her hand on Julie's hip. "Seriously. It's obvious why Dahlia pushed London to go with this color." The green of Julie's jumpsuit perfectly matched the accents in London's jacket. "It makes your eyes..."

Elle burst her fingers out of her fists, like fireworks.

Julie bit her lip. "You promise I don't look weird?"

Julie *felt* weird. The journey to figure out what to wear at the wedding had been a long one, even though Dahlia and London had assured her she could wear whatever the hell she wanted. But when it came to clothes, Julie was discovering that, just like her identity, she had never truly known what the hell she wanted. Had never spent enough time seriously thinking about it. But she'd been learning, recently, the value of practicing new things.

So while she had never felt quite comfortable in dresses, but also felt like an imposter when she'd tried on more masculine suits, she'd landed on this jumpsuit. It was comfortable, even if Julie still felt more exposed in it than she was used to, since it had a rather plunging neckline. But Elle had given her a *look* when Julie had first tried it on—at a small store in Brooklyn, during the long weekend in New York Elle and Julie had managed to squeeze in two months ago, before the fall semester started—a look that had burned into Julie's insides. Before Elle had backed her into the dressing room and kissed her until she was breathless.

So. Julie had gone with the jumpsuit.

"Promise." Elle's hand landed back on Julie's hip, that thumb rub of reassurance Julie was so used to at this point that sometimes she worried she'd start taking it for granted.

But with their new schedule—Elle in Chattanooga most of the week as she started the graduate athletic training program, Julie frantically navigating the chaos of a high school office while taking her own classes at night—Julie didn't take a minute of it for granted. Treasured every text sent during the week. Loved every weekend, when Elle returned home, down to the bones, even when they were mostly spent studying together in the den, falling asleep at eight.

So much of the previous six years of Julie's life had felt like a stretched-out loop of time: each day at work ticking away too slowly, until another year somehow passed by, her middling sadness slowly expanding as the loop started again.

Her feeling of falling behind everyone else only growing.

Until she started coaching the Bobcats. Until she let herself fall in love with Elle.

Now time went by so fast, the rubber band tightened, snapping away every single day. She could barely keep up sometimes. Elle's depression ramped up sometimes, too, in the stress of school, the continued changes to her previously structured life. She still wasn't the best at communicating how she was feeling, what she was going through when her brain started to crash and burn. But Julie was getting better at recognizing her symptoms. She took Elle's distance during these stretches less personally now, even if they often still hurt.

The important part was that they got through it together. Would keep restructuring and finding new rhythms.

Would keep finding comfort in their home—alongside Snoozles, and allergy medication—together.

Julie was trying her best to not take this day for granted, either. Even if she did feel slightly nauseous.

She reached her fingers to Elle's blouse, as equally silky as her own jumpsuit, admiring, once again, Elle's exposed shoulders. Her eyes drifted down, as they had for the last six months, to the new tattoos on Elle's arm she'd come home with one day, a few months after Julie and Snoozles had moved in. An array of rocks and crystals, surrounding the rose, trailing alongside its thorns.

It had taken Julie's brain a few minutes to figure it out. Elle had been standing at the sink, rinsing out a mug, casual as could be when she'd thrown Julie a small smile.

"They're jewels, Jules."

Julie was contemplating, now, how easily their wedding outfits would slide against each other if she moved just a bit closer, how fun that would be—this jumpsuit was made for Elle to slide a leg between Julie's own—when Hank's arm closed around Julie's neck.

"Phew." He dabbed at his eyes with a handkerchief. "Those two up there. The fucking worst."

With only a slight twinge of regret, Julie turned from Elle to throw up a hand in agreement.

"Seriously. How were we supposed to stand there and act normal?"

"I'm still shaking." Hank held out a trembling hand. "A fucking mess. Almost shit myself. I hate them."

"Me too. Hey, do I stink?"

She held a pit to Hank's face.

"You could use some help. Don't worry; I've got some heavy-duty deodorant back in the green room. Nothing natural about it. Solid industrial chemicals."

"Thank god." Julie lowered her arm. "At least someone's looking out for me here."

"I could get you both some alcohol?" Elle asked.

"Yes," Hank and Julie said at once.

As Elle walked away, Hank took a deep breath. "I don't think I'm going to get through my speech."

"Please," Julie scoffed. "You love a speech."

"I know, but." Hank wiped a hand down his face. "She looks so beautiful." His voice broke. "And she's always been such a good sister."

His face crumpled, eyes filling with a fresh wave of real tears, and Julie pulled him into her.

"Come on, brother," she said. "We can get through this."

After a moment, Hank loosened his hold on her waist but kept his head on her shoulder. They rested like that, taking in a minute of peace after the rush of preparing for the ceremony.

"At least you get to go first," Julie said. "I'm going to be dreaming of vomiting until it's my turn."

"But then it'll be over." Hank gave her a small squeeze. "And we'll get to dance and forget everything else for a while. And then we'll get to sleep."

"It is a rather solid setup for a good day."

Elle returned with their drinks, one of London's chosen cocktails for Julie, heavy on the bourbon, and one of Dahlia's for Hank, a peach-infused wine spritzer thing. As Hank finally straightened away from Julie's shoulder, Elle picked up the glass of red wine she'd already been nursing.

Elle still drank sparingly, since Vanessa's departure. And while Julie had had her share of heavy drinking days in her early twenties, she found it surprisingly easy to follow suit now, for the sake of Elle's family. Even if Vanessa no longer lived with them, Elle had made it a point to be present in her and Karly's lives. Wanted to maintain a safe space if Vanessa ever did need to enter their home again suddenly.

Elle still had moments of bitterness that it was always her initiating visits or outings with her cousin, that Karly still seemed hesitant to fully embrace Elle and the rest of the family. But Elle and Julie also knew, from the support group they attended when they could, that recovery from addiction and toxic relationships was a slow, winding road. For now, Karly was still stable, still working at Kroger, although she'd been able to switch to day shifts. Vanessa was safe and doing well. It was more than enough to be grateful for.

But while it was absolutely worth it to model a life of controlled indulgence for Vanessa, Julie had to admit, just then, that the burn of the bourbon in the back of her throat felt good. London had always been a bourbon snob, and the burn made Julie smile. Made the nerves in her gut settle, just a touch. Allowed her to take in the scene around her—the fairy lights, the flowers, the golden autumnal light just beginning to fade behind the trees—a little bit more.

Another familiar arm looped around her waist.

"Jules!" Ben kissed her on the cheek. "You looked *gorgeous* up there."

Alexei waved from his side. "Hi, everyone." His blue eyes were red-rimmed. "That was a very nice ceremony."

"Gorgeous," Ben repeated. "We've been trying to get ourselves together and failing."

"The fucking worst," Hank repeated.

"How are you feeling about your speeches?" Ben raised his own London cocktail to his lips.

"Terrible," Hank replied, at the same time Julie said, "Nervous."

"Aw, friends." Ben threw them his good-natured smile. "I'm sure they'll both be fantastic."

"I feel like mine sounds boring and generic, even though I worked on it forever." Julie pouted. "Dahlia's the writer. And I've already told her every single one of my good London stories. Pretty rude she didn't write it for me."

"That is rude, Jules." Elle patted Julie's shoulder. "But if it makes you feel better, Vanessa just sent this text."

Elle handed her phone over, the screen displaying the photo Vanessa had sent from London and Dahlia's apartment, where she was Schnitzel-sitting. Vanessa was sticking her tongue out while Schnitzel sat next to her, staring at the camera with a dead-eye expression.

This dog is dope, the text underneath it said.

"Aw, Schnitzel!" Ben grinned, scoping out the photo over her shoulder. "That dog hates me so much, and it hurts my feelings." He took the phone from Julie to show it to Alexei, who smiled.

"Makes me miss Delilah," Alexei said as he took a sip from his Dahlia peach spritz. "Although Delilah . . . is very different from that dog."

"*Every* dog is different from this dog," Julie agreed as she returned the phone to Elle. "Who's taking care of Delilah while you're gone?"

"We used to have our neighbor watch her," Ben said. "But recently, we've befriended this farmer from the coast."

"Right." Julie nodded. "Naturally." This was already the most Ben story she'd ever heard.

"Super gay, really loves agriculture. Anyway, he also loves dogs, and he's in town a lot for farmers markets, so before we left we dropped Delilah off at the market with him. We'll drive to the farm to get her when we get back. She'll probably be depressed returning to apartment living after farm life, but what can ya do."

Before Julie could learn more about gay Oregon farmers, she and Hank were whisked away by the photographer for group shots under the trees. And then they were dancing into the reception, and eating the most delicious food that Dahlia had had to convince London they should *not* be in charge of preparing, and then Hank was standing beside London and Dahlia's table, clinking a fork against a flute of champagne.

And the bastard. He totally killed.

Palms sweaty, Julie rose to meet him in the middle of the room when he was done.

"You got this," he whispered into her ear as he gave her a hug.

He passed off the mic.

She took a deep breath. Clutching the mic in one hand and her notes in the other, she made her way to the front of the room, where Hank had just stood. She could give a speech in the middle of a basketball court, but she wasn't used to this.

She faced the room and brought the mic to her chin.

"If you didn't know," she said, "I'm London's twin. And while Dahlia only officially became my sister today, she's already felt like one for a long time."

Julie hazarded a glance at London and Dahlia, but it was a mistake. Dahlia's eyes were shiny with tears. And London...London just looked happy.

Julie blinked back at her notes.

"I've learned so many things from London and Dahlia over the years. Like sometimes, to find love, you have to travel outside of your comfort zone...and find it on the set of a TV show."

This nod to the ridiculousness of London and Dahlia's story produced the chorus of low chuckles Julie had hoped for. Still, Julie's fingers shook as she wrinkled her notes in her hand, the weight of an enormous room of people staring at her hitting her full force. Her throat suddenly closed, and panic that she wouldn't be able to get through it hit her chest.

But then her eyes caught Ben's. He stared at her, eyes warm, leaning forward at his table in concentration. Alexei's arm hung casually over the back of Ben's chair.

Or, Julie thought, *you find it on the Pacific Crest Trail.*

Ben's happiness was overflowing these days, even more so than usual: obvious in the set of his shoulders, the permanent smile lines around his eyes. *"I know Lex has told me we can move on, if I ever get restless and want to try something new,"* he'd told her months ago, when she'd asked how life in Portland was going. *"And maybe I will one day. But I've never felt so right in my life as I am here, Jules. And it's not like I was unhappy in Nashville, because I wasn't. It's just like . . . this place was made for me. And I didn't know, until I got here."*

Julie's eyes slid to Elle's next, where she sat on the other side of Ben. Electric blue. Calm and reassuring. Hers.

It was still hard for Julie to believe, sometimes, when she caught sight of Elle in a crowd like this—still the hottest, most regal queen in the room—that Elle was hers. The silky blouse, bare-shouldered Elle. The athleisure wear Elle. The former star and the future trainer.

Elle fucking Cochrane.

All hers, to admire and love and share life with.

Or you find it on the high school basketball court you never expected to return to.

Maybe all love was a surprise, followed by practice. A step out of comfort zones, followed by hard work. Lurking in all the places you didn't expect, places that become a forever part of you.

"Dahlia and London taught me," she continued, clearing her throat, ignoring the shake of her hands, "what it looks like to love another person for who they are, without reservations or limits. They showed me the joy you can find in a shared passion, always wanting to grow and learn together, as a team. Even when you were, like, literally supposed to be competitors."

The crowd laughed, and the tightness in Julie's throat eased further. She gathered her courage to turn toward London again.

"They taught me that just because love can change and shift as you both grow, it doesn't mean it disappears." And maybe that lesson was just for her. But she was trying to learn it a little bit more, each day. "They taught me that even when you mess up, you try again, until you get it right. That love is a constant, lifelong effort to perfect your favorite recipe.

"They showed me that you should only marry the person who falls in love with the ugliest dog at the shelter." She threw a wobbly smile toward Dahlia, who threw an even wobblier one back. "That you should only marry someone who's always ready to reinvent themself, and who's always ready to support you when you need to do the same. That you should only marry someone who makes you laugh, and never judges you when you cry. That you should marry someone who defends you when you need it, and gives you shit when you deserve it, because they love you."

She turned her watery gaze from London and Dahlia back to the crowd.

"And I know those all probably sounded like generic platitudes. But I knew if I only told embarrassing stories about London from our childhood, they wouldn't let me see Schnitzel for a month." She leaned into the microphone, attempting to channel some Hank Woodson charm. "So find me at the afterparty for those."

A few whistles sounded from the back of the room. From the corner of her eye, she saw London raise their eyes heavenward.

"But the truth is," Julie said, "every single one of those lessons is the most special thing I've ever known. Because they came from London and Dahlia."

Julie reached behind her to pick up a flute of champagne.

"To London and Dahlia." She led the room in raising their glasses. "I love you so fucking much."

And before she swallowed her sip, she heard her mom yell, "Language!" and she almost snorted champagne up her nose. Which made London and Dahlia laugh. Which made the whole room laugh, until the air was only composed of laughter and champagne bubbles, lightness and happy tears.

Julie looked out at the room, full of everyone she loved most in the world, and her hands finally ceased shaking.

"Okay, okay. Now." She smiled into the microphone and raised her champagne once more, harnessing her finest Coach Parker voice when she declared:

"Let's dance."

ACKNOWLEDGMENTS

Thank you to my editor, Junessa Viloria, for once again helping my characters find their funniest, most authentic selves (and dealing with my wordy repetitions, among other things, with patience and skill). Thank you for being on this journey with me, from Burbank to the PCT to Nashville. A special thanks, as I say goodbye to this world, to both you and my agent, Kim Lionetti, for taking a chance on Dahlia and London three years ago. My life has been forever changed because of it, and I can never thank you enough.

Thank you to the incredible Hattie Windley for perhaps my favorite cover of all, to Estelle Hallick and the entire Forever marketing team for your tireless work to get books in the hands of the readers who need them—your work is important and noticed; to Anjuli Johnson, Lori Paximadis, Daniela Medina, Sabrina Flemming, and everyone at Forever who have helped bring my books to life. I am so happy to be on your team.

Thank you to Lindsey Dorcus and Mark Sanderlin, who I was not able to thank in time for the previous books, and to Lindsey Dorcus (again!) and Gail Shalan, for your talent and care with my characters, along with the Hachette Audio team. You are such an important part of these stories' journeys.

Thank you to Alison Cochrun, both for your friendship and

your invaluable help in shaping Julie's story. I appreciate your brain, your time, your vulnerability, and your kindness so very, very much. Thank you to Meryl Wilsner for your astute notes and your endless enthusiasm, which helps me more than you know. Thank you to Kate Cochrane for letting me steal your last name.

Thank you to The Writing Folks, especially Lani Frank, Kat Hillis, and Briana Miano for reading through this draft and providing crucial feedback; thank you also to Katie, Avione, and Piper, who read the first five chapters of a very different draft of this story over two years ago and assured me it wasn't bad (even though it very much was).

Thank you to Beth (also known as b.andherbooks) for helping me come up with a fictitious Milwaukee WNBA team name! And, of course, for everything else you do for the romance community.

Thank you to KT Hoffman, Alicia Thompson, and Manda Bednarik for being the best friends and supporting me in all things, writing or otherwise. You help me get through, and there aren't enough words for that.

Thank you to my family and your loving support of my parenting, teaching, writing, and existing. I'm so sorry I live too far away to have Thanksgivings together. You are always in my heart.

Thank you to everyone who is fighting for justice for queer and trans folks in states that are trying to erase us. I believe that we will win.

Thank you to everyone who has fought for equality in sports—whether for women, BIPOC athletes, or queer and trans inclusion. I believe that we will win.

Thank you to every coach, counselor, educator, librarian, and literally every single person who works in schools who supports queer, trans, and BIPOC students—along with any young person who is simply Having a Hard Time—even in the face of a coordinated, insidious campaign against you. Thank you also to the social workers who are genuinely trying to do the best for kids within the confines of imperfect systems. Your jobs are all impossible, but you save lives.

Thank you to every writer who has blurbed my books, given me a shout on social media, commiserated over DMs, or generally helped me feel a part of this world. You all mean so much to me.

Thank you to every reader who has ever sent me a kind message, to every content creator who has ever tagged me in a kind post, to every human who has picked up my books. Your support of my people makes my heart squeeze so much sometimes that I don't even know what to say. It is often the only thing that helps me believe I can keep telling more stories.

Thank you to every bookseller who has helped put my books in the hands of readers, most especially Laynie Rose Rizer of East City Bookshop, Katie Garaby of Parnassus Books, Joanna Szabo of Annie Bloom's Books, and Christy Peterson of Vintage Books.

Finally, thank you to Kathy, without whom this particular book would not exist, for a myriad of reasons. I love you more with each year I get to parent with you and each sport you valiantly try to teach me the rules of. I know this is sacrilege to say after the book I just wrote, but (Vols, please look away)—go Heels.

YOUR
BOOK
CLUB
RESOURCE

Visit **GCPClubCar.com** to
sign up for the GCP Club Car
newsletter, featuring exclusive
promotions, info on other
Club Car titles, and more.

 @readForeverPub

READING GROUP GUIDE

DISCUSSION QUESTIONS

1. Was Julie's search for the right labels relatable or frustrating to you? Do you wish she had embraced more strongly the words that do likely fit her (like demi) by the end? Or did you understand why she didn't?

2. Did you agree or not agree with CPS's decision to remove Vanessa from Elle's care and return her to Karly's home at Christmas? In an ideal world, how do you think the situation should have been handled—either then, or from the start?

3. Who is the hottest women's basketball player? (If you don't have an answer, googling is encouraged.) How are they *all* so hot? Discuss.

4. How can we make sports break the binary and be more inclusive of gender diversity?

5. *You've Got Mail*: best movie or worst movie?

6. Have you ever changed career paths? What inspired you to make the change? Was it worth it?

7. One thing I have spent a lot of time thinking about lately is mental health representation in romance novels. Often, the partner of the mentally ill character seems to inherently understand both how their partner's illness works and exactly what they need in response. There are no fights or frustrations, just gentle

acceptance and caring. And isn't this the promise of romance novels? What a healing experience to read, each time.

In reality, though, navigating mental illness within relationships can be extremely difficult, for all parties. This is likely a too-personal question for a casual book-club type of discussion, but: Have you ever tried to navigate your own mental illness while exploring a new relationship? Have you ever fallen in love with someone with a mental illness? What are some strategies you think Julie and Elle might have to engage in their future for both of their well-beings?

8. Perhaps related to the previous question: Do you think this book had a third-act breakup?

9. My playlist for writing this book consisted of my regular emo folksy tunes mixed in with more sports-ready jams to get me in the mindset of being ready to hit the court. What are your favorite songs to get you pumped up? For fellow children of the nineties specifically: discuss the best tracks from Jock Jams.

10. As a child, I was one of those people with my head stuck in a book who *mostly* viewed sports as only being for the popular kids, something Not For Me. (Except, okay, I was rather good at field hockey. Someone please write me a gay field hockey book. Lord knows there's an audience.) Experiencing sports as an adult, though—and reading sports romances!—has changed my mind in ways I never could have expected as an angsty teen. Why do you think sports are—or are not—so romantic? Why are they so empowering for queer narratives in particular?

11. Perhaps a niche romance-reader question/mini essay: *How You Get the Girl* was a different writing experience for me compared to the previous books in this series. In both *Love & Other Disasters* and *Something Wild & Wonderful*, the characters experience forced proximity due to an intense, closed-in experience that allows them space to get to know each other very well (and fall

for each other very hard) in a short period of time, mostly free from the distractions of their real lives back home.

For Julie and Elle, however, there were so many things in their real lives vying for their attention, things they had to navigate first before they could truly let the other in. In a way, because of that, I view their story as having more of a happy-for-now (HFN) ending versus a happy-ever-after (HEA). While every couple in a romance book has much more ahead of them after the final page, I think Elle and Julie in particular have a lot more to learn and enjoy about each other over the coming years, which I think they will handle with aplomb, but which I simply didn't have room in this book to cover.

At first I worried this made their story less romantic. But I think one of the big reasons I wanted to write a story like this is because I believe falling in love while in the midst of struggling with complicated daily life—family trauma, unexpected events, hating your job (or alternately, being too committed to your job), feeling unsure about yourself in this big confusing world—that's just as romantic as falling in love while spending months hiking over mountains or being in a bubble of a TV set. In real life, we are often just striving for that HFN however we can. And when we find it on top of everything else? Perhaps that's the most romantic thing of all.

This is all to say: What are your feelings about an HFN vs. an HEA ending? Do you think there is a difference? Do you agree with my own assessment of this one? Do you think most romances end in one or the other?

A NON-EXHAUSTIVE LIST OF
IMPORTANT MOMENTS IN
WOMEN'S BASKETBALL HISTORY

- 1892: Women's basketball is first played at Smith College, less than a year after the sport's invention (for boys) by James Naismith in nearby Springfield, Massachusetts. It's introduced at Smith by Senda Berenson; almost a hundred years later, she will become the first woman to be inducted into the Naismith Basketball Hall of Fame. In other words: even with long-lasting restrictions on *how* they could play, women have been balling from the start.

- 1896: The first official intercollegiate women's game is played between Stanford and the University of California-Berkeley. Women's basketball continues to grow in popularity in colleges and YMCAs across America.

- 1936: The first professional women's team is created in Missouri by C. M. "Ole" Olson, the All-American Red Heads. Gaining popularity through incorporating entertaining tricks and hijinks akin to the Harlem Globetrotters, they also play serious basketball, using men's rules. They travel widely, playing up to two hundred games a season; the league runs for over fifty years. And yes, every woman on the all-white team dyed their hair red, in promotion of a beauty salon. The things women have had to do throughout history are wild.

- 1953: The International Basketball Federation (FIBA), founded in Geneva, Switzerland, in 1932, launches the first Women's Basketball World Cup. FIBA currently has 212 member nations.

- 1972: Support for women's basketball grows greatly after the passing of Title IX, which prohibits gender-based discrimination in any educational setting that receives federal funding.

- 1976: Women's basketball is added as an Olympic sport, forty years after men's.

- 1978: The first professional women's basketball league, the WBL, is founded. It grows to fourteen teams before its collapse in 1981.

- 1982: The NCAA (created in 1906) first sponsors women's college basketball; the first-ever NCAA women's basketball tournament follows. Louisiana Tech beats Cheyney University for the championship.

- 1994: Down by two with 0.7 on the clock after a jump ball, Charlotte Smith of UNC gets a three-pointer to beat Louisiana Tech in the national championship, adding to the history of greatest buzzer beaters in the sport.

- 1995: Rebecca Lobo helps lead the University of Connecticut to a national championship after an undefeated season; Lobo and UConn become stars of the women's basketball world. UConn still holds the record for most national championships, with eleven to their name; the next closest competitor is the University of Tennessee, with eight.

- 1996: The NBA founds the WNBA. Texas Tech superstar Sheryl Swoopes is the first player signed. The first game is televised on NBC in 1997 between the Los Angeles Sparks and the New York Liberty. In 2006, the WNBA earns the distinction of being the first women's team sport league to survive ten consecutive seasons. Starting with eight teams, the league currently has twelve.

- 1999: The Women's Basketball Hall of Fame opens in Knoxville, Tennessee. The building features the world's largest basketball, sitting just outside the Pat Summitt Rotunda.

- 2001: The Los Angeles Sparks are the first professional team, in any sport, to officially celebrate Pride Month.

- 2002: Women's basketball legend Lisa Leslie is the first player to dunk in a WNBA game.

- 2006: Tennessee Vol Candace Parker is the first player to dunk in an NCAA women's tournament game. She later becomes the first player to win WNBA Rookie of the Year and Most Valuable Player in the same year, 2008. She currently plays for the Las Vegas Aces.

- 2012: Pat Summitt retires as head coach of the University of Tennessee Volunteers after thirty-eight seasons. Having never coached a losing season and winning eight NCAA championships, she had been named the Naismith Coach of the Century in 2000. Tennessee is the only school to have appeared in all thirty-six (as of this writing) NCAA women's tournaments.

- 2018: Arike Ogunbowale of Notre Dame hits a last-second shot to beat Mississippi State in the NCAA national championship—after hitting a last-second shot to beat UConn in the semifinals.

- 2020: The WNBA players' union wins a new collective bargaining agreement, significantly increasing pay and maternity benefits, among other wins. There is still much work to be done.

- 2022: Sue Bird retires from the WNBA; she holds the record for most seasons (19) and games (580) played in the league. She won four WNBA Championships with the Seattle Storm, five Olympic gold medals (a record held with Diana Taurasi), two NCAA Championships with UConn, and four FIBA World Cups.

- 2022: Brittney Griner is detained and imprisoned in Russia for five months on drug charges. After being released back to the United States in a prisoner swap, she returns to the WNBA in May 2023. While her case attracts a swirl of opinions, many heavily coded in racism, I include it here to draw attention to how many female athletes, not just in basketball but across sports (but especially in basketball), play overseas during their offseasons, largely due to money. Although the exact amounts other countries pay women ballers is shrouded in a bit of mystery, what is widely known is that it is often significantly higher than what even a star can make in the WNBA.

- 2023: The NCAA women's basketball championship between LSU and Iowa is watched by an average of 9.9 million people, making it the most-watched women's basketball game of all time. While many tune in to watch record-breaking Caitlin Clark of Iowa, LSU is solidly triumphant. Angel Reese is named the tournament's Most Outstanding Player.

- 2023: Diana Taurasi, previously voted by fans as the best player in the league's history, becomes the first WNBA player to score ten thousand points. She currently plays for the Phoenix Mercury.

ABOUT THE AUTHOR

Originally from a small town in the Pocono Mountains of Pennsylvania, **Anita Kelly** now lives in the Pacific Northwest with their family. An educator by day, they write romance that celebrates queer love in all its infinite possibilities. Whenever not reading or writing, they're drinking too much tea, taking pictures, and dreaming of their next walk in the woods. They hope you get to pet a dog today.

To learn more, visit:
AnitaKellyWrites.com
Instagram @AnitaKellyWrites